Praise for Marta Acosta

Amazon #1 Hispanic & Latino Fiction Author
Library Journal Women's Summer Reading Author
Cosmopolitan's Top Ten Latino Must-Read Author

Praise for *The Dog Thief*

"Amazing! *The Dog Thief* has taken preconceptions of how to portray autism and crafted a genre-hopping narrative as rich and diverse as the spectrum itself. Heartbreaking and heart-warming."

—*James Sinclair, Autistic & Unapologetic*

"Pure and heartfelt. *The Dog Thief* is an amazing book. Well-constructed, deftly written and beautiful all the way through. Poetically powerful insight into both animal and human behavior and a satisfying ending. ★★★★★"

—*Amazon Reviewer*

"Maddie is...equal parts brilliant and disastrous. I would enjoy a sequel just because I liked the characters—dogs included—so much."

—*Books on Autism*

"So wonderful! A story of family, relationships, labels that aren't there, growth, and love of all kinds-two and four legged."

—*Goodreads Review*

also by Marta Acosta

The Dog Thief
Happy Hour at Casa Dracula
Midnight Brunch at Casa Dracula
The Bride of Casa Dracula
Haunted Honeymoon at Casa Dracula
Dark Companion
Marvel's *The She-Hulk Diaries*
Fancy That

Coming soon
A Dog to Guide My Soul

MAD DOG DOWN THE ROAD

Coyote Run Book 2

MARTA ACOSTA

Also available in ebook.

www.martaacosta.com

With love, to Anat,
who shares my love of dogs and books

Chapter One

THE TRUCK'S TIRES skidded on loose gravel as I swerved to avoid hitting a couple wearing pale baggy pajamas and dancing down the middle of the road, looking like drunken ghosts in the pre-dawn gloom. Vixen, the sleek German shorthaired pointer in the seat harness beside me, gave a short, sharp bark, and I said, "Your fault. You wanted to come for the ride." Her coat was the dark brown called liver, ticked with white, and she had a solid dark saddle across her back.

A rapid *pop-pop-pop* shattered the silence. I glanced in my rear-view mirror to see the sparks of firecrackers scatter across the asphalt. The deep shadows off the road spilled like ink into a pool of blackness pouring toward the mountains that surrounded Coyote Run. Most buildings on Main Street were dark, but security lights shone brightly from the squat cinderblock building that housed the sheriff's department substation.

The headlights of a delivery truck illuminated the road as it pulled away from my destination, the cavernous old restaurant that now housed Penelope's Catering. I parked and got out with Vixen, going around to the fenced backyard, and heard a deep growl. "Brownie, it's me!" I said, opening the gate.

Penelope Millard's lab mix ambled toward me for a scratch and then greeted Vixen with a sniff. "Hey, Penelope," I called. "I'm here."

A sturdy, middle-aged woman stepped into the open doorway of her kitchen, wiping her hands on her apron. Her silver-streaked hair was tied back by a red polka-dot bandana, and her cheeks were flushed. "Thanks for coming, Maddie."

"Call and I'll come running, hon. Where's the dog?"

"He's inside. He looks in awful shape. I couldn't bear waiting until county animal services opens at ten."

I concentrated in order to meet Penelope's hazel eyes, before glancing over her shoulder, into the kitchen. Rich aromas rose from the stainless-steel vats. "What are you doing up so early?"

"I'm in full-blown party mode until Labor Day," she said. "I wouldn't have even known about the dog, but Brownie kept whining and pacing at the gate. When I checked, this poor fellow was lying there, and..." Her voice wavered. "Come and see for yourself."

The kitchen was already hot and steamy, and I couldn't imagine how hellish it would get by midday. I waved hello to the assistants prepping vegetables and went with Penelope into what used to be a restaurant's main dining room.

There, on a pile of blankets in the corner, lay an emaciated mid-size mutt. I flipped up my palm, signaling for Vixen to stay, walked slowly to the dog, and took in raw injuries and maze of old scars across dull black fur. "Oh, no." The dog's head didn't move, but his eyes found me and, when he whimpered, my throat tightened.

"He wasn't aggressive, so we carried him in here," Penelope said. "I tried to give him water. He doesn't have a collar. Someone's beat him."

My hands hurt. I unclenched them, and my voice caught when I said, "He's a bait dog."

"What?"

"Those jagged scars, old and new, are bites. Someone's used him as bait to train fighting dogs. Look at his paws," I said, pointing to cuts and swelling. "He ran until he couldn't run anymore." I crouched close to the dog. "It's okay, boy. I'm going to check one thing." Slowly and carefully, I lifted the dog's lip to expose stained and chipped teeth. "His gums are pink, which is a good sign in terms of heart failure or internal hemorrhaging, and his breathing is even."

I reached into my pocket and clutched my phone. Ben Meadows, our local veterinarian, had made me swear not to call him before 9:00 a.m. except for "dire emergencies." I could keep the dog stable for a few hours. "I'll take him to my center and make him comfortable until Doc Ben can see him."

"We'll get him to your pickup." Penelope shouted to a brawny cook, who took off his white apron and gently carried the dog out to my truck, placing him on a mat in the back.

Vixen dashed to me, a shank bone between her slim jaws. When she wagged her cropped tail, her entire backside wriggled. "Pen, if you give her treats every time she begs, it reinforces pushy behavior."

"Maddie, we feed every soul that comes to this place, including dogs. Special dogs get special treats, and you said this was your new search dog."

"I said she is *a* dog. She's a beaut, but she lives to hunt, not search." The county board of supervisors had pressured me to accept Vixen as a gift for the Midnight Runners Search and Rescue without allowing me to evaluate her skills and temperament. "She's very amiable. Are you interested in adopting her? She's excellent with other dogs, and Brownie would be delighted with a four-footed companion."

"Oh, no, you don't. Brownie is all the dog I need." Penelope smiled. "I have warm scones."

"That's what she said." This was my only joke. "It was funnier in my head."

"I'm sure it was, sugar." Penelope went to a baker's rack, took three scones and placed them in a white paper bag. "Did you happen to see Dino Ayer on your way here?"

"No, and if I did, I'd give him what-for about those damn Ayerheads. Two were cavorting on the road, setting off fireworks. In the *middle of July*. One spark is all it takes. One spark, and the whole valley goes up."

"As a cook, fire is my friend, but it's a dangerous friend. We all worry," she said. "Dino's been having engine trouble on his boat, but I'm counting on his catch. I make a lovely grilled bass with fresh fennel."

"Why is he selling fish? Don't the vineyard and hippy-dippy yurt village of the brainwashed keep him fully occupied?"

Penelope sighed, and I knew that meant something. I looked down at her shoes, powdered with flour and splattered with sauce, and my shoulders jerked up twice. "What I *intended* to say is that Dino's overextended already."

"Yes, he is, but we all have bills to pay." Penelope handed me the bag. "Two of those scones are for the sheriff."

"It's so sweet that you think these won't be eaten before I see him. I should be able to tell you something about the dog this afternoon."

As I latched the harness on Vixen in the front seat, Dino Ayer parked his truck and began unloading an ice chest. He was an average guy—average height, average features, average husband-with-kids age—and that made it hard for me to identify him when he wasn't accompanied by his stocky little border terrier or his delectable wife.

"Hey, Dino. Penelope's been waiting on you," I said, wondering if I should take the stray home, or stay in town until the Coyote Run Veterinary Clinic opened at 9:00.

"I was working on the boat. Is it too much to ask that the engine hang on for another year?"

"I am not the person to ask since my truck is held together with old bubblegum and baling wire. FYI, a couple of those cult followers were setting off fireworks not half an hour ago."

"I'll tell the institute director to do something about it."

"Director, delusional messianic leader, huckster, ancient mariner, whatever. Tell him to inculcate fire safety protocol at his next brainwashing session."

"That's my brother-in-law you're talking about."

"Then you can ask Emily to tell him. How's Weasel?"

"Getting onto eleven now. Such a great dog, I wish I could clone him."

"Cloning replicates DNA, but only approximates character. If you wanted an identical copy, it would have to be a canine version of an android with the personality programmed in. A *candroid*. Dibs on trademarking that, and don't tell anyone else."

"Okay." Dino shifted his weight to his other foot.

"No doubt there would be a disparity between a dog's actual behavior and the owner's biased and limited perceptions of that behavior, so programming would be a bitch. That could be my company motto. Or, should it be, 'Whitney Candroids: Programming Like a Bitch'? Regardless, the technology's not there yet. I can give you updates on any developments, if you like."

"Um..."

"No worries! I'll add you to my newsletter mailing list. You should be on it anyway to keep up on the latest care practices for senior dogs."

The grease on Dino's face gathered in the furrows of his brow, making it easy for me to recognize that he was frowning. He set down the ice chest with a thud and scratched his chin. Shiny red scar tissue covered the stump where his middle finger on his left hand had recently been cut off in a power-tool accident. "Is there anything else?"

"So much, and I'd love to discuss this further, but I've got an injured dog to take care of."

I started walking away, and he called, "Maddie!"

"What?"

"Do you remember the Jimmy Buffett song you sang at the fundraiser for the women's shelter? 'Breathe In, Breathe Out, Move On'? That was beautiful."

"Credit Dawg O'Donnell, may he rest in peace. He taught me to appreciate Buffett's range beyond whoo-hoo party anthems. Buffett can express such melancholy, acceptance of life's travails, but without defeatism. To me, that song is a quiet celebration of resiliency."

"Yeah, that's how I feel, too. Bye, Maddie."

I made sure the stray was safely on a blanket, stroked a spot by his ears, and said, "Breathe in, breathe out, move on," and then started toward home where I could clean the wounds while I waited to call my veterinarian friend. There were cars on the road now, heading off to jobs at wineries and the hydroelectric plant.

I drove slowly, not wanting to jostle the stray in the back, and, as I neared the entrance to the Ayers' vineyard, a silver-gray Honda Pilot was exiting.

I pounded my horn, and the Honda stopped. I pulled over, hopped out of my truck, and ran to the driver. "Ben, I was about to call you!"

"Is this dire, or can it wait?" Benjamin Meadows, DVM, had trimmed his brown beard to a shadow, the way I clipped a neglected poodle with felted fur. His strong, angular features seemed naked, which made me uncomfortable.

"But you're here right *now*. Come look at this poor dog that Penelope found."

Ben was tall and broad-shouldered, and dressed in his usual

clinic outfit: a blue button-down shirt and dark slacks. He brought his exam bag, and I showed him the dog.

While Ben gave the stray a cursory exam, I looked at the Ayers' place. A hand-painted cloth banner with *Spirit Springs Institute Summer Camp* hung over the gate. An acre had been cleared in the vineyard for a dozen round canvas tents. People in loose white pajamas bustled around a clearing, and smoke feathered up from a large fire pit. The location of the tents in relation to the fire pit was worrisome, especially considering the evening winds. The Ayers' house was at the far end of the property, hidden by enormous willows.

"If you're here, it must be serious," I said, trying to remember all the Ayers' animals. "Who's in trouble?"

Ben held his stethoscope to the dog's heart. "Weasel's an old guy with issues."

"I met Dino five minutes ago, and he said Weasel was fine."

"He's fine for an old guy, so long as his multiple conditions are monitored," Ben said. "Emily might have been overreacting, but it's better to err on the side of caution."

"Emily is lovely, but I'm never sure about anyone who names an animal of one species after another species. It's one of my pet peeves," I said, recalling that I'd seen Emily and her dog at the veterinary clinic the last time I was there, hoping she didn't have Munchausen syndrome by canine proxy.

"Your dog is named after a female fox."

"As you are well aware, she came with that silly moniker. This stray is a bait dog, isn't it?"

"Looks like it. Malnourished and needs stitches on these fresh injuries. The swellings are infected. Broken bones remodeled badly. Does Penelope have any idea of how medical bills for a dog in this condition can skyrocket?"

My shoulders tightened, rising toward my ears.

"Yeah, I thought so," he said. "Maddie, you might want to let this one go. The kindest act would be to take it to the county shelter and let them evaluate. If they have to euthanize, it won't cost you personally."

"No fucking way!" I kicked dirt toward Ben's buffed shoes. "I'll cover the medical bills."

"With what money? Rather than throwing away thousands on a fighting dog that doesn't belong to you, please get a reliable truck. How often has this beater broken down?"

"This dog is what matters to me right now, Ben. Do you want to take him, or shall we meet at the clinic?"

Ben exhaled slowly. "I've got to eat something before the clinic opens, because I can't function if I'm hungry."

"That's not a problem." I went to my truck, where Vixen was nosing the paper bag. I snatched it away and took it to Ben. "These are for you. They're still warm from the oven."

"Oh. That was thoughtful." The corners of his lips twitched up, so I knew he was pleased. "All right, I'll take your stray and do what I can to relieve his pain, but I'm not going to proceed further until we have a serious discussion. Because someday you're going to try to rescue a dog so damaged and dangerous that even you can't rehabilitate it."

He was staring at me, because people always thought I would understand them better if they made eye contact, but it just made me feel like my skin was sliding across my flesh, so I ignored his comment and let down the tailgate on the truck. "Someday? Someday a volcano will erupt with sulfurous particulates that veil the sun, causing worldwide calamity, but that day isn't now."

"Arguing with you is like trying to land a punch on a boxer who constantly bobs and weaves," he said, "You get his back, and I'll get his front."

As we moved the injured animal to Ben's SUV, it whined, and I kept saying, "It's okay. It will be okay. He's an amazing doctor. He'll help." I tucked the blanket over the dog to give some comfort.

I wiped at my eyes, and Ben said, "You're upset. Do you want a hug?"

"No, I'm fine," I said, even though my bones felt too unsettled in my body. "See you later."

Chapter Two

I DROVE BACK to the ranch, relieved that the stray was in a professional's care and thinking about Ben's attentiveness to Weasel. Or was he being attentive to Emily? Although Dino was average, Emily Ayer was a subtle stunner, and my handsome veterinarian pal thrived on attention from women. He claimed he only flirted, but flirting was a complicated game I couldn't follow.

This early in the day, the color of the sky was pale and unfocused, amorphous and unawakened. Thin, filmy clouds shawled mountains verdant with pine trees.

I turned onto our drive, lined with century-old California live oaks, and slowly passed the house that Ben rented from us while his house was being constructed. His wife, Ava, had filled old horse troughs with tomato plants, vegetables, and flowers. Their children's bicycles leaned against the back porch, the way our bicycles once might have leaned, but the house was altogether cheerier than it ever had been when my family had lived here.

The kitchen garden was a lush contrast to the golden fields beyond, bordered by a trickle of creek and vineyards in the distance, stretching to foothills. Last spring, I'd borrowed a neighbor's tractor to mow the fields and turn soil, creating a grid of fire breaks, but the grasses and prickly star-thistle had grown tall again.

If home is where the heart is, this hadn't been home since my sister Kenzie moved away—because she was my heart. Over the last year, the pain of missing her swelled within me, pressing against my lungs, filling my head, pushing out to my fingertips. Without her counterweight, I felt increasingly unbalanced and irrational, and I wanted nothing more than to have compact, energetic, beautiful Kenzie charging through morning chores beside me.

At the end of the drive was a sign, *Whitney Canine Rehabilitation Center* with the WCRC logo, hanging from two beams in front of the parking area. A tall security fence enclosed the compound, which consisted of a huge clearing, kennels, a double-wide trailer that served as the office and training rooms, and a deck with a picnic table and benches.

Immediately to the north was my cottage, constructed of cargo containers. I'd posted bright red *Keep Out* signs to deter staff and clients from wandering into my personal territory. People snooped too much. My assistant, Jaison Bouvier, lived in a gleaming Airstream trailer that was close enough to see, but far enough for privacy. The trailer lights were on, so Jaison was up. I felt safer with people living on the ranch with me, and I felt safest with my dogs nearby.

When Vixen and I went into the center, my beautiful Belgian Malinois, Bertie, came to greet us. He was seventy-six pounds of lean muscle, and the only dog who had free run, going wherever he pleased, but these days, he wanted to leave the compound less and less. I crouched and wrapped my arms around the big dog. He placed his elegant head on my shoulder, his upright ears lying back with pleasure. His long black muzzle was grizzled, and the scar patches marking the thick golden fur on his back had grayed, too, the color of charcoals after the fire has died.

The dogs barked from their kennel runs. Vixen rushed to them, sticking her nose between the links of the fencing. As soon as the kennels were open, the dogs bounded and wandered out: large and small, affable and short-tempered, smooth-coated and shaggy, pedigreed and 57-varieties. Half the dogs were boarders, here for refresher training while the owners were on vacation. The income from the boarding dogs subsidized care for the dogs requiring intensive long-term rehabilitation.

In the double-wide, I set up the coffee maker, and a scruffy little blind dog shuffled to me from his favorite sleeping spot under the front desk. "Morning, Gizmo. How are things shaking?" While the coffee brewed, I brushed Gizmo's coat and said, "I wish your guy was here, because we would have howled with laughter about the Spirit Springs Institute Summer Camp."

Jaison came in and leaned against the wall. In the last year, he'd grown into his bones, no longer a skinny kid, but a rangy man, his teal WCRC T-shirt stretched taut across wide shoulders, his hair twisted into short dreads. "Hey, boss. Why would you have laughed?"

"Because there isn't a natural spring for twenty miles."

"You can find something wrong about anything, except for Bertie."

"Because he continues to be the epitome of his species."

"Vixen is a pretty sleek thing."

"*Thing* is right. She lacks decorum."

Jai chuckled, so I supposed we were joking, and I said, "That's what she said," and he laughed harder, making me relax for the first time that morning. The coffee machine had finished brewing, so I washed my hands and poured two mugs for us. Jai took a carton of caramel-flavored creamer from the fridge.

"That stuff is nothing but chemicals and corn syrup," I said.

"But it tastes good. Didn't your sister tell you to stay off the caffeine?"

My hand jerked, and coffee sloshed in the mug. "Kenzie is not the boss of me. Anymore."

"I miss her, too, Mad Girl. You got blood on your shirt again."

"Occupational hazard." I told him about Penelope's stray, and imagined the dog on an exam table, hopeless and in agony. No, not agony. Ben would alleviate the pain. "What happens to people, Jaison, that they can force dogs to fight and take pleasure in it? Kenzie says, 'Hurt people hurt people,' and I understand to a degree."

"But you don't understand why hurt people hurt animals," he said. "Kenzie is mostly right on this one, but I'm damn sure some people are born evil. You can't blame their parents or anything else, because, at a certain point, we all make our own decisions."

"Maybe it's as simple and complex as a genetic predisposition and opportunity or environment. Like if I was miswired a different way..." I said. "Have you heard about any dog-fighting rings around here?"

"No one in this town tells me a blame thing. Find out from Sheriff Oliver."

"I have repeatedly asked him to update me about any and all criminal activity involving dogs, but he refuses. He thinks I'd interfere. I don't interfere. I assist. It's a major point of contention in an otherwise idyllic relationship."

"No surprise when a nut like you dates a sheriff."

"You're verging on insubordination."

"Am I on the clock? Is there a clock? Cuz if there is, I'm owed considerable overtime."

"We do it for love, Jaison."

"Slick deflect. Who's paying for the stray's medical treatment?"

"I'll tell you once I've figured it out."

Ben called while I was in the yard instructing my teenage intern

Zoe Gaskell how to train a stubborn Corgi to hold a stay through distractions. "Another five minutes, Z."

"This dog has ADD," she said, opening her bright blue eyes wide and puffing out her round pink cheeks. She'd bleached her brown hair silver-blond and added purple streaks.

"*You* have ADD, and the dog can read your frustration. Inhale slowly, exhale, rinse, lather, repeat five times, and then try again with a calm and positive attitude. Treat this as a challenge, not a punishment."

My phone buzzed, and I walked away to a spot where I could observe Zoe's training session without being right on top of her. I answered the call, saying, "What's the diagnosis?"

"Hello to you, too," Ben said. "Your stray needed a blood transfusion. I lanced infected cysts and started him on antibiotics. His right forepaw is damaged and may require surgery. Maybe even an amputation. I'll send an estimate before you—"

"What is this preoccupation with money?"

"Maddie, as radical as it sounds, I like to pay my staff a decent living wage and provide for my family."

"It's odd not having them all here. How are the kids? How's Ava's arm?" Ben's wife had broken her arm when she'd fallen off a ladder hanging outdoor lights.

"The kids are in heaven with their grandparents, spending all day in the pool. Ava is seeing a physical therapist for her shoulder."

"I hope she feels better soon. Back to your well-justified concern with finances," I said, staring into the distance, toward my neighbor's expansive ranch. "Abel Myklebust says he wants to improve our relationship. Well, he can damn well pay for that pleasure."

"Has it occurred to you that you might enjoy becoming acquainted with your biological father?" he said. My close friends knew the family secret that I'd recently discovered.

"I sincerely doubt it, Ben. He wears a gaudy bolo tie every damn day. I'll talk to you later."

I ate lunch on the deck by my offices, watching the dogs play, and gearing myself to talk to my mother's illicit hookup. My mother claimed I was her ex-husband's child, but DNA tests proved I was the offspring of the jerk who had siphoned away our water supply for decades. The only interesting thing about Abel was that his mother was Mexican, so I was Mexican, too.

I told Jaison that I wasn't to be disturbed and then went to my office and shut the door. After ten minutes spent aligning items on my desk and sliding my file drawer in and out, I made the call.

Abel Myklebust answered immediately. "Maddie! Finally. I've left a dozen messages."

I hadn't actually listened to any before deleting them. "I assumed you're as busy as I am, seeing that you have to publish the *Recorder* once a month."

"It's bi-weekly with daily updates, and I always have time for you." Abel was the reporter, editor, and publisher of the *Coyote Run Recorder*. "Can you come?"

"Um, about that, a wonderful opportunity has arisen." I took a breath and counted to three before letting it out slowly through my nose. "I think you would be an ideal sponsor for a special dog."

"I don't want your mutt humping my Bergamascos." Abel had designed his ranch like a landscape painting, with exotic sheep and ornamental sheepdogs.

"Your Bergamascos should be so lucky. This is a Luxembourg flat-coat retriever. An ancient pheasant-hunting breed. I'll adopt out the dog to a select home, but there are a few insignificant medical bills."

"I..." he began, and I knew he was on his computer. "I can't find any..."

"The breed is extremely rare. Color plates of the retriever are at the Royal Academy of Veterinary Science's special collection in Antwerp. It's worth the trip to Belgium, especially if you like French fries, but you'll need prior permission to see them."

"Maddie, that's an entertaining fabrication. I don't believe you have ever left this country, because there's no way you would tolerate a flight. Is this dog the real reason you called?"

"I'm hurt, Abel. I thought you'd appreciate being considered for the opportunity."

"Don't you mean 'shake-down'? I want us to have a meaningful relationship and go public about—"

"No can do, Abel, because then my kind and loving mother would discover that I know about your sordid shenanigans, and that's her secret to keep. I'm sure Mom's made it okay with Jesus, but her new husband might not be as forgiving. Well, who is? Can I count you in as the dog's sponsor?"

"On one condition, Maddie. Participate in the quiz team fundraiser for the library. This Saturday, seven p.m."

"I *already* help raise money for the animal shelter on karaoke nights. I'm overextended."

"Your mother told me you liked the library."

"I always *hid* in the library. Which is different."

"Maddie, if you can't help me, I don't think I can help you. Quiz Night will be fun. We'll have teams of four. Do this, and I'll pay for your purportedly rare dog's medical bills. Bring your guy."

My shoulders shrugged twice. I rolled them to release the tension and then shrugged again. "Okay, I'll come to your stupid thing. Bertie's a homebody these days, but I might bring him if you can give him a steak."

"I didn't say to bring your dog. Invite Sheriff Desjardins. We're not serving steaks, but we'll have snacks. This could be an opportunity for us to let people see we're all friends. It's at Grange Hall."

"Don't expect me to go overboard, friendship-wise," I said. "I can't promise Oliver will be there. Saturdays are the most popular night for amateur criminals, and they're always the sloppiest."

"You're drawing from your personal experience?"

"You may be my biological progenitor, Abel, but don't presume to know me based upon unsubstantiated arrest logs. Later."

When I called the veterinary clinic and told them to bill Abel for the stray's medical fees, the office manager Wylene said, "Doc Ben says you're wanting to buy a truck."

"Not actively. All I need is something reliable."

"A client's neighbor has a Tundra she wants to sell," she said, and told me the price.

Because Wylene was a recent hire, I didn't trust her yet. I shouldn't have trusted the office manager before her, Dawg O'Donnell, the man who insisted I listen to Jimmy Buffett's entire discography, but I still missed Dawg. Life's like that. Sometimes you desperately long for the company of your bad friends as much as your good ones. "What's wrong with the Tundra?"

"Nothing, but she doesn't need an extra truck. She just wants to get rid of it."

"I suppose I have to bite the bullet and say adios to my prehistoric beast. Have her call me."

Half-an-hour later, Jaison and I drove into a gated luxury community on the northern edge of town. The faux Tudor house had a hedge of pink roses and a sprawling, lush, green lawn.

The owner was waiting for me in the driveway by the massive, dark green truck. Donna-June Looper, a middle-aged woman, dressed in pastels and canvas flats, had a fluff of ash-blonde curls and wore glittery diamond stud earrings.

After introductions, I said, "Your lawn's like a golf course. What are your water bills in this drought climate?"

Jai spoke up immediately. "What Maddie means is, does the

truck have any leaks?"

"It's been regularly maintained. My husband only used it to get back and forth from his cabin. I stick to my Prius." Her voice was soft, but firm, the type of voice that works well for dog trainers.

"Is he okay with you selling it?" I said.

"I bought it, and it's registered to me. Gordon hightailed it a week ago. He texted that he'd gone fishing permanently and not to expect him ever to come back."

"If it's only been a week," I began.

"He's taken off before, so it's not exactly a shock. He's wanted to live on a tropical beach all his life. Well, let him live his dream, because I'm already living mine."

Jaison looked studiously away, and I nodded, as if I understood or cared about Donna-June's husband. She handed me a manila folder with the mechanic's paperwork, confirming that the vehicle registration and all repair receipts were in her name.

The brief test drive rattled me because everything was so different from my own pickup, but the Tundra practically swooped up inclines and had an excellent turn radius. Jaison said, "Maddie, if you don't want it, I'm interested. This is a steal."

As we were talking, a bone-thin, hollow-eyed girl in a ribbed tank top and boxer shorts came outside. A violet and yellow bruise bloomed on the inside of her elbow. She pulled her mother away, and their whispers hissed back and forth before the girl went back into the house.

Donna-June flashed a smile and said, "So, what do you think?"

"It's extremely shiny."

Jaison said, "Maddie, Donna-June wants to know if you want to buy the truck."

"Mine still runs most of the time."

"How many times did it break down in the last six months?"

"Fine, whatever." I wrote a check, and Donna-June signed

over the pink slip. I asked Jaison to drive the Tundra back. "I need time to get adjusted to it before I take it on the highway," I said. "I hate change."

"It's a fact of life. See you at the center." He climbed into the cab and grinned. "I won't mind borrowing this."

I stopped at Burger Hut for fries and a strawberry milkshake, snacking as I headed to the ranch. "It's been fun, except when it hasn't," I said to my old truck, patting the dashboard and cranking up the music. I was singing along with Miranda Lambert when I spotted a patrol cruiser with lights flashing on the side of the road.

I slowed and then saw the green Tundra. Jaison stood beside it, his hands raised, while a uniformed stranger paced in front of him. The stranger had his fist drawn back.

In a second, I'd slammed on my breaks, left my truck in the road, and was running to the stranger, shouting, "What are you doing?"

Jaison said, "Maddie, don't escalate, please," and the stranger said, "Lady, get back and do not interfere."

He was short, but bulky with muscles, 210 pounds of mean crammed into a 160-pound sack. His gray, blood-shot eyes peered out from a ranger hat. My gaze slid to his name tag. Richard Kearney. Had Oliver mentioned him?

"Don't you put one finger on Jaison!"

"Don't you shout at me, you loco chica!" The deputy's hand went to the thick black leather belt. "Look at me when I'm talking to you!"

"She can't!" Jaison said.

When I took a step forward, hordes of ants seemed to swarm over my skin, and I waved my arms, trying to cast them off, and Kearney shouted, "Return to your vehicle and put your hands on the hood."

"You clearly don't realize who we are or else—" I said, my blood pulsing loudly in my ears, my body shaking with adrenaline, ants marching over me, and then I heard Jaison call out, "Officer, don't she's—" and my shoulders jerked forward with nerves, and I strained in my effort to hurl the ants away, and the deputy had something in his hand, and he raised it toward me.

And then a force slammed me, and all my nerves froze. I fell onto the scorching asphalt, and each and every one of my twitchy, rebellious muscles clenched and then petrified.

For a moment, I didn't know if that was good or bad.

But I peed my pants, so I guessed it was the latter.

Chapter Three

THE DEPUTY ROLLED me over and cuffed my wrists behind my back. He cuffed Jaison, too, and we were both in the back of the cruiser—me, sitting on a plastic bag.

"You're going to the station," Kearney said.

"That's exactly where I want to be," I said to him. "You are a dead man!"

Jaison said quietly, "Maddie, please, not this time, not this time," and I realized that my experience in patrol cars wasn't the same as his.

"If you both don't shut the fuck up, I'll take a detour and make you shut the fuck up," Kearney bellowed.

I turned to Jaison, wondering if there were bruises under his thin cotton shirt. "Jai," I said, as quiet as I could, "You okay?"

He gave a brief nod. "Occupational hazard," he said, and my eyes welled.

"Shut up!" Kearney said, pounding the steering wheel. We'd entered the center of town, a short strip of shops, food joints, and offices. Kearney called the dispatcher, claiming grand theft auto, assault on an officer, and interfering with an arrest. We had witnesses on the street, all peering into the patrol car, and I screamed, "Bullshit! Bullshit! Bullshit!" so the dispatcher would have my objections on record.

Not that it served any purpose at the moment, since the dispatcher was located thirty miles away at the county seat. But when Kearney turned into the Coyote Run substation, Sheriff's Captain Oliver Desjardins, a magnificent vision in khaki, was waiting in the parking lot. Tall and lean, he was the kind of guy who could run down an escapee without breaking into a sweat. The reddish strands in his sandy hair glinted, and he squinted in the sunlight. His mouth was wide with narrow lips that were in a flat line, and he clenched his jaw.

Oliver opened the patrol car door and pulled me from the car. "What did you do this time, Madeleine Margaret Whitney, and what is that...?" he said, his voice both rough and tender, so much like his twin sister's, voices that reverberated within me and made me feel too vulnerable now.

I couldn't bear to be vulnerable, so I held back my tears and, in a voice, as shaky as my knees, I said, "Hey, Ollie. Could you get these fucking cuffs off us, and you'd pee yourself too if you'd been tased by some asshole sociopath."

Kearney approached, his chest puffed, holding his baton. "I said to shut the fuck up!"

Oliver stared him down. "*Uncuff* them, and all of you come inside. Now."

When we stepped into the air-conditioned station, I shivered, and whispered, "Jaison, did he hit you?"

"No, you didn't give him the chance," he whispered back, and I could have cried with relief.

The desk clerk said, "Afternoon, Dr. Whitney. Been a while since you enjoyed our hospitality."

"Afternoon, but I won't be staying the night this time. Have you met my assistant, Jaison Bouvier? Do you have a pair of jeans I can borrow?"

"You go out with Julie at the grocery," the desk clerk said to Jaison. "She's my neighbor's daughter. Sweet girl, but a bit of a firecracker, am I right?"

"That's what I like," Jaison said with one of his slow smiles.

"Dr. Whitney, will departmental sweats do?" the desk clerk asked.

Kearney's eyebrows were going up and down, and his lips twisted to one side.

"You can all socialize later," Oliver said. "Kearney, you come with me. Maddie, clean yourself up, and I'll interview you and Jaison next." Then he told the desk clerk to keep us separated. While I was in the women's locker room, Jaison took Oliver's Dutch shepherd search-and-rescue dog, Zeus, to the yard out back for a game of catch.

I paced in the lobby, counting my steps and trying to stay approximately two feet from the walls, and the desk clerk said, "Can you sit still for one second?"

"No, I'm all wound up..." I twisted forward and back, side to side, my spine coiled and needing release. "I'll be at the Suncrest buying groceries."

"The sheriff wants you to stay here."

"Not as much as he wants me to have food in the refrigerator when he gets hungry," I said, and went next door to the Suncrest Market.

Julie, a pretty, fresh-faced blond girl, came quickly to me, untying her blue apron. "Dr. Whitney, I heard something happened! Where's Jaison? Is he okay?"

She followed me around the store, and I told her what I'd seen. My hands trembled as I picked up milk, juice, frozen pizzas, a dozen yoghurts, and cookies.

"That's racist!" she said. "I warned Jaison that we need to leave this ass-backwards town."

"It's the nature of the human species to distrust anything

outside the tribe. If you went to a big city, they'd treat you like a hick, and Jai wouldn't be any safer." I hesitated over the beer display, where a new brand, Coyote Runaway, was on sale. I hated new things, but I liked cheap beer. "What's this?"

"It's the microbrewery where that lumber store used to be, behind the hotel. West Coast India Pale Ale. The sales rep says we're supposed to say it's clean and hoppy. Can you tell what's going to happen to Jai?" Julie's clear blue eyes tried to catch mine.

"The only thing I can predict is that I am going to need a drink soon." I put a six-pack of the pale ale in my cart.

"But, Dr. Whitney, the animals can tell you things, right? Maybe the sheriff's dog can tell you something about that Kearney deputy."

I sort of smiled. "I'll do whatever I can to protect Jaison. He's like my kid brother," I said, which was not at all true because I loved Jaison, and I hated and feared my brother, Raymond. I pushed away the horrible images of our last encounter.

Then the store's generic music stopped, and someone announced on the speakers, "Dr. Madeleine Whitney, please report to the sheriff's office. Dr. Madeleine Whitney, please report to the sheriff's office."

I carried my groceries back to the substation and left them in the employee lounge. I opened a bottle of beer, took a few long gulps, and walked down the corridor to a door with *Sheriff's Captain Oliver W. Desjardins* painted in gold and black block letters on the inset glass. Oliver wasn't the sheriff—who was officially the sheriff-coroner based at the county seat—but he was sheriff to us here in Coyote Run, upholder and enforcer, protector and consoler, and rational and empathetic arbiter of the law.

"Close the door behind you."

"Ollie, it's been a hell of a day, and you have lost your damn mind if you think I'm going to..." I gestured with my hand sliding over the bottle.

He blinked a few times and said softly, "You really can't read a room, can you, babe? Close the door because I want a private word."

I slammed the door shut.

"Was that necessary?"

"Hard to say. I'm simmering with rage. Did you fire that dangerous asshole yet? Do I need a lawyer to file a complaint, and will your brother do it for me? Will he give me a special rate?"

"Sure, if it's like your 'special rate' of double-charging annoying clients. Let's calm down and figure this out, okay?"

I could meet Oliver's amber eyes for almost three seconds without much discomfort. His skin was a warm toasty shade this time of year, except for his ears, which were sunburned along the helix. "You keep forgetting to put sunscreen on your ears." My shaking amplified, and I could hear my teeth chattering.

He came to me, kissing me and then pulling me close, and I pressed my head against his shoulder, comforted by his solidity and the rhythm of his breathing, tethering me to the whirling earth.

"Tighter," I said, and he squeezed. "You always smell wonderful, Ollie."

"I'm glad you're okay."

"I am so *not* okay, but at least I'm with you. You have no idea what it's like to be jolted with high voltage."

"Yeah, I do. Being tased is part of our training, but I signed up for that. You didn't, and I wish this hadn't happened to you. You're safe now." When I stopped trembling, he released me and said, "Put down that beer. You're going to have an official interview."

"Has Jai filed his complaint yet? Whatever he says happened, happened. I rescued a dog this morning, all tore up. Someone was using him as bait for dog fighting. Why are people so cruel?" My eyes welled. "Ben may have to amputate part of his leg."

"If the dog is with Ben, he's in capable hands, babe. Interview room."

When I lifted the bottle to my mouth, it clacked hard against my teeth. I took another swig before following Oliver to a small gray room with a Formica table and florescent lights buzzing overhead. A woman in a tan suit and white shirt sat in a straight-backed metal chair, and there was a recorder on the table.

Oliver sat beside her, and I dropped into the chair on the opposite side of the table.

The fortyish woman had thick, straight eyebrows, straight bangs across a straight dark bob, and straight shoulders. Her sand-beige skin was flushed, as if she wasn't accustomed to our summer heat. Her severe simplicity was very attractive, but I was relieved when she didn't try to shake hands.

"I'm Maddie. Who are you?"

"Assistant Deputy Andrea Kleinfeld from Internal Affairs. I've been asked to sit in as a courtesy, Dr. Whitney." She clicked on the recorder and said the date and time and "This interview is being recorded. Would you please state your full name?"

"Oliver can tell you."

Oliver leaned back in his chair. "Humor me, and just answer the questions, Maddie."

"My name is Madeleine Margaret Whitney. A horrible man with high-powered weapons stopped Jaison for no reason than DWB. Zoe's likely executing a loony plot while I'm away from WCRC." I turned to Andrea and said, "That's the Whitney Canine Rehabilitation Center. Zoe is my intern. Super-bright girl, but she has an overzealous entrepreneurial drive. One of my part-timers is supervising her now, but if an emergency comes up, and Jaison and I are stuck here, anything could happen. Because things *do* happen. People move to the country, imagining a simpler life, but life here has a different set of complications. The veterinarian is nearby, but do you know how far it is to the emergency room? The answer is, too damn far. If your arm is pulled off by a hay bailer, you'll bleed out and die before the ambulance even arrives."

"Thank you for that information, but can we get back to the subject at hand?" Andrea said.

Oliver picked up a sheet of paper. "The stop was legit. Deputy Kearney recognized the Tundra and knew Jaison wasn't the owner."

"*How* could he know Jaison wasn't the owner?" I said. "Is there a law—besides DWB—against young Black men driving new-model trucks?"

"Deputy Kearney knew because his wife takes knitting classes at Donna-June Looper's school, and he recognized the *Get Crafty at Looper's* bumper sticker."

Now I remembered seeing *The Crafty Looper* painted on a two-story stucco building off Main Street. "Be that as it may, Kearney was about to punch Jaison."

"Dr. Whitney, would you please relay the events chronologically?" Andrea's voice was even and flat, trying to calm me.

But I wasn't calmed, recalling the excruciating jolt of the taser and the subsequent paralysis. At some point, I jumped up and began pacing, my arms flying out and my voice increasingly strident as I railed against Richard Kearney and demanded violent justice, but no matter how loudly I shouted, I was unable to drown out the buzzing lights overhead and my blood pulsing in my ears.

Oliver said, "I need to do this," to Andrea, and his arms wrapped around me tight as a vise and he was saying, "It's okay, Maddie, it's okay. Jaison's fine. You're fine. We're all fine. That's enough for today."

Most shocking, besides the taser, was learning that Jaison had not filed a complaint against Deputy Kearney. He'd already gone with Julie to pick up the Tundra by the time my interview ended.

I still needed to get my old truck and Ollie was on duty until evening, so Andrea Kleinfeld said, "I'll give you a lift, Dr. Whitney."

I carried my groceries and a plastic bag with my soiled pants—the way I had in grade school, all the times I wet myself. Shame rose in me. "I only use that title professionally for consultations. Call me Maddie. Do you have any dogs?"

She compressed her lips, and then said, "I had a sweet mutt. She passed away last spring at fourteen."

"I'm sorry." I hesitated by her Ford Interceptor.

"You can sit in the front," Andrea said, and we got in. "I don't have time for a dog now."

"Of course you do. You can take it to work like Oliver takes Zeus to the station."

"He's allowed to because Zeus is a working dog. I'm impressed by the Midnight Runners Search and Rescue team, Dr. Whitney."

"We're back to that again. Any dog can be a working dog. The jobs might differ. Do you like to hunt? I have a beauty of a pointer. She's medium sized, about forty-five pounds, and she'd be an excellent companion and-or family dog. German shorthairs are multipurpose. She'd be a fantastic running companion. I can offer you my special rate for training sessions."

I adjusted the window, but the air was blowing too strong, so I had to nudge it back and forth several times, until it was okay, but then the sun shone right in my eyes, so I moved the visor.

"Dr. Whitney, the sheriff's captain explained your condition."

"That I'm his girlfriend? That sounds so juvenile. Americans should have a better term for adult relationships. 'Lover' sounds as if it's used by someone who says ciao and kisses you on both cheeks. I'm talking about people who drink rosé instead of an honest cold beer. I hate those people."

"I don't hunt, but I like to skeet-shoot and I like rosé."

"It's not a hard-and-fast hatred. I make exceptions."

The side of her mouth crooked upward. "The sheriff's captain said that you're neurodivergent, or do you prefer 'autism spectrum' or another phrase?"

"Even if that wasn't an overly personal question, I don't like being labeled. Also, I sincerely doubt he knows any of those terms. Oliver's skill set is crime, sports, and hot women. He'd be ecstatic to uncover a sports rigging scheme perpetrated by a sexy babe. Andrea, have you heard of any dog fighting rings in the county?"

"Andrea is overly personal, and there's animal abuse everywhere."

"That's depressing."

"I don't dwell on the misery. I try to do something about it."

We arrived at my junker, which had been moved to the side of the road. I said, "If you're serious about fighting the good fight, you'll take action against that piece-of-shit Kearney. Thanks for the ride and come visit WCRC soon."

"I may just do that, Dr. Whitney," she said, and waved to me as she drove off.

I got in my truck and took a sip of my melted strawberry shake, before pouring the rest of it on the side of the road. I ate cold French fries as I made my way home.

"Where's Jaison?" My muscles ached as if I'd worked out much too hard the day before.

Zoe was finishing the evening feeding, and she skipped to me, her arms out, and I put my finger to my lips before she emitted one of her teenage screams.

I picked up my sturdy little terrier, Scully, and pressed my cheek against her scruffy fur, breathing slowly, and thinking breathe, just breathe. "Don't get the dogs hyped up, sweetie."

"But! But! But!" she said, hopping from foot to foot with each *but*. She must have grown three inches in the last year and was almost as tall as me.

"Anarchy isn't happiness, Zoe, so be manic on your own time and peaceful around the pack. To reiterate, where's Jaison?"

"He's slow-pace running with Heidi and Bertie." Heidi, a Rottweiler, didn't have much speed, and my beautiful Bertie moved with difficulty. "He told me what happened, and you got a Tundra. What *really* happened? My parents said they heard you got into a slugfest, and you were at the station, and I totally love your cool sweats, but Jai said... well, he didn't say much. He's taciturn. That's one of my vocabulary words. Can you speak Pig Latin? I learned it from Grampa. In Pig Latin that would be *es-hay aciturnay*."

"Jai's laconic. Taciturn has a negative connotation, and laconic implies a laid-back humor. *Ooklay tnay pnay*. I didn't get in a fight. I did get tased."

"Geez Louise! *Eezgay Ouiselay*!"

"Yeah, exactly. It's time for you to go home, isn't it?"

"But!"

"I'll tell you about it tomorrow. I need to get a few things straight with the sheriff first."

She left reluctantly, releasing her long hair from its ponytail, muttering complaints, and admiring the truck. She was a diligent worker, and her parents surely missed her help at their feedstore.

Once in the double-wide office trailer, I threw my soiled jeans and a load of dirty towels into the washing machine.

I took two beers and a glass of water out to the deck as Jai was returning. I handed Jai the water, and he drank half and poured the rest over his head. It ran in rivulets, washing away the dust on his face. We opened our bottles and sat on a bench. Dry leaves tumbled across the yard in the early evening breeze.

Bertie trotted up to me, and I rubbed the thick golden fur

around the dark scar tissue and avoided his hot spots. Old shrapnel, scattered throughout his body, slowly poisoned him and continually pained him. "Bertie, you are the noblest of creatures." I dropped my forehead to his head, grateful that he had come into my life. And then Vixen scooted up, pushing her narrow snout between us.

"We were having a moment," I said, before giving her a scratch. "Jaison, did I make things worse today?"

He shrugged. "For you, definitely. For me, hard to say."

"I thought Kearney was about to hit you. Why didn't you file a complaint?"

"Because I don't want to get shot the next time he sees me, and I plan to keep my distance."

A massive Rottweiler, Heidi, lumbered to Jai and rested her massive head on his knee. When Vixen approached, the Rottie growled. "No, Heidi," Jaison corrected, but Vixen scooted away.

"I wish I could growl, like Heidi, and warn people off," I said.

"No, you don't. Me, I always gotta try to put White folks at ease and reassure them I'm not planning to beat on them."

"Jai, if we were in a nineties movie, we would switch places. I'd be a laconic cool dude with stunning cheekbones, and you'd be the hot weirdo chick, also with stunning cheekbones, and shenanigans would ensue," I said. "Kearney claimed he thought you stole the truck. Do you believe him?"

Jaison rolled the beer bottle over his forehead. "Dude like that is going to automatically assume I'm a criminal. It's like living in a world of fear-biters: no fast moves because they're primed to react."

"Oliver's not that way. He's equally suspicious of everyone, including me."

"'Cept you have a record."

"No convictions, though. That aside, why did Kearney call me a loco chica?" I pressed my free hand against Jaison's arm. "I'm almost as dark as you. Do you think people have been biased against me because of race and I didn't even realize it?"

"You are not near as dark as me, and you got a whole lot of things that will set a person off. Do we have to talk about this now?"

"No." So my friend and I drank quietly under a sky so blue it made my heart break.

Chapter Four

I WAS EATING a bowl of granola in my living room, and Bertie was snoozing on his floor pillow when Ben called and said, "It's a miracle your stray doesn't need surgery. He has a sprain, extensive bruising, multiple lacerations and contusions, on top of the obvious infections. He's significantly underweight and anemic."

"That's wonderful news!"

"He also has a heart murmur, cardiomyopathy. Genetics may be the reason, since he looks part Dobie. You're familiar with it?"

"Yes, one of my clients raises St. Bernards, and it's always a concern. Does that mean no huge medical bill?"

"Depends on your definition of huge. At minimum, he'll have to be treated and observed for the next few days. He's been quiet, knocked out by the meds, and I hope he doesn't turn out to be a canine Mr. Hyde."

"You have a real attitude about your patients lately. Except for one. Why is it that you pay so much attention to Emily Ayer's Weasel?"

There was a long pause on the line, and finally, Ben said, "I'm sure you didn't mean that the way it sounded, Maddie."

"I intended for it to sound dirty, but in a funny way."

"Hmm, I think you need to work on your routine. I'm not ignoring you or your dogs, Maddie."

"Why does it feel like it, then?"

"Maybe you're relying more on everyone else with Kenzie away?" he said. "I heard you got tased by the new deputy. I'm so sorry. Are you okay?"

"I don't want to think about it. Let me enjoy the news about the bait dog, now. Thanks, Ben."

I was relieved about the dog, but angry, drained, and confused. I glanced at the chart on my whiteboard, tracking my goals and progress. I was already fourteen calls over my weekly quota to my sister and this wasn't a discussion I could limit to texts, which I'd also maxed out. Kenzie lived with her boyfriend over the mountain, in an upscale tourist town where there was always something for her to do. She might be out at a fancy restaurant now, or taking a yoga class, or getting a facial, whatever it was that women did in those sorts of places.

When I thought of her now, I became conscious of the dirt in the country. The dirt that always got under my bitten nails. The dirt that dusted up over my boots and my jeans. The dirt that grimed my hands when petting dogs that had rolled themselves dry. The dirt that drifted through every open door and every nook and cranny. I had been unaware of dirt until Kenzie moved away. Now, when I visited her, I felt as if I was contaminating the modern furniture of her boyfriend's condo.

My chart showed that I was overdue to call my mother. I dialed her number, half hoping that I'd get her voicemail, but she answered immediately.

"Madeleine Margaret, it's about time you called! I've had to get news of you from your sister. How is my famous daughter?"

"Kenzie's deliriously happy. She loves living away. She never visits."

"Honestly, you exaggerate everything," she said, and there

was a voice in the background. "Larry says hello. Our church group went to the water park today. Can you imagine? Me, at a water park!"

She was kind enough not to mention the spring break when she'd scraped together enough money to take us to Splash Junction. It was supposed to be a special treat for all of us, but I'd gone into sensory overload and run away, hiding behind a pretzel booth and then kicking and screaming when dragged out. My sister and brother had cried when we'd been asked to leave. "Tell Larry I said 'hello' back. I hope you had fun, Mom."

"It was wonderful! Everything was wonderful—the slides, the lazy river, and the food. I even went on some rides. Well, I had to close my eyes for the scary parts, but Larry was right there, holding onto me."

"Lucky you! I'd need to be put in a straight-jacket before I'd ride anything scary."

"That's what I mean by exaggerating. You do terrifying things all the time. You work with vicious animals."

"They're not vicious. They're like me: tragically misunderstood. How is your farm food giveaway going?"

I filed the ragged edges of my chewed nails while she told me about the food-distribution program for the poor. "It's called a food desert. There are no supermarkets to shop for groceries. At least we had Suncrest Market. Do they still have the bin of bruised fruits and vegetables and dented cans on sale?"

"Yep, they still have that. Oliver says the ugly food bin is like my ugly dog rescues; not much to look at, but bargain treasures."

"How's your handsome man? When will we hear wedding bells?"

"You can check with Kenzie, but she hasn't told me a thing about getting married...because she doesn't call me *at all*."

"Hmm, like you won't call Raymond?"

"That's complicated." The last time I'd seen my drunken

brother, he'd been kicking Bertie and tormenting me. He'd stolen our gun safe and vanished.

"You participated in making it complicated. He's doing well now. He stopped drinking, and he's enjoying his vacation."

"How can he have a vacation when he's never been legitimately employed?"

She was silent long enough to make me squirm, and then she said, "Did you call me only to argue? All a mother wants is for her children to get along and support one another."

"Sorry, Mom."

"Have you been doing anything else? Besides dog things?"

"On the 'famous daughter' front, Abel Myklebust roped me into being in a quiz contest fundraiser for the library."

"Oh, that's nice," she said, her voice a little strained.

"You remember Abel. Weren't you and Dad friends with him?"

"We were neighbors," she said. "Barely acquaintances. How is he doing?"

"Okay, I guess, but I don't pay much attention to him. He keeps trying to be, um, friends. Do you want me to say hello to him for you?"

"No, that's not necessary," she said, and then she launched into a story about her friend's bathroom addition.

I was washing dishes when I heard a car crunching the gravel outside. The dogs barked in greeting, and soon there was a rap on my door, and Oliver opened it.

He had changed into clean jeans and a tan shirt.

"Do you have a warrant?" I said.

"I got your warrant right here," he said, and cupped his hand over his crotch while thrusting his hips.

I laughed so hard I snorted. I was still laughing when he grabbed me firmly the way I liked and kissed me.

He let go and said, "If you're laughing, you've recovered from your trauma."

"It's hysterical laughter. I have hysteria, which comes from the Greek word for uterus. Your sister told me that's why men are never truly hysterical, because they lack uteri."

"She was joking."

"Quite possibly. What are you going to do about that deputy, and who the hell is he, anyway?"

"He transferred in. I told you about him."

"Oliver, I hang on your every word, and I don't recall you mentioning him."

"I absolutely have. You would remember if I said he had a dog. He's good with Zeus."

I pursed my lips. "Even Hitler had his points, I suppose."

"The first one to bring up a Hitler comparison loses." Oliver went to my kitchenette and took a Coyote Runaway bottle from the fridge. "I tasted this at the brewery. I like it." He opened the bottle and pulled me over to sit with him on the sofa. "I'm sorry about the misunderstanding. And it *was* a misunderstanding."

"Like hell, Ollie! He gratuitously tased me!"

"He said you acted like you were high, 'recklessly eyeballing' him, and...and I explained."

My chest rose and fell, and I counted to ten and then twenty and felt my face go red because I realized what I must have looked like to Kearney. Finally, I said, "It doesn't matter what I looked like, and what he did to me. He was going to hit Jaison."

"I'll keep Kearney on a short leash, Mad Girl, until he learns the territory and the rules. I want to give him a chance, because I can sure as hell use someone who wants to do more than collect a check."

"I take in dangerous dogs, but I don't give them weapons!" I said, and I knew my voice was too loud because Bertie's ears pivoted forward and he subtly tensed.

"Do you want me to leave?"

"What for? Am I supposed to deprive myself of good sex simply because you're siding with a psychopath? That makes no sense."

"Only good?" he said in a husky voice, as I took his hand and yanked him toward the bedroom, saying, "I'll have to conduct a full evaluation."

"Okay, very good." I sprawled beside Oliver, my leg crossed over his, and his fingers twined with mine. "Exceptionally good. Prodigy-level sex." My entire body was relaxed, all the muscles uncoiled from the jaggy, erratic tension that ruled my life. "Let's go out. We don't need flashlights. The moon is bright enough."

We dressed and went to the dog center, where he'd left his powerful brindled Dutch shepherd Zeus. We walked along a path cut through the field, with Bertie and Zeus exploring beside us. The dogs looked like wolves in the moonlight as they explored, sniffing the waist-high grasses that waved in the breeze.

Frogs ribbited from the pond, and I said, "At least Abel Myklebust isn't diverting all the water upstream and ruining my habitat. Which reminds me, he's insisting that you go to a library fundraiser at Grange Hall on Saturday."

"Sounds boring."

"Okay, I'll tell him we can't make it because we have official search and rescue business. It's a stupid event, anyway. A quiz team contest."

"I'm the mack daddy of team players. Count me in."

"Are you sure? Won't you be publicly embarrassed if they ask you a question about Greek names for body organs?"

"I've heard of this thing 'embarrassed,' but I've never personally experienced it. Besides, you're not the only intellectual in town, and half the stuff people think you know, you invent. What's the dress code?"

"If Abel's putting it on, gaudy bolo ties and two-tone alligator boots. There won't be any food. Are you absolutely sure you want to go?"

"Don't use me as your excuse. Do you have anything else you'd like to share with me?"

We followed a horse path through neighbors' land, and I told Oliver about the bait dog's condition, and he was quiet for a long time before saying, "You're doing enough to help the dog. Forget about the perpetrators."

"But if I can assist in identifying them, we can stop them from hurting dogs."

"Let it go, Maddie. You have no idea how dangerous those people are," he said. "There was another opioid overdose today. We caught him in time to use Narcan. It was a construction worker who got hooked with legal prescriptions."

"People get injured. Big Pharma preys on that. Speaking of criminal behavior, one of those nuts from the yurts at the Ayers' place was setting off fireworks today. When I ran into Dino, I tried to impress upon him the dangers of setting the whole town ablaze, but he preferred discussing the possibility of cloning his dog Weasel."

The faint light glinted on Oliver's teeth when he smiled. "I'm sure that's an accurate account of the situation."

"It totally is. And what about the fire pit at the Ayers'?"

"They have a permit, but conditions were different when it was issued. I'll have the marshal visit again."

"Do it right away. I don't want an accident—"

"None of us do."

We were quiet for a while, not wanting to revisit recent tragedies.

"Ollie, what do you make of Emily Ayer?"

"She's pretty."

"Quite the understatement. Emily's a Madonna, the timeless

incarnation of serene and maternal beauty. When did the Ayers' vineyard have that pesticide wind-drift from the farmer across the highway? Remember how their grapevines shriveled and died?"

"About four years ago. They lost the lawsuit. Jim said the legal fees wiped them out." Oliver's older brother was an attorney. "Let's hope these vines will finally take."

"Toxins can cause neurological problems or cancerous growths. Weasel's having health problems, and maybe there's a connection," I said. "Corporations have deep pockets and never, ever admit culpability."

"Don't disturb the peace with that rant."

"Okay, but only for you."

We were quiet for several minutes as we took another trail that looped around to what used to be a corner of my family's property. My sister and I had sold a five-acre parcel to Ben Meadows and his wife, who were building a spacious, eco-friendly house.

Oliver said, "Looks like this place is almost finished. You're eventually going to have to find tenants for your house."

"I have already asked everyone who is not annoying."

"You mean Jaison."

"That's what I said. But he thinks it will give his girlfriend ideas about moving in. Kenzie should be helping me with this."

"But you're the one who'll have to deal with the tenants day to day, and your sister is aware of how picky you are."

"Exactly. That's why she should screen them for me."

The rooster's crow announced that it was about 5:30 a.m., and Oliver was rustling around in the dark of my bedroom, getting dressed, when his phone buzzed.

"Desjardins, here," he answered. After a pause he asked questions about the time, location, and details of something. He turned on a lamp and sat on the side of my bed while he put on his shoes. "I'll be there as soon as I can. Dr. Whitney will follow with the dogs. I'll need a search object. Wear gloves and get something from his car with his scent, preferably clothing, and then place it in a plastic bag."

He ended the call and inhaled deeply.

"What's up?" I said.

Oliver looked at me, his jaw set and his shoulders tense. "Dino Ayer's boat just exploded."

Chapter Five

OLIVER LEFT QUICKLY, and I hurried to dress in hiking boots, jeans, and my orange jacket with *Midnight Runners Search & Rescue* on the back. I called Jaison to tell him where I was going, and then I phoned Ben and said, "The situation is absolutely dire. We've got a search and rescue. Can you get someone to cover you at the clinic?"

"Meet me outside the house in a minute."

I buckled Bertie and Zeus in their tracking harnesses. After a moment of indecision, I finally snapped a harness on Vixen, and I put the dogs in crates in the Tundra. I wasn't familiar with the truck's roar when I pressed on the gas, but I tried to quell my unease, and rolled up the drive to the house.

The lights flashed on in the kitchen, and Ben came through the back door, pulling on his *Midnight Runners* jacket and carrying a backpack. He climbed in and said, "Where are we going? Who's missing?"

"Sky Lake. Dino Ayer's boat blew up."

"No!"

I glanced over, and Ben's face looked pale, but it could have been the gloom of the morning. I said, "He's been having engine trouble, but hell. I hope he jumped off in time. Maybe it will be as easy as finding him ashore."

"Did Emily call this in?"

"No idea." I concentrated on driving the unfamiliar vehicle, disturbed by the numerous gauges and weird feel of the seat.

"At least it's not winter."

"It's a warm lake, but depending upon how far out he was, or if he was injured, he might not have the energy to get to shore. *If* he made it off the boat."

"Let's hope for the best. Anyone else joining us?"

"We'll call in another team if we need them. How do you feel about handling Vixen? I've been working with her, but she's not in Bertie's league."

"You don't think any dog is in Bertie's league."

I flashed a smile at him, glad he understood that Bertie was special.

Coyote Run was at one end of the county, and Sky Lake was at the other. When I became accustomed to the truck, I speeded up and said to Ben, "Find some music." Music always calmed me, and he tuned into a Top Ten station, which was better than thinking about Dino sinking into the deep, deep water.

The lake was eighty miles around, and most of those miles were undeveloped forest. There were resorts and private homes, but Dino docked his boat at an isolated marina with a few ramshackle cottage rentals scattered about. I parked in the small dirt lot behind four county patrol cars, a fire engine, an EMT van, and Dino's truck. Dozens of people milled about, talking on radios and phones, and drinking coffee from paper cups.

Out on the lake, dark smoke wafted up from darker wreckage, and search lights from patrol boats strafed water that shone like obsidian. "That must be what's left," I said. "How far is it out?"

"Hard to guess," Ben said. "About half a mile."

Oliver saw us and came over. "Thanks for getting here so

quickly," he said. "One of the vacationers heard a blast and spotted the fire on the lake eighty minutes ago."

"So long?" I said.

"He thought it might be someone partying, or one of the festivals having an event. Another fisherman called in the blaze, but there's no telling if the boat—and not much is left of it—drifted between the blast and its current location."

"Have you called Emily yet?" Ben asked, and I heard the anxiousness in his voice.

"A deputy and a crisis counselor are with her now. We've asked her to stay home on the off chance that Dino hitched a ride and made it back." Oliver sighed and said, "She shouldn't be here if we find Dino's body."

Oliver guided us to wooden picnic tables that were set up end to end. Maps were spread out on one. He introduced us to the boat patrol captain, and Ben said, "I'm a veterinarian, but I have emergency first-aid training."

"Glad you're here, Dr. Whitney, Dr. Meadows," the boat patrol captain said. "These two quadrants are the likeliest spots he might have come ashore, based on the subject's last known position, currents, and distance. Once the wreckage cools, we'll bring her in and check for...remains. We'll keep cruising the lake, and we did a hasty search of the shoreline. It was dark, and we didn't find him, so it's likely that if he did make it, he's well enough to move."

"Do you have a search object?"

"I do," Oliver said, holding up a plastic bag. "A T-shirt from his truck. Maddie, how would you like us to proceed?"

I nodded, appreciative that he made it clear to others that I was directing the search. "Captain, please keep your crew away from quadrants A and B. Because you're covering the water, I think an initial lateral search is the fastest way to find out if Dino reached land. If we can locate that point, we'll search outward. He can't have gone far without hitting a road, or a hillside too steep to climb."

"There's a containment team stationed at likely spots," Oliver said, "and an emergency call went out to homes and businesses on this side of the lake."

"The more eyes, the better. But I don't want anyone distracting us or contaminating the scene any further. If we find anything, we'll send you the coordinates."

"Can I expect a check-in at thirty-minutes?" the patrol captain said.

"Not if we're busy. We're going to be slow and methodical."

The patrol captain called his crew back from their hunt, and my team went to my truck and took the dogs out of the crates. We walked along the road toward quadrant A and then cut back to our starting point on the shore. I opened the plastic bag and held Dino's oil-stained T-shirt to the dogs, letting them sniff, and then we ordered them to search. Bertie walked with his nose down, and Zeus alternated between lifting his snout to the air and dropping it to the ground. Behind us, Ben tried to control Vixen, who coursed from side to side, covering as much territory as she could on the length of her leash.

Vixen froze in place, raised her front paw, and pointed toward an egret on the muddy flats. "A bird dog is always a bird dog. She keeps hoping I'll shoot something," I said.

We sped through sandy beaches by houses and vacation rentals, already covered with too many footprints, as the sun began to rise. Sweat trickled down my back. We trudged through mud flats, pushing aside cattails and reeds, sinking into muck that stunk of sulfur and rotting algae. Fifteen minutes passed, and then another fifteen, and the dogs had no hits.

We didn't speak, and I tried to listen through the rustling of trees, the birdsong, the hum and rumble of machinery beginning the day, for any sign of Dino. Out on the lake, the smoke had faded.

The boat's burned carcass was being tugged toward the resort landing. Soon the brush along the shore was too thick for us to see our point of origin.

"Ninety minutes," Ben said. "Shouldn't we call in?"

Scratches crisscrossed my exposed skin, and an insect bite itched on my forehead. "Let's wait until we reach the end of the quadrant."

But before we could, a voice sounded on Oliver's walkie-talkie. He handed me Zeus's leash and walked out of hearing. Ben gave the dogs water, and I splashed some over my face, wiping it away with my sleeve.

Oliver returned, his face stony. "Time to go back. They found Dino."

"On the boat?" I said.

He nodded, and we were silent, thinking about Dino's terrible fate. Or, rather, Oliver and I were thinking about Dino's terrible fate. I couldn't guess what Ben, so attentive to lovely Emily Ayer, might be thinking about.

"We better get back," Oliver said. "No calls to anyone about Dino until an official statement goes out." He picked up Zeus's leash, and I called Bertie to my side.

Vixen was sniffing farther off at a narrow trail, and she ignored Ben when he called for her. Something rustled up the path, and Vixen flashed after it, the long leash trailing behind like the tail of a comet.

"Vixen, come! Vixen, come!" I called, even as the pounding of her paws became fainter.

"Prancer and Dixon," Ben said.

Oliver said, "Maddie, you don't even try to train that dog."

Ben's eyebrows rose, and his eyes crinkled at the corners. "Maddie's overzealous sense of loyalty makes her believe she's betraying Bertie if she trains Vixen."

"Desire to track can't be trained into a dog." I reached down to pet my beautiful favorite, who was panting and weary. "I'll find her. Take Bertie back to base and give him something to eat, if you don't mind."

I trotted after Vixen. Something landed on my face, and I swatted at it, missing the insect, but hurting my cheek. Mud in my trail boots squished its way down, and each step squeaked.

Vixen avidly hunted birds and critters, and I'd once seen her sizing up a horse, so she could have been following anything. Every few minutes I'd call, "Vixen!" so she could find me if she decided to return. I should have brought Zeus to help me, because I kept backtracking, peering through the thick growth for any sight of the prodigal dog.

I heard a familiar high-pitched yip and moved forward to a branch of the trail that eventually curved back toward the water, and then I jogged until I came to a small clearing with a tidy cabin. A fishing boat, with *Purlynn's Pearl* in script on the hull, was moored at a private dock. There was a tool shed and a grill on one side of the cabin and a stone firepit in front.

Vixen sat alertly by the firepit. She'd been digging, and sand clumped on her wet fur.

"Stay," I said, low and firm, but she came toward me, wriggling her rump. She had something in her mouth. She sat and dutifully dropped it at my feet.

I crouched to examine the dirt and sand crusted object.

I was too sad and exhausted and exasperated to be shocked, but I should have been. The desiccated finger had landed so that it pointed straight at me, and I said, "Fuck you, too, Dino."

After putting the awful thing in a plastic bag, I walked around the cabin. It looked like something in an advertisement for rustic living, with requisite antlers over the front door, green trim, rocking chairs on the porch, and a coir doormat with *You're Reel Welcome!*

Through a window, I could see a comfy man cave of leather sofas and polished pine furniture.

I clanged the brass bell hanging from the awning. No one answered, so I tried the door. Then I tied Vixen to a post and pushed at the windows, because you never know, but they were latched shut.

However, the tool shed, filled with fishing equipment and machinery, was open. *People should be more careful*, I thought. It only took a minute to discover a thin metal rectangle that I used as a shim to unlock a side window of the cabin.

I dropped into a bedroom with twin beds covered with plaid camp blankets and old fishing gear on the walls. Another bedroom was much the same. The sink was clean and dry. The copper kettle on the wood-burning stove was cold.

The refrigerator was stocked with beer and sodas, and the cabinets had a variety of jerkies, granola bars, and candy bars, so I took a selection and shoved them in my backpack.

The living room had a display case filled with model wooden boats, from speedboats to shrimpers to dinghies. Over the stone fireplace was a large needlepoint with a fishing line and hook that read *Get hooked at the Loopers.*

It was too crafty to ignore, so I rummaged through a desk. A few bills and receipts were written out to Gordon Looper, and the billing address was the same as Donna-June's, who'd sold the truck to me. I examined framed photos on the mantel, and there she was, in all her pastel glory, beside a middle-aged man, who I assumed was the runaway husband.

Another prominent photo showed a brown-haired teenage girl, wearing a flannel shirt and jeans, her mouth open in laughter as she held a fishing net over Gordon's head. I tried to connect this girl with the emaciated young woman at Donna-June's house. Perhaps she was a sister.

Other photos showed Gordon on his boat, with his catch, and

in one, he and Dino Ayer grinned like kids as they stood on a sunny beach with fishing poles and icy drinks. In the background was a palm tree thatched cabana with a sign that read *Puerto Azul*.

People knew one another in small towns, spheres traveling along paths that inevitably intersected. Perhaps Dino had buried his severed finger here because this cabin was Dino's happy place, where he came to go fishing with his friend.

Or maybe Gordon Looper was responsible for the amputation.

And maybe the explosion wasn't an accident.

I walked to the road, Vixen at heel beside me, and one of the containment team members gave me a lift back to base. The charred shell of Dino's boat was in a dry-dock, taped off from the crowd that had gathered. A news van idled in the parking lot, but I didn't recognize the reporter talking to the cameraman.

Ben sat on a bench, drinking coffee, with the dogs beside him. "Someone brought us sausages and biscuits. The dogs inhaled theirs," he said, and handed me a cardboard tray with a paper cup and a sandwich.

I tied Vixen's leash on the bench leg and then picked up the sandwich. The cold sausages were too suggestive, so I fed them to Vixen and ate the biscuit, washing it down with lukewarm coffee. "This coffee is terrible. So, what's happening?" I asked.

"They've told Emily. She must be going through hell. She's a sensitive woman."

I glanced into Ben's dark brown eyes for a second, but it only made me feel odd and confused. "Can you get a ride back from someone else? I have to talk to Ollie before I leave."

"Is everything okay, Maddie?"

My arms flew up, splashing the last drops of coffee from the cup. "With me, it never is, Ben."

* * * *

Oliver and the patrol captain were talking, while the county's coroner-sheriff, who had deigned to haul his ass to the scene of a newsworthy crime, addressed a small cluster of reporters. The paramedics van drove away with what I supposed were Dino's earthly remains.

I could practically feel the detached finger in my backpack, commanding me to do something: What? I had no idea.

While Oliver was occupied, I meandered to the repair shed by the dock. A man in coveralls was wiping his hands on a rag. "Quite a to-do," he said.

"It isn't every day you have an explosion," I said. "Are they absolutely sure it was Dino Ayer on the boat?"

"He was missing his fuck-you finger and wore his wedding ring, sort of melted, so, yeah. He was always here, asking for advice and not taking it."

"Is it normal for a boat to blow up like that?"

The mechanic let out a snort. "Not unless you're a total knucklehead, but Dino, bless him, fit the bill. He'd use a pipe wrench to hammer a screw like a nail, and that vineyard of his was a bust, wasn't it? Anyways, he'd just filled up the tank so there was plenty of fuel onboard."

I felt as if someone was running an ice cube up and down my spine, and I tried to shake off the sensation. The mechanic stared at me, and I said, "Sorry, I got the jimmies. I ran into Dino the other day, and the stump on his hand was barely healed. Did you hear about his accident?"

"Sure did. He was messing with a jigsaw and yakking to a buddy at the same time, not paying attention and then," the man said, and made a *bzzz-bzzz-bzzz* sound with a rolling motion of his hand. "Blood spurting everywhere. His friend packed the finger in ice, and they were off to the ER."

"Do you remember the friend?"

"Sure. Gordon Looper. Has a cabin here."

"Gordon Looper? His wife owns The Crafty Looper?"

The mechanic nodded. "He always joked that he used the finger as bait. Him and Dino are—*were*—tight. Like *Brokeback Mountain*, but with fishing instead of homo sex."

"I'll pass on the fishing, but homo sex is one of my favorite kinds," I said, and walked toward Oliver, who waved at me.

I loved the sight of him in all his variations and moods. I loved the way sunlight picked up the copper strands in his hair, the set of his shoulders, his upright posture. I loved the stretch of his legs and the reach of his arms. I loved the practicality and functionality of his body, and the sense of efficiency and competency that he projected.

I grasped his hand and, when he squeezed mine, I felt grounded — as if I wouldn't be whirled off the speeding surface of the earth.

"How's it going, Ollie?"

"Horrible, as expected. It probably happened quickly. I don't think that's going to console Emily and the kids much."

"Are you investigating? Are you *sure* it's an accident?" My stomach felt queasy, remembering how my sister had locked our grandfather's guns away from me. Not that I ever would have... I wouldn't now.

"You and everyone else knew he was having engine trouble, and that's the likeliest cause of the explosion. Dino may be, may have *been*, a Coyote Run resident, but this incident goes to the county, and they'll put as much time into it as it warrants. Or as they *think* it warrants."

"You're off the whole case? You don't have any further responsibility?"

"Nope. Why?"

"Nothing. I kinda hate the fake real sheriff-coroner. You're the only sheriff for me."

He hid his smile behind his hand. "Thanks for coming and

giving us so much of your time. I'm sure you're overdue to commit some infraction of the law."

"You'll be impressed to learn that I'm all caught up today."

Oliver ducked his head, and I knew he was laughing by the way his shoulders shook. "I'm not even gonna guess. Go home, Mad Girl."

Chapter Six

AS I DROVE BACK, I mulled over the many things disturbing me, including the fact that Vixen discovered the finger when Bertie and Zeus had missed it. Perhaps Bertie's sense of smell had diminished as he aged, but Zeus was only three and amazingly adept. The shepherds had kept to the shoreline as directed, though, while the wild little bitch had ranged farther off, inadvertently picking up the old smells from Dino's visits to the cabin.

I'd just entered the center when my phone buzzed. I waved at Jaison and the assistants and answered, "Hey, Sasha, wazzup?"

"Maddie, why didn't you call me immediately? I could have scooped the story, instead of letting a hack stringer grab it," said Sasha Seabrook.

I'd met the pretty young television reporter when everyone in Coyote Run had the mass delusion that I was an animal psychic. Sasha's largest success to date was hosting a series of five-minute dog behavior segments with me. "Oh," I said. "I thought you were only interested in canine-related news."

"You thought no such thing, Maddie Whitney! Sheriff Hot Stuff is in 'no comment' mode. What details can you dish?"

"I can't say anything until the official statement is released."

"The official statement came out ten minutes ago, and the widow's already on her way to identify his, I think they said, his wedding ring."

I changed my muddy boots for a pair of sneakers while Sasha repeated a summary of the county's announcement, and then she segued into a monologue about her career goals. I opened and slid shut my desk drawer a satisfying twenty-six times and replaced the batteries in my walkie-talkie with a new, freshly charged ones before I realized she'd stopped talking.

"Sasha, are you there?"

"Yes and waiting for your response."

"I am at liberty to share a few things with you. Dino Ayer was a terrible mechanic. Also, he loved fishing and Jimmy Buffett's undercurrent of melancholy. Most importantly for you, he had a border terrier named Weasel. That gives you the requisite animal angle for your story."

"I don't care about the dog!"

"It's part of your identity branding, Sasha. You have repeatedly pressed upon me the importance of branding," I said. "Weasel is an idiotic name for a dog. You don't need to include that in your story, because it's obvious."

She sighed dramatically. "Anything else?"

"Yes. There's a nasty new deputy at the Coyote Run substation. His name is Richard Kearney. He's probably a racist, definitely a misogynist, and quite likely a murderous sociopath. You should check to see if he has a history of citizen abuse. Also, Dino Ayer let a fake guru host an adult-summer camp for his cult followers on his land. It's all kumbaya and yurts."

"Yoghurts?"

"No, yurts. They're round tents, originally used by nomadic tribes on the steppes of Central Asia, so what the hell are they doing in Northern California's climate and terrain? And last, there's going to be a quiz team fundraiser for the Coyote Run Public Library on Saturday. It's at Grange Hall. There won't be any food. I'd tell you to eat before you show up, but I've never seen you consume food. I suspect that you subsist on calories absorbed from expensive European body lotions."

"This is the grief I get for turning down a burger with you once! Is that all?"

"I never keep anything from you, Sasha."

As our call ended, my phone buzzed again. It was Abel Myklebust. He left a message saying, "I'm calling in my role as publisher of the *Recorder*. Get back to me ASAP about the Dino Ayer situation. I've got a story ready to run, and I need a quote from you."

I had talked to enough people already, so I turned my phone off and picked up my backpack. I unzipped it only enough to slide out the granola bars and jerky, which I left in the kitchenette for my staff. Then I walked quickly through my compound to the gate, waving to a part-time helper and calling, "I'll be back in ten."

Inside the barn, most of the stalls had been knocked down to create an open space for the dogs in rainy weather. It felt hollow and sad, I thought, remembering conversations with my sister as we mucked out the stalls and stacked bales of alfalfa. Only feral barn cats remained, prowling on the high rafters.

No one ever came in the tack room at the front, which was much the same as it had been, with saddles and riding gear covered in dust. Maybe I should have kept a horse or two. The old refrigerator still held expired equine medications. I shut the tack room door and locked it. Then I reached into my backpack for the evidence bag with the finger. I didn't want to see the terrible thing, so I dropped it in an opaque doggie doo bag and placed that bag inside a brown paper bag.

I taped the paper bag shut and, with a wide-tipped red

marker, labeled it, "CONTAMINATED FECAL SAMPLE. DO NOT TOUCH!! Maddie." I shoved it in the back of the freezer, behind unidentifiable abandoned containers. I had no rationale for hiding the finger, except that it seemed to signify something other than a simple power tool accident.

As I was leaving the barn, a peal of sweet laughter cut through my murky thoughts. Muffled voices came from the handyman's studio apartment on the other side of the barn. Not on my fucking watch! I stomped to the apartment door, banged on it once, and flung it open.

Zoe, my intern, was cross-legged on the rug with her laptop, and the part-time handyman James "Hardwire" Hardworth was perched on the kitchen counter, a baseball cap covering his shaved head. He was a short, reedy young man, his gray eyes bright in a sunburned face.

Zoe shut her laptop, and Hardwire jumped off the counter.

"Hey, Maddie," Hardwire said, and Zoe blushed and said, "I was about to leave."

"You bet you are, Missy. You're supposed to be taking photos of the boarding dogs and sending status reports to the owners. No spelling errors or excessive emojis."

"I already did. I was only saying 'hi' to Hardwire."

"You can do that when he comes to the center, not here. This apartment is off-limits to you without supervision. Now go teach the shelter's glamour girl to sit and stay."

Zoe scrunched her face. "That French bulldog is as dumb as a sack of potatoes."

"Stop being a breedist. That Frenchie is smart enough to make you think it's dumb, and the adoption fees will help the shelter pay bills. Go. Now."

I waited until she'd gone before saying, "Hardwire, what the hell? She's seventeen."

"Gimme a break. She's way too young for me, anyhows. I'm

still looking for a cougar."

"It's how you kill time while waiting for a cougar that concerns me."

He made a face. "Zoe has some interesting ideas. Ways I can monetize—that's her word—my ventures."

"Don't let her con you into any cockamamie enterprises."

"All I'm doing is listening. I could use more money."

"If you can borrow a tractor to clear the fire breaks this week or next, I can give you an extra hundred." I clenched and released my hands. "But I'm paying as much as I can, Hardwire."

"Consider it done," he said. "It's not all on you. I've got this place to live, and I'm thankful for it. But part-time ranch hand and store clerking ain't enough. I want to do something real. And don't offer me a dog job again. That's your thing, not mine."

"We all have to clean up shit, dude."

"I'd rather clean up metaphorical shit, Maddie," he said, and laughed. "I just blew your mind, didn't I?"

I clustered my fingers at my temples and then opened my hands wide. "You did indeed, Hardwire."

Feeding the pack required complete attention, since we were working with food-aggressive and protective dogs. Heidi, the Rottweiler, was becoming agitated by a snack-stealing Jindo. A recently arrived boarding dog had so few canine social skills that he had to be separated before a brawl started. "That one needs private time," I told Jai. "Work with him this afternoon."

"How many sessions did the owners request?"

"None, because they claimed the dog was perfect." We both laughed, because owners always lied about their pets' behavior. "But they signed the contract, which has the 'private sessions as required' provision in it."

"No one ever reads clauses in the contract."

"Not my fault," I said. "Also, Vixen will never be a disciplined search dog. So spread the word that she's up for adoption. She'd be in heaven with a hunting family."

"You can't, Maddie."

"I can, and I will. I'm not the right person for her. I already have the best search and rescue dog anyone could want."

"She has a great nose and endurance."

"That's not enough. In a rescue, lives are at stake, and time is of the essence. The only way she'd bother to track anyone down is if he had a squirrel in his pocket." The pointer had heard her name and came running up to me, giving my hand a sticky lick. "Yes, you're sweet," I told her. "We will find the perfect home for you."

Jai frowned, and I felt all kinds of wrong. My shoulders arched together, like a bow's wire that had been pulled tight. I threw out my fists to release the tension. "I'm exhausted, Jai."

"No worries, Boss. Go home."

Before I did, I called Georgina Maguire, the director of the county animal services division, and told her about the bait dog.

"Maddie, if you want to learn about dog-fighting rings, you have to hang out with the meth crowd, and I don't hang out with meth cookers."

"There's only two degrees of separation between everyone in the county. Surely, someone could get close enough to identify them."

"Who is going to snitch on someone who'll murder them? Let the law handle this, Maddie."

I stared at my phone for several minutes before undressing, and then I placed it on the sink's ledge so I could hear if Kenzie called while I was in the shower. She hadn't called or texted in days. Anything could have happened to her. Anything could have happened to me. Things *had* happened to me, and she must have heard from all her contacts.

If she hadn't called, it was because she didn't care.

Or else, she expected me to handle things on my own.

It was hard enough for me to gauge someone's moods and feelings when they were yelling them right to my face; it was impossible when I only had text on a screen.

For a moment, I wished I had a therapist again, to talk things through. But I stuck my head under the lukewarm shower spray and came to my senses, because I didn't need to pay a stranger to listen to me, when there were plenty of people who would pay *me* to talk to *them*.

Dressed in a sleep T-shirt, I had narrowed down likely candidates when my phone buzzed, thereby making the unlikely choice of therapist for me. Beryl Jensen, a well-to-do, chic divorcee, was calling. She was an excellent source of extra cash.

"Hey, Beryl. Have you finally decided to adopt a dog? It will improve your quality of life exponentially."

"What? No, Maddie, I already have several cats."

"Feral barn cats don't count. My sister was one of those kittens and horses girls."

"I stopped by her place last week to drop off a case of wine that she won in the school raffle."

What school raffle? "Oh, that. She's thrilled to be away from Coyote Run, don't you think?"

"Hmm? I don't like to be stuck here all the time, but it's a beautiful place to visit."

"This isn't about you, Beryl."

There was silence for a moment, and then she laughed. "Right, Maddie. Not about me. Your sister was cheerful, but that could have been because of the marvelous selection of pinot noirs I handed her. Abel Myklebust said you're coming to the library's quiz night. I wanted to tell you not to worry, that it's not going to be postponed because of Dino Ayer."

"I wasn't worried about that. Did you and Kenzie hang out?"

"I only stopped by on the way to my esthetician," she said. "Emily's so distraught. She's not going to have a service until things are settle down. I wonder if she's going to sell the vineyard."

This conversation was completely off-track. "And that's connected to me how?"

Beryl laughed again and said, "You're so clever! Speaking of things connected to you, how's Sheriff Desjardins? Still sexy as hell? Will he be participating on a quiz team?"

"Mmm, he may. He's been preoccupied by the recent crime spree. Not that Dino's death constituted a crime, but the Midnight Runners Search and Rescue team went out, and we're sadly lacking critical equipment. Funds are extremely tight with the county. I was thinking of auctioning off...um, a special training demonstration brunch with my guy as a fundraiser. Even though it would be exhausting for him because of his age."

"Oliver Desjardins always looks as if he has enough..." she began suggestively. "Oh, were you talking about that German shepherd with all the burn scars?"

"Bertie is a Belgian Malinois, which is a type of shepherd dog, but distinct from a German shepherd dog," I told her for about the fortieth time. "An honored military vet, the noblest dog that I have ever had the good fortune to have known. The finest example of the species in the state, maybe the nation."

"Do you actually think people will bid on a chance to have lunch with your dog?"

"You're absolutely right, Beryl. Why go through unnecessary preliminaries? I'll send you an invoice, and you can send me a date for brunch, not lunch. I've had a hankering for waffles. Bertie likes bacon, but he's also fond of sausages. Cocktails would be excellent," I said, because Beryl might tell me news about Kenzie if she was liquored up.

"Well, if that's the only way I can get you over for a drink, I'm in. But the real reason I called was to tell you that I met with Brother Ezra at Spirit Springs Institute, and he told me he'd like a therapy dog. I'll sponsor the adoption and any necessary training."

One phone call and a two-for benefit. "I'm eager to meet Brother Who's-it-whatsit. However, I can't approve any animal until I inspect his Yurtopia. He's possibly unsuited to care for a dog, and I have questions about having animals on that property because major pesticide drift contaminated the soil."

"I guess Emily would have a problem putting it on the market if that's what she wants to do."

"Are you interested in buying the vineyard?"

"I'm merely making conversation, Maddie. You can stop by to see Brother Ezra whenever you like. He enjoys visitors, as do I. I'll have my assistant send you a date for brunch. With your dog."

I could hear her snorting with laughter as I clicked off the call.

"People in this town spend a disproportionate amount of time having fundraisers, auctions, and raffles for questionable causes." I twitched to the right and then to the left.

"You're wearing your fancy bra," Ollie said, and snapped the too-tight back strap.

"Sasha says perky boobs are part of my brand, so now I'm stuck strapping myself into this medieval cantilever device for public events. Which is all Kenzie's fault because she wouldn't let me wear a sports bra for my initial interview, thereby setting an unfortunate precedent." I slipped on a cotton shift with a dog-paw print. "I haven't talked to Kenzie in days. She's living the life of Riley and has forgotten about me."

"I overheard you talking to her yesterday."

"The only reason she picked up is because I told her I was going to have the cops do a home safety check if she didn't. She practically hangs up on me." My skin felt tighter on my body, and my eyes began to well.

"Is that a new dress? You're very pretty, Mad Girl."

I blinked back my tears. "My tax accountant told me I can write off clothing for public events. Will Claire be at quiz night?" I thought his twin would like this dress on me. I always felt a pang when I thought about her, the one that got away — who was also the one I sent away.

"You keep asking me that. She said maybe." Oliver squeezed my shoulder. "If you can't be with the one you love, love the evil twin you're with."

Laughing, I said, "I do." I slipped my arms around his waist and pressed myself hard against his body. "I'm feeling all jumbled about everything. Everything except for you."

"If we weren't running late, I'd offer to unjumble you, but you'd use sex as a way to keep from going to the event."

"What if I promise to make it fast and go with you afterward?"

"Okay, you've sold me."

I was usually the one in a hurry, but this time, Ollie rushed. He yanked up my dress and slid down my panties, pushing me down on the narrow arm of the mid-century modern sofa, where I teetered uncomfortably.

"No leverage!" I said, shoving him away and going to the bedroom. For efficiency's sake, I pushed him down on the mattress and climbed on top. Bracing my hands on his shoulders, I moved roughly, quickly, chasing the sensation that would release the unpleasant tangle of accumulated emotions.

But Ollie kept to my pace, and when I hit my peak, I cried out at the pleasure and momentary exorcism of the haywire energy that had racketed through my body since infancy.

We panted, letting the breeze from the open window wash warm over us. Then I swung my leg over and stood. "Thanks."

He sat up. "Glad to be of service."

But he continued to sit there on the rumpled sheets.

"I thought we were in a hurry."

"I need to do something to get me out of my head. We had another overdose, a twenty-seven-year-old with two kids. Her family is torn up. She'd been clean for years. She gave her children a bath, kissed them goodnight, and left them with the sitter to go to a party. She already had their clothes set out for the next day."

"Smack?"

"Fentanyl, and that's the weird part. She'd been a meth head, so why would she flip to opioids?" His voice went low and thick, and his eyes glistened. "The sitter said she was reliable, never even five minutes late, and when she wasn't back on time, she knew something was wrong."

"Maybe she couldn't score meth?"

"No, year in, year out, no matter what we do, this has always been meth country, and the supply is as steady as ever. The autopsy will tell us more. She got it from a friend, sharing a taste at the party. The friend flipped her dealer. A brainless little shit, dealing to support his own habit. He lawyered up, so we may never learn his source."

"Doc Pete told me once that people prefer drugs that suit their environment. Like, if you live in a ghetto, the last thing you want is anything hallucinogenic to make the nightmare worse."

"That lazy old coot. Wasn't he always trying to prescribe canine valium to you?"

"He saw me at my worst since I had to get extremely agitated to make him do his job," I said. "He was competent enough, but he wasn't in Ben's league."

"Or as good-looking."

"You think so? Because I always had a thang for Doc Pete."

Ollie laughed and reached out to me, pulling me back to the bed. "I love you, Mad Girl."

"Yes, and your feelings are reciprocated, but I don't think we need to be mawkish about it."

"Good, because I don't even know what that is."

Chapter Seven

GRANGE HALL WAS a cavernous brown wood building, forgotten for decades until a tragedy last year had necessitated a space large enough for most of the town's population. After being rediscovered, it held weddings, bingo nights, and dance recitals. A banner over the entrance read *Coyote Run Public Library Quiz Night sponsored by Coyote Runaway Pale Ale.*

We went through the open doors, and wonderful aromas wafted over us. The foyer was filled with people drinking beer and eating sausage and pepper rolls.

Oliver grabbed two bottles from a passing waiter. "You said there wasn't going to be any food."

"That's what everyone told me. You don't have to eat again."

"Free food? Yeah, I do."

The proximity of others, the discordant chorus of yammering, shrieks, and guffaws seemed trapped by the heat, the beamed ceiling acting like a hothouse cloche. I tried not to clench my hand too tightly on the bottle.

"Relax, Maddie, take long slow breaths," Oliver said.

"I prefer taking long slow drinks." I wished I had something stronger than beer to file down the jagged edges of my nerves.

Then Abel Myklebust was in front of me. Per usual, he wore Wrangler jeans, a Western shirt, and an ostentatious Carnelian and silver bolo tie. He was a tall, raw-boned man with olive skin, like mine, and black hair, like mine, but shot through with silver, and dark brown eyes, like mine. He had the same straight eyebrows and the same wide mouth with full lips. How had I ever missed the resemblance?

He held out his arms in a confused way, and I stepped back. "We may never get there, Abel. What are all these people doing here?"

"It's a library fundraiser. Everyone wants to support the library."

"Everyone else must have been told there was food, a courtesy that was not extended to me. Please note that I have fulfilled my obligation and will be leaving."

"I said there wouldn't be steaks, and there are no steaks." Abel held out his hand to Ollie. "Evening, Sheriff. Congratulations on that drug bust. I'm giving it five hundred-words in the *Recorder* tomorrow. Any chance for an interview?"

"Nice try, Abel. Sheriff-Coroner Eastman gave the official statement."

"I prefer hearing from someone who isn't running for re-election. If you don't want to shine that star a little brighter, will you please explain to Maddie that people came to see the resident celebrity? If she leaves, I'm not going to pay the vet bills for the mongrel that she's passing off as a pedigreed dog."

"If Maddie says a dog is valuable, the dog is valuable, pedigree or not. I wouldn't have my awesome Dutch shepherd if she hadn't recognized its full potential."

"You mean, she stole it. Because I featured that story in the *Recorder*."

"Fake news," I said. "Adios, Abel."

But before I could wrap event fliers around a trio of sausage rolls, Abel and Ollie herded me into the hall, which was set up with eight-by-ten folding tables. They plonked me down at one of the two head tables, at a seat with a placard reading *Dr. Madeleine Whitney*. A moment later, petite and glamorous tv features reporter, Sasha Seabrook, swooshed down beside me, wearing an aqua silk camisole dress, and gave me air kisses.

"You're looking glittery tonight, Sasha."

"Someone has to bring sparkle to your flannel-and-denim life. Do you like my frock?"

"Very sexy, but aren't those fake eyelashes heavy?"

"I exercise my eyelids at the gym after my reps."

I thought she might have been joking, but Sasha had fanatical beauty regimes.

We were joined by Donna-June Looper, wearing a bright pink *Capo di Tutti Capi, The Crafty Looper* T-shirt. "Dr. Whitney, what a pleasure to see you again."

"Yeah, well," I began.

"My husband gave me the shirt as a joke. Because my maiden name is Lucchese, no relation. His name, Looper, means someone who runs into the woods, which is too accurate." Her laugh sounded off key.

I was about to tell Donna-June about being tased because of the truck when Sasha introduced herself and asked about the crafting business.

The table was rounded out by Oliver's oldest sibling, who insisted that I call her Principal Desjardins at this event.

"Is Claire coming tonight?" I asked.

"Am I to deduce that you're no longer stalking her?"

"I admit that I may have gone overboard in my efforts to woo her back."

"I'm just giving you a hard time. Claire said you've worked things out. When we spoke today, she was caught up in a papier mâché installation for her gallery."

"Gee, you gals sure do talk purdy," Sasha said, and grinned. "I think I'm sitting at the smarty-pants table. That's to be expected because I have an awesome and impressive degree...in musical theater."

I liked that the beautiful girl didn't take herself too seriously. "I hope you're up on pop culture, babe."

"You can bet your Kardashian on it," she said. "Maddie, how you doing? Your face..."

"Not my milieu." I wiped the back of my hand across my clammy forehead.

Oliver's sister said, "Maddie, terrible news about Dino Ayer. His daughter is a freshman. It's a difficult time for any teen, and now this. When I heard about the explosion, I was hoping for a different outcome, hoping you and Oliver would find—"

"There was nothing to find," I said, quickly. "I mean, *kaboom*. End of story."

Oliver's older sister's eyebrow went up.

"Yes, it's tragic," Sasha said.

Principal Desjardins said, "Donna-June, do you know the Ayers family?"

"Dino and my husband were best friends and fishing buddies. My daughter's close to the Ayers, but Emily Ayer and I didn't have much in common."

Tables were filling up quickly. Oliver was seated with Abel Myklebust, as well as the owner of the eponymous Rudy's Brew House, and my friend, Penelope, the caterer. They'd dubbed themselves Team Hot Biscuits, so Sasha took it upon herself to name our team the Celebrichicks.

"We're not celebrities," I said.

"Speak for yourself," she said. "I've already signed two autographs this evening."

"I don't want to toot my own horn," said Donna-Jean, "but I'm a rock star in the crafting field."

"I'm famous with everyone who went to Coyote Run High," Principal Desjardins said. "And all their families."

Sasha grinned. "See what I mean? It's also a play upon *cerebral*."

"No, it isn't," I said. "Regardless, the Hot Biscuits don't have a snowball's chance."

But I was wrong.

The early rounds had simple questions, knocking out half the teams, which I found predictable, yet disappointing, Subsequent rounds became progressively tougher.

"You're so smart!" Sasha bumped her shoulder against mine.

"Test-taking is a knack. Jack of all trades."

"Master of dogs," she replied. "Please let there be Stephen Sondheim questions. What are you thinking?"

"I'm thinking, *please let this be over so I can finally eat a sausage roll.*" My stomach cramped with hunger, and I slipped my hand into my shoulder bag, feeling around for the jerky stick I'd brought.

Because the questions were skewed toward inconsequential sports trivia, Oliver's team and mine were tied in the final round. He and the brew-pub owner kept pumping their fists in the air. "I'm glad he doesn't do that when he orgasms," I whispered to Sasha. "Or should I be disappointed?"

The event emcee waited for total silence on the final question. "This is a doozy. For our tiebreaker question, name at least two of the five correct answers. 'Supermassive Black Hole—'"

My stomach rumbled, and I slammed my hand on the buzzer, and shouted out the possibilities: "SBHs have a gravitational pull that not even light can escape. They can be found in nearly every galaxy. An SBH can be caused when stellar clusters collapse, or when several small black holes merge. Our own SBH in the Milky Way is Sagittarius A, which is four million times larger than the sun!"

The host read his card, and said, "I'm sorry, Dr. Whitney. That is incorrect. The question is, *Supermassive Black Hole* by the band Muse has been used for video games and TV shows. Name two. Team Hot Biscuits, do you have an answer?"

Oliver grinned at his teammates and said, "I've got this." He hit the button in front of him, "*Guitar Heroes III: Legends of Rock* and *FIFA 07*. And for the hell of it, *The Sopranos*, when Tony's at the Bada-Bing."

"That's correct, Sheriff Desjardins! The Hot Biscuits are the winners!"

I dropped my face into my hands and mumbled, "Sorry, guys. I didn't realize it was going to be such a profoundly asinine question."

Sasha said, "I've never heard you overestimating anyone or anything before, except dogs. That's what you get for sunny optimism."

Oliver made his way through a group congratulating him and said, "Okay, loser, are you going to treat me to a steaming hot sausage?"

"That's what she said," I answered, and everyone laughed, making me feel better. "I would have gotten that question if I hadn't been so hungry."

"You are an unapologetic liar." Ollie smiled. "I won a case of beer and a gift certificate for the annual book sale."

"That's swell." I grabbed his hand and yanked him toward the food table. All the trays were empty, except for one with broken cookies. "What the fuck?"

"Language, Maddie." Abel was suddenly looming at my side.

"You have no right—," I began.

But Abel was already turning to Oliver. "If you won't give me a quote about the drug bust, at least give me one about tonight. Did you anticipate making it to the finals?"

"I don't play to win. I play to play," Oliver said.

"That's ridiculous," I said. "He *always* plays to win." I would have elaborated, but Penelope appeared with a heaping plate of food.

She said, "Sasha told me that your stomach was caterwauling all night long. Eat."

"You are a saint."

I edged away with my belated dinner to an empty corner of the dark hall, where the air wasn't so stuffy and overheated. I sat on a ledge and chewed the cold sausages, remembering the last time I'd been here, with my sister by my side, herding me through the crowd, guiding and protecting me.

I remembered seeing Oliver that night. He'd seemed so generic, then, indistinguishable from hundreds of firm-jawed, fair-skinned cops. I became aware of footsteps. Donna-June Looper had tracked me down.

"That was fun, wasn't it, Dr. Whitney?"

She shifted from one foot to the other, making me uneasy. Was I supposed to say something? Weather was generally a safe topic, so I said, "I hope you are enjoying the summer. It's always the same, scorching hot, but still."

"I'm sure I'll get used to the heat. Dr. Whitney, is there someplace we can talk? Privately?"

I gazed wistfully at the potato salad on my plate. "If this is about the truck, I had a spot of trouble, but it's running fine."

"No, I need you to help me locate someone. Discretely."

I set down the plate and said, "Follow me." I led her through an exit to an alley, illuminated by a single lamp. "Your running-off-to-the-woods husband?"

She shook her head. "He cleared out a significant chunk of cash. He'll make his way home when he's broke, not that I'm going to take him back this time. My daughter, Purlynn, has been gone for two days. She left her phone at the house."

"Is Purlynn the girl at your house? Because she appeared to be over twenty-one."

"She's twenty-three, but something's gone wrong with her, and I'm worried sick thinking she may be in trouble, or passed out somewhere, or... When you're out of contact with someone you love... Anything could have happened to her."

My hands flipped up, palms out. "I'm not dragging her back against her will. Find an intervention group." I began walking to the door, but Donna-June grabbed my arm with considerable strength, which made me like her more.

"I only want to make sure she's all right. If it's too late tonight, I can wait until tomorrow. I have a general idea of where she might be. She's been seen with the regulars who hang out at Curtis's Liquors."

The liquor store was a few miles outside of town, and hookers and dealers loitered in the parking lot. "Tomorrow is better. My dog will be fresh then. I'll check with Sheriff Desjardins to see if he can clear his morning."

"I don't want anyone else to go, especially not the law."

"Is there something I should know, Donna-June?"

"Only that this is private. When Purlynn gets through whatever's going on, she'll feel shamed enough without the whole town gossiping. Name your price, Dr. Whitney."

I appraised Donna-June's pedicured feet in snakeskin sandals and the gold and diamond bracelet on her wrist before I threw out an extremely high, arbitrary fee.

Donna-June agreed immediately. She had done her search and rescue homework and handed me a photo of a pretty, fresh-faced girl, an earlier version of her daughter, and a T-shirt and socks in a plastic bag. "Call me when you find her. If she needs any money..." Her voice trailed off. "They always come back when they need money. That's the curse of being successful, but it's also power. Power helps compensate, but it's not the same as love, is it?"

"Speaking of money, I get paid whether I find her or not."

"Of course, regardless of the outcome, and a flat finder's fee when you locate her."

"*If* I locate her."

"I have a feeling you will, Dr. Whitney. You strike me as a woman capable of single-minded focus. But don't let intellectual overconfidence take you off the cliff like it did tonight."

Like most successful people, Donna-June was accustomed to talking shit and having others listen, so I gave her one of my rote responses. "Sure. I appreciate the advice."

I returned to the hall to find Abel Myklebust standing by the ledge with my food plate. I didn't see any way of getting past him. "'Scuse me, Abel, I haven't finished my dinner." I picked up the paper plate and turned toward the main hall.

"I'm glad you came tonight, Maddie. It's always a pleasure to see you."

"I've been assured by reliable sources that it isn't. Do you have something specific to ask me?"

The big man didn't speak for long seconds, during which I scarfed potato salad. "Our relationship is going to have to evolve, eventually. You're my only child."

"I liked things better before the DNA test. Let's go back to that, and no one will be the wiser." I dropped the plate in a trash bin and left him there.

Oliver was having a heated conversation about the local co-ed softball league, and the shortstop was gazing up at him, occasionally brushing her hand lightly on his arm in a way that made my skin crawl.

I waved him over. "Shortstop is flirting with you. How can anyone endure light-touchers? I'd just as soon chew aluminum."

"Are you jealous?"

"Of being a light-toucher, or being hit on by a light-toucher? Neither," I said. "I have an early morning consult."

"What about additional unjumbling?"

I yanked on his shirt. "I'm looking forward to that. Let's build the anticipation for tomorrow night. In the meantime, don't be a hero."

He grinned. "No can do: it's in my job description."

My caterer friend was heading out, and so I caught a ride from her to the ranch.

Bertie came to the gate to greet me, and I petted him before sending him back to sleep on the deck, where he would be most comfortable in the lingering heat.

I sent a text to my sister: "Came in tops in elite quiz contest! Call me ASAP." I placed the phone on my pillow and thought about Donna-June's anguish about her daughter and my own about Kenzie, and, finally, I drifted off to sleep.

Chapter Eight

KENZIE'S TERSE TEXT, "Congrats, brainiac! In conferences til later," came when I was running down a Basenji that had escaped and was stalking my chickens. My sister was putting me off again. She'd included a link to the *Coyote Run Recorder* story about quiz night, with a photo of Oliver's team holding up the recycled bowling trophy award.

But the headline was about Oliver's drug bust, featuring Sheriff-Coroner Eastman's self-congratulatory statement. There was also a photo of Spam-faced Deputy Richard Kearney standing by a table with a handgun, a shotgun, and an open briefcase turned away from the camera. What a fool: the sheriff-coroner would not be pleased that someone else was trying to bask in his glory.

There was a brief obit for the woman who'd overdosed and a photo of her with her children. If relatives couldn't take the kids, they'd go into the overcrowded foster care system. These were the kind of children that Kenzie counseled, helping them navigate lives of loss and grief, trying to guide them through the labyrinth of human society, where many paths led right off cliffs and few led to joy.

When my morning duties were complete and chores assigned to my staff, I changed into a black AC/DC T-shirt with the sleeves cut off, gathered my tracking gear, and told Jaison, "I'm doing a tracker refresher with Bertie."

"I've been looking all over for that T-shirt. Give it back."

"You shouldn't wear it. The sheriff's department has an institutional hatred for the band."

"I want my shirt back anyway," he said. "Shouldn't you take Vixen, too?"

The pointer whizzed around me with excitement. The dark splotches on her spotted fur shone like melted chocolate. "Has she been pestering you?"

"Not much, but she needs a hard run to burn off all that excess energy."

Because I couldn't think of an excuse, I had to pack her into the back of the Tundra with Bertie. It was too early for any action at Curtis's Liquors, but Purlynn might have left a trail from the night before. My plan was to catch her before she got out and about.

The morning's warmth signaled the heat to come. I took a route past the Ayer vineyards, slowing to spy on the Spirit Springs camp. Sure enough, white smoke wafted from the fire pit. I couldn't wait to lay into the asshole responsible for this hazard.

I fumed through the next few miles, passing vineyards, a trailer park, an olive grove, meadows, and then a scattering of small run-down houses by a mini mall, and turned into the parking lot of Curtis's Liquors. I hoped that Purlynn was within walking distance.

I went into the convenience store, picked up a few snacks and a cold, canned cappuccino, and took them to the counter, where greasy hot dogs rotated in a dirty plastic case.

A yawning clerk rang up my purchases. "Late night for you, or early morning?" I said.

"I'm off in thirty."

"Bet you see all the nighttime party people."

"And those on graveyard shift," he said. "Paper or plastic?"

"Paper. Hey, maybe you've seen a friend of mine, because she said she was moving this way. I lost her number."

He sneered with the natural suspicion of someone who associates with scumbags. "Friend?"

I smiled. "I thought so. Pretty enough to catch your eye." I laughed. "She sure was pretty enough to catch mine. Her name is Purlynn." I took the photo from my jeans' pocket. "She's a few years older now, but I'd sure like to catch up on old times."

He looked at the photo and then at me. One shoulder rose, as if a full shrug was too much effort. My shoulders went up in an uncomfortable mirror reaction.

"I might have seen her."

I pulled out my wallet, then paid him for the snacks. "Sure would help me if you could tell me anything."

"She steal something from you?"

"Only my heart." I hoped he'd be swayed by the fantasy.

"Not my problem," he said, and tipped his chin toward my torso. "Lotta girls wear these shirts like fashion, and they don't know shit about the bands. See you."

"Thanks anyway," I said, picking up my bag. As I walked away, I sang, "*If you want blood, you got it*."

He laughed and called out, "Okay, you win. *You got it*. I think she's out on Elshire Lane. There's a house there, a house share or..."

Bingo! I hazarded a guess and said, "A crash pad? Green, two stories?"

"I suppose you could call it green. It's, like, dirty, and two-level, but only in the back. If you're in the market for something..."

"Thanks, but I'm fine. I mean, I grow my own these days, nothing to brag about, but the price is right."

"You're, like, organic and shit?" he said with interest.

"You could call it that. I don't like to be classified."

We said our goodbyes, and I drove to Elshire Lane, as if a two-mile stretch could rightfully be called a lane. The places here were mostly neglected rentals, surrounded by dead weeds, busted-up appliances, and broken-down vehicles.

I parked at the end of the lane nearest the mini mart and took the dogs out.

Bertie could be trusted to stay with me, but I clasped on Vixen's leash. Crouching down, I presented Purlynn's T-shirt to Bertie and then to Vixen. She bit into the cotton and pulled. "Drop it," I said, and she let go. "Find!"

Bertie lowered his long, dark-furred nose to the ground and began moving back and forth across the broken concrete sidewalk.

Vixen lurched forward, then diagonally, and then began to wind around me. I presented her with the socks, and she sniffed once. "You are displaying profound disinterest. Keep out of Bertie's way," I said and guided her to my side. "Heel."

From behind a slat fence, a pair of boxers charged, snarling and barking. Bertie tilted his head to assess the commotion and returned to tracking, and Vixen whined and edged to the side. "Sit," I told her, making her stay so she'd learn to be calm when I instructed.

The dogs had fawn-brown fur and droopy jowls. "I'm glad to see you're healthy. I hope you get daily walks."

When Vixen settled, I instructed, "Heel," and we followed Bertie, who tracked toward a driveway and doubled back to the sidewalk. He waited at the curb for my direction before moving into the street.

A rusty Audi came behind us and slowed down before the driver blared his horn and then swerved around, but otherwise the street was empty. The rising sun angled over rooftops, causing me to squint as we walked long, depressing blocks.

Bertie moved back to the sidewalk and inspected the paved path to a grimy split-level house. It looked as if it had once been the best place on the block, but now only remnants of a stone border remained. Tattered drapes showed through the greasy windows. I pulled the T-shirt from my backpack and presented it to Bertie again. "I really don't want to go in there," I said. "No one's awake yet."

He smelled the T-shirt and continued to the front door. When I knocked, flakes of paint fell off. My hands clenched, and my shoulders hunched forward. I forced them back and tried to put my lips into a normal shape, but they felt as if they were twisted.

I stretched my mouth wide open, so I could reset my face into something pleasant. As I was lifting my fist to knock again, Vixen yipped, and Bertie's ears pivoted forward, signaling that someone was on the other side of the door.

"Hi!" I said, loudly. "Morning!"

Minutes passed, and the dogs remained fixed on the front door, so I knew I was being watched. I knocked again and called, "Hello!"

The door creaked open enough to reveal a slice of darkness and the edge of a pale face. "What?" said a hoarse female voice.

"Sorry to bother you. Is Purlynn here?"

"Why?"

"Is that you, Purlynn?" When she didn't respond, I said, "We met before. Sort of, but not really. I bought your father's truck."

The door swung open, and the girl threw her arm in front of her face. "Too fucking bright." She wore a tank top and boxers, the same as before, but she was even scrawnier, dark shadows under bleary eyes. "Is this about my dad?"

"No, your mother wanted me to check on you. She's worried."

Purlynn made a scoffing sound and wandered back inside. Leaving the dogs on the porch, I followed her into a filthy living room with a drug-and-sex-den funk. I was glad I wore my hiking boots because I was sure the stained shag carpet was crawling with cooties and had layers of human biological matter.

"You want a drink?" she asked.

"I brought my own. If you don't mind."

"Whatever." She picked up a handle of vodka and glugged it into a chipped mug, and I took my canned cappuccino from my backpack and cracked it open.

"You're Dr. Dog Psychic," she said.

"You can call me Maddie. I'm not a psychic. I'm a canine rehabilitator."

"What's the difference?"

"One-hundred-dollars-an-hour less," I said.

She laughed. "My mother totally fell for that racquet. She was excited to meet you when you bought the truck, which she shouldn't have sold."

"The paperwork's in her name."

"*Everything's* in her name. It's all about Donna-June Looper."

"It's too easy to misunderstand a mother's intentions when we're upset. We should give her the benefit of the doubt," I said, fairly sure I was reiterating something Kenzie told me. "Do you want me to give you a ride back to your Mom's?"

Purlynn finished her drink too fast. Despite the heat, she shivered. "I'll probably die if I stay here, won't I?"

My heart ached, seeing her in this hopeless sunless loveless place. "Purlynn, if you were a dog, I'd haul your ass out, feed you, bathe you, dress you in clean clothes, and let you breathe clean air again until you healed."

Her knees began buckling, and I grabbed her before she fell. She smelled like a sick animal, of stale sweat and fear. "Then take me with you. But not to my mother's. Take me with *you*."

This was a bit over my pay grade, and I was contemplating my options when I heard heavy footsteps coming from the back of the house.

"Purl!" a man yelled. "Purl, where the hell is my stash?"

"Time to go!" I grabbed her right wrist, bent over and put my head under her armpit, and then reached my left arm through her legs, and levered her into a fireman's carry the way Oliver had taught me. The footsteps drew closer as I shifted her weight until she was balanced.

"*Purrll*. You bitch!"

I secured my grip, leaving my left arm free, and I plodded out of the house, grabbing Vixen's leash, and saying, "Heel!"

We were on the sidewalk before a shirtless man lurched through the door, "*Purrll!*"

He lurched forward like a zombie, and in movies, the heroine always trips, because directors never account for the inherent clumsiness of the undead, but I wasn't surprised in the least when this zonked-out jackass stumbled on the broken sidewalk. He fell with a dull thud and an angry howl, and I quickened my steps.

Carrying Purlynn was like carrying a sack of flour: initially light, but progressively heavier. After five minutes, my shoulders and thighs ached. After ten, she was glued to me with some unholy paste of cheap cotton fabric and sweat. Bertie kept to my pace, and miracle of miracles, Vixen maintained her heel.

Getting Purlynn into the high front seat of the truck was impossible, so I rolled her into the back, put the dogs back in their crates, and got the hell out of Dodge.

I called Jaison on my way back and said, "I'll be there in five. Meet me at the car park because I require some muscle."

"Another vicious dog?"

"If only. Caution is advised, however."

He was waiting for me as I pulled up. I hopped out, and he said, "So, whatcha up to?"

"Five-nine-and-a-quarter inches, if I stand straight, and I need you to carry a girl into the evaluation room."

"Any particular reason?"

"Even though I'm not a stickler about legal issues, I hesitate at locking a girl in a kennel until she detoxes."

"You could have told me, instead of saying you were on a tracker refresher."

"It was easier not to explain. Throw her on the sofa, lock up the dog meds, and tell everyone the room's off-limits for now and to keep close watch on their valuables and keys. Give Zoe the rest of the day off. She's going to be too curious."

After I'd splashed water over my face, I went to the evaluation room. Purlynn was curled under an old, flowered sheet, and Jaison had left a turquoise Gatorade on a side table. Her face shone damply, and she breathed unevenly. I pushed the sheet down to inspect her arms and the backs of her knees, but I didn't see any tracks.

"So, what is your poison, Purlynn?"

She stirred when I spoke and then sank back into her dreams. I brought in my laptop and worked on my accounts, watching over her. She woke once, and I held the bottle of Gatorade, helping her drink and feeding her a few aspirin. "Go back to sleep."

Jai brought me a PB&J sandwich at lunchtime. "There's one for her, too, if she gets hungry. She looks familiar, and why's she here?"

"You met her before. Donna-June Looper's daughter. She was on a bender, and her mother wanted me to find her."

"For a fee?"

"Of course, not that I plan to add 'bounty hunter' to my list of services." I brushed crumbs off my jeans and said, "I thought things would be easier by now, but I'm barely scraping by. Zoe's always badgering me to 'scale up,' but expanding means more staff, more staff means a bigger payroll, et cetera, and I find myself stuck with paperwork all day long."

"It's either a business, or a charity," he said. "I don't especially want the law around twenty-four-seven, but since Ben's family is moving out, have you considered renting the house to Oliver?"

"That's a terrible idea. He's delighted in his condo, and I'm delighted in my little place." I chewed on a fingernail. "Beryl Jensen has hired me to meet with the hipster guru at Spirit Springs Institute and provide a therapy dog. That fee and Donna-June's finder's fee will give us a little cushion. I miss our psychic reading money, though."

"That was a stupid fun scheme. If I ever leave here, I might pick up that gig."

I grabbed his wrist. "You're not going to leave me!"

"Calm down. I'm just saying, 'if ever.'" He stared at Purlynn, who jerked uneasily in her sleep. "I have to consider the future though, cuz I love this place, but not a day goes by that I don't miss being with Black folk and different kinds of folks. I'm drowning in the beige."

I sighed. "Yes, this town was founded by people trying to get away from 'the Blacks,' but that was a long time ago. Everyone likes you. I *love* you."

"It's too complicated to explain. I'm not grouping you with the rest; you know what it's like being different, not just inside, because people can hide that, but outside."

"Yes, but I realize that I get a pass because my parents and grandparents lived here," I said, glumly. "I'm not the most empathetic person in the world, but if you ever want to try to explain, I'd listen."

"Thanks, Mad Girl," he said, "but some things you have to live to understand."

A few hours later, when Jai and I were putting the boarding dogs through standard recall lessons, Purlynn meandered out of the office trailer. Her hair was wet, as if she'd washed up in the small bathroom, and she was wearing a set of extra clothes my sister had left behind. My heart flipped when I saw the faded pink jeans and striped T-shirt.

"So, this is where I am," Purlynn said, "the dog place."

"Officially the Whitney Canine Rehabilitation Center. 'Dog place' is expeditious but lacks specificity. Purlynn, meet Jaison. Jaison, meet Purlynn."

They waved to each other, and Purlynn asked him, "Does she always talk like this?"

"'Course not. She swears a hell of a lot, too, when the interns aren't around. I'm gonna excuse myself to take over the lessons." He didn't even bother to hide his laughter as he left.

I went to Purlynn and said, "How you feeling?"

"I could be better, but I've been worse."

I lifted my hand toward her elbow. "I noticed the bruise when I bought the truck." When she didn't answer, I said, "You're aware that I'm neglecting my dogs for you."

She took in a breath. "When I was fifteen, a boyfriend got me into speedballs, but my parents got me to treatment. I haven't touched that stuff since. I'm trying to deal with something, so, yeah, I hit the booze."

I didn't believe her, but this wasn't an intervention. "You hungry? I can scramble eggs and make coffee. That's the extent of my cooking repertoire."

The resident Rottie rumbled over to inspect the visitor, and Purlynn bent over to scratch behind the dog's ears. "I can cook."

"No, get a little sun on that skin. That's Heidi." I watched Purlynn, who appeared to be relaxed, but could have been worn out. "How much do you know about canine behavior?"

"What's to know? They're dogs."

"They're prey animals and pack animals. You run, and they'll chase you. You get riled up, and they'll get riled up. Keep quiet and stay put. I'll be back in ten."

She sat on the edge of the deck, and Heidi lay beside her,

resting her head on Purlynn's thin thighs, providing comfort without judgment, or obligations, or agendas, and I instantly liked Purlynn better.

In my cottage, I scrambled two eggs and filled a plastic mug with cold coffee and ice cubes, and dumped in plenty of milk and sugar. I made sure all accessible windows were locked, and I locked the front door behind me. I took the food out and said, "You better sit at the picnic table. Otherwise, Heidi will chow down the second you turn your head."

"Cool dog."

"She is, but, like all of us, she has issues, and you don't want to get on the wrong side—which is the inside—of those jaws." We both went to the table and sat on the bench.

She ate a few forkfuls and then pushed away the plate, drinking her iced coffee instead.

"You're not hungry?"

"How is it possible to ruin eggs?"

"Kind of a gift. It keeps me from cooking for others. Shall we call your mother?"

"I don't feel like going back there now."

"Like they say at closing time, you don't have to go home, but you can't stay here. Do you have any relatives or friends who aren't junkies or dealers?"

"I'm not always like this," she snapped.

"I was contracted to locate you, which I have done, and I'll inform your mother in order to collect my fee. You'll understand if I want to go about my business now."

She attempted to catch my gaze, perhaps to convey something nonverbal. "Why do you keep looking away?" she said.

"People's faces are confusing. They're like...like mirrored funhouses, where everything is distorted and deceptive, reflecting things where they aren't, obscuring things that are. It's not only you, it's everyone."

"That must be a bummer. And all those weird twitches?"

"My body functions as well as I need it to. Why do I spend so much of my life trying to explain myself to others? Why should I give a damn if they feel uncomfortable around me? Because I don't give a damn. In fact, my quirks eliminate extraneous bullshit people from bothering me."

"I'm seeing a pattern here." She let out a short, sharp laugh. "Knitters always see patterns. Go ahead, call my mother and tell her to come get me. I'm missing my bed and her liquor cabinet anyway."

I made the phone call, and Donna-June arrived within the hour.

And, after the Capo di Tutii Capi of the Crafty Looper handed me an envelope with a thick stack of twenties, I thought I was well rid of the both of them.

Chapter Nine

SOMETIMES IT'S BEST to start with a clean slate. I wiped off my whiteboard with its log of phone calls and texts, and then I called my sister. And called again and again until she picked up.

"Kenzie!"

"Mad Girl! What's the problem?"

"My problem is that my only sister never returns my calls and only responds with curt notes to my texts. I miss you!"

"I miss you, too."

"You sure don't act like it. All kinds of things are happening here. We haven't even discussed Dino Ayer of Ayer Vineyards, dying in a boat explosion."

"You told me."

"Yes, but we didn't *discuss* it."

"I didn't see the point. Why do you care about him?"

"I don't, but Ben has been making frequent house calls for his mutt, and now he's comforting the beautiful widow, Emily."

"And that matters because?"

"*Because* do you think something might be going on? Ava and the kids are away with her family in Virginia for the summer, and I hardly see Ben anymore. He's moving this week."

“Maddie, is it possible you’ve been taking advantage of your work-husband’s veterinary services?”

“I would never! Besides, he always bills me. You haven’t even asked about the quiz night. I went with an extremely positive attitude to fundraise for the library. Abel Myklebust was there, ugh. I could have used your moral support.”

“Didn’t Ollie go with you?”

“Yes, and then he stole the first-place win from me on a technicality. Which I forgave, because I don’t hold grudges, except about an awful assistant deputy he hired.” I waited for her to say something, but she didn’t. “You’ve don’t even care that I was tased, Kenzie. I mean, what the fuck?” My throat grew thick.

“Of course I care, sweetie. It’s awful. I wake up at night freaked out about what could have happened to you. But we’ve been over this incident a dozen times already. *Please* stop barging into situations, because it scares me to death.”

“I’m fine, and I’d do it again. I’d do anything to save Jaison.”

“But he was okay. You were there, and he was okay.”

“The asshole deputy was going to hit him.”

“You made that assumption, and your people-reading skills are limited.”

“Kenzie.”

She sighed loudly.

“When can I see you?”

“You can see me when you come to see me. How often have I invited you?”

I frowned at the thought of driving over the mountain so I could sit in her boyfriend’s too stark and too-carefully maintained condo, or an upscale tourist town bistro. “Why don’t you come here instead? We need to decide what to do with the house, and you can meet the latest boarding dogs.”

“My patient just walked in. Talk to you later.”

“Promise?” I said, but she’d already clicked off.

I was staring at my phone, wondering what she meant by "later," when Ben texted that the dog fighting victim was ready to be picked up.

I took Bertie with me to the veterinary clinic. "Hey, Doc Maddie, how ya doing?" said the office manager.

I wasn't used to seeing Wylene sitting at the desk, which she'd decorated with hippopotamus cartoons, bookends, and figurines. Her top featured a pink hippo with *Faster, Meaner, & Smarter than You Pink!* in a childlike font.

"Hi, Wylene. You've changed things around here."

"Isn't it fun? Can I give Bertie a treat?"

"Thank you for asking, and, yes, he'd like it. Do I have to sign anything?"

"No, Mr. Myklebust covered everything. He must really like you a lot."

"He feels it's his civic obligation to support small businesses."

She raised an eyebrow. "Uh-huh."

"Speaking of Coyote Run issues, is Emily Ayer's terrier doing any better, or does he have a permanent medical condition?"

"You can ask Doc Ben yourself. Weasel had an appointment yesterday. Go to exam room one, and the doc will bring the stray to you and talk about aftercare."

"Mind if I leave Bertie here in the meantime?"

"It's always a pleasure having his company."

I grinned. "He's considering running for mayor."

"He'd win in a landslide!"

I poked through Ben's animal-centric books in the exam room while I waited for Ben. He had a photo of the lab who'd passed away years before. When Ben came in leading the bait dog, I said, "Ben, it is well past time for you to adopt another dog. Your kids need one."

"Ava has enough to do without caring for a dog, but she agreed to two kittens. Don't you want to know about your stray?"

"Yes." I crouched down by the dog and looked at the shaved areas with black stitches. His brown eyes met mine, and his tail wagged slowly. He'd put on at least five pounds, and his thick black fur, though still dull, was clean. "Hey, fellow. How ya doing?"

"He's building back muscle, and he moves easier every day. He'll need to finish his antibiotics. Keep him from rough play for another ten days," Ben said. "He's timid with dogs, understandably so, but he's okay with cats."

"How old do you think he is?"

"About three. You don't intend to bring him into the pack now, do you?"

"I need to observe him." I ran my hand down the dog's back. "I'll introduce him to Bertie for now, but he'll be different when his strength returns."

"Maddie, even you, with all your gifts, won't react fast enough to prevent disaster every single time. Err on the side of caution."

Ben was at his most appealing like this: doctor, priest, and confidante. "How's Weasel doing?"

"What?"

"Emily Ayer's dog."

"I don't discuss my clients' pets. Patient confidentiality."

"That's not a thing. Dogs don't care if you discuss their health."

"The owners do," he said. "I've hired Hardwire to help me move. We should have things clear in two days. Are you sure you don't want me to repaint?"

"You've made significant improvements already. It will be strange not having you right there."

"Maddie, I'll only be a five-minute walk away."

"But now I can yell real loud, and you can hear me when you're in the yard."

"I might not miss that."

"Of course you will." I sidled closer to him. "Am I still your friend?"

He put his arm around me, pressing down to make it heavy on my shoulder. "I'll always be your friend. We're the Midnight Runners, aren't we?"

I nodded. "Our last Midnight Run was a bust. It wasn't midnight, and Dino wasn't actually missing."

"It should be a relief that no one else has vanished."

I considered telling him about Purlynn but didn't. "By the way, if you come across a young dog like Bertie, and no one's like Bertie, but with similar composure and tracking instincts, tell me, because Vixen is not working out."

"No."

"No what?"

"No, I'm not going to find another dog for you to reject. You want everything to be in a state of stasis with Bertie. But dogs grow old, Maddie, and he has a spectrum of injuries. The kindest thing you can do for him is to give him a break from grueling searches."

"Ben, I came here to pick up a dog, not to pick a fight." I shrugged his arm off my shoulders. "Because I could share my opinions about *your* behavior that you might not appreciate.

He stepped back and raised his hands, palms up. "Truce, then. A truce for now."

Halfway down our lane to the WCRC, I parked. I hauled out the dog crate, set it on the gravel, and called Bertie to sit nearby. Then I unlatched the door. The injured dog cowered inside, so I gently, but firmly, tugged the leash, pulling him out.

His hips were low, his tail between his legs. I reached over and lifted it, because mood can follow position. He didn't growl, which was a plus.

"You'll feel better when you're moving," I said. "Let's go!"

I began walking briskly into the field and signaled for Bertie to join us. The bait dog veered away from my Bertie, and I held the leash to bring the dog's head higher. "Happy stance, happy heart." I began trotting, and the dog had to trot with us.

I took in the sun-warmed air, the birdsong, the golden grasses rustling against our legs, Bertie's coat shining, the sky, the sky, the sky a blue that was pure and deep and light and nothing and everything all at once. "This is the beginning, and it's going to be beautiful, and your name is..." I pondered the damaged, but healing animal by my side. His black fur flicked a black-blue like fountain pen ink. "Beau Blue," I said, "for the beautiful blue sky today. Beau Blue."

When we reached the pond, I stepped into the muck at the edge. Bertie waded in, lapping the water. Beau hesitated and turned his head toward me, warily. Realizing that he was used to being struck made me want to cry.

"Not here, fellow, not anymore." I looked from him, so he could relax. As I listened, I heard splashing. Beau stood next to Bertie, drinking. His small steps were huge leaps of courage, and as much as I liked teaching others to work with dogs, I cherished these tiny private successes.

I led Beau to the barn where two stalls had been converted to isolation wards. I placed him in a smaller one with water and easy-to-digest kibble.

Bertie and I walked over to my center, and Zoe said, "Hey, Maddie, where's your rescue?"

"His name is Beau Blue, and he's in the barn."

"That's a lot of Bs, Boss. Why didn't you bring Beau Blue boy back here? Does he have *ubonicbay agueplay*?"

"*Onay, otay ubonicbay agueplay*. He's had enough challenges for one day. I'll move him to the far-end recovery kennel tonight after the others are settled in. You can make sure it's clean and put a dental chew in there for him."

"I wish you would give me interesting tasks, instead of drudge work."

"Show me where you are with the Frenchie."

She called to the French bulldog, who was playing chase with a terrier mix, and the dog came instantly.

"Sit, Snickers," Zoe said, and the dog sat.

"Snickers?"

"I renamed her, because Snickers bars are delicious. Prepare to be amazed." She flipped her hand, and the Frenchie rolled over. "Speak," she said, and the dog barked. "Dance." Zoe began to chicken-dance, and the dog cavorted around her. She stopped and pulled a treat from her pocket, saying, "Catch!" to the Frenchie who snatched it from the air. "*O-say?*"

"*O-say*, I am totally amazed, especially since you were so negative about Snickers."

"I was until you mentioned the financial aspect. I think we can ask an extra two-hundred for her now."

"Zoe, you realize that any adoption money goes directly to the rescue group, don't you?"

She stuck her hands on her hips. "Course I do! Which is why they'll be glad to give us an endorsement with the Frenchie-owning hipsters, who'll want to board their snorfling dogs here for special training!" Looking down at Snickers, she said, "I didn't mean Snickers. Her snorfling is adorable, but worries the heck outa me. What is the deal with purebred dogs? Didn't anyone learn about hybrid vitality in biology class? Hello? Hip dysplasia and congenital blindness and deafness anyone? You say *purebred*, I say *inbred*, potato, po-tah-toe," she said. "How does this sound? *Dr. Madeleine Whitney's Advanced Course in Performing Arts*."

"It sounds eerily like your *Professor Whitney's Clown School for Wiener Dogs* and the adjunct *Whitney's Wonderful Weiner Dogs Traveling Circus* proposals.

"You remembered!"

"Remembered? Heck, I'm scarred for life. Now, go prep the isolation kennel before I put you on doo-doo duty."

"I feel totally unappreciated," she said, huffing off.

From noon to early evening, I watched Hardwire's truck, hauling a trailer, make a dozen trips, from our house to Ben's. I went to my family's house and glanced through the open door to the empty kitchen with its clean white walls and bare windows. Ben came in from the hallway, carrying a broom and a dustpan.

"Hey, Maddie, I'm about finished here."

"It always surprises me how different this place seems from when we lived here." Kenzie loved bright colors, knickknacks, bric-à-brac and whatnots. She had an indiscriminate passion for fresh flowers and an abiding belief in potpourri's contribution to civilization.

"I remember the first time I came here. You were in a state of shock."

"To be expected when one finds a corpse on a hike. It put me off trespassing for weeks." I shook out my arms, trying to dispel the ragged energy running from my fingertips upward. "I was sure you wouldn't stay in Coyote Run long after that grim introduction. Truth is, I was pretty sure you wouldn't stay *before* that incident. Newcomers romanticize small-town life."

"Sometimes dreams come true."

My laugh bounced in the empty space, and I said, "For the most part, I like living here. I like the familiarity of everything and everyone. It goes without saying that I hate living here for the very same reasons."

"Because everyone's always 'up in your business,' as you put it." He leaned on the broom. "Ava threatened to kill me in my sleep when I bought the clinic." He grinned, tilting his head. "She knew from the start that I wanted to be a small-town vet."

"She and the kids went away that summer, too."

"You're fishing, Maddie. Ava stays sane by taking breaks from her workaholic husband now and then. When she's gone, I can even sleep at the clinic, a bad habit, but when I have critical animals, it's hard to break away."

"Animals like Weasel?"

His brow furrowed and his eyebrows lowered, and I wished he was a dog because then I'd understand what that meant. "I'm always here for you and your dogs when you need me, and you can be damn sure people have gossiped, Maddie, but I don't let their suspicions interfere with our friendship."

His voice was too loud, and I knew it was happening again: I'd said the wrong thing and was fucking things up. "I'm sorry, Ben. Maybe I'm jealous you spend time with Emily, or maybe I'm jealous you spend time with Weasel instead of my dogs. Or both. Kenzie calls you my work-husband."

To my relief, he grinned. "Ava says that we bond on our love for animals as well as our obscure paranoias."

"You're the only one I know who understands the dangers of zoonotic disease transmission. Everyone else goes blithely about life, ignoring the obvious: that we're going to be subject to global pandemics that make HIV and Ebola seem like nothing. Those goddamn wet markets are going to kill us all."

"And you're the only one *I* know who's fascinated by maggot debridement therapy, which continues to astonish me, since you have bugs-crawling-on-your-skin issues."

"One of my great fears is that I'll develop a disease that requires MBT to clean out a complex, festering wound."

"If that should ever happen, I'll hold your hand while they apply maggots."

I smiled toward him, letting my eyes connect with his hazel brown ones for a second.

He propped the broom on the wall. "You'll be interested to learn that I'm going to participate in a study on MBT on animals.

Because of antibiotic resistance, there's renewed interest in the old methods."

"Tell me about it while we do a walk-through, just to be official about the landlord-tenant thing."

I glanced at the three bedrooms, two-and-a-half baths, and living room: so clean, light, and anodyne that I had a difficult time connecting my miserable childhood to it. I lingered in Kenzie's old room, a sharp ache going through me because I so wanted to see her colorful clothes piled on chairs, and her makeup and jewelry scattered atop a dresser. I missed the faint lavender from her sachets and candles.

After I gave my okay on the move-out, Ben and I walked down the road to his house because he wanted to show me his study. The room had built-in bookshelves, a work counter on the longest wall, industrial laminate flooring, and a glass and stainless-steel cupboard for medical supplies.

"This is perfect, Ben. So close to my center!"

"Dream on. This is my sanctuary for study...and the occasional dire emergency, because I'm only going to keep the bare minimum of equipment here. I am not your concierge veterinarian."

"Oh, I'm pretty sure you are."

"Okay, maybe I am, but that's only my side hustle."

"So long as we have an understanding. Hey, Ollie's working swing shift so I'm free tonight. Do you want to go to the Brewhouse for a burger?"

"Thanks, but I'm beat and covered in grime. I'm going to unpack until I can't keep my eyes open anymore."

We said our goodnights, and I returned to the center, finished my chores, and went into my cottage. It seemed cozy, but lonely, which wasn't an unfamiliar sensation for me, but odd in this particular space. I sent several informative texts to Kenzie, microwaved frozen macaroni and cheese, and watched two *iZombie* episodes.

Oliver called to say he was running late. "I won't be there until two at the earliest. Maybe three."

"I love your booty calls, but only when I'm awake enough to participate. Go catch the crooks, Ollie, and let me catch my z's."

I decided to bring Bertie to the cottage to keep me company the way he used to. He stood slowly from his favorite spot on the deck. I didn't want to drag him away and make him jump up on the bed, so I sat beside him and massaged his tired muscles until he closed his eyes and began snoring softly.

Vixen danced around me, and I capitulated, letting her invade my private space. I pointed to the rug beside the bed and said, "Here."

When I awoke, drenched in sweat in the middle of the night, she'd snuck in between the sheets and was stretched out alongside my body, her paws in my face.

Chapter Ten

IT WAS HIGH TIME I visited Ayer Vineyards, especially since I'd earn a consultation fee for merely meeting with Brother Ezra.

I took Bertie and Vixen with me and drove to the front entrance. The last time I'd been here, I'd been too upset to notice that the sign for the winery's tasting-room hours had been removed. A banner reading *Love is Truth—Truth is Love* now hung from two rough-hewn posts. Cult followers, wearing their ivory pajamas, had already started making breakfast. In a clearing, a long-haired woman led a group in yoga poses. They made me think of mimes, and then I recalled Zoe's Wiener Dog Circus, because there was definitely a scammy performance element to both.

I parked in the shade and took the dogs with me toward the firepit.

"Morning," said a too-smiley woman with a long braid. "Welcome to Spirit Springs. Would you like to join the yoga session?"

"No, but I'll take coffee."

"We are a drug-free community, but Brother Ezra's organic herbal tea blend is a wonderful way to start the day."

Drug free? Those cultists I'd seen dancing on the road weren't high on life. "Thanks, but I'd just as soon drink boiled star-thistle and dirt." Imagining the grit of dirt made my shoulders jerk. "I'd like to talk to Brother Euripides. I'm Dr. Madeleine Whitney. He's expecting me."

"I'm sure you mean Brother Ezra."

"Sure, whatever. He's interested in a therapy dog."

She looked at Bertie, who had lain down at my feet. "He's beautiful. Scars are our warrior marks."

"Not for everyone, but definitely for Bertie. He's not the therapy dog candidate," I said. "She may be available." I pointed to Vixen, who was squatting and peeing on someone's jute satchel. "There must be something in that bag making her mark it."

"Well, um, I'll tell Brother Ezra that you're here. Dr. Whitney, correct?"

I paced near the firepit, noting the approximately twenty foot clearance around it. A canopy covered a dining area, set up with long trestle tables, decorated with jam jars filled with wildflowers.

"Hello, I'm Brother Ezra," said a pleasant, well-modulated voice.

I turned to see a slim man in a thin white T-shirt and an ivory cotton kilt. His shiny caramel-brown curls hung below his shoulders. He had fine, elegant features, wore clear lip gloss and black mascara, and his fingernails were painted blue.

Emily was the sweet-natured girl next door, but Brother Ezra's sexual energy hummed like a '70s glam rock star's, and I wouldn't trust him as far as I could drop-kick him. "Commodious tent. Gussy it up, and it would do swell for weddings."

"Are you planning on getting married? I would be honored to officiate, and our events manager could coordinate the wedding and reception."

"Marriage is a legal contract. All you need is a pen. Expensive hootenannies are unnecessary."

"I'm also available for quick and dirty hoedowns," he said with a suggestive smile.

"I bet you are," I said, noticing how quickly he'd read me. "Your firepit is a hazard to the entire community. If you want to cook, get portable induction units."

He continued to smile, but his tone was less friendly. "The fire marshal inspected it recently and extended our permit, but I appreciate your concern. And you are?"

"I'm Dr. Madeleine Whitney," I said, fuming. "Beryl Jensen told me you're looking for a therapy dog, and I'm here to evaluate your needs and the premises."

"You're the dog rehabilitator."

"I'm also on Coyote Run's K-9 search and rescue team." I dropped my hand to Bertie's head and scratched through his thick fur.

"So many are lost." Brother Ezra gazed at me.

"And now you've lost me, dude." I tried to keep eye contact for the recommended three seconds, but that was two seconds too long. "Have you ever lived with a dog before?"

He dropped the magic juju attitude. "Emily was the dog fanatic. She had a standard poodle and a cocker spaniel, and my college roommate had a mastiff mix."

Vixen had mysteriously acquired a bagel and was running, tossing it up from her jaws and then catching it again. "Vixen, out!" I commanded, but not too enthusiastically, because I was wondering where she got it. Vixen dropped the bagel and then held it down with one paw in order to rip off chunks. "She has an undefinable charm, don't you think? I'll take a bagel with cream cheese."

"The bagels are gluten free, and we have faux cream cheese made of tofu."

"You say *faux*, I say *fake*. I cannot comprehend rejecting a thing in favor of an unsatisfactory imitation. Things should be themselves. I mean, if you don't want to eat dairy, eat something else, instead of manipulating a non-dairy food into dairy-product consistency. If you don't want to eat processed flour, don't eat processed flour. Don't advertise things that have never ever had gluten as gluten-free. Don't attach a moral value to a goddamn cookie!" I realized that my voice had grown a tad strident. My only decent therapist had taught me to use rote phrases to smooth over situations, so I said, "But that's merely my opinion!"

"Beryl Jensen told me you have interesting opinions."

I flipped through my Rolodex of banalities. "Thank you for sharing that. Did you help care for your family's dogs, and do you think you can make the commitment to be the primary companion to a dog for its lifetime?"

He said he'd walked and fed the animals, but no one ever admitted to being neglectful. "Anything else, Dr. Whitney?"

"Yes, where will the dog live?"

"Here at the vineyard in the warm months. We'll see about the cold months when winter comes. If things work out, I'd consider another. We have room."

"If you want to keep a dog here, I'll need soil samples to make sure this isn't still contaminated by that pesticide wind drift that killed off the grapes. And no matter what the pesticide company 'proved' in court, I don't believe them."

"You're aware that my sister is Emily Ayer, right?" When I nodded, he went on: "Even though she and Dino lost in court, the pesticide company agreed to scrape off and replace the topsoil. Tests show it's safe."

"But who contracted the tests?"

"Do you think the results were tampered with?"

"Not necessarily. I've spent time in labs, and it's a simple enough task to predetermine desired results and structure tests to achieve that end," I said. "Maybe that's the reason your sister's dog has such serious health issues."

"Weasel has health issues?"

"If you want to adopt a dog, you should be attentive to the ones around you. Talk to Emily and get tests from an environmentally responsible laboratory. If they come out okay, I'll be delighted to find a therapy dog for you. How is your sister doing?

His body slumped a fraction, like a tire with a pinhole leak. "She's grieving, and I can't do a thing about it except to tell her she won't always feel this awful. She and Dino have...*had* such a deep bond, one of love and devotion."

"Dogs give us love and devotion." I realized that I was opening and clenching my hands, making my palms sweat. I spread my fingers against my jeans.

"It's not on the same level as a spiritual connection between humans."

"That's merely your opinion. I don't adhere to speciesism, and wearing that skirt here is ridiculous."

"Well, *I* don't adhere to gender-defined roles," he said. "Do you have a problem with a man in a skirt?"

"No, and neither will any rattlers you come across. Sure, we have rattlesnake antivenom, but it's expensive and people are never the same afterward, kinda like when someone's struck by lightning. Merely my opinion."

I drove to Penelope's Catering, happily considering the bill I'd send Beryl for the consultation. I was in luck, because my friend was inspecting appetizers and desserts for a party. "Mind if I?"

"Afternoon, Maddie. Keep your hands off the trays, and I'll get you a plate. Where's Bertie?"

"In the truck with sneaky Vixen. This is a fast-food stop. Because I'm fast, and you always have food."

She laughed. "Sweet or savory?"

"A little of both. Is that roast beef? Those chocolate thingies are tempting. Did you like the photos of Beau Blue I sent you? Doesn't he look like a different dog?"

"It's amazing. Nutritious food and affectionate company are good medicine."

"I concur. You won't believe the appalling breakfast they tried to force-feed me at Spirit Not-Anywhere-Near-a-Springs Institute at the Ayers' place."

"Tell me all about it."

So, I set to talking and eating while she worked. I polished off a lemon verbena and thyme cookie and said, "That concludes my full and accurate reporting of events that transpired with Brother Whatever. What the fuck were Dino and Emily thinking, letting him set up camp here?"

"That's a riveting tale. Why don't you write it up and submit it to Abel Myklebust for the *Coyote Run Recorder*?"

"Oh, Pen, when we met, you were one of those deeply sincere, salt-of-the-earth lesbians. What happened?"

"Maddie, do you even hear yourself? Doesn't it bother you at all that Dino Ayer died in a terrible accident, and now his wife is all on her own raising the kids and trying to manage the vineyard? Dino was always friendly, and Emily a gentle soul."

I blinked too many times and too fast, and she said, "I'm sorry. I didn't mean to be so harsh."

"It's okay. When I veer off course, I need someone to steer me right," I said, thinking she sounded so much like my sister, the angel on my shoulder, scolding me for being a jackass. "Thanks for breakfast. Come by and see Beau Blue when you get the chance."

I called Zoe into my office and said, "How would you like to be on television, showing what that Frenchie can do?"

"Are you serious!" she shrieked. "Are you serious!"

"Your words are in the form of a question, but your tone is exclamatory. Yes, I'm serious. I'm demonstrating agility training on Sasha Seabrook's weekly feature. Filming is Friday morning, eight a.m., and I need you here by seven-thirty sharp. I'll take Sheriff Desjardins' dog over the obstacle course, and then you can run through a few tricks with Snickers. She'll be our adoption spotlight for the French Pug rescue. Sasha's sending a release form that your parents have to sign."

"Holy Pokeman! What should I wear? Do I get to say anything? Will I be interviewed? Can I use a title like 'Associate Canine' something, or will that make it sound like I'm calling myself a dog? What's our adoption price strategy, because I listened to a negotiation expert and—"

"No negotiations, because this is not a hostage situation. Wear your WCRC T-shirt. You'll have sixty seconds, and you can say hello to Sasha. Not a word about traveling circuses."

"But!"

"Say thank you, Zoe."

"*Ankthay ouyay, Oezay.*"

"Very funny."

She flung her arms around me and said, "I totally mean it, Maddie. Thank you! I heart you so much."

"Me, too, sweetie." I hugged her, and then she skipped off.

Jaison walked over and handed me a paper bag. "Julie made these organic dog treats. She wants your opinion. She'd like to do something besides clerking at the market."

The bag held about a dozen bone-shaped treats in multiple colors. "I'll try them out on Bertie. He's very discerning."

"Bertie eats bugs and frogs. What was the hug about?"

"I told Zoe she can show off the Frenchie's training on Sasha's show."

"Girls. Dog cookies and tv shows and customizing things. Taking pictures of everything they eat and everything they wear."

"*I'm* a girl."

"Not that kind," he said. "Do you still want your rescue, Beau, to meet the others? He was okay with Bertie, wasn't he?"

"Beau was weak then. He'll likely react differently now, and the last thing I want is for Bertie to get into a scuffle with a younger dog," I said. "Run over to the sheriff's station and pick up Zeus. If Beau starts anything, Zeus will put him in his place."

"Are you seriously asking me to go to the station? I have been avoiding that goddamn deputy every day. I don't even pick up Julie at the market anymore."

My face grew hot, and my arms swung out once, twice, three, four, or five times. "Sorry, Jai. I didn't think... But you'll be fine there since he knows Ollie has your back."

"I hate this. If you want Zeus, you go get him." Jaison stomped away, dust clouds rising with his footsteps.

Careless, thoughtless clumsy bitch, I thought. I wanted to run after Jai, but knew I'd only make it worse. Because I always did. I yanked up the hem of my shirt to dab my eyes and told myself that he'd forgive me.

By the time I returned from the sheriff's substation with Zeus, I'd become so anxious that I couldn't stand still for even a moment. My fingers fluttered as if each was participating in a stadium wave, and my lips tugged to the left and then the right.

I walked with Zeus through the gate, thinking *breathe, just breathe*. I looked nervously toward Jai and waited. "Hey, Jai, I was wondering..."

He didn't hesitate, but came to me and took my hand, weaving his fingers with mine. "Stop jumping outa your skin, girl. I ain't gonna bite."

"I was...that was my White privilege, wasn't it?"

"Yeah, and maybe it was your *I am the hot chick who bangs the sheriff privilege*."

When I opened my mouth, the laughter carried away all my

anxiety. "You're not mad at me?"

"If I was a dog, you'd already read that we're cool."

"I'm never going to figure things out on my own, Jai, and I shouldn't have to ask you to educate me about race—"

"Huh, that's some enlightened shit coming from you."

"I can't take any credit. Kenzie continually sends me articles because she thinks I need to get in touch with my ethnic identity."

Our conversation was interrupted by a shriek from across the yard, and we saw Zoe standing in the kiddie pool with the garden hose and dogs jumping around her.

"I'm wild about that girl," I said. "But I miss ending afternoons getting lit with you and not having to be careful about what we say and how we say it."

"Me, too, Boss, me, too."

"That's what I get for trying to be a role model. Speaking of which, it's time to evaluate Beau's temperament."

Beau had been moved to the end kennel, where he'd adjusted to the pack's sounds and smells, but at a safe distance. He was accustomed to me and no longer crowded into the corner. As I had done on my previous visits, I clicked my tongue and gave him a treat. His tail wagged a few times. Most labs had strong food motivation, and this lab mix was no exception, which would work in our favor.

I clipped a leash on his collar, and he yawned, a sign of his nervousness. I took him from the center through a side exit and began a slow trot through the grasses until he began to lag. I circled to a clearing by the barn.

I loudly clicked my tongue and, when he acknowledged me, gave him another treat. I whistled to signal Jaison to approach. He came from around the barn, with Zeus by his side.

The second Beau saw the Dutch shepherd, he stiffened. I clicked my tongue, but he was fixated. "Reset," I called out to Jai.

He moved out of sight again, and I took Beau farther off. I

whistled, and Jai and Zeus returned, getting the same reaction from Beau.

I clicked my tongue, but he kept watching Zeus. We repeated the exercise, but no matter the distance, Beau was too traumatized to turn his gaze from another dog. I took him back to the isolation kennel. I sat on the ground beside him with a treat in my palm. After four or five minutes, he came forward and gingerly took the treat.

"This is going to be a long process, isn't it, Beau? Your whole world is fear and pain, and my heart goes out to you. But you're going to get better. Zeus and the pack are going to help. It seems impossible, but you'll be happy soon."

He let me put my hand on him, and I scratched his back, wanting to cry when I felt the scars under the fur. "If I ever find the bastards who did this to you, Beau, if I ever find those bastards, I swear, I swear..." That was the problem with revenge: the only righteous punishment was as barbaric as the crime. "Humans are the worst animal, Beau. But you know that."

When Oliver came over in the evening, I told him about Beau's progress, but became riled as I expounded on Brother Ezra and his crew. Ollie responded by turning the TV on to a baseball game.

"You are not taking this fire hazard seriously," I said, twisting the hem of my AC/DC T-shirt. "You weren't even listening about Brother Ezra and the Inferno of Danger and the fire marshal's criminal apathy."

He sighed and pulled me close. "I'm sorry, babe. I have got a lot on my mind lately. I visited the place myself. They've promised to bank and douse the fire by ten every night. It's safer than most home barbecues."

"I disagree."

"You've expressed that—because they have 'stupid names,' 'stupid fake food,' and 'stupid clothes.' None of those are crimes, or your ratty T-shirt would be. I told you to throw that thing away."

"I don't tell you what to wear, so don't you tell me what to wear," I said. "Besides, AC/DC rocks, and I'm sure that cult listens to stupid noodley music. They undoubtedly have stupid sex."

"I'm going to hate myself for asking, but how can sex be stupid?"

"Okay, *some* stupid sex is acceptable. Take off your clothes, and I'll demonstrate."

Oliver left well before dawn, and I couldn't get back to sleep. I dressed and was outside with Bertie as the sun's rays edged over the mountains. We strolled to the far end of our property, just the two of us in the quiet coolness.

Quiet, except for a door slamming in the distance and then voices. I walked toward the sounds. In the distance, two figures embraced by a car parked by Ben's back porch. The figures parted, and one went to the car and opened the door, setting off the interior light.

Emily Ayer, Weasel nowhere in sight, slid into the front seat, started the engine, and drove away.

Chapter Eleven

ZOE SHOWED UP at 7:00 A.M., bringing zucchini-raisin muffins and orange juice. "Hi, Boss. I came early so we can confab about our presentation."

I picked up a muffin and bit into the still-warm pastry. "These are scrumptious, thanks, and I wouldn't confab unless under threat of torture." Bertie ambled over hopefully. I picked the raisins from a muffin and fed it to him. "Zoe, be careful. Dogs shouldn't eat raisins or grapes."

"And onions, chocolate, caffeine, macadamia nuts...as if I'd share macadamia nuts, and you made me memorize that list, but my mom baked the muffins for Sasha, not for the dogs. Your shirt is inside-out."

"It was dark when I got up. I'm not even changed yet. Take the Frenchie out for a run."

"To relax Snickers?"

"To calm you both, because you're giving me contact jitters."

"I don't understand why most training is making dogs relaxed," she said. "They sleep eighty hours a day. If they were any more relaxed, they'd be in comas."

"We use everything in our arsenal to teach dogs how to calm

themselves, so they don't go on overdrive when they're in an unfamiliar situation or threatened."

"You don't teach Vixen anything. She runs around like a wild animal."

"She's not a client dog."

Zoe puffed out her cheeks. "*Ouyay. Ateverwhay.*"

"*Ankthay ouyay, oney-bunnyhay.*"

Sasha and her cameraman arrived a few minutes late, and she said, "Sorry I'm tardy, hon. Who's the cutie?"

I introduced them to Zoe, who was hopping from foot to foot in delight. She offered them muffins, and we all went to the obstacle course in the barn. I told Sasha, "Agility training is a fun exercise that also engages a dog's mind. My pack has not been trained at competition level, but most enjoy the activity. I'll be introducing a newcomer who's never been on the course so people can learn how to encourage a novice if it balks."

"Can't you use Bertie? Everyone loves seeing him."

I reached down to touch Bertie, my talisman and friend. "No one is surprised when he excels at anything. We want to show that any dog will benefit from this activity."

Zoe, who was hovering behind the cameraman, said, "And it's an excellent way for people to bond with their canine companions, too."

Sasha smiled and said, "Someone's an excellent student!"

"Teacher's pet," I said, "and *someone* should fetch the beagle."

Zoe ran off, during which time I endured Sasha powdering my face and messing with my hair, while I pushed her hands away and said, "It's fine, it's fine!"

Zoe returned with Vixen, who wore a silver bow around her neck.

"Where's the beagle?" I asked.

"He jumped in the pool and rolled in the dirt before I could get the leash on him."

Vixen wiggled up to Sasha, who petted her and said, "What a pretty girl!"

"Pretty silly. Don't get your hopes up," I said, "because every time I've tried to teach her obstacles, she takes off after mice."

Sasha cringed. "Are there mice here?"

"Not anymore. She got them all."

The segment began with an introduction and a short Q&A about agility training. Then I called Vixen to the start of the course, a children's play tunnel, and, using a squeaky ball as her reward, directed her to run through.

She zoomed through the tunnel and proceeded to leap onto a platform, climb a ladder, drop down into a kiddie pool, pausing only to shake herself, jump through a raised ring, and then cross a seesaw, all in record time.

"Wow, that was amazing!" Sasha said toward the camera.

I was so astonished that I stumbled over my commentary about the need for patience and repetition. "Accept that most dogs won't get this right the first or second or even the tenth time," I said, my shoulder jerking upward. Vixen chewed manically on the squeaky toy. "This is more about gradually building trust than about, um, winning a timed race."

"She sure loves that toy, Dr. Whitney. Is it appropriate for all dogs?"

"Only with supervision. Dogs can chew through the toy and swallow the rubber pieces and the metal squeak mechanism."

"Why do dogs like squeaky toys so much?" Sasha asked.

"Because they sound like the death cries of small animals."

"Oh!" she said, but her smile didn't falter. "Okay, and you have a special adoption candidate to show us, don't you?"

After Zoe gave her demonstration, Sasha pulled me outside to a shady spot under an oak and hectored me with personal questions while the cameraman filmed. After ten minutes, I said, "Enough with the inquisition. You must have accumulated hours of footage, and I can't find any theme running through your questions."

"I told you, it's my special project. I'm collecting everything you say like a word cloud, and eventually the theme will reveal itself to me."

"Word clouds are the worst diagrams. They don't organize or illustrate anything."

"You are an unusually prickly character. Most people totally suck up to me for attention, like your little friend Zoe. She was wonderful, by the way. She's got a hundred-watt smile. I'm going to edit out your death cries comment, though."

"Fine, go ahead and cut out the most interesting part of the segment," I said. "Sasha, I'm having a moral dilemma, and I wonder if you can weigh in. What would you do if you discovered that a friend is cheating on their partner, but your friend denies it to your face?"

She tapped her forefinger against her chin while she thought. "Why does it matter?"

"Because I adore the friend's partner, so I feel as if I'm complicit if I don't tell them. But I don't want to interfere, and I'm furious that my friend is lying to me.

"Too many unknowables, Maddie. Are you sure your friend is sexing up someone else?" When I nodded, she said, "Your friend and the partner might have an open relationship."

"They both told me they're monogamous."

"I did a five-part series on alternative relationships, and people have legitimate concerns that they'll lose their jobs or be shunned if others find out they're not monogamous. Ironically, most 'traditional' people don't realize that monogamy is far from traditional. Read the Bible or the Quran; polygamy and keeping women as chattel were the norm until relatively recently."

"But my friends know that I don't give a damn about society's mores. They have no reason to lie to me."

"Ah, that's not a moral dilemma; that's a wounded ego," Sasha said. "If you like your friends, why don't you respect their privacy? Does that help?"

"Yes, it really does," I said, even though it would have been easier to set aside my preoccupation with Ben's sex life if Dino was still cluelessly puttering about town.

"Relationships are horribly complicated, which is why I'm determined to hold my ground as proudly and permanently single." She grinned. "See, there's more to me than a pretty face."

"I've always acknowledged your superior intellect."

"You lie like a rug, Maddie Whitney." She smiled and tossed back her shimmering, honey-gold hair. "Anything else on your mind?"

"Yes, do you recall Dino Ayer, who died in a boat explosion recently? He and his wife had to lease land to a cult to make ends meet. The fanatics live in yurts and wear pajamas and build fires every day, which is a safety hazard for us all. The leader has messianic tendencies."

"Maddie, you can't mean Brother Ezra, because he's wonderful and wildly photogenic! He's already invited me to his Light Hands Healing Workshop. I've pitched an alternative medicine story to my producer, so fingers crossed."

"'Light hands' sounds like a nightmare. Don't be fooled by his mellifluous voice and bleached-teeth smile."

"You trash him like an ex."

"No way! Nevermind. I was only trying to help with your," I said, and then used one of Zoe's phrases, "your career trajectory."

"You want to help? Get me a juicy crime to report. I love the cutesy beat, but my dream is to write about blood alley."

"Sasha, the very next time I discover a marauding gang, I'll call you," I said, and we burst out laughing.

* * * *

Jai and I worked with Beau Bleu, and by the end of the week, he could stand within fifteen yards of another dog and accept a treat. He no longer cowered when I appeared and allowed me to sit with him and brush his coat. I only spoke to Ben briefly about my scruffy dog Gizmo's stomach rash and a Weimaraner's hot spots.

Zoe overheard the call, and, when I finished, she said, "I don't understand hot spots. How can a spot hurt without an injury?"

"Not every injury is visible, and pain also migrates along the nervous system."

"You mean like how acupressure works? Because my mother had an acupressure session at Spirit Springs Institute, and now she's all revived and stuff. She acts like she's not a senior citizen anymore."

"Zoe, your mother isn't even forty."

"That's what I said – a senior citizen. Geez. When are we going to be on Sasha Seabrook's show again? I'll watch videos to learn canine acupressure for my next demonstration. Bertie can be my patient, and shouldn't I be paid for my appearance?"

"*We* are not having another show soon. *I* am, and I'm not paid for them."

"You *should* be paid. You're a professional, and professionals are paid for their expertise. If they can't pay you, take your talent somewhere else."

"It's not all about money, Zoe. I'm glad to teach people how to understand and care for their dogs. It's also unethical to pay a source for a story."

"Then get out of the news and produce your own show, so you wouldn't have to worry about your bills so much."

I should never have let her help with the accounting. "Precociousness is not a universally beloved quality," I said, and walked away, out of the compound and down the lane to our house.

The bicycles and toys by the front porch were gone, and the

kitchen garden had wilted. My grandfather had grown vegetables and sunflowers here, and my mother favored berries, fruit trees, and roses. My sister introduced heirloom tomatoes and annuals that reseeded, and finally Ava had added herbs and pansies. A little of everything had survived from the past, and I didn't want to be responsible for single-handedly killing it all through neglect, so I turned on the hose and watered the most forlorn plants.

While I watered, I considered my finances. If I wanted higher rent, I'd have to upgrade the appliances and replace the swamp cooler with air conditioning. I didn't want to deal with someone who would flip out every time a bat flew inside or ladybugs infested the bed linens or the well stopped pumping or a dog stole a roast chicken off the dining room table.

Ben and Ava never minded those things.

My phone binged, bringing me to the present, and I stepped away from a muddy rivulet and turned off the hose. Claire Desjardins had sent a message: "Lunch? Meet at pup school."

For as long as I could remember, half the town's population ran wild and feral until they'd entered kindergarten, and the rest attended Coyote Pups Preschool. Because I'd been unmanageable, I'd been kept at home, but my siblings loved Coyote Pups, or maybe they loved getting away from me, shrieking and throwing myself on the floor. Whatever the case, I was fascinated by the open building with its art displays, bookcases, and toys racks.

Oliver's beautiful twin was in the art room, helping toddlers label colorful papier mâché animals. She was willowy, and her long wavy hair was a golden red. She wore it in a low ponytail, tied with an azure velvet ribbon. She had a constellation of freckles scattered over her creamy skin, golden-green eyes lined with kohl, and a wide sensuous mouth. Most of her tattoos were hidden, but at the base of her throat was a gold star, and a new one on her shoulder intertwined *C & O DeJ* above their birthday.

She wore her favorite paint-splattered overalls over a vintage ivory camisole.

I waved to her and then sat atop a children's workbench to wait.

The toddlers were herded out to the lunchroom, and Claire went to the sink and washed the paste and tissue paper from her hands. She came over and kissed my cheek. "Sorry to keep you waiting. I thought I'd be done by now," she said, in the rough, honey voice that I'd fallen in love with.

"I like watching you."

"You look better than ever, Maddie. You're growing out your hair."

"Not on purpose. The moment it starts to itch my neck, I'll get out the scissors. Ollie said he could trim it, but I wasn't sure if he was joking."

"He's got a steady hand. We used to cut each other's hair until he joined the sheriff's department. I went overboard with the buzzer."

"I like your twins tat. When did you get that?"

"Last week. We can skip lunch and get yours finished," she said, because I'd jumped from the parlor chair in the middle of inking a floral scene on my breast as a tribute to her last name: the gardens.

"Oliver already offered to draw in the rest with permanent markers, but I'm convinced you grabbed all the artistic talent while you were still in utero."

"That I did." Claire steered me out of the building, and we walked over to Main Street. I turned right, but she turned left. "Claire, you're going the wrong way. If we don't get to the Brewhouse soon, we'll have to wait for our burgers."

"I want an herb salad and grilled salmon."

"Oh, not the Country Squire! We're not dressed right."

"I'm an artist, and I have artistic license. You're a renowned dog trainer, and you have...dog license," she said, and began laughing. "Come on, you never minded the Squire when you prowled for hookups with wine country tourists."

"*Of course*, I minded it, but what were my alternatives?" I said. "I was frozen out of all the LGBTQ-XYZ-whatever massage circles and sourdough-starter exchanges and square dances because of you."

"No, because you make comments like that, and you were stalking me."

"I wasn't stalking. I was transitioning, albeit slowly, from our relationship."

"You don't do well with change."

"True. It's possible that I may never describe something as 'artisanal' instead of 'overpriced crap made by someone with a master's degree in philosophy.'"

The sheriff's substation was directly ahead, and I slowed down. Claire put her arm through mine and said, "Ollie isn't there. You'll have to settle for me."

"Oliver says the same thing, that I'm settling for him, which I am not. He's wonderful," I said, and then I saw Deputy Richard Kearney step out of the station's entrance.

He saw us, too, and tipped his hat.

"Hi, Rich!" Claire called out, and now I was the one hurrying her along.

"I can't believe you said hello to that asshole! He tased me and was going to beat up Jaison."

"It's awful that you were tased, but Rich told me a different version. He says you were threatening him and acting, well... He regrets the whole thing."

"Yeah, he regrets it, and *I* got fifty-thousand volts. If I ever see him walking on a dark road, I'm going to put my pedal to the metal and rid the world of one monstrous skinful of nasty."

We'd arrived at the Country Squire's brass-trimmed front

door. Claire smiled and said, "Sometimes I miss your righteous anger," and I warmed right through.

"Okay, Claire, for you, I'll endure this place."

We walked into the air-conditioned chill of the upscale restaurant with white tablecloths, vineyard murals, shiny brass fittings, and innumerable crystal gimcracks. I glanced at the long bar and was glad to see that Abel Myklebust was not at his reserved seat there, scribbling in a notebook.

Like half the town, the hostess knew Claire and led us to a window table. Claire waved off menus and ordered salads and steamed salmon for us and a bottle of a local rosé.

"I wanted a burger and a beer."

"You don't eat enough vegetables." She lifted her chin toward the bar. "Your dad's not here."

"I wish Ollie never told you that."

"We tell each other everything. Most everyone guessed years ago anyway."

"Well, it was a secret to me," I said. "My mother doesn't know that anyone else knows."

"Of course she does."

I repositioned the shiny flatware and the water and wine glasses until they were satisfactory. "I'm the reason my legal father left her."

"According to my aunt, Jesse Whitney was a complete asshole, which is why your mother fell into Abel's lecherous arms." Claire stopped talking while the server brought our food and poured our wine. When we were alone again, she said, "I think you should come out."

"I've always been out, Claire."

"I meant that you should come out as Abel's daughter."

I buttered a slice of baguette. "It would serve no purpose."

"Unlike Jesse Whitney, Abel is gregarious, interested in the world, and smart to boot. Will you at least think about it?"

"All right, already, I'll think about it."

"No, you won't."

"No, I won't. Can we discuss something else? I thought I could handle my sister being away, and I managed when I was preoccupied with the construction of my cottage. Lately, though, I have constant low-grade anxiety. Everything feels skewed, but so infinitesimally it's not consciously perceptible. Subconsciously, though, my apprehension keeps growing. Does that make sense? I'm glad Kenzie's living the life in her photo-worthy condo, with her well-adjusted friends, but it feels as if she's drifting farther and farther from me, as if she's a different person when she no longer has to play caretaker to the village idiot."

"Don't flatter yourself; Coyote Run has idiots galore," she said. "A reliable source told me you're constantly calling and texting Kenzie. I'd do the same if Ollie moved away. Not that he would."

"You used to swear that you were going to move somewhere where the beer was cheap and the girls were free, or vice versa."

"That's my daydream. How could I ever leave my family?"

"Build a papier-mâché airplane and fly away."

She laughed and began telling me about the sculptures she was creating for a gallery show in the winter. I wished I understood what she was talking about, but I didn't, so, I smiled and nodded and admired the sunlight glinting on her hair and the pink blushing on her cheeks and the tiny silver hoops along the helix of her ears. I admired the way her graceful paint-flecked fingers punctuated her sentences. And, while I didn't understand the art she created, I understood the art that she was, and the sculpture of her clavicle, framed by her camisole and visible above the worn denim bib of her overalls, was unspeakably beautiful.

We'd ordered profiteroles, and she'd refilled our glasses when someone said, "Hello, Dr. Whitney. I thought you hated people who drank rosé."

Andrea Kleinfeld from Internal Affairs stood by the table. She was dressed casually, in blue cotton pants and a blue sleeveless button-front shirt.

"Yes, and now I'm consumed by self-loathing," I said.

Claire smiled at Andrea. "I'm Claire. Would you like to join us and have a glass?"

"I'm Andie, and, yes, I'd love one."

So, she sat, and the women smiled at each other, and I stared at the ceiling, decorated with blown-glass grape clusters.

"Andie likes skeet shooting, but she doesn't want to adopt a dog," I said by way of introduction. "Claire is an artist, and her family has lived in Coyote Run forever. She has a wonderful flower garden, but the fruit trees get ransacked by vermin."

The women laughed, and somehow both jumped in chatting about too many subjects to follow. Claire leaned back in her chair, that way she did when she flirted, encouraging the object of her interest to lean forward, and then we were sharing the profiteroles and ordering iced coffee.

Claire and Andrea. Well, Coyote Run had a limited dating pool, and eventually everyone hooked up with everyone else, which, I supposed, accounted for my mother and Abel Myklebust, who was, in fact, hulking across the restaurant to his favorite barstool. I pulled a few twenties from my pocket and set them on the table. "Excuse me, but I must touch base with someone." To Claire, I said, "I'm going to talk to Abel. Are you happy now?"

"Ecstatic," she said, and I left the women, wove between tables, and sat on the stool next to Abel's.

A new bartender came up and said, "The usual for you, Mr. Myklebust, and your..." and he looked from one of us to the other, and I said, "Ah, fuck," because the resemblance of our reflections in the bar mirror was so obvious.

Abel said, "Maddie, cease cursing, and what will you have?"

"Nothing, I'm fine." My shoulder jerked forward, and a nerve by my right eye pulsed. When the bartender served Abel a whiskey and left, I said, "I need you to find out something for me."

"Good to see you, too. How's that rare Luxembourg flatcoat retriever fraud of a dog?"

"Almost ready for the heritage breeds show. Have you met that jackass living on the Ayers' land? He's conned everyone in town. He calls himself Brother Ezra."

"Probably because that's his name, or a version thereof. Emily's maiden name is Brothers. He's Ezra Brothers. He's bright and friendly, a useful addition to the community."

"Fine, drink the Kool-Aid with everyone else. Now that Dino is gone, the whole place might be converted to a feel-good rainbow orgy yoga commune."

Abel sipped his whiskey. "What's your agenda? Because you always have an agenda."

"Brother Ezrat wants to adopt a therapy dog. I'm concerned about the soil being carcinogenic."

"Ezrat, really?" Abel rolled his eyes, which was not an attractive look on a middle-aged man. "That concern is a scintilla more credible, but your supposed worry is unwarranted. The topsoil was scraped off, carted away, and replaced."

"Newly planted vines have died, though."

"Dino overreacted after the pesticide drift. He thought the clean soil deserved clean stock, and he planted *Vitis vinifera* that hadn't been grafted onto American rootstock."

"I'm not following you."

"European vines are susceptible to Phylloxera, a louse that sucks the life right from the roots. There's no pesticide for the louse, but native vines have Phylloxera-resistant rootstock, which is why they're used for grafting. Surely, you're familiar with the Great French Wine Blight in the late 1880s."

"Excuse me if I've never bothered to study enology."

"Oh, your sister told me you were randomly exploring college majors alphabetically, so I thought you must have covered that before crash landing on forensics."

"My exploration was alphabetical, not random, and my degree was in criminology, not forensics, thus my ignorance of enological history. For your information, I successfully completed the doctoral program and was gainfully employed."

"Then why did you quit?"

"I prefer the company of dogs," I said. "You are an exceedingly annoying conversationalist. When did you talk to Kenzie?"

"The annoyance is mutual. I invited her to Quiz Night. She couldn't make it but assured me you'd do well because of your expansive knowledge of nothing-in-particular."

"I'm sure she didn't put it that way, and I'm not comfortable with you talking to my sister about me. If the soil is safe and Emily can grow louse-resistant grapes, why doesn't she do that rather than lease valuable acreage?"

"Now that Dino's dead, she won't need to. He had a multimillion-dollar life insurance policy."

"What!"

"Dino was always careless, scaring Emily to death. After he hacked off his finger, she said he had to either give up his hobbies or get life insurance to support the family if he killed himself."

"How can you be sure that Emily's motive wasn't to make Dino more valuable dead than alive?"

"The Ayers were having financial problems, but so are you, and I doubt you're going to put out a hit on me for an inheritance."

"Abel, if I was going to kill you, I'd do it personally. Their marriage may have had a dark side."

"Do you know why I sit here every day? Because people can find me easily, and they like to gossip, the way you're doing now. I've been friends with the Ayers for years, and Emily is a genuinely sweet lady. She's always been head-over-heels for Dino."

"I find that hard to believe."

"Love is blind. Or, in Sheriff Desjardins' case, deaf as well, because listening to you is aggravating. I hope you're nicer to him than you are to the general populace."

"Men say *nice* when they mean submissive and unquestioning, and they reserve that adjective for females. You can quote me on that."

"Why should I? Every time I've asked you for a quote, you manufacture some out-and-out lunacy."

The bartender, bringing a refill for Abel said, "Families, right?"

"Presuming much?" I said to the bartender, who apologized and left.

"Maddie, I suppose I should be grateful that you're talking to me. But you make everything so difficult."

I felt a twinge of something. "I've been told that my whole life, Abel, how I make everyone miserable."

"I didn't mean—"

But I was already off the barstool. I waved to Claire and Andie on my way out, but they were too engrossed in their conversation to notice me.

Chapter Twelve

ABEL MUST HAVE gone directly to the *Coyote Run Recorder*'s office, because he immediately sent a message with a copy of the Ayers' soil analysis. I scanned it and googled the testing laboratory. It seemed legit.

I called Georgie Maguire at the county's animal shelter and told her I needed a therapy dog for Ezra Brothers at the Spirit Springs Institute. "It will be living in a commune, so already people-friendly is highly desired."

"But I count on you to help with our most problematic rescues."

"And you always can. I don't want to invest excessive time rehabilitating a dog for this doofus, but I'll gladly take a totally funky dog that's not likely to be adopted otherwise."

"We brought in dozens from a hoarder last week," Georgie said. "No one would describe any as cute."

"Excellent. Send me pics and info on your candidates, and I'll select two...no, three, to work with. Let's do a small, medium, and large combo platter."

"I'm not complaining, but didn't your client request a single animal?"

"As a general rule, Georgie, I try not to get stuck on technicalities."

As I set down my phone, Jai leaned breathless inside the doorframe. "I went to the barn, and you can't believe what I saw!"

A shiver went through me: the finger in the paper bag. "There's an explanation," I began, a thousand needles prickling my skin.

"Yeah, the creek's running because Abel released water! In the summer."

"That's what I was going to mention."

"Even the pond is full."

"Hot damn! Let's go for a swim."

Taking the pack to the pond required extra hands, and a volunteer offered to join in the muddy venture. I changed into shorts, a tankini, and water shoes, and Jaison put on cut-offs. We sprinted across the field and then did a perimeter check for rattlers on the boulders around the pond. Heat reflected from the rock surfaces onto our skin, and the sun burned down, and we jumped in the cold water.

The dogs played chase and splashed around us. We threw sticks for them, and we did cannonballs from the largest boulder. We sprawled on the rocks to dry, and the dogs rolled in the dirt and grasses. We closed our eyes against the bright light, and Bertie, muddy and content, leaned against me. I rubbed his head and said, "Why aren't there more words for sky in English? I can't think of any that people use in normal conversation."

"There's no need for any others," Jaison said. "It is what it is."

"It is what it is," I said, pleased enough with the sky above me, my friend beside me, and the dogs all around, and on such a day, in such a place, it was easy to ignore an amputated finger hidden in a freezer. Because what difference did it make to a dead man? I sank into the pleasure of this day and my companions. A sparrow's call tweaked like a door pushed back and forth by wind, a red dragonfly glittered across the pond, and a dog snuffled.

When I stood, Jai opened his eyes and said, "Are we going back already?"

"You stay. I'll be working with Beau Blue. He should be enjoying this, too, and soon he will be."

"Your father is obviously trying to help you," Oliver said, crossing the patio to check on the steaks grilling. Zeus and Bertie lay nearby, hoping for the canine Holy Grail: a steak that slipped from the tongs.

"I cannot ascertain his motives. He made dark implications about murder for hire."

"That's ridiculous," Ollie said. "No one would have to pay to murder you when there's a long line of eager volunteers."

"Let me guess: It's funny because it's true. You said dinner would be ready two hours ago. Don't tell me you were at a meeting, because your shirt smells like beer."

"I was at a meeting with the Coyote Runaway brewery partners. They had an attempted break-in, but mostly wanted to introduce themselves."

"They should make friends, then, instead of taking up your time, especially when your time is really my time."

"It goes with the job, Maddie."

He slung his arm over my shoulders, and I leaned against him. "You're so busy these days."

"Crime rises with the temperature."

"You want to share anything?"

"Thanks for offering, but Claire listens to the 'mundane details' without grimacing."

"She understands better than I do. Has she said anything about meeting Andie, a.k.a. Andrea Kleinfeld at the Country Squire?"

Fire flared on the grill, and Oliver got up and sprayed it down. "You should have told Claire that Andrea was IA before inviting her to lunch."

"I didn't invite Andrea. Claire did, and what difference would it make if I said, 'Hi, this is Detective Andrea Kleinfeld of Internal Affairs, and she questioned me when I was tased'?"

"The difference is that Andrea isn't a random acquaintance. I walk a tightrope with IA. I don't want any dirty cops around, but I don't want anyone, including myself, to be falsely accused."

He'd said "falsely," but we knew that Ollie didn't go by the book when it conflicted with his personal sense of right and wrong, which was finely calibrated to consider all the casualties of a crime, including innocent family members of both victims and perpetrators.

"You should have warned me off Andrea even before I let her give me a ride."

"I would have, but you were raging out. You wanted me to shoot a deputy."

It sounded vaguely familiar. "I'm sure you're exaggerating. I might have said something about issuing a warning to a racist cop via a minor flesh wound. Ain't no crime in that."

"Actually, it's several."

As Oliver looked down to inspect the charcoals, his torso shook.

"Go ahead and laugh. I am so not over it."

He plopped the steaks on plates, and I followed him inside. His condo was like him: efficient, unfussy, and well-constructed. Over the past year, he'd acquired several dog toys. He kicked aside a tug-of-war rope and put the plates on the round dining table, which was already set with a salad, roasted corn-on-the-cob, and red wine.

Before he sat, I noticed the way his jaw clenched. I waited until we'd taken a few bites and said, "Ollie, what's going on? This isn't about the little stuff, is it? Does it have something to do with Internal Affairs?"

"There are things I can't tell you. Does that matter?"

"I have my private life. You have yours. Just like I have my home, and you have this place. I'm content with us being together apart. As for living with you full-time..." I shook my head. "And you wouldn't be able to stand it either."

His jaw relaxed, and he smiled a little. "That's something my ex-wives never understood. Distract me with something interesting."

I told him about my conversation with Abel, and Ollie said, "I heard about the insurance policy. It was the smartest move Dino ever made, aside from marrying Emily. She's a prize."

"Ben Meadows apparently thinks so." I raised my hands and shook away the tension. "I know, I know, I shouldn't resent him paying attention to other women, but I'm possessive. I enjoy his company, and he's the best veterinarian I've ever had. It's a miracle he's stayed here, and I don't want anything, including a divorce, driving him away."

"Emily's not the type to cheat."

"How can you be sure?"

"Because before you, when I was on the loose, I made my moves. Claire did, too, in fact, because, I mean," he said, and stretched his arms out. "Who's gonna pass on this?"

"Passing on you, I understand. Passing on Claire...she's every straight chick's kinky fantasy. I thought she didn't hit on women in relationships."

"We were all young, so stupid, and careless about our hearts and thoughtless of others then. Maddie, don't you dare give the rest of that ribeye to the dogs," he said, but it was already too late.

"Five minutes, and I'm going to go home. Rub my shoulders." I rolled onto my stomach, and Ollie straddled me and began massaging, but our skin was still sweaty, and I wiggled away. "Ollie, you're too goddamn hot."

"That's what she said."

We both laughed. "How come I never tell that joke right?"

"Because you use it indiscriminately. You don't need to use gags. I think you're hilarious."

"Most of the time, unintentionally. I feel all sorts of off these days."

"Your business?"

"Yes, and family. I owe my mother a long-overdue phone call. I have a hundred questions about dreadful Abel Myklebust. I'll never forgive him for not helping her when she was breaking her back to raise us."

"Maybe he *did* help her out. Why don't you ask her?"

"If my mother had wanted to tell me about Abel, she would have told me. I've asked her repeatedly if I was adopted."

"But you weren't. Maddie, as much as she deserves her privacy, you deserve information about your history. Your mother doesn't live here anymore, so does it really matter if you recognize Abel as your father when it's clear as day?"

"I've made her life difficult enough already. As far as day is concerned, I've got a long one tomorrow. Go to sleep, babe, and I'll let myself out."

He was breathing evenly before I'd even pulled on my jeans, his arms akimbo across the rumpled sheets. I treasured these opportunities to watch him when he couldn't watch me, so I stood there as his chest rose and fell, filled with a painful tenderness for him I was incapable of expressing with soft words and gentle embraces.

Rancho Vista Animal Services, the county's central shelter, was underfunded and overloaded by irresponsible owners and backyard breeders, as well as those who could no longer care for their pets because of health or financial problems. I waved at the receptionist and said, "Georgia's expecting me."

"Hi, Dr. Whitney. Go on through to her office."

I slumped as I passed the kitten hotel with its glass window displaying adoptable furballs playing and snoozing. Kenzie had always wanted a house cat, but cats weren't safe with all the dogs.

Georgie Maguire was at her desk, her cheeks flushed under skin weathered by the outdoors. She stood, wooden bracelets clattering and tiered earrings swinging. She'd pulled her long blond and silver hair up into a bun and wore an embroidered kaftan. She was like a wild rose open to the day: generous and sensuous and carelessly lovely.

"Hey, Maddie. It's going to be hot as hell today, isn't it?"

"Hey, you're ready for the beach."

"I'd love a vacation. Where's Bertie?"

I picked up her stapler and began squeezing it, letting the spent staples drop into a metal trash can. "He wants to stay with the pack these days." I counted out ten staples, eleven, twelve, twelve was a satisfying number, before putting the stapler down, parallel with her desk mat and approximately three-and-a-half inches from the desk's edge.

"It's thoughtful to let him be, but it must be a difficult transition for you."

I nodded, not trusting myself to speak.

Georgie said, "Okay, let's go meet your therapy dogs."

We went to a large central hall with chain-link gates revealing available animals. I was familiar with the chorus of desperate cries, whimpers and yelps, a chorus that broke my heart each and every time I heard it.

"I'm glad you're taking three," she said. "A Bay Area rescue is coming to pick up a dozen dogs, but we're still maxed out."

"I'll reach out to my regulars and see if I can rustle up foster homes." I paused at each gate, making quick assessments.

"I think these are the best six for your purpose, but you're welcome to check out the others." She pointed to three gates with red RESERVED FOR WCRC signs. "At least the hoarder fed them. They had ticks and the usual problems. Doc Ben and another vet did assembly-line neutering, spaying, and immunizations. These have pent-up energy, but they're friendly enough."

I crouched to better see the dogs, which included Chihuahua-terrier mixes curled together on a mat, mid-size pitbulls leaping against the gates, and hounds baying above the din. "The pitties are fine," I said. "The Chi mixes won't do well sleeping in tents come winter, but I have another client who's seeking two small breed dogs. I'm going to pass on those hounds. They'll take off wherever their noses lead them. Show me the others."

I snapped a few photos and sent them to the client. Then I looked at the hoarder's other dogs. I kept circling back to a homely mutt with a scrub of reddish fur and stubby legs. It thumped a thick tail on the cement floor, got up, and trudged over to sniff at me.

"It's golden retriever and maybe corgi," Georgie said. "The fur was a matted disaster, so we clipped it down."

"This is exactly the amiable ugly I want." I also chose a funky 51-flavors dog with mottled fur. As I was completing the adoption forms, my client called to say that she would love the chi mix duo.

When I snapped on the leashes, the dogs lunged this way and that. "Can you take the little ones, Georgie?" She carried them to my truck while I gave the others a brief lesson in heeling on a walk.

I loaded the dogs into crates. "They're well-balanced, considering."

"The owner cared enough to have the bitches spayed at our mobile truck, which is where we met him. We've been working for over a year to convince him to give most of them to us," Georgie said. "They'll have a much better fate than a dog that came in yesterday. We had to put it down immediately."

"Without the three-day waiting period?"

"A cyclist found it on the roadside about seven miles from here. The dog was ripped to shreds and in agony. I wasn't going to tell you, but I figured you'd learn sooner or later from Oliver, since a report was filed."

"He might not have heard yet since it's outside his region. There was a mountain lion sighting recently."

"Mountain lions kill quickly and feed on their prey. This was destruction. I think this dog was used in a fight."

A shiver ran through me. "Did it have any identification?"

"We found an ID chip and called the owner. She'd advertised it for free a few weeks ago, and a young couple came in, asking for a family pet."

"I really wish people wouldn't give dogs away without a home inspection."

"Me, too, but most people rehoming pets don't have any experience vetting an adopter. The ones giving away dogs for free are clueless that they're prime targets for abusers and hoarders. The owner was shaken up. She said the couple were friendly and polite. Honestly, any adoption can go wrong. We can be handing our animals to polite monsters. In my dream world, we have the time and staff to do frequent surprise inspections."

"That's an admirable dream, Georgie. Could you give me the owner's name and phone number? Because I'd like to have a chat with her."

Georgie resisted until I swore that I wouldn't harangue the owner, and she said, "Share anything she tells you with Sheriff Desjardins and let him handle things. Dog fighters are in criminal syndicates, and you can't help abused dogs if you're dead."

"I'm only making a phone call. That's it, and I'll tell Ollie whatever I learn."

* * * *

I brought Zoe into the evaluation room to meet the stubby dog, and she said, "Boy, what is that fugly thing?"

"Beauty is in the eyes," I said.

"And the nose, too. P.U.!"

"You'll be giving her a bath afterward. Right now, you're going to help me evaluate her temperament. What's the first step?"

"Take her on a walk?"

"How?"

"Mmm, go into the field and see if she charges ahead or shows timidity. See how she reacts to sounds and if she's smelling things or using her eyes mostly. Then bring another dog in and see how she reacts."

"Okay, that's what we'll do. Put the leash on her."

Zoe tried to drag the dog out of the room, and I said, "You remember all my instructions, but pick and choose when you practice them. You need to guide a dog's behavior, not force it."

"No one's going to want this dog anyway. It's a big ol' stinky mess."

The dogs may have frustrated Zoe, but not as much as she frustrated me sometimes, so I sent her to do chores and evaluated the dogs on my own.

By evening, I'd successfully integrated the hoarder dogs into the pack. I was worn out, yet felt a sense of accomplishment, when Ollie called and said, "I wanted to see you, but things have gotten hectic. How late will you be up?"

"It's been a long day. I'm amazed that my eyes are open now. Tomorrow?"

"That would be better."

"Ollie, did you hear about the dog a cyclist found out by Rancho Vista? Georgie said it was torn up, like it had been attacked by dogs. Or maybe one vicious dog."

"It was in the daily briefing."

"I have the name and address of the original owner, who gave it to a 'friendly couple.' Can you go with me tomorrow and talk to her?"

"Send me the info and, if there is time, I can have a deputy call, but—"

"But there *won't* be any time, will there, because you're understaffed. Everyone is understaffed. We can have charity drives year-round, but we still can't raise enough money to cover everything the town needs."

"You do what you can, Mad Girl, and that's a lot, especially since you're an existential nihilist."

"I wish I'd never told you that, and I don't think you fully comprehend what it means."

"It means that nothing I say to you matters and that you're going to do what you're going to do, irregardless, which is hassle me to ticket clueless citizens for things like giving away dogs and having bonfires and selling cappuccinos with artificial whipped-cream topping and using *irregardless*, instead of *regardless*."

"So, you do understand," I said, smiling. "I could not love you more, Oliver Desjardins."

"We live to fight another day, Mad Girl."

Chapter Thirteen

IT WASN'T YET 10:00 A.M., but it was so hot that my bandana couldn't keep the perspiration from stinging my eyes. I enjoyed washing and brushing sibling Dalmatians that were being picked up by their owners today. In the two weeks they'd boarded with us, the city dogs had grown sleek from exercise.

"I wish we had a Dalmatian at the fire station," Zoe said. "That reminds me of my dream last night. I was at the Bonanza Days parade behind the fire truck, and I was stark naked! Principal Desjardins was there, and she said, 'Zoe Gaskell, you were supposed to be in your drum majorette uniform!' and everyone booed me. Isn't that totally insane? Because I've never even been a drum majorette. What do you think it means, Boss?"

"Dreams are mental Dumpsters, all the miscellaneous scraps and junk. Trying to interpret them is like trying to cook a meal with garbage. You can do it, but you don't want to serve it to anyone you like."

"That's not what Mom says. She says that dreams reveal our innermost hopes, emotions, and fears. Maybe different people dream for different reasons. Like, maybe your dreams are garbage dreams, but Mom's dreams are totally mystical."

"That's entirely within the realm of possibilities, Zoe. Do you have anything else to share?"

"I got an A on my essay about hybrid vitality. My teacher said it was 'very passionate and well-reasoned.'"

"Congratulations!"

"I'm doing so well with online classes that I've decided not to go to State in the fall."

"But, Zoe, if you attend State for two-years, you can easily transfer to one of the U.C.'s and earn a valuable degree."

"You said you hated college."

I shook my head. "I hated the social interactions, but I loved the classes and opportunity to learn from amazing professors and scholars. You're outgoing like my sister, and she had a wonderful time meeting people, joining study groups, and going to parties. Don't cheat yourself out of the college experience."

"You're totally quoting from brochures now. I don't believe the 'college experience'—frat parties and pizza nights—is worth digging myself into debt for the next thirty years. Besides, a degree from an elite school is only useful if you want that kind of life. Like, if I wanted to be on the Supreme Court, I'd have to go to Yale Law School, right, because they *all* go to Harvard or Yale Law. I totally don't understand why our whole government is ruled by these Ivy League sons-of...and no one even questions the one percent pulling our puppet strings. It's like we're living in a dystopian novel, but the resistance hasn't risen up yet. I don't want to be a douchebag like the Facebook guy with his Harvard degree and all those Silicon Valley misogynist pigs with their disruptor B.S., a modern variation of medieval feudalism. I think Pig Latin must be the native language of male chauvinist pigs, don't you?"

"I'd never considered it," I said, amused and impressed by her passion.

"I want to be Steve Jobs, who didn't finish college and wasn't a male chauvinist pig—that's what my grandma calls my grandpa all the time. I don't know what languages Steve Jobs spoke besides English and Pascal."

I petted the Dalmatian beside me and came to the realization that Zoe had, in fact, been listening too attentively to my various ravings during her internship. "Be that as it may, I think you should seriously consider the advantages of a traditional college education. Talk to your parents."

"My parents are cool with it." She beamed. "I'm gonna put these guys in the kennel so they stay clean until they're picked up. See, I show initiative."

After Jaison and I reviewed our policy for holiday bookings, he said, "Zoe told me she's ready to move on from being a training intern to our marketing director."

I looked out my office door and listened to make sure we had privacy. "When I gave her the internship, I felt guilty about taking her from her parent's store. Now I wonder if the Gaskells were glad to have her move on. I can barely handle business as it is; I don't want or need a marketer."

"It's always the little ones that are the most power-hungry," he said, and picked up the blind little mutt, who'd wandered our way. "Isn't that right, Gizmo?" The dog nuzzled Jai, who rubbed his belly, before setting him down. "Zoe's a Miss Smarty, like you. What were you like at her age?"

"Self-righteous and furious. Prone to stream-of-consciousness tirades. Highly reactive and still kicking and spitting and throwing myself on the ground."

"Yeah, I figured." He closed the office door. "Boss, I love that bananas girl, and she's a real hard worker, but her energy is not in rehabilitation. If you're going to keep expanding the pack, we need a full-timer with the right-mind-set to be a serious trainer."

"You think I should let Zoe go?"

He raised his hands, palm forward. "That's your call, but you should definitely stop adding dogs."

"Okay, and these last ones won't stay long.

"Thanks, Boss," he said, and left.

My phone buzzed. It was the Spirit Springs Institute benefactress. "Hi, Beryl. Did you see the photos I sent to Ezra?"

"Yes, and I also received an installment of your bill. I said one dog."

I pulled the file drawer out and slid it back seven times. "Three dogs are easier to care for than one, because they provide activity for one another."

"Do they? That's not the point, Maddie."

"Trust me on this, Beryl. Brother Ezra is going to love all three dogs, and I've already started training them."

"We had a deal, Maddie, and you've been ignoring my invitation to brunch."

"I must have missed it. No matter. See you at one!"

"Don't you ever check your messages? Today is Dino Ayer's memorial, and everyone expects you there."

"And the memorial is, um?"

"It's at Spirit Springs Institute. Brother Ezra will conduct the service. You should call him immediately about your part in the program."

"My schedule is, um..."

"Penelope Millard is catering."

I called Oliver and said, "Do you want to swing by and pick me up for Dino's memorial? Penelope's catering."

"My afternoon's jammed, and I've already paid my respects to Emily. Please try to be sympathetic to her. She's in a bad way."

"I'm not a complete monster. I intend to observe politely."

"Your intentions are debatable. Your actions are what really count."

"Every time someone lectures me, it makes me miss Kenzie's scolding and puts me in a funk."

"A funk is the right mood for a memorial. Stay funky, babe."

I cleaned my favorite boots and slipped on a navy shift dress. After smoothing my hair with water, I went to the center to get Bertie.

He rested in the shade, panting, as the younger dogs wrestled and played. I crouched beside him, and he gazed at me soulfully. "I'll bring you a treat, Bertie, something delicious. I have a plastic bag in my tote with your name on it." I dipped my head to the velvet fur of his snout.

Vixen waggled up, and I hesitated, but guessed that dogs probably weren't welcome at funerals. Still, I felt vaguely guilty as she stood at the gate and watched me leave.

Cars were already parked at the Ayers' vineyard. I hopped out of my truck, gripping sunflowers from the garden, and followed the crowd to the dining tent. Benches and folding chairs faced plastic banquet tables that displayed photos of Dino with his family and friends. A sound system played Jimmy Buffett's "Trying to Reason with Hurricane Season," and I shoved the sunflowers into a huge standing horseshoe arrangement, making sure my handwritten card was visible.

I picked up a tart, icy margarita from the refreshments table and intercepted a server with travel-friendly teriyaki beef appetizers. I ate one and saved four in the plastic bag.

"Dr. Whitney!"

I was so startled by Brother Ezra standing right behind me, I dropped the bag. "No need to shout."

"Sorry to ruin your food. Let me throw that away." His antique linen nightshirt wafted when he stepped forward in a gold lace-up sandal.

"It's perfectly fine." I picked up the bag, dusted it off, and slipped it in my tote. "Still throwing caution to the wind with sandals, I see."

"I asked Emily about rattlesnakes, and she explained that the field cats clear away rodents. Without that food source, snakes don't come into the vineyard."

"Biodiversity is admirable in theory, although balance is impossible. Cats wipe out birds, and coyotes kill cats. You can tell because coyotes leave the heads rolling around. It's quite macabre, and town newbies always think a local psycho is torturing animals. In addition to snake aversion, I suppose I'll need to train your dogs to leave cats alone."

"I requested one dog to start."

"Three amazing therapy candidates became available, an incredibly rare opportunity, so I made an executive decision." I scanned the crowd and pretended not to notice Beryl, who waved at me. "I better get a seat."

"Sit on the aisle. Your song will be at the end."

"What song?"

"I left you a message. Dino wrote his last wishes for his service, and he wanted you to sing 'Breathe In, Breathe Out, Move On.'"

It was strange to think back to that morning when I'd last seen Dino. Had he already written his last wishes then? "He told me he liked it."

"I'll accompany you on guitar. We should have practiced."

"If you can plunk a few chords, we'll figure it out as we go. Coyote Run sets a low bar for entertainment."

"Would you like me to introduce you as Dr. Whitney, or... Everyone else calls you 'Maddie.'"

"Everyone else doesn't use their last name as a title."

He tilted his head. "Emily's always called me Brother Ezra, and there's a story to the name, but today is not the day for it. My friends call me EZ."

"That's what she said," I replied, and when he laughed, I liked him better. "Introduce me as Maddie Whitney, since I'm not here in my professional capacity."

"Your doctorate is in...?"

"Yes, it is. Wow, this place is really filling up."

The crowd went silent as Emily Ayer, leaning on Ben Meadows, and her children entered the canopied space. The force of her grief was like a sonic boom, sudden and shocking and visceral, and my throat tightened, and my jaw ached.

She'd become as thin and fragile as a leaf in winter. Her black dress hung off her frame, and her cheeks were sunken, making her dark eyes huge. Her caramel brown hair hung in a braid down her back. She moved hesitantly, as if in a daze. She took a seat in the front row, pulling one child on her lap and circling her arms around the other two.

"Excuse me," Ezra said, and moved toward his sister.

I sat in the back row and sipped my margarita while listening to Buffett sing about surviving "*'til I see you again*," and I wondered if this was Dino's playlist.

Donna-June and Purlynn Looper greeted Emily and sat in the second row, right behind all the relatives. Even though Purlynn's eyes were red, she'd gained enough weight to look healthy and pretty the way country girls do, feminine, but capable of changing a tire or hauling a lamb out of a mud pit.

Men with weathered faces filled the middle rows, and Brother Ezra's pajama-clad followers passed out memorial leaflets.

Abel Myklebust stood by the entrance, which gave him clear sightlines. He scribbled in his leather-bound notebook and chatted with the owner of Rudy's Brewhouse, who dabbed his face with a pale blue handkerchief. He waved at me, and I tipped my head by way of acknowledgement.

The service began with Brother Ezra giving a welcome address and sharing personal stories about Dino and his family.

Friends and relatives followed with memories of holidays and milestones.

I leaned forward when Purlynn took the podium and said, "It's no secret that my father, Gordon Looper recently bailed out of town like it was a leaky boat, but he wanted me to tell everyone how brokenhearted he is by Uncle Dino's passing and to send his deepest condolences to Aunt Emily and the kids." She looked at Emily and placed her hands over her heart. "When I was little and my mother was working night and day to get the Crafty Looper off the ground, my father and Uncle Dino babysat me. You can imagine what that was like." She paused, and the audience laughed.

"They thought every five-year-old should be taught how to string worms, bait hooks, and what test line to use for what fish," Purlynn said. "The rule was, you catch it, you eat it, and there were a few terrible meals, but a hundred awesome ones, and we always had s'mores for dessert. Like all fishermen, they had tall tales. They told me about pirates' treasures, desert islands, white-sand beaches, and water bluer than the sky. They didn't sing well, but they made up for it by singing *really* loud."

The crowd laughed again, and she continued: "I wouldn't trade those days for anything. My father prays that Uncle Dino will spend eternity with a cold drink in one hand and his fishing rod in the other, barefoot, relaxed, and happy in his knowledge that he'll eventually be joined by those he loves most."

Several weathered men now took turns telling fishing stories, and I was losing my battle to keep from dozing off in the stultifying heat when Andie Kleinfeld, in a crisp pink button-down shirt and black slacks, sat in the empty chair beside me.

"Afternoon, Dr. Whitney," she whispered.

I kept my voice low and said, "Are we doing that again, Andie?"

She flashed a smile. "Were you a close friend?"

"We bonded over dogs. Why are you here?"

"Meeting the citizenry."

The citizenry in general, or me in particular? Or was Andie really here because of the young widow and the insurance money? I glanced toward Emily, still beside Ben, and then stared at my boots and tried not to look suspicious—because *everyone* has done things that could be misunderstood out of context. Perspiration ran down my back, and I began blinking too fast. My skin contracted over my flesh, and it was too damn hot.

I became aware of silence. I lifted my head, and everyone was staring at me.

"Maddie, if you'll come forward..." Ezra held a guitar.

I stood so abruptly that I banged against the seat in front and walked up the aisle. The crowd was flushed, and foreheads shone with perspiration, but Ezra seemed cool and collected in his nightshirt.

We noodled a bit until he'd tuned his guitar to my voice. He played well enough to seduce college girls by a campfire or entertain his grandparents at Christmas. I counted down for him to begin, and then I opened my mouth and released my voice, the very act making my body relax. I sang to the lovely Emily and her children, and I wanted the words to mean something to them, *breathe in, breathe out, move on*, and I remembered listening to the song on a mixtape made by Dawg O'Donnell.

He taught me that sorrow can be beautiful in its purity and sincerity, and I was grateful to him even though he'd tried to kill me. Could Andie have discovered the truth about Dawg's death?

No, because only Ollie and I knew the truth. *Breathe in, breathe out, move on*, I sang, and lost myself in the words and emotion.

Then the song was over, and people were crying, and Ezra said, "Thank you, Maddie."

The service concluded. I made my way back to the refreshments table. I guzzled ice water so quickly it dribbled down my neck. I searched for Andie and saw her talking to Penelope. Maybe Andie was here just to meet people.

Ben came to me with Emily, and she said, "That was beautiful, Maddie. Dino would have loved it."

"I was glad to. I'm so sorry, Emily." My shoulders jerked up hard. I forced them down and returned to my canine comfort zone. "How's Weasel?"

She glanced at Ben, and they exchanged a series of microexpressions I'd never decipher. Ben said, "Weasel's a comfort."

"I'm so lucky to have him," Emily said. "Especially now."

"Would you like another dog, Emily? Another companion for you and your kids?"

"I, um, I can't think about anything right now. It's so hard..." Her voice faded, and she twisted her hands together.

Other guests hovered nearby, wanting to offer their condolences, and I felt them all closing in on me. "Whenever you want, Emily," I said. "Later, Ben."

On my way out of the tent, I ran into Penelope, who lifted the corner of her *Penelope's Catering* apron to fan her face. "That was perfect, Maddie. Sad, but perfect."

"Why haven't you passed out? It must be one hundred and ten."

"One-sixteen outside by our burners. It's wonderful that so many people support that poor woman and her children."

"That's the upside of small-town life. The downside is that there's always a pariah. I speak from personal experience."

"You're not a pariah."

"Not much these days, but I'm always cognizant that this burg could turn on me like I'm a rabid dog jerking and twitching down the road."

"Like in *To Kill a Mockingbird*, when Atticus Finch shoots the mad dog?"

"Exactly. The dog's name was Tim Johnson, beloved by the town, a point that was glossed over in the movie. When he died, I wailed. That dog was an astonishingly convincing actor, even though he wasn't even listed in the credits. Don't you think that's shocking since he's absolutely critical to the story?"

"Yes, well," she said, "How is Beau Blue?"

"His recovery physically is coming along, but emotional recovery is a slow process."

"I'm sure you'll do wonders," she said. "I saw you talking to Andie Kleinfeld. She dropped by last week and asked if I catered sit-down dinners. She's throwing her parents an anniversary party."

"I met her through Oliver. She's based at the Sheriff-Coroner's headquarters," I said. "My core temperature is approaching the liquid magma stage, and I've got to get back to the center. Let's continue discussing canine actors next time."

"Oh, I can't hardly wait," she said.

I grabbed a handful of mini meatballs and was out of the tent, wanting to be home with a cold wet towel over my head, and longing to talk to Kenzie about loss and grief and how we go on when our hearts are broken.

But Donna-June and Purlynn Looper stood by my Tundra. The open field offered no easy escape from the mother, and I was intrigued by the daughter, so I said, "Hi, Loopers. I missed talking to you inside."

"We can talk better out here," Donna-June said. She fanned herself with a memorial flier so that Dino's grinning face flashed back and forth like a windshield wiper.

"That was a moving tribute, Purlynn."

"Uncle Dino would have loved the ceremony and your song. It's so hard for the whole family. The little ones don't understand." She wiped her eyes, already red from crying.

Donna-June nodded. "Everyone's talking about the insurance,

but that's not going to make it up to Emily. Dino meant the world to her and the kids."

"I'm maxed out on human interaction now, so..."

"I'll get to the point, Dr. Whitney. Purlynn's told me how much she liked your dog school, and we've seen your training videos and read up on the missing person searches."

"You mean the rehabilitation center and the Midnight Runners Search and Rescue K-9 team."

"Right," Donna-June said. "Purlynn manages my retail shop, but she'd like to—"

Purlynn rolled her eyes. "I don't want to work in retail or teach crafting. I want to work for you."

Well, that was unexpected. "I could definitely use help. But before we go any further, show me your arms."

"What?" she asked, stretching her arms out and rotating them. Her skin was clear of tracks or bruises.

"Are you clean? I mean, clean enough? I don't care if you smoke weed or have a few drinks on your own time, but I can't have anyone with drug issues dealing with dogs. You have to be clear-headed and able to react instantly."

Donna-June said, "Go ahead, Purlynn," and the girl said, "I was in a dark place. I smoke and drink normal, I guess. Not on the job. I don't like to make mistakes."

"Purlynn is precise and detail-oriented," her mother said.

"Did you grow up with dogs?" I asked. "What's your experience with them?"

"We have cats, but I really love dogs. Uncle Dino usually had one at the cabin, and I always dog-sat for my aunt. She was impressed and thought I should start a dog-walking service."

"Why didn't you?"

"Purlynn's always had a knack with animals, but she was busy helping me," Donna-June said. "She's worked at the shop since she was twelve, and I expected that she'd become a partner for the expansion." Donna-June shook her head. "Maybe she'll be interested later."

"Expansion?"

"Yes," Purlynn said. "My mother has a ten-year plan that includes franchises. So, do you have any jobs available?"

"No, but I have an idea," I said. "Donna-June, how would you like to swap employees? My intern Zoe Granger, who's as sharp as a tack, is more interested in growing a business than dog training. She needs to move up with a promotion and a pay increase. Now, if you would agree to meet with Zoe, and would like her to work for you, it will free up funds for me to hire Purlynn."

"Granger as in Granger's Feed Store?"

"Yes, and she'll be eighteen soon. She worked the front register from the time she could stand on a stool to reach it, and her skills include bookkeeping, inventory, and customer relations. She has business acumen, insight into cross-platform marketing, and is eager for challenging endeavors," I said, repeating Zoe's buzzwords. "She'll be taking college courses, but she's balanced work and school while she's been with me."

"She's been coming by the store since she was little," Purlynn said. "We've talked about what it's like to work in a family business."

"My canine rehabilitation center is already too small for Zoe's dreams. I can offer you minimum wage to start, and there will be a trial period. Working with animals isn't for everyone. The majority of the people I hire quit after a few weeks because the job is hard, dirty, and occasionally hazardous. I'll have to clear it with Zoe."

Donna-June said, "Well, honey, what do you think?"

Her daughter smiled. "If it's okay with Zoe and she fits in at Looper's, I'd like to try it."

* * * *

When I told Zoe about the opportunity, she was ecstatic. "*Yuck esyay*! I would totally love to work at the Crafty Looper. Their online business is insane, and it's so cool inside with all these arty things and classrooms."

"I'm the only one who didn't realize Looper's was such a success. I hope I'm not making a mistake, letting you go and inviting Purlynn to work here."

"I've talked to her at the store," Zoe said. "She manages the retail shop, which is like this place, in a way. The amateurs come in, enthusiastic to volunteer, but they don't realize it's work. It runs on a schedule. You need to be reliable. Are you going to miss me?"

"No, because you'll always be visiting, won't you? Besides, you don't have the job yet."

"Please, bitch," she said, and giggled.

"That's 'Boss Bitch' to you."

Chapter Fourteen

EVEN THOUGH IT WAS WELL past sunset, the air remained heavy, or maybe it was my own body that felt heavy: a heavy head that ached from excessive heat, heavy limbs exhausted by chores, and a heavy heart from longing for those living and dead.

"What would I do without you?" I said.

"Are you talking to me or Bertie?" Oliver asked from the shadows of his patio.

The lawn sprinkler rotated *swish-swish-swish* in my direction, where I lay on a patch of lawn with Bertie, staring into the constellations, and sprayed us with cold water. "Both. And Zeus, too. Where is he?"

"Inside on the kitchen linoleum. Stay the night with me."

"Your body generates too much heat."

"You never let me use the air conditioner."

"It's noisy, and it never feels normal."

"How would you know what 'normal' feels like?" he said. "Regardless–"

"Irregardless," I said, and he laughed. "I have to confess something. Both *regardless* and *irregardless* are acceptable, but *irregardless* is non-standard. I was being a dick correcting you."

"Maddie, my sister's a principal, so I think I already knew that. I want you to stay."

"I feel as if needles are piercing me behind my eyes, and I'll be miserable company. But when it cools down..." I said. "Ollie, there are innumerable things I can't figure out."

"Not Ben and Emily again. I can't understand you and Ben being 'just friends,' either, but I've accepted it."

"I hardly see him anymore. I guess that's what he does: moves on from one female friend to another. But I wasn't talking about Ben. Days like this, I miss Kenzie something awful. We talked for a few minutes, but it wasn't enough. It's not the same as seeing her and hugging her. I'm sorry if I go on too much about this."

Swish-swish-swish, cold water sprayed across my face, blending with my hot tears.

"I don't mind listening. I only wish you could find a way to live with the distance. Maybe a family therapist could help you and Kenzie work through things."

"Multiple attempts have proved futile. I always try to outsmart therapists, because I'm stupid that way, and Kenzie tries to out-analyze them. Let's put that on the back burner," I said, as Bertie got up from my side and shook droplets all around before padding into the condo. "Did anyone in the department contact the woman who had owned Beau Blue?"

"I checked on it. The couple who took her dog gave a fake address and fake names. There's nowhere to go."

"She must recall something that can help identify them. Did you prod her memory? If they're not stopped, they'll continue to hurt and kill animals!"

"Maddie, I told her to get in touch if she remembered anything else. It's still on my radar." In the dark, without the distraction of his expressions, I could detect the exhaustion in his voice.

"Thanks, Ollie. I'm sorry I'm such a mess tonight. I feel as if,"

I said, crossing my hands over my chest, "as if multiple elements are building toward *something*. I can't make out what it is, but it's coming. Today's memorial made me think about Dawg O'Donnell. Andie Kleinfeld sat right by me. Why would she do that? Do you think she suspects something? Could we get in trouble with Internal Affairs?"

Oliver moved in the darkness. Ice cubes tinkled against a glass. "You're not going to get in trouble for escaping attempted homicide. Besides, IA doesn't go after civilians."

My skin goosebumped. "Is Andie investigating you?"

"It's normal for IA to go on fishing expeditions. Usually far less productive ones than Dino's." Oliver came to me and crouched down, one knee on the wet cement. "Maddie, I need you to promise me something. Can you do that?"

"Tell me what it is first."

"Everything is conditional with you." When he smiled, his even teeth shone in the faint light coming from inside the condo. He gripped my hand, making me feel grounded there, lying flat on the revolving earth, seeing what *was*, a history of the stars' light, like letters lost for millennia finally arriving with ancient and obsolescent news. This temporal discordance usually reassured me that no matter how terribly I'd fucked up, my misdeeds were irrelevant. But now my joints creaked uneasily in their sockets, and my skin shifted uncomfortably over my flesh.

"Maddie, promise me you'll trust that I love you. No matter what I say or do, or whatever anyone else says, or whatever happens, promise that you'll believe what I'm saying to you now: I love you and only you, and I will continue to love you."

"I don't understand, Oliver." Drenched by the sprinkler, I shivered. "Tell me what you mean."

"I mean what I'm saying. The situation at the department may get problematic. I don't want you to get drawn into it. I may keep my distance."

"Distant like the moon, circling, waxing and waning, or distant like Haley's Comet, shooting past once and disappearing for decades?"

He lay on top of me. "I couldn't say yet. Maybe like a shooting star: Watch long enough and you'll see me, dragging a blaze, burning in the atmosphere, and crashing hard, Mad Girl."

"Are you in danger?"

"My name is danger," he said, and when he laughed, his chest pushed against me.

"Be serious."

"What is it you always say when you get bitten or knocked over? Occupational hazard. Generally, the hazard is isolated. This time it may have a longer reach. If I keep away, know that I'm coming back. Whatever anyone says, whatever *I* say, I love you and only you."

I put my arms around him, already feeling the loss. "That's too complicated for me to understand with such limited information. People are too tangled."

"Tangled and jumbled and in knots. Do you promise?"

"A promise is an intention, a hope that may or may not be fulfilled. Whatever comes, I trust you absolutely, Ollie."

"Stay the night."

And, though my head pounded and my limbs ached and my heart hurt, I stayed with him, and we made love on the bedroom floor because the bed was too warm and soft, and I needed an unyielding surface, and I felt a sense of dread and overwhelming love for my partner and dearest friend.

We rose at 5:00 a.m., and he said, "If you need anything..."

I thought of the sorts of crises one thinks about in silent darkness, about raging fires and catastrophic earthquakes, torrential storms and floods, locust invasions and antibiotic-resistant bacteria, financial collapse, and deaths of those near and far. I thought of Kenzie, miles away, so she'd be safe if anything happened here, and my mother, protected by her devoted husband, and my brother, who always escaped the trouble he caused.

"Ollie, if I need anything, I'll ask a friend."

We hugged, and parted, and I loaded Bertie in my truck and drove away. Entering the pre-dawn world was like returning to a familiar land that had been intrinsically altered, and its very familiarity made every miniscule alteration all the more glaring.

Or maybe I was overreacting.

Zoe's interview with Donna-June went well, and she was offered a job. Our center would be shorthanded for a week since Purlynn would be training her before joining us. I sent Purlynn the WCRC handbook and training binder and hoped she would show up having prepared.

I texted Oliver once. He didn't reply immediately, but this wasn't unusual with us. It was easy to forget the rest of the world when I was with the pack. Jai had already taught the therapy dogs the basics, and we practiced drills to reinforce their training. Practice, take a break, practice, take a break. They were amiable, but the little one was snappy and the large one was too eager to bestow sloppy slobbery licks on anyone nearby.

Beau Bleu came right over when I entered his kennel. I brushed his bristly coat, clipped on a leash, and walked him to the creek. I pulled off my boots and socks, and we stepped in the cool water that flowed over smooth gray stones and volcanic rock. I became so engrossed in trying to puzzle out my last conversation with Oliver that I was taken by surprise when Beau jerked away so hard that he yanked me off my feet and pulled the leash from my grip.

I scrambled up and saw Beau yards away, stiff-legged with fur ridged along his spine. And there was Vixen, prancing toward him with an enticing sideways waggle.

"Beau, sit!" I commanded, but he was fixated on the spotted pointer.

I consciously quelled my anxiety, because I didn't want to stoke an already dangerous situation. I took one slow step toward Beau and ordered, "Stay," in a clear, loud voice.

And Beau, to my relief, sat, but I could still see the rigidity in his body, the desire to explode.

And then that mad little bitch ran right up to him.

I tore toward them, anticipating sharp teeth, torn flesh, and blood, but Vixen was presenting her rump to Beau and then rolling on her back, waving her legs in the air, as friendly and non-threatening and vulnerable as a bunny.

Beau's hackles dropped, and he sniffed appreciatively. He endured a lick and a nudge. When Vixen popped up and went into play position, he hesitated. She dashed away and then approached. She repeated the action with a high-pitched yip.

I watched amazed as Beau began to play chase with her, the leash dragging behind him.

Beau was entering a familiar land, intrinsically altered by experience, but he still remembered what it was to play. I swiped the tears from my eyes so I could watch the two dogs, running through the golden grasses under a scorching sun and a cornflower-blue sky. And my heart warmed for Vixen, who'd challenged Beau to discover the spirit that had been buried in suffering and fear.

Jaison ran to me, breathless when he said, "Sorry, Maddie. I got here as fast as I could. Am I seeing what I'm seeing?"

"Yes, Beau's playing!" I said. "But who the hell let Vixen out of the center?"

"She did. I was in the office and heard noises on the roof. I go outside, and Vixen's climbed up somehow and then leaps over the fence. She's kind of amazing."

"Amazingly reckless."

"She doesn't have Bertie's laid-back control, but it's possible her instincts about dogs' temperament are as good as his."

"Stop talking crazy," I said, turning my head to hide my smile.

Oliver never got back to me, which didn't deter me from calling, texting, and sending emails detailing my activities and thoughts. I called and texted Claire a few or possibly a dozen times. She blocked me again, but I discovered she and Andie were a thing these days. It would be easy enough to visit her at home or at Coyote Pups, but I didn't want to add to my restraining-order incidents.

I did a deep dive into the history of Dutch shepherds and compiled a monograph that I dropped off on Oliver's porch. I thought he'd be interested in beer-making, so I order a craft brewing kit and books to be shipped to him. I stopped by the substation once, twice, or three, or several, times and was told that he was in meetings, which was fine, since I was already much too busy.

Ben, who had been a constant presence since I stepped into his office a year before with a semi-feral dog, was out of sight, but not out of mind. In the gloaming, I'd wander across the fields until I was close enough to see his house. Sometimes lights would be on, and sometimes the whole house was dark, and my ranch seemed every bit as lonesome as it had before the Meadows family had moved here.

Chapter Fifteen

EACH MORNING I WAS GRATEFUL for the dogs who kept me occupied and gave me perspective, and I was singing along with a yowling hound when the Coyote Runaway Ale Company partners called.

"We need a consultation as soon as possible."

"What's the problem?"

"Our company dog has been going nuts: barking a lot and acting up. He used to be fine, but today he reacted to a customer."

"I can schedule you in next week."

"Um, actually, he sort of nipped the customer, and, um, we promised to get help ASAP. Our vet, Dr. Meadows, says you're the best trainer he's ever seen."

I felt a fizzle of pleasure. "I can always make time for a red-zone dog. I'll be there at about six-fifteen."

The Coyote Runaway Brewing Company occupied a converted lumber store with a fresh mustard-yellow paint and steel trim. I led Bertie and Vixen through a sea-green glass door and into the cool, dark tasting room, where a few customers sat at plank tables. Fans revolved high overhead, and the air was redolent of malt and yeast. At the far end of the room were enormous stainless-steel tanks.

A bearded and tattooed young man came forward and introduced himself as Cody. "Thanks for coming, Dr. Whitney." His lips moved up and down, and maybe this was how he smiled. "Fenster doesn't get along with other dogs."

"Bertie and Vixen will help evaluate Fenster," I said, thinking, *heinous name*. "They can stay here for now." I signaled for the dogs to sit and looped the handle of Vixen's leash to a chair leg.

"Will they be okay?"

"Bertie will stay. Vixen may unless she sees something interesting. Do breweries have mice? Wineries do."

His mouth moved up and down again. "Our brewery meets all sanitation codes. Fenster's upstairs."

I followed him up a staircase to a balcony with a lounge and offices. Muffled barking came from behind a closed door, which shuddered and thumped occasionally.

Cody introduced me to his brewery partner, Mike, another bearded hipster in jeans. Or maybe Mike introduced me to Cody, because I was already confusing one for the other. I sat on a leather Chesterfield sofa and said, "What's the problem?"

Cody or Mike rattled on about their awesome shop dog, who had suddenly become "a little mouthy." He gesticulated when he spoke, giving me ample opportunity to see scabs on his arms. "He completed puppy training and knows basic commands. He's a little over two, and we think he must have been abused, and that's why he's acting out."

His partner said, "He doesn't like strangers coming upstairs. He's perfectly fine downstairs."

"I checked with the county's animal services. There were previous bite and running-loose complaints. The rule of thumb is that for every actual complaint, there are ten that haven't been reported. How often has he bitten you?"

Both did the up-down smile.

"Okay, I'd like to meet Fenster. Bring him out."

Cody or Mike went to the door and cracked it open. "Sit! Sit! Sit! Come! Okay, heel! Fenster! Fenster!"

A massive spotted dog with a black splotch over one eye pushed him aside and charged toward me. I stood up to my full height, head up and shoulders back, and ordered, "Sit!" and signaled with my hand palm forward.

The dog practically left skid marks.

I said, "Down," and moved my hand palm parallel to the floor. Fenster held his head sideways, eyeing me, but not directly. He took a step forward. I clicked my tongue, "*Tch!*" and blocked him from moving to Cody or Mike.

We did a little do-si-do, him repeatedly moving toward his nervous owners, and me blocking him. When the partners began complaining on Fenster's behalf, I glared their way, and they shut up. "The key is outwaiting him."

Fenster knew that, too, and persisted for another ten minutes. He finally lay down, still giving me the side-eye. I sat on the sofa, and Mike/Cody stepped toward an armchair close to Fenster, who began to rise.

"*Tch!*" I repeated, and the dog sat. "Cody, Mike, don't go to him. Come to this sofa and let's chat. What is he? Argentine dogo?"

"And Catahoula leopard dog."

"And he's your first dog?"

Both men nodded.

"Was he here during the attempted break-in? How did he react?"

"What attempted break-in?"

I took my eyes from the dog momentarily. "The sheriff said you had a security problem here."

"No, everything's fine. You're on the K-9 search team, right?"

"Yes, Midnight Runners Search and Rescue."

"Sheriff Desjardins told us about it at our promotion party at the Triangle Lounge. He's kind of a wild guy for a sheriff."

The comment threw me off. After the nearest dive bar was shut down last year, the scumbag clientele migrated farther out of town to the Triangle Lounge, locally referred to as the Bermuda Triangle because people who drank there vanished for days. "Wild? How do you mean?"

"Like how he hangs with a hardcore crowd. Lost five hundred dollars on the pool table and doubled down, lost a thousand, and laughed it off. Some hot women there, but I wouldn't want to look under the hood because the engine would be filthy. No offense to women, of course."

Oliver had told me I'd hear things about him. "Back to Fenster. So, for your first dog you got a powerful hunting and guarding mix?" I imagined the pressure his jaws could exert.

"We thought he could help guard and also be our mascot. He was a huge puppy, only seven weeks old, so cute you can't believe. He's not mixed. It's a new breed. We found him on Facebook." They told me the insane price they'd paid for him.

The dog seemed wary but wandered to me. I scratched his well-shaped noggin. "How often do you exercise him? Do you go running or biking with him?"

I took a treat from my pocket and held it slightly out of reach, moving it around. Fenster stared at it. I lowered it toward his nose, because smelling should be his primary instinct, but he kept staring. I put it in the flat of my hand and gave it to him.

"He's exercised all the time," they said, "Several times a week. We throw the ball for him in the yard. He won't walk on leash. He pulls too hard."

"'Several times a week' means a few times a week," I said. "Throwing the ball in the yard is insufficient. He needs daily exercise. We're going for a walk." There was a thick chain leash hanging from a hook, but I took a simple rope leash from my pocket and introduced it to Fenster. He moved his head away for a few seconds. When I held it to him again, he let me slip it over his head.

"That rope's too thin," one owner said.

"It's enough."

Now excited, Fenster lurched forward, and I corrected him with a "*Tch!*" flicked the leash, and said, "Heel." I kept the leash high on his neck in order to have better control.

He lunged at angles before realizing that the only way to move forward was to move with me. We went downstairs to the bar. A server, cleaning a tabletop, quickly stepped away from us, another indication that everything had not been "fine."

When Fenster saw Bertie and Vixen, he growled low in his throat, and I flicked the leash and put him in a sit.

Vixen wriggled madly, wanting to join us, and Bertie came to investigate, nose forward. Fenster stiffened, so I kept him close to my side, holding him so that Bertie could sniff at his haunches. The massive dog resisted and growled again, before relenting.

Bertie was vaguely interested in the dog and, after several seconds, wagged his tail, giving me the okay. When Fenster relaxed, I encouraged him to give Bertie a reciprocal sniff.

I signaled for Bertie to move to my right and kept Fenster on my left, and we walked past Vixen. I led them out of the building and down the sidewalk with Mike and Cody trailing behind.

"Watch out!" one said, and the second said, "I can't believe he's doing this!" By the end of the block, Cody and Mike were singing hosannas about witnessing a miracle.

"Okay, your turn," I said, and both men slumped. I handed the leash to the closest one and said, "Stand tall, relax your shoulders and your arms, be confident that this will go well."

He took two steps, gripping the leash tightly, sweat beading on his forehead.

"Stay calm and confident, and relax your arm and hand," I said, and Fenster lurched toward the street, yanking the hipster almost off the curb.

I took hold again and made them both practice for another hour. Finally, they managed walking their dog for half-a-block without a problem. I called out, "Okay, come on back. We'll do this again tomorrow."

"Only as far as those trees!" Mike or Cody said, and he headed in the opposite direction.

And then from around the corner came a young man walking with a toddler.

Time slowed, and I could see the instant that Mike or Cody panicked, jerking back the leash, and Fenster, realizing his owner's fear, snarled and braced his legs to leap forward, and the young father swooped up the child in his arms, creating dangerous excitement.

I cried, "Go!"

And Bertie, his aches and pains nothing now, streaked forward and stood between Fenster and the child, and Bertie's lip curled up and he gave a deep rumble that I could hear because I'd raced there, too, and I breathlessly watched as Fenster froze and then...understood that the man and the child presented no danger, that he should stand down.

So, he did.

"Give me the leash," I said to the sweating hipster. To the father, I said, "I'm sorry about this."

He was too shaken up to say anything and, clutching his child, walked away.

I wanted to slug the Coyote Runaway bros, but I couldn't react near an unbalanced dog. My body twitched and jerked as I took deep breaths in and let slow breaths out, and the two hipsters stared, and one said, "You see what we mean! He's dangerous."

Finally, I spoke. "Your neglect and incompetence are what's dangerous! You specifically chose this dogasaurus because of your macho and snobby pretentions. Instead of adopting a stable rescue dog, which might have 'a filthy engine,' you got an untrained puppy. Fenster is an overgrown goofball, and you've set him up for failure by not providing structure or exercise. He doesn't want to lead your little pack, but neither of you is taking that role. He reads your fears and anxiety and that's why he was trying to protect you from a child. *He* is not safe with you."

"I guess we'll sell him back to the breeder," one mumbled.

"The *backyard* breeder who ripped you off with a puppy too young to have left his mother! They never take responsibility, and you're lucky Fenster didn't have Parvo and die before he was three months."

"Someone else will buy him then."

They grumbled on the sidewalk while I went into the tasting room to collect Vixen. When I returned outside to march past them with the three dogs, Cody or Mike said, "You can have him for what we paid, which doesn't include all his immunizations and supplies."

"Cody and Mike, I think I speak for the township of Coyote Run when I say fuck you, fuck your clueless purebred pretensions, and fuck your 'no offense' misogyny!"

And that is how I came to steal Fenster.

Righteous indignation propelled me home and carried me through introducing Fenster to the dogs at the center. He quickly submitted to the pack's cumulative strength and reverted to his true playful nature, galumphing after Heidi before I kenneled him for the night.

On rare occasions, the first steps of rehabilitation were just that easy.

I called the general line at Coyote Run Veterinary Clinic and said, "Wynona, this is Dr. Whitney. The dudes at Runaway Brewery asked me to take Fenster. Would you please send all his health records? Thanks."

I wondered if Mike and Cody would come here and try to take the dog. I stayed in the office trailer, listening for cars and noises as the night wore on. The blind scruffball curled on my lap, and I said, "Gizmo, I don't feel so brave anymore. Fenster, terrible name, will eat buckets until he's ready to adopt out, and I've still got Beau Blue to care for. Oh, but you should have seen Bertie today!"

As I waxed eloquent about Bertie's bravery, my phone buzzed: Ollie was calling. My heart thumped, and my throat tightened. I answered, saying, "Is this Oliver Desjardins or the doppelganger who parties at the Bermuda Triangle?"

"Hey, Mad Girl, it feels like so long."

"I've been trying..." I didn't trust my voice anymore.

"I'm calling in my capacity as Deputy Sheriff," he said in a quiet voice. "You've been accused of Grand Theft Canine."

My emotions were trapped in a labyrinth of M. C. Escher stairs, twisting and turning upon themselves, and I was laughing and crying and Oliver was saying, "Did you really tell them, 'If you want your dog, try to get him, dickheads,'?" and I was saying, "Why can't I see you anymore?"

"I'll get them to drop the charges, but you'll have to pay them for that dog or give it back. I'm sure you'll figure out a way to protect the dog and screw the owners," he said. "Ah, you goddamn beautiful felonious mad girl... I have to go."

"No, not yet, Ollie! Talk to me. I miss you so much it hurts all the time."

There was silence then and dead air, and I called him back five times. When he didn't answer, I crept back into the memory of Bertie's magnificent deed to give me solace when nothing else made sense.

* * * *

The Coyote Runaway Brewery emailed an invoice for Fenster. I crossed two zeroes off the end, divided that amount by two, and mailed a check. I was rubbing the huge mutt's back, and Jaison said, "Nice dog. Heidi doesn't want to kill him, and even Gizmo likes him. When are you going to give him back?"

Gizmo leaned against Fenster's hind quarters and snored.

"Like, never ever. The Runaway dudes are much too nervous and weak to own a powerful dog."

"Is he ready for adoption?"

"Not yet. He was descending into the red zone and has a record of aggression. At heart, he's a lover, not a fighter, and I want to be sure he's stable."

"Another mouth to feed."

"We always manage, don't we?"

My sister and I spoke sporadically and too briefly. She answered every call with, "I'm on a deadline," or "Chris and I were just sitting down to dinner," or, "Good grief, Maddie, I feel horrible that you were tased and that Oliver is ghosting you, but we've already talked this through a hundred times! Déjà vu all over again from when Claire dumped you, and, no, I can't be your therapist. Have you contacted anyone on the list I sent you?"

"Why should I when you're a licensed psychologist? Also, if I can make time for extraneous people, I'd think you could make time for a single solitary conversation with your favorite sister. Oliver's not ghosting me. He and everyone else I know have been replaced by faux doppelgangers."

"I hate myself for asking, but how can doppelgangers be faux?"

"Because *real* doppelgangers make a sincere effort to haunt and have meaningful interactions. They don't need to be chased down, because they appear of their own volition! I may as well be marooned on a desert island."

"Maddie, if you care about me, you'll make the modest effort to come here, but, no, and of the last ten times we got together, I had to drive to you nine times. Draw a pie chart to illustrate the imbalance. Who are the extraneous people?"

"Beryl Jensen continues to pressure me to have brunch with her. She is the epitome of extraneous. If she were a body part, she'd be a vestigial tail that you'd be eager to lop off."

"You're wrong, per usual. Beryl's cheerful, chic, and generous. You were supposed to meet with her weeks ago, and you're supposed to be training Ezra Brothers with those heinous mutts you're foisting on him."

"I do not appreciate the negative spin, Baby Girl. Why did you say, 'Ezra Brothers' instead of 'Brother Ezra'?"

"Ha! I *knew* you knew his real name, not 'Brother Ez-rat.' or 'Brother from an Idiot Mother.' If you ever stepped outside your canine microcosm, you could have attended the Board of Supes meeting two years ago when he proposed his institution's summer camp. Don't you remember me telling you about it? Why do I bother asking? Yes, he's unorthodox, but he's highly intuitive and doing remarkable things, especially with cognitive behavioral therapy. I attended one of his seminars, and my conclusion was: super-hot and sexy."

"Who is this? I ask because my sister had a taste for conventional bros in polo shirts."

"Chris is not a bro, and it was merely an observation."

"You've gone to the dark side. Ezra Brothers is a charlatan using his looks to bilk the tragically gullible."

"So says the former animal psychic. Hang on a sec." After a few minutes, she said, "Maddie, a client is waiting. Talk to you later."

After texting her a few choice words, I texted Beryl that Bertie and I would be delighted to join her for brunch the next day.

* * * *

While I ate my dinner, berry yoghurt and graham crackers, I logged my attempts to contact Oliver on the left half of the whiteboard. I was sure Zeus must miss playing with Bertie and the pack, so I phoned, texted, and wrote postcards to Oliver's home and to the substation, inviting Zeus to visit.

Returning to the whiteboard's right side, I wrote *Concerns* and under this heading I listed: *Dog Fight Couple, Ben & Young Widow, Rent House, Paternity*, and *Financial Equilibrium*. Now was as good a time as any to address these issues.

I didn't want to wait until the Rio Vista Animal Shelter opened tomorrow morning, so I called Georgie McGuire directly, and she said, "Do you know what time this is?"

"Time is a construct, and this is critical. Can you give me the contact info for the woman whose dog was used as fighting bait?"

"Sheriff Desjardins said he'd follow up on it."

"Ollie's slammed with work and lost her number. He asked me to conduct a brief interview."

After grumbling at length about her personal life vis-à-vis her professional life, Georgie gave me an address and phone number for Heather Porter, who lived twenty-five miles beyond Rancho Vista.

I thanked her and put a check mark beside *Dog-Fighting Couple* on the whiteboard.

Next, I called Ben Meadows and said, "Hey, stranger."

"Hi, Maddie. I've been meaning to talk to you. I ran into Cody at the barbershop. He was upset that I recommended you as a trainer."

"I've never met anyone named Cody."

"He's a Coyote Runaway Brewing Company partner."

"Oh, *that* Cody. What a maroon."

"He said you stole his dog."

"Really? Because he accepted payment for Fenster, who's

adjusted beautifully at the center. He would be a wonderful dog for your family."

"I won't let my children anywhere near that beast."

"You must be talking about another dog. My Fenster is an adorable, clumsy lug. Why don't I see you anymore? When was the last time we had a movie night?"

"You made me watch *Galaxy Quest* and a documentary about the making of *Galaxy Quest*, which was approximately three hours too much of *Galaxy Quest*-related media."

"Don't be ridiculous. You loved it. You'd love it even more if you watched the original *Star Trek* and grokked all the meta references. We can do that! Season one, episode one. Where are you? Do you want to stop by and have a drink tonight?"

"No can do. I'm still at the clinic. A high-roller at the casino is on his way with his pet iguana. It was run over by a housekeeping cart. I'm doing a crash course on removing the broken part of a tail and reattaching it. With luck, the tail will regenerate."

"Sounds like fun," I said. "Ben, do you ever feel as if you've been replaced by a doppelganger? Of course, that would mean that I'm talking to the doppelganger now."

"I'm not that complicated. Do you ever think you're a doppelganger, Maddie?"

"I don't think I'm worth the trouble to doppelgang, but I'm no expert," I said. "Do you have a Heather Porter in your patient files? She rehomed her dog, and he was torn apart like Beau Bleu. County Animal Services had to put him down."

After Ben checked, he said, "There's nothing on Heather Porter. If I hear anything from the other vets, I'll tell you."

"Ben."

"What?"

"I miss us spending time together."

After an extended silence, he said, "Me, too, Maddie. We'll have dinner soon."

Ben had been friendly enough, but he was friendly to everyone. I put a check mark after his name.

Chapter Sixteen

I'D ARRANGED MY SCHEDULE to give me free time midday. I wore an aqua skirt with an ivory cotton shirt that was businesslike enough for this climate. I touched up the chipped purple polish on my toenails, only smearing a little as I slid my feet into sandals. After a cursory inspection, I snipped my hair at the nape and managed to cut off a chunk somewhere in back. I grabbed my bangs, pulled them forward and hacked off an inch or two.

Then I tackled the next thing on my list. I drove to the husband-and-wife real estate team in town that had handled the sale of our parcel to Ben. I showed them recent photos, and we talked about lease agreements and tenant requirements.

"You'll be competing against completely renovated open concept houses. Won't you at least upgrade the appliances?"

"Surely you can find someone who values vintage charm," I said, eyeing the electric pencil sharpener and a dozen yellow Ticonderogas on the credenza. I stood and inserted a pencil into the sharpener and listened to its satisfying whir. I blew the wood shavings off the pencil tip, set it to the left of the sharpener, and picked up another pencil.

"Dr. Whitney, we understand that your family home has deep emotional value, but a few cosmetic updates can dramatically increase your rental fee."

The real estate agents continued to speak, but one pencil tip broke and I had to start sharpening again very carefully. Even so, the pointed tips varied in length and angle, and I focused on the delicate task of making them uniform. While I did this, the couple filled forms for my signature.

I drew from my generic expressions and said, "I appreciate your effort and am confident you'll do a great job!"

This task completed, I drove to the Rancho Vista address Georgie had given me. Heather S. Porter, Notary Public and CPA, had an office in the strip mall I'd seen on my way to Curtis's Liquors. I pushed the door open to a small room with basic oak furniture and gray industrial carpeting. Standing fans barely stirred the sweltry air. A silver-haired woman in a beige shirtdress sat at an orderly glass desk with framed certificates displayed on the wall behind her.

She stood and smiled. "Good morning. Do you have an appointment?"

"No, I just have a few questions." I smiled and looked at her eyes, counting to three.

"Do we know each other?" she said.

"You're Heather Porter, right? I'm Dr. Madeleine Whitney. You may have seen me somewhere talking about dogs." I hazarded another look at her face and noted the vertical lines between her eyes. "The sheriff's department asked me to gather details about the unfortunate incident with your dog." I sat in the guest chair, and, when she realized I wasn't about to leave, she sat, too. "Ms. Porter, I have a special interest in your case because I recently rescued a dog that had been used as bait to train fighters."

"I never would have given Toppy away if I'd known what would happen!"

"Criminals target people who are too nice to suspect anything, Ms. Porter. Can you describe the people who took your dog?"

She'd advertised Toppy online and tacked flyers in local shops. "They told me their names were Bob and Mary Smith. I remember because they joked that their names were so common, they were unique. They wanted a dog for their son's tenth birthday."

"Did they say where they lived, or offer additional information?"

"They said they had a house at Vineyard Garden Estates. I was surprised because they're so young and it's pricey, but they told me they were in tech and worked remotely, so Toppy would always have company." Heather clasped her hands. "Afterward, I checked the address. It wasn't real. I should have checked."

"Is there anything else? Did you see their car?"

"It was a gray SUV. Gray or silver," she said. "Mary and Bob looked the way all young people do. Brown hair, tattoos and piercings, expensive phones, jeans and T-shirts. He had a beard. She was pretty with a curvy figure, a sexy girl. I thought they seemed a little...rough, but I didn't want to judge because it's generational, isn't it? The styles the young ones have. How do you tell them apart?"

"I can't tell most people apart because I have significant prosopagnosia, or face blindness. I never forget a dog though. Did you walk to the SUV with them?"

"Yes." Heather's eyebrows drew together as she remembered. "It was a late model, but dusty. I can't remember the make. They had a dog crate in the back, and when they loaded the dog, I noticed a tattoo on the side of her throat, mostly hidden by her long hair, and I thought that must hurt, getting a tattoo there. It was like a Jules Verne thing."

"A Verne portrait or something steampunk?"

"Steam-what? I don't want to talk about this anymore. I keep waking up in the middle of the night and feeling sick to my stomach, and I can't undo it, so can you please leave me alone now?"

I stood and gave her my card. "If you remember anything else that could identify them, please call me, and for heaven's sake, please spread the word that dogs should not be given to strangers for free. Home checks and follow-ups help protect our pets."

I dashed off an alert to Georgie and nearby shelter directors about the dog fighting couple before grooming Bertie for our brunch date. I cleaned his ears and brushed his coat. "Your nails will need trimming soon, Sir Bertram, but you look splendid as always."

His tail thumped and his ears flattened back as I scratched his chin, which showed grayer every month. Vixen had snuck into the office and was tempting Bertie to play tug-of-war with a sock from the laundry basket.

"Drop that," I said, and she did, leaving it soggy with spit. "Jaison! Are you there?"

He came to the doorway. "Hey, Boss. Wazzup?"

"Kenzie always says that when she tries to be cool," I said, and sighed. "Wazzup is I don't want Vixen in the trailer without supervision because she's figured out a way to open the dog-proof trash bin."

"I didn't let her in. She's got her ways, though. Do we have a meeting scheduled?"

"You mean my skirt? Bertie and I are going out to brunch with Beryl Jensen at one, and we'll be back by two. Check out my legs! I can't do anything about the scars, but they're tan, and I only have a few bruises."

"Hot stuff! Do you mind..." He brushed his hand roughly over my shoulders. "If you gonna barber, you gotta put a towel around your neck. Your bangs are whack, and the back's funky."

"It will grow out. Can you get Zoe to take photos of the therapy dogs so I can share them with Beryl?"

"You'll have them before you get there."

Beryl lived less than a mile away, and her ranch was a well-landscaped, ten-acre parcel with a small vanity vineyard, ornamental stone and metal sculptures, a lavender and rosemary garden, and a gravel drive lined with tall Italian cypress. Olive trees in huge terra cotta pots framed the entrance of a French farmhouse-style home.

We got out of the truck and Bertie lapped at the fountain. When he was done, I wiped his muzzle dry with the hem of my shirt. "I gotta say, Bertie, that I do not hate this place. Let's see what's on the menu."

"Yoo-hoo! Dogs' best friend!" Beryl crunched along the gravel drive, glamorous in a gauzy lilac slip dress, huge sunglasses, and gold bangles. She was a pretty woman whose age was highly disguised, and she could have been thirty-five or fifty-five. Her smooth bob was a shimmery platinum pink, and her tan was evenly coppery.

"Hi, Beryl. I like this hair color."

"I'm going to hug you the right way." When she put her arms around me and squeezed hard, she smelled pleasantly of something green, like eucalyptus. She was sensual in a way that made me both alert and wary.

We parted, and I said, "Who clued you in?"

"Kenzie. She told me soft touches creep you out. Lunch is by the pool." Beryl led the way through the front door into a spacious hall with sisal rugs on wide plank floors. Paintings covered the high walls.

When I paused in front of one of Claire's abstract landscapes, she said, "Yes, I own several Claire Desjardins works. She's talented, isn't she? Does your dog shed a lot?"

"Bertie sheds the optimal amount. He's exemplary."

"So you keep saying." She walked through an open concept dining/living space with floor-to-ceiling sliding glass doors to a terrace that stepped down to a freeform swimming pool. "Well, he did help you find that senile old lady last year."

"Bertie also saved my life, his military handler's life, and only the US Army knows how many others."

Beryl led me to a table under a wisteria-covered pergola. Platters with food—olives, cheeses, roast chicken, salmon, grilled corn, ripe tomatoes, salads, summer fruits, vegetables, delicate pastries—and bottles of rosé crowded a long sideboard.

"This is quite the layout, Beryl."

She smirked. "You mentioned bacon. It's under the covered dish."

I lifted a silver cloche, revealing a vintage pottery dog food bowl with chunks of beef topped with thick slices of bacon. I set the bowl on the ground, offering it to Bertie, who came forward eagerly. "You've made his day."

"Shall we?"

We sat, and she picked up a bottle, displaying a *Rosy Beryl* label. "You may have expertise about terriers, but I have expertise about terroirs, and this rosé was custom made for this weather and this place."

She filled our glasses, and we began drinking and eating. Bertie, already finished, lay contentedly on his side in the shade. My shoulders shrugged slowly, loose and easy in the heat, and I let them shrug again, and half-listened to her chatter about Coyote Run's need for a luxury day spa, her exercise regime, and city life vs. country life.

"It's a constant effort to keep up this place," she said. "I have the worst time getting someone to haul furniture back and forth from my homes."

"Jim Hardworth, my ranch hand, has a truck and is reliable. I'll tell him to call you."

"He's not one of those grizzled country skunks, is he? The ones with pinched nerves who make a woman do the lifting?"

"I can't vouch for his back, but he's not grizzled," I said. "Beryl, I'm thinking you're right about this goddamn rosé. The food is delicious. Thank you for thinking of Bertie."

"You're welcome. What is the timeline for the therapy dogs?"

Lulled by chilled wine and warm weather, I recited the steps required to properly train the rescued dogs. She asked thoughtful questions, and I was enjoying myself as we discussed the psycho-social benefits of human-pet companionship. "I hope everything goes well, but if any of the dogs is unsuited for this role, I'll rehome it elsewhere and find an appropriate replacement."

"Maddie, I consider you a community resource, which is why I indulge your socialist distribution of wealth to the needy four-legged."

"What? What? I don't...um, *you* were the one who asked me to find a therapy dog."

"One, singular," she said. "You're doing good work, so I don't mind. I'm sure Abel feels the same way."

My effort to stay motionless only made my hands clench and unclench. I hid them under the table against my jittering knees. "I don't understand what you're implying, Beryl."

"Implying? Oh, I thought I was being direct." She laughed.

"Great, I'm a joke. The truth is that no matter how many dogs I save, it's never enough. People won't stop breeding them. They want puppies, even though puppyhood is so brief, and this makes me furious and desolate. Kind and loyal dogs are euthanized every day because they're not cute enough or they have a physical or behavioral issue. Or because their owners grew bored with the responsibility or lost a job or a home and had to give them up," I said, and stood, bashing against the table and knocking over my glass. Bertie stood, too, and came to my side. "These beautiful animals—these sentient, loving creatures—have no control over their lives. They are entirely at the mercy of the most vicious, selfish, heartless species on the planet. But at least the situation gives you a few laughs!"

Bertie's head nudged my hand, and I thought of the meal that Beryl had made for him. "Thank you for brunch. Bertie enjoyed it."

"Don't be angry. We haven't even had dessert yet, and I was going to give you a doggie bag, but if you must rush away..."

"A doggie bag for me or for Bertie?"

"One for each," she said. "Maddie, I try not to take myself too seriously, but I don't appreciate being treated like a joke either. I was laughing at the tactic, not your goal or you."

I twisted my hands. "I apologize for yelling. I'm incapable of reading people. I'm always afraid that if I ask for exactly what I want, I'll be turned down."

"Apology accepted. Maybe you need to learn a better way to ask for what you need. Dessert?"

"Thank you." I sat again, and Bertie lay down, resting his head on my feet.

She dabbed the spilt wine with a napkin. "You fascinate me because I'm never sure what you're going to say or do."

"Neither am I. When I concentrate, I can control my behavior to a degree, but not for long, because my mouth hijacks my brain."

"You don't seem to make much effort controlling your behavior around me."

"Now that you mention it, I don't. My sister constantly sings your praises."

"Kenzie's delightful. I wish she still lived in town, but it's easy enough to visit when I go over the mountain. What do you think of her boyfriend?"

"Christopher is bright and has an easy, low-key personality. It must be relaxing for her to be with him instead of her wackadoodle sister." I needed to stop moping. "More fascinating, did you hear that Dino had a huge insurance policy?"

"That was the only practical thing he ever did. Everyone with a business or dependents should have life insurance at whatever level they can afford."

"I don't."

"Well, that's foolish. You could have died in that fire on Mt. Hale last year, and then where would that leave your family and your center? I'll have my broker call you."

"Right, and then I'll suddenly have an 'unfortunate accident' with a woodchipper. No thanks."

"I seriously doubt that Emily killed Dino. However, your handsome veterinarian friend spends considerable time with her."

"Ben Meadows was home when the boat exploded. I picked him up to go to the search for Dino, and he wouldn't have had time to get back from Sky Lake by then–even if he was the type to murder for passion, which he's not," I said. "Probably not. People are unpredictable. Next topic: What is it you do, exactly, besides being social?"

"Kenzie said she told you." Beryl's eyebrows arched high, like a teacher waiting for an answer.

"If she said she told me, she told me. I'm a terrible listener."

"My consulting company coached young women to pursue financial careers. I sold it when the market was right. Besides being social," she said, grinning, "I founded a group to mentor and invest in women entrepreneurs. Your sister mentioned your difficulty with your center's finances. I'm happy to review your business plan."

"I appreciate your offer, but the only way you could help would be to clone me, and nobody wants that. The last time Dino Ayer and I spoke, we had a fascinating conversation about animal cloning."

"My offer is open if you come to your senses."

Beryl served iced coffee and dessert, and I learned that she'd married and divorced once when young and had a son in

Philadelphia. "I wish he lived here, and he wishes I lived there, but we have daily videocalls and spend holidays together. We're not in each other's hair."

"I'm particular about my living space. That's why Oliver and I have our own places."

"Now that you mention the hunky sheriff, would you mind if I asked him to dinner?"

"You can, but I can't promise to come with him, especially if you invite a load of extraneous people."

Her face slightly twisted. "I'm a little confused, Maddie. You and Oliver aren't together anymore."

"Yes, we are."

"But on his social sites, he says he's not in a relationship. He has photos of himself with someone else."

"I don't even bother with those because he keeps them exclusively for departmental information and sports propaganda."

Beryl went to the sideboard, where she'd set her phone, scrolled through it, and held it out toward me. "Here!"

And there, on the screen was Oliver with his arm around a young woman with shaggy sandy-blond hair, hoop earrings and a nose ring, with her hand on his thigh. She wore a tube top, shorts, and cowboy boots. He wore my black AC/DC T-shirt with cut-off sleeves and beat-up black jeans. I felt numb, but then I focused on the clothes and remembered what Ollie had asked me to do.

"You're shocked," Beryl said.

"That's a doppelganger, not Ollie. Ollie and I are completely together. Feel free to tell anyone who asks. Now, about those doggie bags..."

Chapter Seventeen

THE LEFTOVERS WERE a huge hit with my staff, and they were chowing down when I took a dented whiteboard and tripod from the supply closet. Jaison said, "You're not going to make another flow chart for us, are you?"

"No, I'm taking this home. My life now requires three boards."

I opened all the windows in my cottage without noticeable effect, and Bertie tramped to the bathroom and flopped on the tile floor. I splashed water on his fur and placed a wet towel under his head, imagining him in the sweltering desert with his young handler, both wearing full battle gear. "When I think of you then, Bertie, I have to pull myself back from feeling sorrow or pity, because you were with a brave handler who loved you. I wish he could have kept you, but sometimes we're forced to leave those we love, and we endure and recover and find joy again."

Bertie's black-tipped golden tail thumped a few times, and he licked my hand. I lay near him on the cool tile, closed my eyes, and listened to his steady breathing. I cleared my mind, and my limbs' erratic energy dissipated.

I awoke in the dark, confused and stiff on the floor. After splashing my face with cold water, I propped the third whiteboard next to the others and wrote *Oliver Doppelganger* across the top. I wondered where the doppelganger was tonight, what he was doing, and who the girl was.

The photo in the bar was cropped tight on the couple, only showing an edge of heavily shellacked pine counter and shelves of booze. Dusty Christmas lights and a red stop sign with *Politics Free Zone!* written on it adorned the mirror. The tourism council had printed and distributed the signs after too many bloody brawls during the last election.

The girl appeared sexy, but I didn't know if I'd be attracted to her in real life. I'd have to hear her voice and feel her touch. Ollie wasn't as particular, and I knew for a fact he'd dated some who over-perfumed or whisper-talked.

I examined the website for the Triangle Bar, aka the Bermuda Triangle, a no-frills landing page with the address, hours, and a street-view photo of the building. It would be simple enough to confirm that the bar in the doppelganger's photo was the interior of the same building.

The mystery girl was relevant only regarding the doppelganger. Who was he and why had he taken Ollie's place? Thinking about Ollie and missing him, missing everyone, hurt my heart, and if I stayed by myself, I knew I'd do something foolish.

I gathered Tanqueray, tonic water, and limes and left Bertie at the center, where he could snooze on the cool deck. I changed my mind about visiting Ben and detoured to the glowing light of the barn's apartment, reminding myself yet again to dispose of the fingersicle in the tack room freezer.

"Hey, Maddie, over this way," Hardwire called from the shadows of the small porch that fronted the apartment. He wore only frayed cut-offs and was barefoot. His nickname suited his body, skinny with ropy muscle, and he had a truck driver tan, his left forearm much darker than the rest of his body. "You finally come to seduce me?"

"Do you have ice cubes?"

"Kinky! I'm sorry as hell to turn you down, but it's too damn hot to screw even with ice cubes. Whadaya got there?"

"Gin, tonic, limes. It's G and T weather."

"Hoity-toity. I'll stick to beer but let me get you a glass. Gimme a lime, you fancy sissy."

A few minutes later, we creaked in wood rocking chairs on the dark porch, drinking and singing along with Sam Hunt on the apartment's rinky-dink sound system.

"I should replace those speakers," I said.

"Save your money. I'll be rolling in it soon enough. *Ruber*. What do you think?"

"Rubber?"

"No, Ruber for whenever you need a country rube to do a job. Need to install granite countertops? Ruber. Dig a well? Ruber. How about fencing? Ruber."

"Can you do all those things, Hardwire?"

"No need. I'll contract the jobs out for a percentage. Zoe came up with the idea. People all over town have skills, need extra cash, and don't mind driving to a job. They don't always got time to hustle for the work, though, or have people skills to negotiate."

"Not a bad idea if you're willing to manage people and be available twenty-four-seven. There's also licensing, background checks, taxes, and insurance."

"That sounds like a hassle."

"It is for me, but I hate the business duties of the rehabilitation business. If you're interested in extra work, Beryl Jensen needs someone to haul furniture. She made it sound like it's something she does on a frequent basis."

"Who's she?"

"Rich lady who owns a ranch here and other properties. I'm warning you, though, she's probably picky. Don't load expensive furniture if you've recently hauled manure." I described where she lived, and he said he'd drop by and introduce himself.

"You're hanging with high society these days."

"I prefer hanging with society that's high," I said, and held my pinched fingers to my lips and inhaled deeply.

"Funny, thinking about the way we met."

"Which time? When you asked me for a BJ at Bonanza Days, or when you were calling me names while driving by in your truck?"

"You always gotta bring that up."

"Our friendship's special because we worked for it, Hardwire."

We listened to the music and crickets and a coyote yipping in the distance. "I don't want to be a snitch, but you're my girl."

"Say what you need to say."

He let out a breath. "Okay, so I'm a Rudy's Brewhouse man, because who doesn't like free peanuts in the shell, but I dropped by the Bermuda Triangle with a buddy who gets his pharmaceuticals there. Anyways, I was surprised to see Sheriff Ollie D sitting at a booth when he's been so scarce around here."

"You're not snitching. People have said things."

"There's this chick. Not your class..." Hardwire said, kindly, because I was coated in a patina of sweat and dust. "I go to him and am like, 'Dude,'—cuz he wasn't in uniform—'Dude, what's going on?' and he's like, 'If you bust my balls, I'm gonna bust your head,' and his crew were snort-laughing like it's hilarious, and it wasn't even a joke, but they were already embalmed. And I was like, 'Dude, I don't even know you!' and walked away."

"Ollie's going through something,"

"PMS?"

"You mean PTSD? He'll come back."

"But do you want him back?"

"Yes, always, no matter what," I said. "He'll return like a dog that's been lost for years and reappears with a gray muzzle. No one knows where he's been and what adventures he's had. The only thing that matters is that he's found his way home."

"He'd be a damn fool if he doesn't come back, because the moment you're free, I'm making my move."

I laughed. "I thought it was too hot and I'm too young for you."

"I'd make an exception." He tipped back his beer, stood, and took my glass. "Time for a refill, and I just remembered, my aunt Carlene sent you some gifts."

Maybe it was the gin, but it was probably Hardwire's company that made me feel better as I listened to him rustle inside the apartment. He brought drinks and a shopping bag that he set at my feet.

"Your aunt didn't have to give me a thing. How's she doing?"

"Real good. She's grateful you trained Moxie not to eat remotes and phones, and she's getting the right dosage and staying on schedule with her diabetes meds. Moxie makes sure she walks twice a day."

I reached into the bag and found jars of plum jam wrapped in tissue paper with pretty, decorated labels, handmade soap, hand lotion, and a tin of cookies. "Oh, this is perfect! I can never have enough homemade jam. I try to stock jam for an apocalypse, but I always end up eating it."

"Ever since Auntie got better, she's making arty stuff. She practically lives at the Crafty Looper. Miz Looper gives discount coupons to the diabetes support group on account of her brother died of diabetes."

"Her daughter, Purlynn Looper, will start working here tomorrow, and Zoe's going to work for Donna-June Looper."

Hardwire laughed so hard, he practically choked. I slapped his back, and he said, "It's like a hostage exchange! You're trading the dangerous fanatic for someone sensible."

"Purlynn is sensible?"

"Compared to Zoe, sure, who isn't?"

* * * *

On waking, I became aware of the soft warm air, the summer light, and then, sharp pain at my temples, but drinking and bullshitting with Hardwire had prevented me from spiraling into desolation.

I'd asked Purlynn to come to the center at 7:15, but she was waiting at the gate, dressed appropriately in jeans and boots with a *Get Crafty at Looper's* baseball cap, when I arrived at 7:00. She scratched Bertie's nose through the fence.

"Hi, Purlynn. The pack didn't tell me you were here."

"Hi, Maddie. Whatever Feng Shui is with animals, I have that."

"Come on in. Stay calm, walk straight ahead, and ignore the dogs." We entered the yard, and the pack circled around us, sniffing the newcomer. "A few residents have hall passes and are free to roam as they please, but the problematic dogs are kenneled until they can be supervised when Jaison comes at seven-thirty."

After a brief tour of the facilities, I showed Purlynn how to use the coffee maker, and she filled out her job application and tax forms.

As she signed the last page, she said, "I've studied your training videos obsessively, but you never say exactly what your philosophy is."

I squinted at the bright light angling through the window and rubbed my temples. "The general idea is to respect the species by learning to read their body language and behavior. Don't project human emotions and motives. Reward healthy behavior and provide steady guidance. Be humble about your skills and realize that you need to learn from the experience of others. Rule number one is: Follow Jaison's and my direction without hesitation, questioning, or second-guessing, because I can't have our dogs or staff hurt. We can discuss techniques afterward, but not in the moment. Got it?"

"Got it."

"Jaison's your supervisor, and he's fair and calm. Take your questions to him. I'm difficult, and I'll piss you off. I'm blunt, and I inadvertently say things I don't mean at all. I'm screwed up that way, so be warned."

She smiled. "I have a thick hide, which is why my mother let me handle customer relations. You have no idea the hell some knitters will give you if a dye batch is a fraction of a shade different. Honestly, sometimes I'd rather scrub out the toilets!"

"Ideal attitude since you're responsible for morning poop patrol. We clean continually because no one wants to step in crap or smell it, and a clean yard prevents the spread of disease. If a dog has diarrhea, tell me, because we need to address health problems ASAP."

Throughout the day, I watched Purlynn perform her tasks and interact with the dogs, and I forgot about my headache and my misery. Because she kept her cool when a scuffle broke out, separating the dogs without shouting. Because she waited patiently for a dog, cowering behind a planter, to come to her. Because she sanitized the grooming equipment without complaint. And because she relaxed into the morning with a palpable contentment.

When Jai came to me and said quietly, "She's good," I said, "Very good. You can't teach that intuition, but it's early days."

"I wouldn't have believed it after seeing her passed out on the couch, but she's got something you can't teach, an instinct for reading the dogs' body language. Count me in on the Zoe love train, but her manic energy doesn't jibe with canine rehabilitation."

I told him about Zoe's Ruber concept, and he told me she'd once floated the idea of escape room parties, "but once a group escaped the room, they'd also have to escape bloodhounds. I had to school her about all the racial shit of dogs tracking convicts and protesters. Why are White people so damn ignorant about their own history?

"Most people are damn ignorant about most things, including yours truly, which is not an excuse, but an observation. I can't even find out why Ollie won't call." My headache returned with a vengeance, and my eyes watered, and my throat tightened. "I've made it all about me again, haven't I?"

Jai said, "If you ever want to talk about Oliver," and I said, "I'm fine. I'm fine. Everything's fine," because I thought if I kept saying it, maybe I'd eventually believe it.

Chapter Eighteen

ZOE EVENTUALLY PERSUADED me that selling branded merchandise would be a fairly passive form of revenue, so I visited the Crafty Looper on my lunch hour. I expected a toxic cutesy aesthetic, but I stepped into a modern and airy retail shop with crafting equipment, yarns, and fabrics for sale.

A young and pretty woman with obsidian-black hair that fell to her hips stood behind the counter, attaching price tags to oversized wooden knitting needles. Despite the warmth, she wore a long-sleeved T-shirt. She smiled and said, "Welcome to Loopers! Can I help you find anything?"

My eyes met hers and then veered away and landed on a pickle jar half-full of coins and crumpled bills, labeled *Support Diabetes Research!* "Hi. Could you tell Zoe Gaskell that Maddie's here?"

While she phoned, I took another glance at her. Ice-blue eyes, late twenties, lovely breasts, and a firm ass in tight jeans. She projected a sexy dirty girl vibe, the kind of girl who was up for anything after the bars had closed, and she was so familiar I wondered if we'd once tumbled into bed together.

She finished the call and said, "Go down the hall to the

staircase. Zoe's on the second floor, and her desk is by the front window."

"Thanks."

The young woman kept looking at me, as if she expected something from me, or I had done something wrong to her, or perhaps I was supposed to buy something. My shoulders rocked forward, and I said, "Um, have we met before?"

"No, but I know who you are: Dr. Maddie, the dog trainer who does the search thing, right? Do you work at the sheriff's station?"

"No, and the last time I was there was because I got tased and hauled in for completely bogus shit and have yet to bring up legal proceedings against the county. However, I do volunteer on the K-9 search team if someone goes missing. My dog rehabilitation center takes up all my time."

"I've seen your show. I really want to get a puppy, but they're so expensive."

"Only if you want a purebred puppy, but the Rio Vista shelter has a wide selection of dogs."

"They won't let me adopt because my landlord doesn't allow dogs, but I could keep the pup at my boyfriend's and bring it to work, too."

"Your boyfriend can adopt it then. I strongly recommend an adult over a puppy."

"He doesn't want another dog and says it should be in my name," she said. "I guess I'll keep asking until I find someone with a litter."

She wasn't even listening to me, so I said, "Your hair is absolutely stunning."

She swung it back. "Thanks. My best friend is a stylist."

"Well, it's fantastic. See you."

I walked to the back of the shop and into a hallway. On either side, students wearing *The Crafty Looper* aprons sat at work benches in glass-walled studio-classrooms. Half of the second floor was closed off, and half was office space. Zoe sat on a plastic bounce ball and chattered on the phone.

She finished her call, jumped off the bouncy ball, and threw her arms around me. "'Bout time, boss! How do you like my command post?"

"Very organized. I want one of these," I said, pointing to a long, frosted-glass dry-erase board.

"You're so in love with charts that you should marry them. Are we still going for burgers?"

"Of course. Show me what you need to show me first."

She grabbed my hand and pulled me out of the office and down the stairs to a basement and said, "This is our current stock, mostly sold through our online store." She opened a box and pulled out a small gold storage bag with the company logo. "Look at this cute needle case! Branded items are over fifty percent of our revenue. Responding to trends is super-fast and easy since we already have suppliers in place."

"I'm glad you're having fun here, honey."

"I am, and Miz Looper doesn't make me write footnoted reports like you! Anyways, you could do this with WCRC. Collars, leashes, food bowls, clothing, toys, all with a design that reflects your corporate identity. The money would roll in, and you'll be sitting pretty."

"I'd need a building to store everything, and how much time does it take to pack and ship orders?"

"You wouldn't have to do a thing if you outsource fulfillment. I wish Miz Looper would do that, but she likes to keep stock in-house. What do you think?"

"I think it's time for lunch."

"Can we eat *inside* the Brewhouse?"

"Can you try to be nondescript?"

"*Ofway oursecay iway ancay*, but I don't think you can."

On the way to Rudy's Brewhouse, Zoe gossiped about her

coworkers, and I said, "The girl in the shop was friendly, but she wants a purebred puppy."

"Not everyone dumpster dives for grungy used dogs, Maddie. Isn't her hair amazing? She just got those extensions. You should totally get extensions!"

Zoe continued to natter as we bypassed the to-go window and entered the bar's gloom. Peanut shells already layered the floor, and we snagged a booth as construction workers, leering at us, left it.

Zoe stuck out her tongue at them and said, "What a bunch of male chauvinist pigs!"

"Why do you keep using that old-school phrase?"

"Because it's fun! My grandmother calls my grandfather that when he asks for clean socks. Her favorite movie is *Nine to Five* with Dolly Parton. Dolly is like our queen. Do you think male chauvinist pigs speak Pig Latin? They totally should. *Eythay otallytay ouldshay.*"

"*Esyay, eythay ouldshay*. You stay here, quiet like a bunny, honey, and I'll order. How do you like your burger?"

"Well-done with extra mustard, cheddar cheese, and bacon. I want a chocolate shake and onion rings."

"No shakes here. I'll get you a Coke." I cleared the dirty dishes and put them in the plastic tub by the kitchen.

Rudy manned the cash register, his glasses halfway down his nose, wearing a faded *USMC Veteran*'s baseball cap over his frizzled gray hair. Every year, his leathery skin shrunk more over his frame. "Hey, Maddie, haven't seen you at karaoke night lately. Your old man keeping you at home and outta brawls?"

"Karaoke is not the sheriff's thing. I didn't start that last fight, and he's the one who gives me tips on how to defend myself."

"I enjoy a catfight as much as any red-blooded American man, but 'no politics zone' means 'no politics zone,' and you still owe me for those broken pitchers. I sent you the bill."

"I'll pay next month. I'll have my usual, and also a burger, well-done, extra-large order of onion rings, and a Coke."

After he rang up the tab, Rudy said, "You can wait here, but eat outside, because Zoe Gaskell is underage. The sheriff may turn the other way for you, but we try to respect each other, which means I make an effort not to be goddamn blatant."

"Can I have peanuts while we wait?"

He thrust the yellow plastic basket of nuts at me and said, "Next!"

The trio of now-housetrained therapy dogs walked well on leash and followed basic direction. Two were especially people-oriented, had decent recall, and would leave things and fetch on command. The third was dog-oriented but would do well enough to round out this mini pack.

I took Purlynn with me to the Ayers' property, and, as we went through the entrance gate, she said, "I called Aunt Emily last night. Her brother's been helping her get through this awful time."

"Everybody seems to love Uncle Ezra."

"Don't you like him?"

"I'm peculiar."

"He's an amazing guy. Unique. That's what my father always said. Says."

"Have you told your dad about this job?"

Her face scrunched in a way that I didn't even try to decipher. "I talked to him about Uncle Dino's memorial. He wished he could have been here, but I think he's...he's moved on, body and soul."

"What about you?"

"I'll see him again sometime."

I wondered if I sounded as naïve when I talked about Ollie returning to me. "When you love someone, they live in your heart, existing in memory and emotion, and also living wherever else they are, in people's hearts and memories, simultaneously." I parked in the bare patch by the main yurt.

"Do you believe that?"

"Yes, I believe thoughts and feelings are as real as this truck, those mountains, the hawk perched on that post." I recalled Ollie's smile, the tender roughness of his voice, and the movement of muscle under skin. I recalled the taste of his mouth and the weight of his body on mine, and all the silences we shared, and my profound amazement that I loved and was loved. And I told myself, *this is real, and this is real, and this is real, and I will hold on to it forever.*

Then I brought myself back to the present. "Unload the dogs while I find Ezra."

Ezra Brothers held court in the yurt lodge with corporate types, whose summer casuals were not casual enough to keep them cool in the rising temperature. Ezra dressed absurdly in a white tank and teal parachute-silk cargo pants, plus gladiator sandals, his long hair drawn up in a high ponytail. I resented his black eyeliner, because I was a total sucker for it.

He stopped mid-blather to say, "Friends, this is Dr. Madeleine Whitney, Coyote Run's renowned canine rehabilitator. Please carry on your discussion while I greet the newest members of Spirit Springs Institute's family."

He walked over and attempted to hug me, but I dodged. "So, you're gonna be that way," he said, low enough for only me to hear. "And I dressed up especially for you."

"I shudder to think of your closet, Ezra, because I'm sure you don't own any practical boots," I said. "But that's neither here nor there, since I shudder all the time anyway."

"My closet is a wonderland." He grinned widely with too even and too white teeth. "Don't let your irritation about the fire pit interfere in our relationship."

"It's not irritation; it's flat-out opposition to a hazard that endangers the entire valley, and I don't know how you conned the fire chief otherwise."

"There's no mystery about it. I demonstrated our strict safety measures," Ezra said. "We got along. I like to get along with everyone."

"Stop using the fire pit, and we'll revisit our relationship. In the meantime, let's hope your Mr. Magic juju extends to the canine world."

He and Purlynn greeted each other warmly, and he said, "I can't believe your mother let you leave her business."

"She hopes I'll come back, but I don't think so." Purlynn held the dogs' leashes with a relaxed arm, and they stood when we approached, their ears pivoting forward: curious, but not anxious. "I love spending my days outside."

"Like father, like daughter," Ezra said, reaching out to squeeze her arm.

"Ezra, meet your pack: Slater, Tiffani Amber, and Zack." I handed him a leash. "We're going to go for a walk to get acquainted. No, don't tighten up. Keep your arm loose, dropped down by your side."

"I think I'm capable of walking a dog," he said. "I planned to pick out their names based on their auras, not... Are those names from *Saved by the Bell*?"

"Are you the dog guru now? If not, listen and learn."

He winked at Purlynn and said, "Ouch!"

"Hey, don't expect me to save you," she said. "I'm only the magician's apprentice."

"Keep pace," I said. "Eyes straight ahead. Don't let the dog herd you, Ezra." I reached to the leash to give a tug, and I clicked my tongue. "If you must give a correction, do it immediately. A short sideways pull works. Never correct in anger. Be the boss, but don't be a bully."

"You made that sound. *Tch.* What about the clicker method?"

He tried to get out of Tiffani Amber's way.

"Keep walking straight and claim your space," I said. "Proper clicker training is a great method, but what happens when you don't have a clicker handy? Well, you always have your mouth. You can make any sound you like as long as it's distinctive and you're consistent."

Only twenty minutes later, he was successfully walking all three dogs, and he'd shown me a fence around the yurts where the dogs would sleep.

"Nice set-up. You'll need to keep the dogs close until they bond with you, and then they'll stick around. Even after they bond, you don't want them running loose and getting hit by a car or accidentally shot by a hunter. You *really* don't want them skunked. Be sure to read my special de-skunking recipe on my website." I steered them toward the small grove that blocked the little gem of a Victorian house from view. "Let's visit your sister and Weasel."

"She may not—" Ezra began.

"Your dogs should meet Weasel properly so there won't be problems later on," I said, but stopped when the house came into view. In the years since I'd last been there, the creamy white paint and green trim had peeled, and shutters now dangled from windows. Cobwebs and dust shrouded a dead juniper border. A Chevy rusted on blocks by the garage. Children's toys, sun-faded and cracked, cluttered the yard.

A dog yipped from within the house. A moment later a stocky, short-legged terrier pushed the screen door open and scampered to us, his tail wagging a mile-a-minute. "Hey, Weasel."

Weasel's tan and grizzled coat was thick, and his eyes were bright in his whiskery face. When the dogs sniffed hello, the therapy dogs didn't show the hesitation or fixation common when sensing illness. A hanging shutter creaked in the lethargic breeze, and wind chimes clinked like broken china. "Ezra, what the fuck happened to this place?"

"Every cent went to lawyers and for the replacement vines." Ezra said. "Now Emily has to try to work things out without Dino's help."

"How are the little ones doing?"

"They're too young to understand anything other than their father's away and their mother's sick. Our mom and dad took them home after the memorial. It's easier for them to be away right now."

When I gave Weasel a rub, I felt the neat layer of fat under his coat. "Weasel looks as fit as a fiddle."

Ezra said, "He's really improving."

"Especially after Aunt Emily started feeding him organic homemade food," Purlynn said.

"What exactly was wrong with him?" I asked.

"Cancer?" Purlynn said.

"Yes, cancer, and Dr. Meadows has been treating him," Ezra said. "Remarkable vet, isn't he? He's at the forefront of the field, to be expected from someone from a UC Davis DVM/PhD. Maddie, you have a doctorate, too, right?"

"Yes, and I'm here in my professional capacity, so it's 'Dr. Whitney,'" Ezra was remarkably specific about Ben's credentials. "Was it hemangiosarcoma? Did it affect internal organs?"

"What was your field again?" Ezra said.

"My sister Kenzie always says I'm outstanding. Out standing in a field," I said.

Ezra raised his hand and hit the chimes, sending them clanging, and called out, "Hey, Sis, we're here for a visit."

Which left the score even at Home Team 2 — Visitors 2.

Emily's voice came softly from inside. "Hang on."

While we waited, I gave the dogs water from a hose and left them in the shade of the nearest tree. "If she's too busy," I began.

"She may not be up to answering questions about Weasel's

medical condition," Ezra said.

The young widow, clutching a thick sweater closed over her dress, came outside. She was like the house: something once beautiful and cosseted, rapidly deteriorating. Her intoxicating sexual undercurrent—because, of course, yes, I'd desired her, we'd *all* desired her—had become a dying ember smothered with ash. Her grief, dark and heavy with tears, enveloped us.

"Brother Ezra," she said. "You should have told me you were coming. I would have made lemonade. I have water."

"No, don't go to any bother." Ezra put his hand to her cheek. "You're cold. You're not over that flu. Summer flus are the worst."

"I start feeling better, and then I can't..." she said. "Hi, Maddie, thank you for coming by. And Purlie, you've started your new job! Is it exciting?"

"Hi, Aunt Emily. I broke up two dog fights already—so it's a lot like a clearance sale at Mom's!"

Emily's weak laugh devolved into a cough, and then she cleared her throat and stared at the ground.

"Is there anything I can do or get for you?" Ezra said, compressing his lips and furrowing his brow, and I thought, *if flu means heartbreak, it's early days.*

"It's only a bug. I'll get over it." She shivered, which made me shiver, and suddenly I recognized that she was traveling on a path that could easily be mine.

I slid my arm around her narrow shoulders, pulling her close, and breathed in the faint scent of CK One perfume; I'd thrown away my sister's bottle because I could smell the nutmeg in it, but I didn't mind it so much today. "A dog can be such a comfort when you're sick, like you were a comfort to Weasel when he was sick."

"He's my special little guy." She practically creaked when she slowly bent over to pet her dog.

"Go back inside, Sis. I'll bring dinner later," Ezra said. "Get some rest."

When she smiled, it seemed like an act of tremendous courage and a benediction. She walked slowly into the decrepit house, Weasel at her heels.

I closed my eyes and thought, *please stay safe, please stay safe,* wishing that magic was real, that prayers made things so, that I could recite an incantation to protect those I loved, and despairing because I was so powerless even on this unremarkable and insignificant planet.

I opened my eyes and Ezra was standing close and staring at me. I turned my face away from what was undoubtedly a sensitive and penetrating gaze that impressed his followers.

"Maddie, are you all right?"

"Today's session was satisfactory. We'll be here day after tomorrow, same time. Purlynn will send you a list of supplies you'll need."

On the ride home, Purlynn said, "Why don't you like Ezra?"

"Because he runs around calling himself Brother Ezra." I thought for a second. "I barely made it out alive when Mt. Hale went up in flames last year. It's infuriating how people here ignore and downplay the dangers of living in a tinderbox. I also resent those who glide by on charm and looks. My therapists could tell you theories about that."

"Therapists," she said, and made a scoffing sound.

"What do you have against them?"

"Nothing, I guess. My dad always said...*says* that going fishing solves most problems, including what's for dinner." She tapped her fingers rapidly on the dashboard. "There's Brother Ezra, the Spirit Springs Institute founder, and he's flash and show, and there's Ezra Brothers, a friendly guy with a sense of humor. He goes out of his way to help others, and he can talk a fast line, but he's an even better listener, and that means a lot to me."

"Okay."

"Okay, what?"

"Okay, I'll try not to actively dislike him. But gladiator sandals? In rattler country? He's practically begging me to mock him."

"He likes dressing up," Purlynn said, and laughing with her felt as if I'd released a breath I'd been holding too long.

Rehabilitating and training consumed my working days, and I filled my solitary evenings by searching for reports on lost and missing dogs. I wrote a newsletter to WCRC subscribers on the dangers of giving away pets for free and a tribute to canine actor Tim Johnson *for Barking Mad Reviews*, my anonymous animal actor website: "The dread builds as Tim lurches and jumps awkwardly down the unpaved road toward his awful destiny. In the novel, Jem pleads for a closer inspection and confirmation of rabies before taking action, but fear vanquishes compassion. In both the film and novel, implacable Atticus Finch raises his firearm, takes aim, and remorselessly executes the once-beloved town pet. He orders his children to stay away from his victim's body, eliminating potential discovery that he might have needlessly slaughtered poor Tim Johnson. The communal celebration of Atticus's brutal behavior is marked by cheery music."

I penned letters to Oliver in careful script, describing my activities in his absence. Rereading Sarah Waters' *Fingersmith* put me in a swoony Victorian mood, so I twisted a lock of my cropped hair, snipped it off, and taped it to a card: "Please accept this keepsake as a symbol of my eternal devotion and undying affection. Miss Madeleine Whitney." I mailed the card in an envelope that had been sealed with red wax.

After a follow-up training session with Ezra Brothers, I visited Emily and gave her a basket of fruit, cheese, and crackers. She hadn't yet recovered from the "flu," so I stayed only a little while, asking questions about her childhood pets, a topic most people enjoyed. Her grief felt genuine, but I still believed she was hiding something. But what? Could the pesticide corporation she and Dino had sued be responsible for the so-called accident?

I dragged the sofa out my cottage and onto the small deck to make space for the five whiteboards that required continual updating, preventing me from paying any attention to Abel Myklebust's frequent texts and messages.

Upon reviewing the *Kenzie* board, I began to see that she might have a valid complaint. I called and offered to drive to her place, but we could not settle on a date. "Wednesday," she suggested, and I said, "That's the County Shelter's Karaoke Night Fundraiser," and she said, "You can come for lunch and still do karaoke at night," and I said, "I can't do too many things in one day," and she said, "You're impossible. Give me a date, any date." So, I did, but she was scheduled for something boring, and we both promised to figure out a mutually agreeable time.

"Emily Ayer wears CK One. Back in the day, you drenched yourself in that perfume."

"Geez, I saved so long to buy that bottle. I wonder what ever happened—"

"Okay, go through your calendar and send me dates you're available. Talk to you soon!"

And, at ten every night, I drove to the Triangle Lounge and parked across the street, behind a Dumpster hidden from the men loitering by the entrance. Oliver usually arrived soon after, in black jeans and metal band shirts, and the regulars greeted him with nods and shouts, one armed hugs, and fist bumps. He'd grin and respond in ways that made the others laugh.

There is a particular ache being so close to someone loved and yet unable to hold and hear and smell them; an ache contracting densely into itself, a black hole of pain, devouring even light.

Then Oliver would vanish into the Bermuda Triangle, and I'd drive home alone.

Chapter Nineteen

A BROKEN SOUL heals when it heals: it can be helped along, but not rushed. Soft new fur grew over Beau Blue's wounds, but he'd been moved back to the isolation stall in the barn, since he'd shown aggression to every dog except Vixen. Purlynn spent one-on-one time with him in the afternoons, and I worked with him at the end of every day when the heat had died down.

Gusts as stale, vegetative, and rough as burlap scratched over my skin. Vixen trotted by my side as we collected Beau from the barn and meandered into the field. When the wind gusted again, it carried a whiff of smoke. I rotated in place, searching the landscape until I saw the orange flames licking upward and black smoke billowing, high on a far hill.

I reached into my jeans, but once again I'd left my phone in my office or truck. I ran toward the barn, which had a landline, the dogs at my side. Beau Blue began lagging, and so I tied his leash to Vixen's and ordered, "Stay!" and took off again.

My foot caught in a gopher hole, and I crashed down onto rocky soil. I rose and stumbled the last few yards to the barn. Ignoring the pain in my palm, I began to wrench the barn door open when the *thup-thup-thup* of a chopper's blades pulsed the air.

I looked back to the hillside, where a helicopter dumped scarlet-orange retardant on the fire.

I bent over catching my breath and trying to quell my anxiety. *Breathe in, breathe out.* My knees quavered as I returned to the dogs. Through the grasses I saw Vixen standing by Beau Blue, who was lying down. She pushed her nose at him, and I expected to see his paws lift in play. But they didn't. And my panic exploded as I sprinted to the dogs.

Beau Blue lay there, each breath wracking his body. His dark eyes met mine, and his tail thumped once. His entire body shook when he coughed.

"No, boy, no boy! Hold on!" I struggled to lift him, but he was too heavy for me to move without hurting him, so I stood in the field and screamed, "Help! Help!"

When I glanced toward Ben's house, the sun's rays mirrored gold, and I couldn't tell if anyone was home, and I screamed for help again, and I stroked Beau's fur, and said, "Hold on, I'll be back, please hold on!" and I dashed to the barn, dragging the door open, and stumbling into the tack room.

The vet's phone was on speed dial, and a message played, "You've reached Coyote Run Veterinary Clinic. Please call during office hours, between nine a.m. and five p.m. If this is an emergency, please call—" I slammed down the phone, picked it up again, and dialed my office line.

It rang and rang and rang, and then Jaison answered, "Whitney Canine—"

"Get the truck right now. Beau is having a heart attack! Call Ben's personal phone."

I reached the dogs interminable seconds before Jai rumbled through the field in the Tundra. Vixen whined and circled us as I continued to stroke Beau's side.

"Ben will meet us at the clinic," Jai said. He lifted Beau gently and placed him in the truck bed.

I handed Vixen's leash to Jaison, and he said, "You're a mess. Let me take him."

"No, he's my responsibility." I climbed in the truck, and tore through the field to the drive, and then sped toward town, only slowing at stop signs to check for oncoming traffic.

At the last intersection before the clinic, I tapped the brakes, glanced left and then right, and too late spotted the sheriff's patrol cruiser on the verge. I floored the gas again, burning rubber, and my heart pounded, my hands sweat and slipped on the steering wheel, and a siren screeched behind me.

The cruiser hung tight to my tail as I slowed on Main Street, with its busy summer mix of tourists and locals, driving, walking, and shopping. I turned into All Animals' parking lot where Ben waited. I almost tumbled out of the truck as he picked up Beau from the back and carried him.

"We were running, and he slowed down, and he started coughing," I said, trailing after Ben toward the clinic door. "He couldn't stand. Is it his heart?"

"Stop!" someone yelled, and I said, "Not now, Ollie!" even as my brain was registering that the voice wasn't Oliver's.

A hand gripped my arm. I tried to yank away, but Assistant Deputy Richard Kearns didn't let go.

Attracted by the loud voices, people on the street walked our way and watched as Kearney shouted, "Goddammit, I said stop!"

Ben stood in the doorway and said, "Maddie, do you need me?"

"Take care of Beau and then call Ollie," I yelled. "Tell him that this racist misogynistic asshole is assaulting me. He's tased me before without provocation. Will someone please tape this?"

"There's one over the entry," Ben said, indicating a security camera mounted on a post. He hesitated, and I said, "Go!" and he entered the clinic, the door closing behind him.

Two teenagers on skateboards held up their phones to record

us, and Kearney released my arm and announced, "I'm *not* assaulting you. You violated the speed limit and ran a stop sign."

"I stopped! It was an emergency."

"'California stops' aren't legitimate stops, Whitney. Show me your license and registration."

Of course, I didn't have my license. "And you aren't a legitimate cop. I'm not talking to you. Call Sheriff's Captain Desjardins. You know I own the truck."

"I'm following procedure. Any weapons on your person or in the vehicle?"

"Like I'd give you an excuse to shoot me. Which is to say, no, no weapons. I'll get the registration. Remember that you're already on record for being abusive."

"Lady, I don't give a shit what you think about me, but I'm the real law and order, not like some...get the goddamn registration."

"Please note that I'm moving extremely slowly so you won't mistake a reflection as an AK-47, or the registration slip as an incendiary device." I kept my eyes on him as I stepped back toward the passenger side and opened the door. I narrated my actions: "I am now opening the glove box. You will note a rubber bone and an Almond Joy candy bar wrapper, because some days you feel like a nut and some days you don't."

"How the fuck did Desjardins ever stand listening to your constant stream of bullshit?"

"I am picking up the registration slip. I am bringing it to you."

His florid face grew redder every second, and this time he spoke low, so that only I could hear him and his breath was hot and I could feel the spittle as he sneered, "That's why he dumped you, you crazy bitch. Course he already has another crazy bitch to suck his cock. At least the current bitch is a hundred percent woman, not some freaky spastic dyke."

I knew I shouldn't antagonize him, but knowing is not the same as doing, and I said, "If you need me to read the registration aloud to you, I can do it in Standard American English or in your native language, Pig Latin." And, even before the words were out my mouth, I hated myself for being weak enough to be hurt and foolish enough to take his bait.

Someone in the crowd said, "Snap!" and someone else said, "Oh, no, she didn't!" and another voice, a familiar voice, a voice I loved, said, "That's enough, Dr. Whitney," and in harmony, a sweeter voice said, "It's okay, Maddie."

I turned and my vision narrowed on the Desjardins twins in the crowd. Claire's long golden-red wavy hair fell loose over her shoulders. Oliver's recent buzzcut exposed his sunburned ears, and both squinted in the angled light. Individually, each was beautiful, but together they had an otherworldly quality, and I wondered what they were silently communicating to each other as they bore witness, but did not approach me, and my vision pulsated with the heat and my desire to beg for their forgiveness and receive their solace.

"I didn't mean..." I began, and I wondered how many times I'd started a sentence that way, and how many more times I would utter it over the next month, the next year, the next decade, the entire course of my clumsy, inadvertent life.

Kearney snatched the registration slip from my hand.

I couldn't look anywhere, and so I looked everywhere, nauseated, dizzy and seeking a point of focus, and eventually my gaze came to Kearney's dilated pupils, red veins mosaicking his sclera, the thin pale lashes, and I smelt his cloying coconut aftershave. I wanted to kick him and strike him and shriek and flail.

But my body had different ideas, and I was as surprised as Kearney when my mouth gaped open—and I projectile vomited all over him.

Commotion ensued. I was vaguely aware of Kearney jumping

away, of the crowd gawping and noses crinkling in disgust, of my knees crashing on the asphalt, of the severe cramping in my gut as I hurled again and again. Although suddenly drenched in sweat, I shuddered with cold. My eyes watered, and I wiped my mouth with the back of my hand.

Ollie, as still as stone, gripped his sister's forearm, and Claire's lips formed her sad mouth, a pout with the corners turned down.

I remembered being seven and throwing up on my desk during the Pledge of Allegiance and a teacher handing me paper towels and saying, "Clean it up," while my classmates tittered and *ewwh*ed with disgust. I braced myself and rose to my feet. "I'll clean it up," I said in a shaky voice.

Kearney stomped from side to side, cursing, "Shit, fuck, shit, fuck, fucking bitch, she did this on purpose! I'm charging assault on an officer of the law!"

"Maddie, you're sick." Abel Myklebust came forward.

"Don't you think I know that? I'm sick. I'm a mess. I've always been a mess!" Tears blinded me, and my arms swung to and fro like a wind puppet at a used car lot.

Oliver put his fingers to his mouth and whistled sharply. "Okay, everyone, time to go. The show's over." He stared down the crowd, and a few people began to drift away. "Abel, that goes for you, too. There's nothing newsworthy here.

But those who stayed to see the show's final credits enjoyed the bonus scenes when Abel grabbed my shoulder with his broad meaty hand and put the other against my forehead. "No, you're *really* sick. You're burning up. I'm taking you home."

"She's not going anywhere but to the station. Bystanders can't interfere," Kearney said. "Sheriff, back me up on this."

"I'm not a bystander," Abel said. "I'm her father, and I'm taking her home. If anyone has a problem with that, talk to my attorney, James Desjardins.

* * * *

As Brother Ezra observed, summer flus are the worst. Though the sun is out, you feel nothing but chills. Abel asked me to stay in his guest room, but I insisted on going to my cottage because I needed to be near the dogs. I stumbled inside, knocking over a whiteboard in my hurry to make it to the bathroom in time to vomit again, but there was nothing left in my stomach.

I cleaned my face, brushed my teeth, managed to change into a sleep T-shirt, and crawled into bed while Abel lumbered about. I was aware of his footsteps, doors and cupboards opening and closing, and the low tones of male voices.

He entered the bedroom with ice water, hot tea, crackers, and my phone on a tray. "I didn't know if you wanted something cold or hot to drink," he said, setting the tray on my bedside table.

"I get hot, and then I get cold," I said through chattering teeth. "I thought Emily Ayer wasn't sick. I thought she was mourning. But being sick and being in mourning aren't mutually exclusive."

"Summer infections are inevitable with all the tourists coming through. Jaison stopped by, and I told him what happened. He brought your phone, and he's coming later to check on you."

"No, tell him he has to stay away and stay well so he can care for the dogs. Can you bring me a blanket? There's one in the hall closet."

He was gone and back with the blanket, tucking it around me, and if I hadn't been so weak, it would have felt too strange to endure, this looming man's awkward mimicry of a father's care... Not that Jesse Whitney had ever bothered to do anything beyond hand us cherry Kool-Aid popsicles when we had fevers. So, there was that.

"Do you have a thermometer?" Abel said.

"Only a dog thermometer, and I'm not using it." I sipped the tea and nibbled a saltine. After waiting a minute, I finished the cracker and ate another.

"Let me call your doctor. Where's the number?"

"I'm fine."

His laugh reverberated in the small room. "You are the most difficult person I've ever met. Why don't you ever call me back?"

"I'm sick. I can't talk." I shoved my face into the pillow.

"I need to tell you something, Maddie."

"Thanks for your help and kindly allow me to suffer in peace."

"It's about the sheriff."

I didn't speak, and he finally said, "His recent bust, the case against the heroin dealer, was dismissed today. The haul turned out to be crushed over-the-counter ibuprofen and starch."

"A mistake was made."

"Not a mistake. It originally tested as heroin. Adulterated, sure, because street product is always cut. But at some point, after the initial test and now, it was switched. It was an inside job, and only a few people could have made the substitution."

I spoke into the pillow. "Why would anyone do that?"

"Someone either stole it to sell or was paid to destroy the evidence." He paused. "Maddie, Oliver had access."

"It's not him. He could never be bribed to sabotage a bust, and he'd never steal for personal profit."

"He's hanging out in low-life bars and throwing around cash. I saw your boards. You wouldn't keep them unless you thought he was up to something. What's going on with you two?"

"Nothing. Everything's hunky-dory."

"We've all seen Oliver with another woman, Maddie, and we've all seen you parked down the block from the station watching for him. Do you realize what people are saying? 'There's Mad Girl Whitney stalking another Desjardins.'"

"He's not another Desjardins. He's a doppelganger."

"What are you talking about?"

"Go away, Abel. You left me alone for decades, so you sure as hell can do it now."

"I'm not going to—" he started, but I rolled off the bed and stumbled to the bathroom, slamming the door.

The scant contents of my stomach attempted a rapid exodus. During the course of this painful and noisome episode, I heard Abel's heavy footsteps and the front door closing.

I existed in a state of suspended animation, barely mobile and vaguely aware of time passing. My phone kept buzzing, so I turned it off.

Jaison visited, bringing Bertie and Vixen. Bertie panted in my stifling cottage, so I mumbled, "Why did you bring him here when it's too hot? Take him where he's cool."

"You asked me to bring him this morning when I made you toast, remember?"

"Yes," I said, but I didn't. Vixen leapt onto the bed with me, licking my face and stretching beside me. "Get her out," I said, but my arm was already over her back, holding her close.

"You want anything, call me. I don't care if it's three a.m."

"Is it three a.m.?"

"No, Boss. Go back to sleep. Get better."

Penelope stopped by with bone broth. I gave half to Vixen and saved the rest for Bertie.

Hardwire brought wine and said, "Thanks for getting me the job with Beryl. She said you love rosé."

Which was funny because now it was true but laughing made me throw up again.

I didn't mind them coming by, but I was afraid of who would come next, because my blurred thoughts had resolved enough to make out dogs in the field, orange flames, billowing black smoke, a helicopter's *thup-thup-thup*, so I staggered to the front door and locked it.

I wanted so much to be wrong, but eventually Ben knocked on the door and called, "Maddie, may I come in?" The doorknob rattled and he called my name again. When I didn't answer, he rounded the cottage and peered through my bedroom window, open to the nighttime breeze. "I'm sorry, but... Let me come in. I need to tell you something."

"No. Please don't. Please don't say it."

"I'm sorry. I did everything I could," he said. "I'm so sorry."

"Beau, poor Beau." My crying was ragged and ugly, and Vixen nudged me, the way she'd nudged Beau, which made it both better and worse.

Chapter Twenty

DAYS MELDED INTO nights, and nights melded into days. I ate ice chips when my fever spiked and drank hot tea when I shivered. My bones ached, and it hurt to swallow. I ignored my phone and communicated with Jaison through the window. "You can't come in anymore. I have the plague," I said. "I'm contaminated."

"I haven't gotten sick yet."

"You may be willing to take that chance, but I'm not. Stay well, Jai."

I didn't answer when Ben came or called, even though I knew he hated his role as the ferryman on the River Styx. I thought that the only way he could deal with their deaths was if he loved animals in a clinical, theoretical way, and not as individual creatures, each special, to be mourned and remembered for a lifetime.

When Bertie visited, I sat upright and stroked his fur and fed him treats, and promised we would take a swim together soon, and I sent him away from my sickbed into sunshine and fresh air.

I kicked Vixen out, but she snuck back in, and when I went to my bedroom, a gray lump adorned my pillow. I thanked her for the gift and threw the dead mouse in the trash.

My eyes hurt too much to read, so I listened to music, mostly Jimmy Buffett, and my dozy thoughts floated around my distant sister, hapless Dino, exquisite Emily and sickness and Ben, the dispassionate caregiver, and Oliver and Oliver and Oliver, and, every now and then, I thought about the amputated finger in the barn, a frozen *Fuck you, Madeleine Margaret Whitney*.

I woke alert in darkness. I flicked on a light, and Vixen, her head on my pillow, stared at me, thumping her tail. Like a cold engine sputtering before starting up, my brain began to sort out things: the summer flu, Beau's heart attack, the scene at Coyote Run Veterinary Clinic, Abel's public paternity announcement, the doppelganger framing Oliver.

A perverse masochism lured me to check my phone. Kenzie and friends left urgent messages of concern. Strangers and reporters attempted to contact me. I deleted the latter without reading the texts or listening to the contents, except for Sasha's, who said, "You've gone viral. Let me help you fix this. Call stat!"

Zoe's cryptic message said, "I-*yay ouldn'tshay ave-hay* encouraged you, but I am making this totally okey-dokay!"

The real estate agency texted that they no longer wished to represent my house as a rental property, and Abel had called several times. I didn't listen to his messages, but I didn't delete them either.

Although my mind had cleared and I believed I was well out of the contagious stage, my body still ached, and all I wanted was to soak in a tub, drink, think, and possibly drown myself. There was an old-fashioned clawfoot tub at the house, but it no longer felt like my house anymore, so I dithered for an hour before I gathered a towel, soap, and the bottle of rosé and walked up the drive taking Bertie with me. "Old times, Bertie. Remember when we lived here?"

He ambled at his slower pace, but once we entered the

garden, he stopped. His ears pricked up at attention, and he whined, but it wasn't a warning whine. It was a *wanting* whine. Perhaps Ben was here.

I approached the back door slowly, keeping Bertie beside me. I turned the knob, which was unlocked. I pushed open the door, and Bertie shot past me and into the house. "Bertie!"

I went after him, dropping the towel and clothes. I ran down the hall and then up the stairs, calling, "Bertie!"

Pausing at the landing, I peered through the shadows. The bedroom door stood open. I approached it slowly, brandishing the wine bottle. Then I jumped in front of the doorway and said, "Who's here?"

And my beautiful little sister turned from the window and held her arms wide. "Are you planning to offer me a drink, or beat me to death with that thing?"

I set down the bottle and threw myself at her. "Baby girl!"

And when she wrapped me in a bear hug, I pressed my face into her thick dark brown hair, smelling her rosemary-lemon shampoo.

"Maddie, you're squeezing me like an old tube of toothpaste!"

I let go and stepped back. "What the hell are you doing here?"

"I have had a number of reports that you are spinning out of control."

"More than usual?"

"Yes, more than usual."

"Do you mean about Oliver? Or when I threw up on the cop? Not to worry. I'm perfectly fine," I said, and then I burst into tears.

I sobbed, and Kenzie filled the bathtub and said, "Get in."

I slipped into the water and continued to blubber while she balanced on the tub's edge and scrubbed my back with a soapy washcloth. I dunked my whole body under and held my breath until I composed myself enough to tell her about Beau Blue.

She wrung out the washcloth and hung it over the spout. "You gave Beau safety and affection while he was with you."

"It wasn't enough."

"You never feel it's enough. You did what you could do."

"In *Galaxy Quest*, Gwen DeMarco—she's played by Sigourney Weaver—"

"And you love her as Riley in *Alien*, too."

I smiled. "I love her in everything. Gwen says, 'I have one job on this lousy ship. It's stupid, but I'm going to do it, okay?' Well, my lousy ship is Planet Earth, and I don't think my job is stupid, but many would consider it unimportant, but I'm going to do it, okay?"

"Okay," Kenzie said. "Come out before you're as wrinkled as a brain."

She left me, and I stayed in the tub until the skin on my fingers puckered. After drying off and dressing, I followed wonderfully familiar aromas drifting from the kitchen.

Kenzie placed a mug of Campbell's Tomato Soup and a crustless grilled cheese sandwich, cut into triangles and wrapped in a paper towel, on the counter. "I only brought a few basics."

"It's exactly the meal I wanted. Stay in the cottage with me."

"That cottage is set up for you and you alone, Maddie. I have a sleeping bag."

Looking at Kenzie now in the bare white room, I noticed the dark shadows under her blue-gray eyes, her pallor, the way her wrist bones stood out, and how her top hung off her shoulders. "Baby Girl, do you need to tell me something?"

Her lips twitched as if she was trying but failing to smile. "Chris and I broke up."

Dark feelings swirled in me: sorrow for her sadness, greedy joy that she was back, and guilt for my selfish reaction. "I'm so sorry! What happened? Why didn't you say anything?"

"Because I'd made such a big deal about moving out and us

living independently. Chris is a sweetheart, but—and I swear to god, Maddie, I'll *kill* you if you repeat this—I became so bored in that nice condo with nice furniture and polite conversations about how nice dinner was, and nice evenings out with nice friends, and returning home for nice sex afterward. I thought I wanted everything to be 'nice' and that I would like a relaxing life, but I wanted to punch my fist through the wall. I feel terrible."

"Why do you feel terrible?"

"Because I used a genuinely decent man as an excuse to leave my eccentric sister, and then I used my eccentric sister as an excuse to leave a genuinely decent man, so what does that say about me?"

"You told me you loved him."

"I did. I thought I did. I loved what Chris represented: stability, sanity, and kindness."

"He loved you, though. How could he not? Did you break his heart?"

She smiled at last. "You'd think so, wouldn't you? But he didn't bother trying to change my mind and may even have been relieved to have his place to himself again. He said that we enabled each other and that we're co-dependent."

"How do I enable you?"

"You don't mind when I shout and blow off steam the way I can't with clients. You keep life interesting."

"Hmm, I never thought of you benefiting from the drama. Are we co-dependent?"

"Absolutely, the way we should be: sisters who love and help each other," she said. "Is our furniture still in the barn or did you dump it?"

"You said you didn't want it. Our family stuff and your what-nots are in the attic. What about all the things you took to Chris's?"

"We didn't need duplicates, so I had a sidewalk sale.

Everything else is in boxes in my car, which I left at Beryl Jensen's. I stopped there on the way over, and she kept refilling my wineglass."

"Did Beryl tell you I was freaking out?"

"Maddie, it would be faster to name the people who *didn't* tell me than those who did."

"Oliver. Oliver didn't call you, and I'm sure his doppelganger didn't either."

"Now you're making *me* freak out. Why do you keep going on about Oliver and a doppelganger?"

"Do you have a dollar?"

"Why?"

"I need one now."

She left the room and came back a few moments later with a crisp bill in her hand. "Here. Consider it an advance on your Christmas present."

"Thank you." I held the bill to her. "Kenzie, I would like to hire you as my therapist, wherein our communications will be in confidence per your professional code of conduct. This dollar is payment for a session."

She hesitated and then took the dollar. "I accept your payment for my professional services. Would you like to start now?" When I nodded, she said, "What's with all the bonkers talk about doppelgangers?"

"I think Oliver is not Oliver because he's undercover, and he's doing something dangerous and needs to keep me away. Is he keeping me away to protect his cover, or to protect me, or both?"

"Or maybe he's broken up with you and didn't want to tell you directly so he's ghosting you."

I shook my head and rejected all her efforts to influence me otherwise, but I knew the difference between a ghost and a doppelganger, and countered every argument by saying, "We're partners. I trust him," until she finally gave up, and said, "I trust you, and if you trust him, then I'll try to trust him, too...for now."

We talked until dawn, and, if we had no solutions to our problems, at least we had our companionship. "Kenzie, I feel horrible that I'm overjoyed you came home. It isn't home without you."

"You have no idea how much I missed you. I was impressed with how well you were doing on your own, though, and things were great with Chris until the novelty of living in a sane household wore off. I didn't want to give up on my relationship without really trying, but I kept taking on water and floundering."

"I have something to confess, Kenz, because love is truth. The word you want is 'foundering,' which means sinking, not 'floundering, which means thrashing about.'"

"But you *swore* to me it was 'floundering,' and that everyone else was wrong."

"Because I thought it was funnier, like a flounder fish with its eyeballs on top of its head. As Ollie says, irregardless, you can always tell me your problems. It might be best, however, if you think of me the way I think of my dogs when I talk to them: because, like a dog, I can't help beyond appearing to be a concerned listener."

"I can always use a concerned listener. How are you still awake? I have to crash."

"I've slept for most of the week. Go to bed."

As I walked to the center, the rooster began crowing. In the few days that I'd been sick, the season changed. The wildflowers bore seedpods, and grasses had gone brown. We'd survived so far without terrible fires, but we wouldn't be safe until the November rains.

Someone had brought my truck back, washed it, and replaced

the Looper's bumper sticker with stickers for Midnight Runners Search & Rescue and Whitney Canine Rehabilitation Center.

I'd fed the dogs and wrote "Welcome Back, Kenzie!" on construction paper and taped it to the trailer's front door. I was tempting fate by drinking coffee when Purlynn arrived at 7:15.

"You're here early," she said. "How do you feel?"

"Thrilled that my sister Kenzie is back at our house, but otherwise awful on a multitude of levels: physically, emotionally, and spiritually. But alive, which is always better than the alternative. Or alternatives."

"There's only one alternative to being alive, isn't there?"

"Excellent question. I'll leave it for greater minds to ponder," I said. "My priority is returning to work."

Dogs live in the moment, and when I was with them, I did, too. I showed Purlynn a technique to acclimatize Fenster to noises, and I spent an hour with a sheepdog who hated being groomed. Jaison led dogs on a morning run, and a volunteer took charge of cleaning our kitchenette and evaluation room.

A client brought croissants and fruit salad when she came to pick up her dogs. She was usually over-eager to talk to me, but she barely looked my way and spoke only to Jaison. So, whatever shit I was in, there was a silver lining.

Around mid-morning, Jaison said, "Take a break and walk with me, Boss Lady. What's making you smile non-stop?"

"Kenzie's back! She's at the house."

"No shit! Why didn't she come say hi?"

"She's probably still asleep. We stayed up talking all night."

Jai and I strolled to the juncture of the stream and the pond. The pond must have dropped a foot, but the stream still trickled. "At least Abel Myklebust hasn't diverted the water again."

"He helped you a lot this week."

"He outed our biological connection against my express demand that he never do so."

"You and your million rules. No one cares about something that happened back then."

"My mother does, and she won't even admit to me that I'm not Jesse Whitney's daughter," I said. "You never talk about your family, Jai. Too personal?"

He picked up a flat round rock and skipped it on the pond's surface. "I don't like sharing things with people I don't know, and when I came here, I didn't know you. I thought it was strange that you hired me when I didn't have any experience. I thought it was strange how you gave me keys, let me handle money, and rented the trailer to me when you didn't know me from Adam. I thought it was strange how you treated me better than your own brother."

"Nothing strange about it. I trusted you because you interacted so well with the dogs. You could have bullshitted me, but you can't bullshit them. As for treating you better than Raymond..."

"Now I understand, but I didn't then." Jaison smiled. "Anyway, you never asked, and I didn't mind keeping things separate."

"I was respecting your privacy," I said. "Okay, love is truth, and the truth is that it's enough for me to keep up with my friends, let alone all their friends and miscellaneous relatives, about whom I couldn't give a shit."

"Yeah, it didn't take long to figure that out, and I didn't want to waste your 'fucking precious time' with personal stuff," he said, and we laughed. "Mother and father married forever. Two older brothers, I'm the baby. Huge extended family. Some doing okay, and some getting by. They all want me to move back to Louisiana, which I miss. But every time I think about going, we have a day like today." He lifted his eyes to the sky. "I didn't mind humidity when I lived in it, but now that I've lived without it..."

"It's so damn beautiful here." *Breathe, just breathe.* "Did you want to talk to me to tell me you're leaving?"

"Someday, Mad Girl, but not today. I wanted to say that the shit has hit the fan with the video of you and Kearney. I don't think Sheriff Ollie's watching out for us anymore."

"No, he is. I'm sure he is."

"He didn't step up for you."

"He couldn't because I was running stop signs and speeding." My fingers fluttered.

"I figured. But you're on record for calling a cop a pig."

"Blame Zoe's goddamn Pig Latin. You know how things get stuck in my head."

"That's what she said."

"Is it really time for jokes?"

"Maddie, I was giving an example. You had 'that's what she said' stuck in your head for so long I was about to smack you to get it unstuck."

"You should have told me to stop saying it."

"Naw, cuz after a while, it was funny because *you* thought it was funny," he said. "We've had cancellations and hate calls, too."

"Hero to zero," I said. "Do I need to do anything about it?"

"Customer relations is not your strong point. We've shut down comments on the website, and we're screening all calls. Purlynn's touching base with our regulars and explaining that you were delirious with fever."

"That sounds better than 'batshit crazy.'"

"Yeah, I thought so, too, but I recommend you stay under the radar. You got a lot of people hating on you right now."

"I'm used to it."

"Not like this, Boss. Be careful."

Chapter Twenty-One

LATE IN THE AFTERNOON, I saw Kenzie's blue Subaru Forester by the house, so I took a break and found Kenzie and Hardwire sitting on cardboard boxes in the kitchen, drinking rosé from plastic cups. She wore a blond wig, styled in a long bob.

"Hey, Hardwire, Kenz. I thought that wine was supposed to be for me."

"Aren't you going to ask about my hair?" Kenzie twisted her head right and then left.

"No, because there's no excuse for the heinousness." I filled a cup with wine. "Okay, I give up. What's the deal with the hair?"

"I participated in an experiment on bias, like the famous blue-eyes/brown-eyes study. Turns out blondes *do* have more fun."

"If you mean that blondes get away with more crap, then I could have told you that if you'd bothered to ask," I said, glancing up at the kettle-shaped clock on the wall. "I hate liking this wine, and I hate that you brought back that ridiculous clock. A clock should not mimic the shape of another appliance."

Kenzie started laughing and said, "It wouldn't be home without you complaining about Mom's clock."

"Well, I'd love to hear you girls bicker, but I got to get getting on. My woman's waiting for me." Hardwire rotated and thrust his hips. "Ba-boom!"

"What?" I asked, and then it dawned on me. "Beryl? *You* and Beryl Jensen?"

"I've been telling you I wanted a cougar from day one, Maddie." He promised to take Kenzie to pick up furniture from Beryl's storage and left.

"Beryl's giving you furniture now?"

"Yes, and I appreciate it. She told me about your brunch."

"She harbors the delusion that I'm interesting. There's a Chinese curse, 'May your life be interesting.'"

"That's a pleasant association. Are you here for a therapy session? Because I can start the clock."

"If this was a Venn diagram—"

"Your favorite kind."

"Parabolic graphs are my favorite, but Venns are easy to draw and understand. Anyway, my visit has a ninety-three percent crossover of sisterly companionship and therapist consultation."

She refilled her wine. "I'm listening."

"I don't want to tell Mom about Abel's public announcement, but I don't want her to find out via gossip. You break it to her."

"You and Mom should accept that this is public knowledge and beyond your control."

"Larry's not going to forgive her. It will be my fault for screwing up her life yet again." The empty plastic cup cracked in my hand.

"Exactly like you to take the credit for her marriage to Dad. Let's see, how old were you when that happened? Oh, yeah, you weren't born for another two years."

"Are you this snarky with all your patients?"

"Maddie, I refuse to continue reassuring you that you haven't ruined anyone's life...yet. Besides, Larry's often commented on how different we look, so I'm sure he suspects.

“He already thinks I’m going to hell.”

“But he likes you anyway and keeps hoping that you won’t.”

“Only because Larry respects the fact that I’m banging a man who packs heat.”

“You have such a lovely way with words.” Kenzie sighed. “Larry’s head-over-heels for Mom, and she’s capable of managing her marriage without compromising her relationship with you.”

“That’s why I want you to talk to her. You can express all the intricate emotional crap. Every time I’ve even approached the topic of my paternity, she shuts me down.”

Kenzie closed her eyes for a few seconds. “All right, here’s what I can do. I’ll tell her Abel let the cat out of the bag, so she’s prepared. In return, you have to write a letter to her sharing your feelings. You don’t have to mail the letter. You can use it to organize your thoughts and read it to her later. Promise?”

“I promise.”

Kenzie made me raise my hands to prove I wasn’t crossing my fingers and then said, “What’s next on the agenda?”

“Legal stuff.” I set my phone on the counter, put it on speaker, and returned Jim Desjardin’s call.

“Thank you for *finally* getting aback to me.” He named a date to appear in court for verbal assault, simple assault, and reckless driving.

“Contempt of cop isn’t illegal,” I said. “It was inadvertent. I was sick, and I drove fast because of a medical emergency.”

“Abel Myklebust asked me to represent you, but I informed him that it would be a conflict of interest. Also, I’m a family lawyer, so your situation isn’t my bailiwick. Your father should hire a defendant’s attorney.”

“My only connection with Abel is an accidental biological one, and I wasn’t calling Richard Kearney a pig because he’s a cop. Ollie can vouch for my character?”

“I’d rather not discuss my brother now, and he’s requested

that I ask you not to contact him. It might be seen as interfering with a witness."

"That's bullshit!"

"Oliver doesn't want to file a restraining order against you for stalking and harassing him."

My sister's jaw dropped in surprise or dismay, or both.

I said, "Okay, I understand. Tell Ollie I'm here whenever he needs me. I'll *always* be here, no matter what."

Kenzie waved and mouthed, "No! Stop!"

"Anytime Ollie needs me for anything, I'm here," I said. "Tell Claire, too."

"Find a good lawyer, Maddie. Goodbye."

The phone went silent, and Kenzie said, "Why did you keep going on when I waved for you to stop? Stalking is a form of emotional abuse and a serious crime."

"I'm not stalking him. I'm watching so I can protect him."

"That's *exactly* what stalkers say."

"We're not going to agree on this. I believed everything Oliver told me our last night together, and I believe it still. But if it's what you want, I'll keep my distance until he asks for help."

"You should be doing it for yourself, not for me."

"The result is the same, isn't it?" I said. "Let's move on to the next item on my list: Beau Blue."

"Do you want me to handle it?"

"Thank you, but I promised Beau that I'd care for him, so I need to do this myself."

Wylene at the clinic answered my call and said, "I'm sorry for your loss. The cremains were returned to us today. If you want to talk to Doc Ben, he's meeting with a pharmaceuticals rep."

"That's okay. Please tell him to bring the cremains when he can. Thanks, Wylene."

I stared at the phone in my hand and told Kenzie, "I don't think Ben wants to be close friends anymore."

"His wife warned you he's a serial flirt. Frankly, I don't see why she puts up with it."

"Ava says it gets him revved up and sexy for her. She keeps a few admirers on the line, too."

"Yes, it's all fun and games until somebody gets hurt. In this case, you. Shouldn't Ava and the kids be back by now?"

"Ben says her shoulder is still healing, and she needs her parents' help. He keeps himself occupied with Emily Ayer's Weasel."

"You're the worst. Emily isn't a calculating black widow, and if you hadn't been snooping at her house, you wouldn't have caught her flu."

"I wasn't snooping. I was delivering a get-well basket."

"As a pretext for snooping. What's next on your list?"

"You, but you're here so we can move on. I suppose I have to come to a rapprochement with my biological father, which isn't as important as identifying the dog fighting ring."

"Cross that off your list. Hurting animals is a precursor to killing people. Let Oliver and his department handle it. How are you going to fix the mess with Deputy Kearney? Have you even read the social media?"

"No, because why? The trolls I can bear, but the constant stream of advertisements throws me into conniptions. As for the data mining, I strongly oppose treating citizens as mere commodities to be monetized. For example—"

"If I hadn't heard this paranoid lecture a dozen times, I'm sure it would be fascinating, Maddie. I made the mistake of watching that video and reading the feedback, and it's horrific. Since your clients are cancelling, you should make a public apology."

"No need. Zoe assured me she'd fix everything."

"Zoe? As in *Zoe Gaskell*? The girl who once asked me how to trademark psychological counseling based on the concept 'It's not your fault; they screwed up'?"

"I still think that's genius."

"Of course, you do. You can't rely on a teenager for something this critical."

"Teenagers invented social media crises. They are the experts. Irregardless, I'm scheduled to deliver therapy dogs to Ezra Brothers. Come with me and you can witness the weirdness with your very own eyes."

"Like I'm not doing that now," she said. "Why do you keep saying 'irregardless'? You told me it was incorrect."

"It used to be, but it isn't anymore. It's okay for things to change. Ollie taught me that. The *real* Ollie." My vision blurred, and I wiped my eyes.

"Okay, hon, I'll go with you, but only because I can't believe you own a vehicle that is not on the verge of total collapse."

"No one can."

On the drive to the Ayer vineyard, I told Kenzie, "It's great that you're not doing anything and can spend time with me. We're so lucky the house wasn't rented."

"I probably shouldn't have walked away when I was establishing a solo business, but it was either renew my office lease or come here. What are we going to do without rental income, especially now that you're losing clients?" She sniffed. "This smells only a little doggy."

"Enjoy it while you can. Do you want to start your animal therapy business again? We can rebuild the stalls in the barn..." I hesitated, considering the frozen finger in the tack room.

"I love working with children and families, but I don't miss the labor and expense of keeping horses."

"If you change your mind, I'll do whatever I can to support you. I miss being able to ride sometimes, and it's strange, isn't it, not seeing the horses grazing?"

"I miss them, too. Thanks, Maddie."

I turned into the Ayers' drive and said, "Here's the pup tent city."

"The yurts are wonderful!"

"Please note that these nutjobs have a huge fucking firepit with no concern for the risk to all and sundry. Fire Chief Lunts refuses to do a damn thing about it."

I parked, and we hopped down from the Tundra.

"There's a clearance around the pit, but I see your point," Kenzie said. "When the winds come..." As she spoke, a breeze blew her hair across her face. She pulled it back and twisted it into a knot.

We unloaded the dogs and led them to the main yurt. A Kool-Aid drinker directed me to a fenced area with three yurts and tomatoes growing in wine-barrel planters.

Ezra Brothers, wearing a tank top and a floral sarong, waved us in.

"I told you: He wears skirts in rattlesnake country," I muttered to Kenzie.

"Skirts are comfortable, especially in this climate."

"Well, you won't see me tempting fate. I'm sure Ezra does it for maximum attention and to let his big dick swing in the breeze." I opened the gate and called, "Hey, Ezra!"

"Maddie, welcome! And you're..." He gave Kenzie a long, sultry gaze with his dark-rimmed eyes.

"I'm Maddie's sister, Kenzie. You probably don't remember, but we met when you gave a talk in Marin on living by your personal truths."

"Truth is love, and love is truth," he said. "You were seated toward the back of the room. I was touched by what you said about horse therapy programs for children with developmental disorders. I'm sorry I didn't catch your name then."

"I'd be surprised if you did," she said. "There must have been two hundred people there, and everyone wanted to participate."

"Yes, reminiscing about conferences is delightful," I said. "Ezra, this is a well-constructed fence. Can you call the dogs' primary handlers so we can take a short walk together?"

The handlers joined us, and I examined the yurts, each with dog beds and bowls for water and food. While we wandered around the vineyard, I reviewed care and training tips with the handlers. Kenzie and Ezra lagged, caught up in their own conversation.

When I felt assured that Slater, Tiffani Amber, and Zack were in reliable hands, I said, "Learning to live together is a process that takes time. Call me if you have any questions or want to talk about the dogs, because it's always fun to share stories. Send me pictures, too!"

"Thank you so much, Maddie," Ezra said. "Is there anything I can do for you in return?"

"Yes. For god's sake, if you're not going to wear pants and boots, get a walking stick to clear the path before you."

He glanced at Kenzie and grinned. "No, I meant something to help you with your public relations problems."

"Oh, that. A social media expert has already volunteered her services. Come on, Kenzie."

Instead of following me, she stared goony eyed at Ezra, who said, "It's been a pleasure. I'd love to hear about your experiences with families with multi-generational neurodiverse conditions. Perhaps over dinner?"

"Don't do it, Kenzie," I said. "He'll feed you foraged bitter weeds dressed in vinegar and moral rectitude."

Kenzie blushed pink, but Ezra laughed, and said, "I'll take her to any restaurant she likes."

"I haven't been to the Country Squire in ages," Kenzie said.

I waited in the truck while they settled on a date. She'd unknotted her hair at some point, and it whipped away in the breeze. A foot taller than my petite sister, Ezra leaned forward to talk to her. I couldn't remember seeing her smile or laugh so much in forever. Shouldn't I have paid attention to that before?

She was grinning when she climbed into the truck.

I started the engine and began driving home. "Ezra is full of shit, but he's not the worst man in the world. What I mean is, I don't mind if you date him."

"How magnanimous, Maddie. He's barely on my radar."

"He's not your usual style, but you sparked with him."

"Maddie, just because I don't go out of my way to shock people, doesn't mean I'm narrow-minded. As for Ezra, being charismatic is his thing."

"You weren't sparky with Chris."

"No, but I could count on him. I knew he cared for me. Besides, sparks die out."

"Except when they explode into a firestorm."

"You know how Mom doesn't like us to say 'earthquake' because she thinks it's unlucky? Well, please stop saying 'firestorm.' We're all aware the danger is constant, but you need to work through your trauma."

My shoulders jerked, making my steering a little uneven, and Kenzie said, "Okay, I'll talk to Ezra about the firepit."

"Everyone's already tried. He won't listen."

"Maddie, if I can persuade you to wear an underwire bra for public events, I think I can persuade an egotistical cult leader to take basic safety precautions. Especially one who was conned into adopting heinous mutts named after 'Saved by the Bell' characters."

"Tiffani Amber is the actor, not the character. Ah, Tiffani Amber!"

"Irregardless, Mad Girl."

I couldn't stop smiling as we drove down our lane, under the wide branches of the California live oaks, to our house, to home, because home is where the heart is, and Kenzie was my heart.

* * * *

When my sister came to my cottage for dinner, she took one look at my whiteboards and notes, and said, "Charting again, Maddie?"

"They keep me organized."

"Or do they feed your OCD? What's this?" She leaned forward to read a sheet of graph paper. "Around the Moon, A Floating City, The Fur Country..."

"That's Jules Verne's bibliography. The dog fighting woman had a Jules Verne tattoo, and I'm trying to figure out what that could be, beyond the obvious hot air balloon, based on the inaccurate movie, or a submarine. Verne was prolific, and I may have to read all his major stories. Not in the original French, of course."

"*Quelle surprise.*" She pulled the note off the board. "I think it's time to let this one go, don't you?"

It had taken me almost an hour to copy all the story titles. "If you think it's necessary."

She smiled and crumpled the paper. "Let's clear these off. Then you can start with one board, and one board only, and list three reasonable actions. These actions should exclude locating dog fighters, snooping on the Ayers, and obsessing over Oliver."

"I'm not obsessing. I'm devoting an appropriate amount of attention to the person I love."

"Maddie, you're one step away from boiling a bunny in his kitchen. Do you have anything for dinner?"

"I have eggs. Well, I didn't quite have time to collect them this morning."

So while she gathered eggs and foraged for vegetables and herbs in the kitchen garden, I peeled notes from the whiteboards, snuck them into a drawer, wiped the boards clean, and set three boards and easels outside.

Kenzie banged about with pots and pans, I fussed over my goals, and finally reduced my list to the essentials: 1) write a letter to Mom and talk to Abel re: relationship; 2) public apology for ticket incident; and 3) ask Beryl for help with business plan.

I bit into the frittata Kenzie had conjured. "How do you make everything taste incredible?"

"Fresh ingredients and giving a damn. Mom says that you've been donating to her church's farm-to-table program."

"I wish she'd had access to something like that when she was scraping every cent trying to put food on the table."

"Mom's proud that she provided for us. You should admire her, instead of anguishing about her difficulties."

"I do, but she wouldn't have had to go through that if our fathers had helped her. Or if I hadn't constantly needed so much. If I could go back in time—"

"I would like to enjoy this meal without you getting stuck in this loop again. If *I* could go back in time, I'd tell Mom to leave you in the forest to be raised by wolves."

"I would have liked that, but I'd miss having you for my sister."

"You could visit me. We could have had a secret howl, so you'd recognize me."

"You probably wouldn't have howled as often as you should have."

"You probably would have told the wolf pack that I never howled at all, despite the fact that I was howling myself hoarse." She pushed her plate aside. "Okay, I'm going to the house to call Mom and tell her the jig is up. Start composing your letter."

A few moments after Kenzie left, I heard a high-pitched howl, which set half the dogs at the center howling, and I flew outside and howled, too.

Chapter Twenty-Two

I SAVORED MY FIRST cup of coffee before I called Jaison to my office. He closed the door behind him and plopped into a chair. "Ready to talk, Boss Lady?"

I shifted my keyboard to the right and then a bit back again until it was centered properly. "I thought Zoe was going to manage the backlash."

"She did." He took out his phone, scrolled, and then handed it to me so I could watch a video.

Zoe had snagged an interview with Sasha Seabrook, wherein my former intern announced, "It's actually because Dr. Whitney and I were discussing gendered oppression at Rudy's Brewhouse on Main Street, home of the five-star charbroiled burger, and I used the phrase 'male chauvinist pig' because of the iconic movie *Nine to Five* starring Dolly Parton. It got stuck in Dr. Whitney's head. She's got a condition like Tourette syndrome, I think, because she cusses like you wouldn't believe. So saying 'Pig Latin' wasn't an insult to law enforcement, but an objection to institutional sexism. Oink, oink! Also, shout-outs to my bae Billy Zlotnik, the crew at Gaskell's Feed Store, the pride of Coyote Run since nineteen-seventy-five." Zoe took a deep breath and continued, "And don't forget to visit the Crafty Looper, home for all things crafty and creative!"

I watched it twice and then hung my head in my hands, and said, "At least, she managed to promote one movie and three businesses. Maybe Sasha has a suggestion. I have to talk to her anyway about the next training segment. Any ideas?"

"How about dental health?" Jaison said. "The right chew toys, kibble, and bones for every size of dog."

"Great topic. I'll pitch it to Sasha."

"About time!" Sasha said when I called. "My goodness, Maddie, the poop has hit the propeller! So many things happening. Your friend Zoe—"

"I just saw it. She was trying. I wish she hadn't mentioned the Brewhouse since she's underage. Well, that's over and done with."

"I feel horrible about the whole thing, Maddie, although I have to say, viewers love her. I'm glad you understand and hope you'll still give me deets on the search."

"Understand what and what search?"

"Understand that our dog training features have been cancelled." She paused. "And there's only *one* search. Isn't that why you called?"

Sasha and I engaged in a clumsy polka of words, spinning in circles, unsure of who led, and tripping over each other. I finally realized that her station had cut ties with me because of the Pig Latin incident and that a hotel guest had gone missing from Towering Pines Casino.

"I can't believe Sheriff Desjardins hasn't told you this already. The guest lost over three-hundred grand last night of payroll money he 'borrowed' from his company. He didn't sleep in his room and left everything, including his phone. Towering Pines' cameras show him walking away from the complex at one a.m. but not returning. His wife sounded the alert because she thinks he's suicidal," Sasha said. "The moment you and the Midnight Runners find him, everyone will fall in love with you all over again, and my manager will beg for you to be back on-air."

"Thanks for telling me. I'll head there right now."

"I'm almost there! See you soon."

I grabbed my backpack and pulled on my high-view orange *Midnight Runners Search & Rescue* vest.

I went out to the yard, where Bertie dozed in the shadows of the potted bamboo plants. "Hey, boy, time to rock and roll."

He opened his eyes and stood slowly, and I thought of the rugged terrain around the Twin Pines Casino. "You'll limber up once you get going," I said, as I strapped a harness on him.

"What's up?" Purlynn said, coming over.

"A Towering Pines hotel guest took a hike and never returned."

"I thought Vixen was your search dog. Do you want me to get..." Purlynn began, but Vixen had already insinuated herself, winding around my legs.

"She's not a reliable search dog," I said as Vixen licked my hand and then nuzzled Bertie's face. "Okay, whatever. Call the sheriff's office and say we'll be there as fast...as it is legal to drive."

I fumbled with my phone as I crated Vixen and harnessed Bertie in the front. "Hi, Wylene. Dr. Whitney here. I need to talk to Doc Ben about an emergency. We've got a search and rescue."

"I don't think he can do it. He's in surgery on a dog that ate a box of nails. We're all worried."

"Okay, all right. Tell him to get in touch as soon as he's available."

"It's gonna be awhile. Be careful!"

My heart thudded as I thought about being alone with Oliver and the dogs, running through the woods, smelling the greenness, slipping into the shadows, on the hunt. Because that was how we'd bonded.

It hadn't been so long ago, when Bertie was beginning to slow down. I reached over and rubbed his head. "I won't push you hard. Oliver and Zeus can charge ahead, and we'll go at a reasonable pace. We'll be thorough."

I turned onto the highway, which was clear save for a tour bus and a few RVs. The vineyards had shifted gold, red, and violet, heavy with clusters of indigo grapes. The fruit on persimmon trees had ripened into scarlet-orange. Where had the summer gone?

Glancing in my rearview mirror, I made out a patrol car behind me, but the sun's reflection obscured the driver. I was five miles over the limit and immediately slowed down. The patrol car drew close to my tail and then hit the siren and the gas, blowing past me.

As soon as I was in the clear, I sped up. The vineyards gave way to lush woods at the mountain's base where Towering Pines Casino & Resort Hotel was located. Emergency vehicles, media vans, and a crowd were gathered by the enormous water fountain in the center of the sprawling parking lot. Ollie was somewhere in there, and I was struck with a painful yearning for the sight of him, the smell of him, the taste of him, the sound of him.

The moment I led the dogs from the truck, the crowd directed its electric hum toward us. I shivered in the heat, shook out my arms, and made my way to the first-responder vehicles. The casino was a powerful force in our county, and the event had drawn the presence of Sheriff-Coroner Eastman, who looked exactly like the pre-packaged political jackass he was, wearing shiny medals and pins on his jacket. I waved to Jeanne Gallego, the casino's CEO, in her trademark business attire and tooled red leather cowboy boots, and Sasha Seabrook, who were being fitted with microphones for an interview.

"Welcome back to Towering Pines," said someone behind me.

I turned to see Jeanne's husband, wearing a security guard's uniform and squinting in the sun. "Hello, Professor Gallego, shouldn't you be at State, inspiring and-or berating your students?"

"Not for another two weeks, Dr. Whitey."

"I can't tell if your tone is more sarcastic with 'doctor' or 'Whitey.' I'll have you know that I have indigenous blood."

"Ordering a la carte from the menu of identities, are we? I heard that Abel Myklebust claimed to be your father. We'll share a dried stockfish dinner sometime. You can pontificate about the oppression and vilification of the Viking people, and I can pretend to sympathize."

I grinned. "Delighted to pontificate on any topic of your choosing. Have you seen the sheriff?"

"Ollie D was interviewing a witness. Imagine he'll be back soon," Professor Gallego said. "Pretty little bird dog you've got."

"I'm willing to part with her. You hunt, right? That's what she lives for."

Vixen sniffed his boots, and he reached down to scratch her head. "I wanted the one with the soul."

"Vixen is intelligent and ingenious."

"I don't doubt it, but she's got the wily grin of a trickster god about her."

"You're so flippant about assigning Native American archetypes to my dogs, but I think it's a little unkind to send me into a time-sucking research vortex."

He laughed. "OCD is an academic's best friend. Trickster spirits aren't exclusive to Native American folklore. I might have been referring to your Norse god, Loki."

"Were you?"

"No, because we're in Coyote Run, not Lillehammer. A trickster is an agent of chaos," he said. "Could it be that *you're* the trickster?"

"Is a trickster aware of his or her role?" I scanned my

surroundings for Oliver, but the parking lot was cluttered with *Not Olivers.*

"They relish their roles."

"That's not me then," I said, trying to adjust my spine because of the pressure building inside me. "I have a dog you may like, a purebred Catahoula-Argentine dogo. An impressive dog for an impressive man with a high level of earned confidence."

"Flattering me into buying a 'purebred' mutt, eh? My retriever could use a companion besides the boss's yappy little Pommies. Send me a photo and info."

"I will. He's a terrific dog." My shoulders twitched back and forth. "I hate crowds."

"We would have preferred to search for the guest without all the publicity, but someone in local enforcement leaked the news."

"Not Ollie?"

"No, Ollie D respects our sovereign authority over tribal land," he said. "There's your man now."

The copper-gold of Oliver's hair gleamed out from below his baseball cap as he walked from the casino's administrative offices. He wore a tan departmental polo shirt and jeans, and Zeus was beside him. We were partially hidden by the crowd, but brindle shepherd raised his snout and froze. Then Zeus leaned forward eagerly.

I released Bertie's leash, and he ran to his pal, sniffing and jostling in greeting. Zeus's joy showed in his open mouth and ears that tipped back.

Ollie quickly tugged Zeus's leash, ordering him to sit, and the Dutch shepherd showed his confusion because he hesitated for a split second before complying.

I was confused, too, because now another search and rescue team came from around the fire engine. I called, "Oliver!"

He turned his back on Bertie, who returned to me, whining low. "It's okay, Bertie. I'll figure this out."

People had stopped speaking and stared at us as we walked to Oliver. "Hi, Oliver."

"Sheriff's Captain Desjardins," he said. "What do you want?"

"We're here to help. Who's leading, and can you catch me up?"

"I didn't call you," he said loudly, so he could be heard by Sheriff-Coroner Eastman, who had come our way with ruddy Dickhead Kearney a foot behind him.

"Ms. Whitney," the Sheriff-Coroner said.

"Dr. Whitney," I replied.

"I reserve the title of Dr. for those who've earned medical degrees," he said. "You can go now. Tomorrow you'll receive official notification that the county's contract with you is terminated."

"You can't do that."

"Actually, I can. Didn't you read the morals clause?"

"No one ever reads contracts," I fumed, and saw Kearney grinning like a jack-o'-lantern.

"That's *your* problem," the sheriff-coroner said. "Now leave the premises before I have you arrested for interfering with an official duty."

I was so desperate that I tried to do what normal people do: make eye contact with Oliver. He finally looked right at me, and my ribcage constricted until breathing hurt, and I mouthed *Oliver, please!* and then he took Zeus toward the other K-9 team, and the crowd watched me before turning away.

"You see, Ms. Whitney, that no one wants you here," Sheriff-Coroner Eastman said, and he and Dickhead Kearney left to join Ollie.

If I keep away, know that I'm coming back, Oliver had said. So, I didn't chase the doppelganger. I didn't drop to my knees and weep. I didn't scream out my love and need and sorrow. I began returning to my truck, glancing at the hotel wing of the resort.

After the fire last year, I spent a few hours recovering in a room here. Ollie and I sat by the window, looking into the night, and we'd talked about death and our responsibility to the living, and my growing attraction to him deepened into respect and admiration, and we swore a pact that would forever connect us.

My ragged fingernails cut into my palms, and when I relaxed my hands, Vixen's leash slipped from my grip, and she pulled away, racing to the fountain, leaping in, frolicking with the water splashing around her, and I dropped Bertie's leash and said, "Go ahead," and he trotted to the fountain and jumped in.

As I watched the dogs, Sasha came to me and said, "Dang, girlfriend, what was all that about?"

"I'm persona non grata big time."

"Then why are you smiling?"

"Look at the dogs. Look how they're celebrating."

"Celebrating what?"

"Celebrating life. Celebrating the sun's warmth and the water's coolness. Celebrating movement and play and friendship. Such simple things, yet so significant. The world can be falling apart, and dogs will still show us how to find happiness," I said. "Sasha, I screwed up. I always screw up."

"What do you mean?"

"Insulting Deputy Kearney with my stupid Pig Latin comment. He tased me once, and I don't like him. He scares me. I had a dying dog in my truck, and my only thought was to get him to the vet. Zoe and I had been talking in Pig Latin, and that came out."

"You're different, Maddie. You don't have a filter."

"A filter presupposes that I've conceived ideas before speaking, but that's not the way it is for me. I'm as surprised—and often as appalled—as anyone when I hear myself. It's *always* been this way. It will *always* be this way for me. I'll spend the rest of my life apologizing. With dogs, I never have to explain myself.

They understand that..." I paused trying to find the exact words. "They understand that my love is truth. That truth is love."

My friend slipped her arm around my waist and pulled me tight. "You're a kind person underneath all the prickles and whacked-out opinions. I love you and promise you'll rebound from this."

Since Kenzie was frantically looking into renting an office for a solo practice, I didn't share what had happened with Ollie and the search for the missing man. But through the evening and into the night, I checked local news reports, and, when the man was found, I was saddened, but grateful I'd been excused from the team.

The K-9 team discovered his body at the bottom of a steep ravine, his bare feet torn from walking on rough terrain, empty prescription bottles at his side, and apologies to his wife and coworkers written on hotel stationery.

I was mulling over those notes when Zoe called and said, "I made it worse, didn't I?"

"Not at all, honey bunny. I'm going to have to wait this one out, but thanks for trying."

"Whew, that's a relief. Guess what? Miz Looper is letting me produce promo videos for our classes! I'll be the host, asking our instructors questions and showing samples of completed projects."

"I bet Sasha would give you tips on interviewing."

"You think?"

"Absolutely. She thinks you shine on camera. So do I."

"Thanks, Boss. I hope things get better for you."

"Talking to you has already made them better. We'll get together for lunch soon."

Chapter Twenty-Three

A DAY PASSED and then two and then three. A letter arrived from the Sheriff-Coroner's legal team, officially terminating my duties with the department and ordering me to return all departmental property, including my encrypted walkie-talkie. Live by unread contract clauses, die by unread contract clauses. If they wanted their property back, they could come get it.

Professor Gallego was interested in Fenster and came to meet him one afternoon. They connected instantly. We introduced Fenster to the professor's stable energetic lab and let the dogs go for a run with the pack.

"What's this purebred mutt cost?" Professor Gallego asked.

I told him what I'd paid the Coyote Runaway hipsters and said, "But I've invested time training and feeding him, so I'd like to be compensated."

"Runaway Brewing Company is one of our suppliers, and they told me you dognapped Fenster. I'll reimburse your actual cost and match that with a donation to the shelter."

"I can live with that, and the shelter will appreciate the gift. I'd like to work with him for a few days longer to reinforce basic training. I'll bring him to you when he's ready."

"No rush. I haven't broken the news yet to the wife."

"In the meantime, you can think of a name for him."

"If he answers to Fenster, that's fine with me. I don't hold a dog's name against him."

"You hold *my* name against me."

"Only for a cheap laugh and because you always react, Dr. Whitey."

"When I have the time, I am going to do something to come to terms with my recently discovered heritage. Something beyond liking Mexican food."

"Maybe your grandmother can help."

"My grandmothers are long dead. I've given up my psychic readings gig, and I'm not going to have a séance to call the spirit world."

"Your grandmother, Carmen Fuentes Myklebust. When she visits Abel, she always stops by the casino."

"That I am not ready for. What is she like?"

"Bright and effervescent. A fiend for the one-armed bandits. Keen on our buffet dinner. Delights in complimentary tipples."

"Consider teaching poetry, Professor. Call me if any problems arise."

"I'd be a fool to ask a trickster to solve my problems," he said, laughing.

Professor Gallego aside, most adopters had lots of questions. Ezra Brothers called for help with a student so afraid of dogs she refused to participate whenever one was nearby. "Can you do anything?"

"Ezra, have you seen Sheriff Desjardin's dog Zeus?"

"The scary German shepherd with the tiger stripes?"

"Zeus is a Dutch shepherd with a brindle coat. The sheriff used to be afraid of dogs, too. Now he's devoted to Zeus. Bring your cult follower to my center."

"You have your cult, and I have mine," he said. "Bow wow."

Ezra, resplendent in a long, embroidered tunic and colorful wood bead necklaces, arrived with a pajama-clad woman who was showing typical signs of human distress: pallor, dilated pupils, slumped posture. I avoided shaking hands with her because I suspected she'd flop her hand out like a corpse.

Ezra winked at me and pulled up his tunic enough to reveal snakeskin cowboy boots. I grinned and sent him to visit with Purlynn so he wouldn't interfere.

"There are too many dogs!" the woman said, backing away from the gate.

"Sometimes it's better to dive right in," I said. "I want you to trust me that no harm will come to you. As a general practice, you should never believe a stranger who asks for immediate trust, but I'm a stranger with established credentials. You don't have to do this if you don't want to."

"I don't want to, but I don't want to be afraid of dogs anymore. It's so stupid."

"Fear is not stupid. We should always pay attention to it because it's central to our survival. But healthy fear can become outsized and take control. I'm going to teach you when it's safe to approach dogs, what warning signs to watch for, and the proper way to react in a dangerous situation." I saw the exaggerated rise and fall of her chest. "On a scale of one to ten, how anxious are you now?"

"Ten."

"Good, because you can't get any more anxious. Most panic attacks last less than half an hour. Do you want to ride this one out?"

She blinked too much, but nodded.

"Okay! Breathe slowly, in through the nose and out through the mouth. We're going to enter together. You only have to do one thing: walk straight across the yard as calmly as you can. The dogs will come to inspect you. They'll circle and sniff you, which is how they learn. Completely ignore them, which means no eye contact and no petting. No running or fast movements, because dogs are prey animals."

I made her repeat my instructions three times while she did jumping jacks. I smiled and said, "Now I'm going to open the gate," and we went into the yard.

I'd done this exercise dozens of times, and every time I succeeded in helping someone overcome their fear of dogs, I felt a warm fizz. I lived with a multitude of fears, and this, at least, was one I could manage.

When she felt comfortable with the dogs, I handed her to Jai to teach her basic leash skills. While they took rumbly Heidi and sturdy Scully for a walk around the ranch, Ezra joined me on the deck.

"You're regal today," I said. "Like an Egyptian king."

"Or queen. I'm not particular so long as I'm center stage."

"The less anyone sees me, the better."

"Emily feels the same way. My mother's the general director for the community theater back home in Oregon. They produce a six shows every year on a shoestring budget, mostly musicals, but we felt like we were one step away from Broadway. Emily had a real gift onstage, but she never cared about acting. Me, I'd do whatever was needed—help build sets, go on coffee runs, sell tickets, and play any role they'd give me."

"And wear costumes," I said, wondering if his sister was still a talented actor.

"That was my favorite part. I wanted to wear costumes every day, and the women had the most dazzling costumes. I loved seeing these small-town caterpillars transform into gorgeous butterflies. I didn't think I could ever do that for myself until D'Andre Riggs auditioned for the lead in *Mame*."

"Nice that a small town would make that casting choice."

"'Nice' had nothing to do with it. D'Andre had perfect pitch and a short fuse," Ezra said. "I look damn fine in a three-piece suit, but this weather is too damn hot for even tropical-weight wool."

"My sister forces me to dress up for public appearances." I twisted my torso until my spine aligned. "She believes in presenting a professional image."

"When I met Kenzie at the conference, I was wearing a button-down shirt and slacks. She might have been surprised seeing me like this."

"You're fishing. Weren't you going to take her to dinner?" I said.

"She keeps putting it off." He shrugged. "I thought she liked talking to me."

"She's been busy exploring her professional options: if she wants to have a solo practice or work with the school system. But I'll share one thing about my sister. She can scope out a gym rat faster than my dog Vixen can catch a real one."

He smiled and said, "I'm not a gym rat. I do CrossFit."

"Different name, same jock strap. Let's see how your student is progressing."

Hardwire delivered enough furniture and accessories for Kenzie to fill the house. She arranged it in a way that was all hers and said, "Beryl's hand-me-downs are exactly what I'd buy if I could afford them."

"Odd, how this place has transformed," I said. "When it was Mom and Dad's, it was depressing and a little shabby with Grandma's dusty things. When we came back, we tried to make the clutter of leftovers warm and comfortable, but it was sadly half-assed."

"I thought it was cozy!"

"It was cozy enough. Nothing like this. This is like you. Feminine and colorful, but not old-fashioned or kitschy."

"A little kitschy. I still have the teapot-shaped clock."

"I'm seeing it in an entirely different light: as a way to poke at me."

"Why don't you move back into your old room?"

"No, no, and no. But it's wonderful having you in arm's reach."

"Have you mailed that letter to Mom yet?"

"I've started it a dozen times. My feelings are beyond confused."

"For heaven's sake, Maddie, just call her."

"You said she seemed fine about it."

"'Seems fine' and 'is fine' are two different things. She's relieved that you finally know, but she's worried her old friends here will think badly of her. Her minister is counseling them through it."

"What the fuck is Larry's problem? It's not like Mom cheated on him with Abel Myklebust. Ugh. Thinking of them together is extremely distressing."

"Yet you fail to understand why she had difficulty with some of your relationships."

"Not 'some.' All of my relationships with women and people she couldn't pigeonhole. How do you think Mom's going to like your cult leader?"

"She won't approve of the way he presents himself, but he's heterosexual, even if he isn't exactly heteronormative."

"Wow, you make that sound so sexy, another reason I hate labels. Since you care about those things, you may want to confirm where he likes to park in the sexuality garage."

"He's definitely Kenziesexual, and what matters is that I'm not naively falling under his spell simply because he's pretty."

"You better hope he's seeing you as something beyond a pretty plaything, too," I said.

"Are you seriously giving me relationship advice?"

"Strange, isn't it?" I said and grinned. "When Mom flips out over Ezra's mascara, be sure to remind her she voted for a man with bleached hair who slathers himself in foundation."

"I certainly will not," Kenzie said. "Have you completely given up on your list?"

"A few clients have returned, so I don't need to make any rushed decisions about my center." I aligned mercury glass ornaments on the coffee table. "What about you? Are you going to work for the school district or go the private practice route?"

"I keep hitting a mental wall, so I've decided to spend a few weeks at Spirit Springs Institute to try to find some clarity."

"You've fallen for Ezra and his shtick. You're going to start wearing those terrible pajamas."

"Maddie, there were years when you refused to wear anything but pajamas. Maybe it's my turn to wear loose, comfortable clothes." She smiled and thrust her hip. "And hide this body? Who am I kidding?"

Ben, carrying a big cardboard box with a wooden box atop, knocked on the frame of my open cottage door. "Hi, Maddie."

"Come on in."

He entered, set the cardboard box on the sofa, and handed me the wooden box. "This is for you."

"Beau Blue?" I said, and he nodded. "Do you want to spread the ashes with me?"

"Sure."

"What's in the carton?"

"Coyote Runaway IPA. Mike and Cody sent it as a truce. They're still not happy with the way you took Fenster, but they realized you were right and admitted that living with him scared them. They hope you'll help them find a suitable dog."

"They need extensive training or perhaps personality transplants before they can be trusted with another dog. If they don't have time to properly care for a dog, they can get a cat."

"Cat people aren't bad."

"No, but they're different. They're people who take vacations without going through separation anxiety."

"Most dog people are like that, too, Maddie. Where's Bertie?"

"At the center. He has room to roam there and find cool spots when it's hot and warm spots when it's cool."

"Maybe he's trying to teach you something." Ben opened the cardboard box, took two bottles, used a Swiss Army knife to flip off the caps, and handed me a chilled bottle. "When is the last time you took a vacation?"

I tucked the wooden box under my arm and walked outside. "Come here and look at our stars, Ben. I never need a break from them."

"Other places have beautiful skies, too," he said. "I heard that the county finally released you from your search and rescue obligation. You wanted that from the start."

"But *only* at the start. It was so exhilarating, wasn't it—our first search together with Ollie, running in the darkness, covered in mud, torn up by brambles, and singing to Eileen?"

"That evening started a little like this one, drinking and talking about dogs. You were heartbroken over Claire Desjardins. Are you heartbroken now?"

"This is different. Everyone thinks I'm a fool for trusting that Oliver will come back." We began walking toward the creek, and a mild breeze sighed over my hot cheeks.

"Everyone thinks Ava's a fool for trusting me," he said. "But the only rash thing she's done in her entire life was to marry a man who dragged her to the boondocks.

We were both too aware that I mistrusted him. "So here we are. In the boondocks. It's okay if you stay with the Midnight Runners."

"I don't think I will. You're the lynchpin, Maddie. I only untangle leashes and carry another flashlight."

"You provide vital medical support. Kenzie once asked me why you didn't pursue human medicine. I thought it was an inane question."

"I realize you think I don't care about the animals as deeply as you, but it's agonizing every time I lose one. I cannot imagine dealing with sick and dying human patients every day."

"But you give emotional support." I couldn't shake what Ezra had said about his sister's acting ability. "How's Emily doing?"

"As well as can be expected. I think stress weakened her immune system. She hasn't completely recovered from the flu."

"It hit me like a freight train and moved on." I stopped at a curve on the path, listening to the slip and slide of the creek. "We're here. Beau liked this place. He never had a chance, did he?"

"You gave him a few comfortable weeks, Maddie, and he didn't suffer long."

Inside the box was a plastic bag filled with ashes and small bits of bone. I sprinkled the ashes where Beau had met and played with Vixen, and Ben shook the rest into the field. When the rains came, the minerals would give nutrients to the soil, and Beau would live again in the spring flowers, and bees would pollinate those flowers, and there would be honey, and the seeds would fall and birds would eat them and fly far off, and Beau would still exist in myriad ways, part of the universe.

After Ben left, I'd made another attempt to write a letter to my mother and then stayed up late recreating my whiteboard charts in a spiral notebook, but the letter-size pages didn't allow me to visualize the scope of information. Now I moved in a daze toward the barn to rearrange the agility equipment. Perhaps today I would dispose of Dino Ayer's frozen digit. Burying the finger or hiding it in the compost heap wasn't an option with Vixen prowling around, as she did now, running forward to inspect mole holes. Despite keeping my bedroom windows and door closed, she always managed to sneak in to leave morbid valentines on my pillows: a tiny sparrow, two mice, and a much-mauled squirrel's tail.

I didn't have a garbage disposal in my cottage, and the manky old disposal in the house routinely balked at cruciferous vegetables. I could drive down the highway and hurl it out the window—except that women throwing fleshy objects from moving cars always raised suspicion.

Maybe Emily Ayer would like the finger. She could cremate it or bury it or do as she pleased to memorialize Dino. I imagined the macabre thing suspended in a pickling solution in a place of honor, like the mantel, and I wondered if Oliver, the real Oliver, kept the lock I'd sent him.

I was so wrapped up in my thoughts it took me some time to realize the creek was no longer running,

"Freaking Myklebust!" As I was pulling out my phone to call him, Vixen gave a high-pitched yelp.

She was at the corner of the barn, doing a skittering dance around something.

"You silly girl, come here."

There are some sounds you only need to hear once, and, forever afterward, you'll instantly recognize them. So even though a vintage biplane flew overhead and the dogs at the center barked, I heard the low, hollow rhythm of a rattler's tail. I followed the sound to make out the large adult snake, coiled and ready to strike, its brown pattern easy to miss against the packed dirt. Though younger ones are as venomous, this rattler had a longer reach and was stronger.

"Vixen, come," I said, aware that my words meant nothing because her prey drive was fully engaged. Her entire body froze, with one paw raised, her dark elegant muzzle pointing at the rattler.

"Vixen, *come!*"

If I tried to grab her, I'd put myself in striking distance. I could call for help, but she might get bitten before anyone could get here. If I used the hose to spray the snake, it would slither away, and Vixen would chase it.

I slowly circled to the open barn door. Tools leaned against the inside wall, and the flathead shovel had a handle long enough to keep me out of the rattler's strike zone. I needed to lure Vixen away from her prey, and I knew I couldn't bribe her with the dog treats in my pocket.

But a rotted prize might be irresistible.

Now inside the barn, I moved quickly to the tack room and opened the freezer. I reached into the back, pulled out the icy brown paper bag, and tore it. I tugged open the Ziploc bag and took out the horrible frosty finger. I needed desperately to wriggle and flap my arms, but there was no time, so I grabbed the shovel with my free hand and slipped back outside.

Holding Dino's finger between my left thumb and forefinger, I hissed, "Vixen, come!"

Her eyes flicked too quickly to see what I had, but her nose twitched, and then twitched again. Because she not only smelled the finger, she *recognized* it.

She neatly backed away from the snake until she reached me. She sat at my feet, a silly grin on her face. "Here. Knock yourself out," I lowered the finger, and she delicately took it in her teeth and sped off, out of harm's reach for the moment.

When the rattler began to slither away, I aimed the shovel's edge behind its head and slammed it down with all my might. The rattler writhed and twisted, and I shoved harder to end its suffering. Sweat beaded on my forehead and a splinter slid into my palm. Another push, and the head separated from the body.

I smashed the head with my shovel, crushing the skull. "I'm sorry. This isn't personal, but I've got to keep the dogs safe, even the slippery escape artist."

The dog in question was nowhere to be seen.

I shoveled the dead snake into a trash bag, tossed in the Ziploc and plastic bags, and tied the top tight and dumped it in the bin. After scrubbing my hands with hot, soapy water until they were red, I locked the tack room, and stormed back to my office trailer.

Jaison was coming out of the evaluation room with a silky-haired little Yorkie. "Hey, Boss, what's up with the dish-rattling stomping?"

"Rattling! I just killed a rattler by the barn. Why aren't the cats doing their job, eating the vermin so the snakes don't come hunting?"

"Because the dogs keep pestering them. Vixen is the worst."

"God help us if she ever figures out a way to climb the barn beams," I said. "What's up with the Yorkie?"

"The owner inherited Shambles from a relative, and the little thing needs help overcoming phobias." Jai set the Yorkie down, and it came to sniff me. "See, he's already walking on linoleum, which used to terrify him. I gave the owner a thirty percent discount, but he bought a two-week session."

"We'll take what we can get," I said. "Also, the creek is dry. When did that happen?"

"It was running yesterday. Not much, but trickling along."

"I suppose I have to talk to Myklebust." I went into my office, closed the door, and called Abel before I found a reason to procrastinate.

The moment he picked up, I said, "Where's my water? Why are you diverting the creek?"

"Maddie, if you want the creek to run, you need to come to my house because I have something important to tell you."

"Next week."

"It can't wait until next week. Today."

"If I come, will you release the water?"

"Yes."

"I have a consult here in an hour. I'll be there after that."

I had to call Kenzie three times before she answered, saying, "Maddie, I was in a meditation session, and now I have a yoga class. What's the problem now?"

"Abel Myklebust is extorting me by blocking our water. He won't release it unless I see him. How soon can you get here?"

"Nah-uh, you're doing this on your own. You need to talk to him anyway."

"Even if I agreed with that, it should be voluntarily, when the time is right."

"The time will *never* be right for you," she said. In the background, voices chanted, and chimes tinged. "Mmm."

"Mmm, what?"

"Someone served me iced hibiscus tea. It's wonderful. Have fun with Abel."

"But—"

"But Ezra and I are going out for dinner."

"Have you talked to him about the firepit yet?"

"Yes, and he suggests that you're projecting your generalized anxiety. Maddie, I've observed evening gatherings, and the firepit is safer than home barbecues. The Institute doesn't use it when there are breezes."

"You're brainwashed. Next, Ezra will tell you my worry about snakes is sexual repression, but I had to execute an innocent rattler by the barn today."

"Good grief! Why wasn't that the first thing you told me?"

"A snake can strike one person at a time. A wildfire can devastate thousands. When will you be back?

"Late, unless you need me home now."

"Do what you need to do, Kenz. After all, it isn't like we haven't had rattlers before."

Chapter Twenty-Four

THE SHORTEST PATH to Abel's house was following the creek to the wire fence, climbing over the fence, and cutting across gently rolling pastures. Spectacular Old Norwegian sheep dotted the landscape, and shaggy Bergamasco sheepdogs came to inspect me. I knew the dogs from previous visits to borrow Abel's tractor, using a key conveniently hidden in the hollow of a fake granite rock.

Perspiration dripped down my back, and I wiped my brow and hands as I approached the house, a modest single-story ranch, white with dark green trim. I was wondering if I should have changed into clean clothes when I noticed him. He wore dark wash jeans and a faded *Coyote Run 10th Anniversary Bonanza Days* T-shirt as he raked leaves under a persimmon tree.

He saw me and said, "Let me finish up," and he scooped the leaves into a plastic barrel and then put the rake in a tool shed. When he returned, he said, "A place for everything, and everything in its place. Come inside."

I followed him around the house to the front entrance. He dusted his boots off on the straw doormat, and I did the same.

I expected the home's interior to be as shiny and ornate as his turquoise and silver jewelry, but the small entry room had off-white walls and dark hardwood floors. I sniffed and hoped we'd go toward the enticing aroma of chicken and spices, but Abel took me into a shadowy living room with older brown leather furniture and a flat-weave blue rug. Generic landscape paintings hung on the walls, and there were black and white photos on the brick mantel. He'd set tall glasses and a pitcher on a marble-topped coffee table.

"I keep the curtains closed because it gets too hot. I can open them if you like," Abel said.

"It's fine. I thought you'd have the air conditioning cranked up high."

"I never use it unless a visitor complains. Do you want lemonade?"

"Thanks," I said, and sat on the sofa.

He filled the glasses and handed one to me. "Well, you showed up."

Nothing in the room seemed familiar. "Have I ever been here before? I mean, any time *after* I was born?"

"Once when you were a few months old. We—my wife and I—had a Christmas party. Your parents didn't stay long." He wrinkled his nose, and I realized I'd seen this particular twitch before. Then he set his glass on a cork coaster and adjusted it until it was centered.

"Everyone must have suspected I was your offspring. I suppose that's one reason my mother moved us to Arizona; and it couldn't have been easy for her to see your comfortable life when she was struggling to raise your child without any assistance."

"I offered to support you, Maddie, but Charley swore up and down that you weren't mine. They didn't have DNA tests in those days like they do today."

Hearing him use her nickname caused me to clench and unclench my hands. "Or maybe you weren't too eager to press the issue. After all, I wasn't exactly a darling little angel baby. Irregardless, what's so important?"

"It's 'regardless.' 'Irregardless' means," he said, and stopped when I smirked. "Smartass. What do you know about the sheriff's recent behavior?"

"I'm not going to be your anonymous source. Ask him yourself." I sniffed the tantalizing aromas and wondered what was cooking.

"Of course, I asked Sheriff Desjardins already. Didn't you read my story about the switched drug evidence?"

"The *Coyote Run Recorder* is not at the top of my reading list."

"You never tire of putting me down," Abel said. "The sheriff bends the rules sometimes, but it's always been to give people a break; i.e., kids partying or you stealing tractors."

"Borrowing."

"Without permission," Abel said. "If Oliver was motivated by money, he could have pursued a law degree. Jim hoped he'd join his firm.

"I can't see Ollie behind a desk all day. He likes action."

"Maybe that's what took him in the wrong direction. Maddie, he's being investigated by Internal Affairs."

"Do you mean Andrea Kleinfeld? She's only hanging around because she's got a thing going on with Claire."

"You're deluding yourself. You think I don't care for you—"

"Because you've proved the case over the decades."

"Oliver's made it clear he's done with you, so keep away from him for your own sake. If he goes down, I don't want him to drag you with him. You can barely function as it is."

"Gee, thanks. I thought I was an accomplished and highly respected expert in my field."

"What happened to your rare dog?"

I bit a hangnail. "He had a congenital heart defect and died. He deserved a better life."

"All that money wasted."

My head jerked up. "That money gave him a few weeks of relative comfort and happiness."

"What *else* could it have done? I'm careful with what I have. Your generation has expensive cars and oversized houses with unmanageable mortgages, credit card debt, and all the latest gadgets."

"Who the fuck are you lecturing? Because that's not me. Sometimes you act as if I'm about to shove you into a woodchipper for an inheritance, and other times you spout paternalistic hogwash," I said. "I expressed my desire to keep our biological connection private. You've damaged my mother's reputation, and she is a wonderful woman who didn't deserve that!"

"No one who met Jesse Whitney would blame your mother for stepping out on him. People here are more understanding and forgiving than you give them credit for, so don't use her reputation as an excuse to reject me." He gripped his knees, leaned forward, and was quiet for a minute. "If we spent time together when you were growing up, I might be able to figure you out."

"There's nothing to figure out. I'm very straightforward."

Abel laughed and said, "It's possible you believe that. Are you hungry?" He didn't wait for an answer. "Come on."

I followed him past a formal dining room to the kitchen, which was spotless and twice the size of ours, but just as dated. At least the wall clock was clock-shaped. A Formica table was set for two. "You cook?"

"I can make a few things, but Estrella, my housekeeper, cooks twice a week for me. There's nothing like Mexican home-cooking. It's what I grew up on."

"I never realized you were part Mexican until the DNA test. Okay, I'm a quarter Mexican, Latinx, Hispanic, whatever. I have no idea what it means."

"It means whatever you want it to mean. Of course, you must factor in how you experience the world based on people's assumptions about you. If I'd had my mother's last name, Fuentes, I would have been treated differently, especially the way I look. My father was blond with blue eyes. His parents emigrated from Norway to Duluth, and he found his way here." Abel took a skillet with a roast chicken and vegetables from the oven. "It has a chili rub, but I told Estrella not to make it too spicy."

He served thick slices of chicken with potatoes and tomatoes, and drizzled juices over the meat. "I'd offer you a beer, but I'm concerned about your drinking."

"I need to drink in order to be around you."

"I'm not exactly comfortable around you either." He took two bottles from the fridge, opened one, and poured beer into a glass for me before sitting across the table. He offered me a warm tortilla from a pile nestled in a kitchen towel, saying, "They're homemade."

"Thanks."

He rolled a tortilla and set it on the side of his plate, and then opened a jar of pickled jalapeños, and placed a few on his chicken, before holding the jar toward me.

"No thanks." I enjoyed a few bites of tender garlicky roasted potato.

"What are you thinking?"

"I'm thinking that we get along better when we don't talk."

"Hmm. You could be right."

We ate the rest of our meal in silence. He cleared the plates and brought out watermelon frozen pops specked with black seeds.

When I finished mine, I said, "Dinner was tasty. Please thank Estrella for me."

"Remember what I said: be careful around Oliver Desjardins. Don't fall into an illegal scheme you can't B.S. your way out of."

"Sure, and you should remember what I said about dogs."

"You didn't say anything about dogs."

"Didn't I? I think you should write an investigative piece about dog fighting in rural communities."

"I'm not getting caught up in your monomania."

"If that's how you feel, I'll see myself out," I said, and left the room. I didn't hear him following, so I opened doors to see a linen closet, a bathroom, and a study as neat and sparse as a monk's cell.

The study was small and relatively cool, with the sort of indestructible oak furniture you see in public libraries: a broad desk, file cabinets, and a credenza. A slight breeze shifted the closed curtains, and I opened them to let in enough light to read the books' spines. Abel had placed all the nonfiction in the largest case: political histories, biographies, and journalism. Rows and rows of identical notebooks filled another bookcase. The last one held a mix of hardcovers, but mostly paperbacks, several thin and old, and I turned my head to read the names: Asimov, Clark, Heinlein, Herbert, LeGuin...

I pulled *Foundation* from the shelf and flipped the cover to see a signature.

"It's not autographed to me," said Abel, making me start. "I found it at a garage sale."

"You like science fiction."

"The classics, primarily. I like to reread my favorites." He plucked the book from my hands and returned it to the case.

I scanned the books on the bottom shelf. "If I told you I had a Jules Verne tattoo, what would you think?"

"I think you'd never stay still long enough to get a tattoo."

"I said *if*—it's hypothetical. Would you think of a submarine or a hot air balloon?"

"I'd think of a roto-copter powered by electric batteries, or a solar sail."

"But what would most people think?"

"Something inaccurate based on a Hollywood movie, not text. Do you know that Verne conceived of tasers?"

"Yes, but I'm not going to hold that against him." I pointed to the shelves of notebooks. "Do you keep everything you scribble?"

"I have a storage room filled with notebooks. Memory isn't trustworthy."

"Maybe facts aren't facts. Perhaps we don't merely disagree; we've actually had different experiences."

"I'm not interested in nonsensical metaphysical discussions. Aren't you leaving?"

"Yes, and stop diverting my water."

"I legally hold those water rights."

"Some laws are merely arbitrary, but inherited water rights are downright egregious. Night, Abel."

On my short walk back, I mulled over my evening, especially Abel's twitches, his obsessive-compulsive behavior, blunt speech, and propensity for intruding on personal space.

When I arrived home, I once again tried writing to my mother.

Hours later, I had a pile of crumpled papers, so I abandoned that project. I wiped down my single whiteboard and brought two whiteboards from the closet. After reconstructing and updating my *Oliver* board, I began one headed *Abel Myklebust*. Just for the hell of it, I started a word cloud of his traits and behaviors.

When I was satisfied with my project, I took Bertie for a walk to the house, and Vixen followed, dashing back and forth, and, to her delight, Bertie played chase with her.

Kenzie wasn't home, so the dogs and I circled the fields. Water trickled in the creek bed now, and optimism sparked within me. If only all my problems might be resolved as easily as this one had. But when I went to my cottage and turned on the bedroom light, the filthy gnawed finger on my pillow only mocked my efforts.

Keeping my eyelids partially shut to limit my vision, I wrapped the finger in aluminum foil and buried it in my freezer behind ancient bags of frozen peas.

At our morning staff meeting, Jaison said, "I've got good news and bad news. The bad news is that you've been 'uninvited' from your presentation at the state's northern division of shelter trainers, so you've lost the honorarium. The good news is that you won't have to prepare for it or travel to it."

"I'm not crushed," I said. "How are next month's bookings?"

"We're still getting cancellations. So long as it's temporary, maybe it's a good thing because we all need some down time."

"In light of our reduced caseload, if anyone wants to use personal days or take unpaid time off, tell me."

An assistant said, "Maddie, are you sure there's going to be enough work later on?"

"I'm strongly inclined to think so. People may not like me personally, but they need help with their dogs."

"No one else can do what Maddie does," Jai said. "They'll be back."

"Thanks, Jaison," I said. "On the positive side, the creek's running again, so there may be enough water in the pond for an afternoon swim."

When the meeting was dismissed, I called Purlynn to me. Tan and healthy, she now resembled the pretty outdoorsy girl I'd seen in photos at her father's fishing cabin.

"Purlynn, I'm taking Fenster to his new owner today, so can you please give him a workout and a bath?"

"Yes, Boss. I'll be sad to see him go." Her phone pinged, and she checked the screen and set it on the table.

"Go ahead and answer."

"It's my father." Her face shifted expressions, and her voice was thick when she said, "I miss him."

"It must be wonderful to have a father you love. You probably heard that the neighbor is my biological father."

She nodded. "The newspaper publisher."

"Publisher is a big title for someone who puts out a tarted-up penny rag."

"Well, I like it. He always runs stories about Looper's classes and events, and I like the coupons."

I sighed. "I'm probably a little hard on Abel. I didn't learn he was my father until recently. It's different for you."

"My father's so wonderful. I love him," she said.

"Maybe he'll come back to your mom."

"No, he'll never come back." Her eyes welled, and she said, "Excuse me," and left the trailer.

She'd forgotten her phone, and I picked it up to return it to her. I tapped on the text beneath Gordon Looper's profile photo, and read, "Purly-girly, amazing fishing. There's always a room for you here. Come when you can. OX" There was a snapshot of rowboats on a white-sand beach and turquoise water, and I thought, he's living the Jimmy Buffett life that he and Dino dreamed about.

I set the phone on the table, went into my office, and sang, "*Just enjoy this ride on my trip around the sun...*" I understood the allure of leaving complications behind, but I didn't think it was possible. Simplicity wasn't simple; you had to continually fight entropy, the universe's inexorable drive toward disorder. You might as well stay where you were.

After delivering Fenster to Professor Gallego, I detoured to a few local tattoo studios. The closest one was a run-down stucco building near a tire store. The tattoo artist remembered inking a hot air balloon for a man who operated tourist balloon rides, so that was a bust.

The second studio was in an old bungalow, next to a café and beside a music shop. A bell over the front door tinkled when I pushed it open.

The burly tattoo artist gazed up from his work on a woman's calf. "No," he said. "Whatever you want, *hell, no*. Get the fuck out."

I smiled and tried to make eye contact. "I have one quick question."

"I remember you! You're the one who screamed and kicked and busted my nose!"

"I *already* apologized, and it wasn't entirely my fault. Your touch was too light."

"That's not a thing." He set down his needle. "Do I need to throw you out? Because I will. I still can't breathe right."

A few men came from the back to watch, and I said, "I don't want any work. Have you done any tattoos of hot air balloons, submarines, floating ships, the moon, or tasers?"

"Shit," a man said, "That's where I seen her! She's the 'Don't tase me,' barfing chick!" The men burst into laughter. "The cop hater." They playacted the scene and made oinking and barking sounds.

"I don't hate cops," I said. "Okay, I do hate one person who happens to be employed as a deputy. But that's neither here nor there. Have you done any of those tattoos?"

The burly artist lumbered toward me and kept moving forward, forcing me to back up right out of the salon.

I stood on the sidewalk and yelled, "So is that a 'no'?"

A loud creak and snickering caused me to look up, but I didn't move quickly enough to avoid the bucket of cold water dumped out a second-floor window. The day was hot enough to dry me off as I walked to Coyote Pups Preschool. Parents, clustered in front, stopped talking and gave me sideways glances, the human equivalent of the canine whale eye. I didn't wait for them to start fear-biting; I crossed the street and leaned against a wall.

A few minutes later, the lunch siren sounded, and children

surged out of the front doors, waving paper flags and paintings on thin newspaper. I walked in a tight circle, thinking, *Claire is putting away her supplies now, Claire is washing her hands now, Claire is picking up her backpack and saying goodbye to her cohorts now*... But I had to repeat the sequence repeatedly and, by the time she finally exited the building, only a few parents and children lingered.

Children ran to her, and she leaned over to better admire their artwork, her coppery waves falling forward. I felt both astonishment and pride that she had once chosen me.

I called, "Claire! Claire!"

She turned until she spotted me. I smiled and waved and forced myself not to rush to her. She stood still, her pale blue dress barely moving in the exhausted summer breeze, and then she crossed the street. "Hello, Maddie. Did you go swimming?"

I pushed my damp hair back. "Someone dumped water on me. Are you seeing Andie Kleinfeld?"

"I'm fine. Thanks for asking, and, yes, I've been keeping company with Andie."

"'Keeping company' makes it sound as if you go for buggy rides after supper, which is not the point. Abel Myklebust told me that Internal Affairs is coming down on Ollie. What has she told you?"

"Andie doesn't talk shop with me, and I'm not going to discuss Oliver with you now."

"Oh, that's rich, seeing that you couldn't stop talking about him when we were together even though you knew I didn't want to hear it."

"Be careful what you wish for...."

"Claire, I can endure waiting for Oliver. I can do that. But if he's in trouble, please tell me how I can help, what I can do." I tried to meet her eyes, but my focus flitted away to her green backpack, a bicycle locked to a post, the heat wavering up from the asphalt.

"Oh, Maddie." She wrapped her arms around me, drawing me tightly to her, and I ducked my head against her neck, inhaling her familiar citrus fragrance, and she said, "Leave him be."

I tried to hold on to her, but she pulled back and walked away, and I shouted, "Tell him, Claire. Tell him I'll help."

She didn't turn around, but that was all right because I knew she would pass along my message. Because, even when the twins didn't talk, they told each other everything.

Chapter Twenty-Five

AFTER A FEW DAYS without any public blowup, I decided that Abel had been overreacting about Oliver. The *Coyote Run Recorder*'s lead story was that Emily Ayer had received Dino's life insurance claim and already sold her property. The moment I read this, which happened to be a little before six in the morning, I pulled on my sneakers and hurried to the house, Vixen beside me.

We went up the stairs and found Kenzie sleeping prettily, on her side, the thin cotton blanket a mess around her. I straightened the blankets and was folding the top of the sheet as evenly as I could considering the circumstances, when she opened her eyes, and scrambled upright.

"Maddie, what the ef!"

"Your blankets were askew. I was fixing them. Did you hear about Emily? Did Ezra Brothers tell you? He must have. You should have told me!"

"I should clobber you. What time is it?"

As if in response, our rooster crowed, and I said, "It's late. He's been crowing for hours now. Get up and let's have coffee and chat."

"No, I'm comfortable. You come here."

I slid under the blanket and, after I'd arranged the pillows behind my back for a few minutes, Kenzie slapped my hands and said, "Stop that. I only found out about the insurance payment yesterday, and I was sworn to secrecy."

"There is a sister exemption in secrecy pacts. What's the scoop, poop?"

"The reason I've been spending so much time at Spirit Springs is that Ezra will be going away with Emily and the kids to help them move, and he wants me to help manage the Institutes' relocation to—and you will never believe this—the Lakeview Cabins Motel."

"Holy shit! He's going from a springs location that's nowhere near an actual spring to a lake view location that doesn't have a view of a lake."

"I knew you'd appreciate that. Coyote Runaway Brewing Company scored venture capital backing, and they're buying the Ayers' property at a rock-bottom price. They plan to put in a visitors center and a beer garden."

"That's better than selling to a corporate winery. But managing someone else's institute isn't the same as practicing therapy, Kenz." I wove my fingers with hers. "You're a wonderful therapist."

"I'm not giving it up, and this is only temporary. After the transition, which will take several months since the motel rooms have to be remodeled—"

"And thoroughly disinfected, ugh. I hope Ezra's going to pay you with more than a flash of muscley calf and a bouquet of wildflowers."

She laughed and punched my arm. "Oh, he absolutely tried to charm his way to paying less, but Beryl coached me to negotiate exactly what I wanted in terms of responsibilities and a compensation package. I can't believe I'm creating my dream job, and it's here in Coyote Run."

"That's fantastic, baby girl! Is Emily leaving for real, or only moving to Vineyard Garden Estates?"

"She doesn't want to stay without Dino, and she's rented a villa in someplace called Positano so the kids can learn Italian."

"*Only You* with Marisa Tomei and Robert Downey Jr. has scenes shot in Positano. I've seen that movie three times.

"You and your celebrity crushes. Your point is?"

"My point is that Positano is a fishing village. Dino's best friend Gordon Looper took a permanent fishing vacation, too," I said. "Do you think Emily and Gordon...? But Gordon left Coyote Run well before Dino's accident. Or maybe he never left."

"Have you ever met Gordon Looper? Because he's an ordinary middle-aged man who strongly resembles a baked potato."

"And that's bad because?" I said, trying to puzzle it out.

"Terrible example, because you love potatoes," she said. "The Ayer-Looper relationship was between the buddies."

"Gordon invited Purlynn to visit whenever she wants," I said. "If he was in cahoots with Emily..."

"If Gordon Looper was having a murderous affair, he wouldn't want his daughter dropping by. As exciting as it sounds, I doubt that Emily is a black widow, Ezra's a maniacal cult leader, and Weasel's a notorious crime boss."

"As if Weasel has that skill set." I looked at Vixen's hind quarters, visible as she rooted around Kenzie's closet. I hoped the pointer wouldn't spring out with a mouse and disrupt the sisterly moment. "Vixen, however, is capable of anything."

"You sound as if you admire her."

"I respect her as a force of nature." Pressing my palm against my sister's, I said, "Your hand is so small and ladylike, it's a wonder you managed to shovel shit for much of your life. Do you miss it?"

"There's some satisfaction in the brute physical labor. I want another horse, but not yet."

"Kenz, do you ever miss Dad?"

"Do you? He was your dad longer than he was mine."

"He never acted like a father to me. Now, I understand why."

"Sometimes I miss him for five minutes, and then it passes," she said. "He was apathetic and negligent, but not actively toxic. He and Raymond manage to have a relationship. Male bonding."

"Jerk bonding," I said. "It's so freaky being with Abel and suddenly recognizing a physical or behavioral similarity. I wonder if I've always recognized them subconsciously."

"Um, maybe. Maybe not. It's easy to see things we're seeking. Will you please get out so I can go back to sleep?"

I flipped the blanket over and swung my legs off the bed. "Kenzie, I miss Oliver so much it hurts. I miss him all day long, every day. I go to sleep missing him. I wake up missing him."

"Practice what you preach, Mad Girl. The pack heals. Go be with your pack."

The pack heals, and the dogs taught me to live in the now, to enjoy the simple act of running in the sunshine, resting in the shade, leaning against a companion and breathing the clean air. Now that Kenzie was contributing toward the bills, I tried not to worry about finances.

The loss of business was a guilty pleasure, and summer felt like summer: Staff took days off, we had barbecue lunches, and we started a group project, *Camp Canine Chronicles*, silly videos of the dogs solving mysteries. Our friends came over for drinks, relaxing in the balmy evenings, and they urged me to go out again, but too many people in town harbored animosity toward me.

Purlynn was a wonder, and, with her help, Jaison could take a long-overdue vacation to visit his brother's family in Las Vegas. I only fretted a bit and said, "You promise to come back?"

"I have no choice. You're holding Heidi hostage." He stroked the dog's broad back. "Take care of her while I'm gone."

"Of course, I will."

"I was talking to Heidi," Jai said. "But the other way works, too."

"Drive carefully. Call me if anything goes wrong. Call Ollie first. I'm sure he'll still answer your calls."

"Relax, Mom," Jai said. "Julie's spent the last week preparing for the drive. She bought a dashboard camera and has been watching way too much Court TV. Her favorite expression is 'I'd like to speak to your supervisor.'"

We laughed, and I hugged him for so long he had to pry himself away.

"Wait a minute!" I ran to the trailer and came back with a *Midnight Runners K-9 Search & Rescue* bumper sticker that I stuck to his dark blue Toyota Corolla. "Okay, you can go now."

Jaison waved as he drove away, and I was still staring at his car when Purlynn tapped on my shoulder and said, "Can you give me a few tips on bathing that Labradoodle? She rolled in chicken poop and refuses to go in the tub."

We practiced exercises, and I said, "She's not afraid of the grooming basin. She's nervous about the steps leading up to it. Get her outside of her head and following her nose, and you can encourage her to follow the scent of a snack up the stairs."

I watched as Purlynn lured the dog with a treat and then approached the stairs from a different direction. When the dog began to balk, she massaged the hind hips, urging movement, and the dog stepped forward onto the tub's platform. Purlynn lathered, rinsed, and dried the dog to a golden fluff.

"Well done. You have a natural instinct," I told her.

She smiled. "I can't believe I'm paid to do this. Thanks for taking a chance on me."

"I almost didn't. I was concerned about your drug use. Everything going okay now?"

Purlynn ducked her head. "I should have told you at the time, but I was in a state. Those bruises were from the 'Take a Needle, Get Needles' blood drive we did for the American Red Cross. Everyone who donated got knitting needles or a crochet hook. My veins are deep, and the phlebotomist stabbed me like a pincushion."

It sounded plausible, particularly since she used the word "phlebotomist," but I didn't care so long as Purlynn wasn't using anymore. "Hardwire told me how your Mom gives gift certificates to women in his aunt's diabetes support group."

"Type 1 runs in my family, and half the county has Type 2, so Mom does everything she can. Ask her what she thinks about health care in this country, and you'll get an earful."

"I'm all for extended rants," I said. "I'll say hi to your mom when I visit the store again. Zoe wants me to check out dog accessory prototypes she thinks will sell well."

"Low-cost, high-markup small items are Looper's bread and butter."

"There was a girl at Looper's retail counter who resembled someone I knew, but I didn't recognize her from town. Not that I can recognize people, but she stood out. Long black hair down to her hips, tats, kind of a rocker chick."

"You mean Beth. Why?"

"She went on about getting a puppy, but she didn't have the right set-up. People underestimate what a pain in the ass they are. Do you think she's responsible enough?"

Purlynn rubbed away a spot of dirt on her hand and didn't answer right away. "I don't know her well enough to make that call. She only helps when shipments arrive. The rest of the time, I think she parties with her boy—I mean her friends. She's popular."

My phone buzzed. Sasha's number was on the screen. "I've need to take this," I told Purlynn, and walked away. "Hey, sexy lady."

"Hey, hot legs!" she said. "How is everything?"

"That question is overarching and unanswerable. On a specific topic, business sucks, which gives me time to hang with friends. Come for drinks tonight? I will even serve you rosé."

"Oh, no, don't be like normal girls! Stay eternally my Maddie. That would be an excellent romance title, wouldn't it?"

"I couldn't say. I've only ever read one romance book because Georgie Maguire highly recommended it. It's called *Forever, Amber*, and it includes a harrowing and historically accurate description of the Black Plague. Do you realize that there have been bubonic plague cases every year in Western states?" I warmed to my subject. "We think of epidemics as medieval, but the Black Death was introduced to the States in nineteen-hundred, carried in on ships. Of course, the government denied it, because they were afraid the economy would tank. Can you imagine being so morally corrupt? You're always searching for your Big Crime Story, and inaction in the face of human devastation is criminal. Research the bubonic plague and the ways it could easily spread exponentially if it gets into cities."

"Ugh, no thanks. Maddie, you know all the footage of you I've been taping? I'm seeing the theme, and my manager thinks I'm onto something. It's not a Big Crime Story, and it needs editing, but I've never been so excited by a project. I'm double-checking to make sure you're okay with me sharing it."

"I can't imagine why anyone would want to listen to me blathering, but sure, as long as it helps improve human-canine relationships, go ahead," I said. "Seriously, Sasha, consider reporting on the Black Plague and pandemics. We escaped Ebola because it's an obvious, easily identifiable disease that kills quickly, but emerging viruses are fiendishly insidious. Maybe it's not a virus, but a firestorm, or an earthquake, but I feel in my bones that *something's* going to come, and I'm terrified we're not going to be ready."

"If we aren't, I'll bunker down in your cargo container house, and we'll survive on all that jam you've been hoarding."

Panic is a cold-weather emotion, goosebumps and nerves and tension, the desperate need for the nearness of things: firelight, bodies, companionship. Desolation is suited to the lassitude of summer, scorching days and stifling nights, pushing away blankets and sweating limbs and shuttering out the sunlight.

While Kenzie dove into her role at Spirit Springs, I tried to stave off the doldrums by spending every moment with the dogs. They expected me to fulfill my duties as one of the pack. Because they wouldn't enable my self-pity, I didn't presume to ask for it, especially from Bertie, who'd experienced unimaginable horrors.

It was easy enough to ignore the rest of the world and hide at the ranch. I ate eggs or cereal or whatever Kenzie might cook. I studied old shows and commercials and added a "Vintage Dog Actors" section to *Barking Mad Reviews*. I wrote dozens of versions of The Letter to my mother, all unsatisfactory.

On Friday, my team finished their chores early, and I sent them off and basked in the late afternoon's sunshine. Most of the dogs dozed in the shade, including Bertie, who sprawled under the picnic table. I closed my eyes and was drifting off when the atmosphere changed, and the dogs stood and turned their heads toward the drive, hearing what I couldn't.

I stood, too, and soon saw a patrol cruiser coming our way. Oliver! I raced out of the center, bashing my leg on the gate, in my hurry.

The setting sun mirrored the windshield, and I was already gripping the passenger side handle. I stumbled backward as Deputy Richard Kearney got out of the car.

"I haven't done anything," I said, cursing myself for closing the center's gate behind me, shutting myself from the dogs, who could protect me.

"Yeah, you have, Whitney. That's why I'm here to serve you a restraining order." He reached into his pocket and pulled out a folded envelope.

"What the fuck! I have stayed as far away from you as I can get!"

He laughed his ugly huh-huh laugh, holding the envelope toward me. "Read it and weep."

"This is bullshit. You have nothing on me!" I snatched the envelope, ripped it open, and unfolded the sheet inside.

"Not yet, but you've been harassing Sheriff's Captain Oliver Desjardins, and the court now prohibits you from contacting, stalking *and* sending messages, including electronic messages to Oliver Desjardins, to stay at least one-hundred yards away from his workplace, his home, *and* his vehicle, *and* from disturbing his peace. If you violate this restraining order, you can be sentenced to jail—again—pay a fine, or both."

My hand shook so much that the paper fluttered. Oliver had taken out a restraining order on me.

"See," Dickhead Kearney said, "even a dirty cop doesn't want you."

"Oliver's not a dirty cop. Get the hell off my property." My breathing was too fast and shallow, and my skin prickled all over.

"It is my fucking pleasure."

Kenzie found me sitting on the floor of the evaluation room holding Gizmo, Bertie's head resting on my ankles, and Vixen trying to nose her way under my arm.

"What are you doing here? Why haven't you answered my calls?" she said.

"Ollie issued a restraining order against me."

She reached out and pulled me up. "Put down Gizmo and come on," she said, and yanked me after her to my cottage and threw open the door. "What the hell, Maddie?"

I'd had to lean the sofa vertically upright to make space for all the whiteboards. The yellow and pink Post-its layering the walls like fringe fluttered in the draft.

"Have you ever used word cloud diagrams, Kenz? It's unclear how productive these will be ultimately, but I'm discovering unexpected associations. I feel as if I'm staring at a pattern, yet not recognizing it."

"What happened to your three reasonable goals?"

"Life is not reasonable. Put on your therapist hat: Abel Myklebust told me Oliver's being investigated by Internal Affairs because drugs from a bust went missing. He needs me to be ready to help at any moment."

"Because he stole drugs?"

"Ollie wouldn't steal evidence."

"He has a high-pressure job. It's so easy to take one step and then another and soon you're far from home."

"You're being uncharacteristically delicate about telling me that corruption is easy. Sure, it is for most people, but Ollie's not most people. He has Claire, and they have something akin to a Vulcan mind meld, *Star Trek* first-generation telepathy, which gives them superior emotional strength."

Kenzie twisted a strand of hair and sighed. "Sweetheart, I've known you every day of my life, but I still don't understand half the things you say."

"Exactly my point! Oliver and Claire have never spent a moment of their existences being misunderstood, or should I say 'un-understood'?"

"You can say whatever you like, but I'm not leaving you by yourself tonight. Wash up and put on a decent outfit, because we're going out to dinner."

"I can't. I am reviled and attacked everywhere I go. The village idiot."

"Nonsense. You're a hero here."

"Oliver's their hero, not me. I'm Tim Johnson until he's accused of having rabies, and he's lurching and twitching, and everyone hopes Atticus will shoot me in the street."

"I've told you a hundred times, *To Kill a Mockingbird* is not a tragedy about a dog. We're having a little going-away dinner for Ezra at Penelope's, so you'll be in a safe space. Beryl and Hardwire will be there, and Ezra said Purlynn is coming, too."

"Jaison is in Las Vegas, and I'm not in the mood."

"He always skips these things and, besides, he's coming back tomorrow, so you can damn well get in the mood." Kenzie stomped into my bedroom, and I was comforted by her familiar bashing around and huffing. She returned and shoved clothes in my arms. "Bathroom, shower, now."

Too dispirited to argue, I did as I was told, and when I came back, wearing a violet camisole with a denim skirt, the sofa was back in place, and all the whiteboards had been put away.

Kenzie pushed my hair back and smoothed down the sides. "I don't suppose I can get you to wear jewelry, but this is a start. Where's your TV makeup?"

"I don't have any. Sometimes Sasha smears hers on me."

"Liar."

Kenzie found the plastic case under my sink and made me sit while she dabbed and brushed crap on my face until I couldn't stand it anymore and said, "You'll paint me like a clown."

"A clown, an idiot, a mad dog, what do you care?"

She shoved me into her Subaru, and I slid down in the seat, hoping no one would see me.

Chapter Twenty-Six

WE WENT INTO the spacious hall that had once been the old restaurant's main room, decorated with ivory paper lanterns and strings of white lights. Long tables, dressed in white linens and dahlia-filled vases, had been pushed end-on-end so everyone could sit together.

Penelope greeted us and said, "It's only leftovers from a wedding brunch. I hope you don't mind."

"Pen, we live for your leftovers," Kenzie said.

Penelope took my hands in hers. "I'm so sorry about Beau. I hope you're okay."

"Maddie's in a funk," Kenzie said. "I brought her here hoping she'll eat her way out of it."

"Or drink my way out," I said, "Excuse me." I went to the bar, nabbed a bottle of beer from a bucket of ice, and ducked into the alcove where wine crates were stored. I sat atop them in the shadows and thought of the last time Oliver had called me and the sound of his laughter.

The light flickered, and I saw Ezra Brothers standing in front of me, wearing a butter-yellow silk chiffon ruffled shirt, half-unbuttoned over a smooth tan chest, and indigo jeans, sexy as hell. When he brushed back his long brown waves, gold chandelier earrings twinkled.

"Ezra, you're the most glam person ever to grace our humble village."

"That's a pity. Next, you'll tell me no one in Coyote Run owns a sequined gown. You look fabulous for someone hiding under the stairs."

"It's my costume. I'm passing as a normal human being."

"Kenzie said you were upset. Are you going to stay here all night?"

"Yes."

"I'll be right back."

He left and returned with a plate of food and another beer. "Come out when you want."

I ate by myself and listened to the bustle and clatter from the kitchen and the laughter and conversation from the main hall. I recognized my friends' individual voices but couldn't think how to join them without being obvious.

About thirty minutes later, Ezra came by with peach crumble and a glass of brandy. "Do you want to share anything? Why are you so blue?"

I drank half the brandy before I said, "Have you ever believed in something, *someone*, and everyone else tells you you're wrong? I've been appallingly wrong before. I exercise bad judgment on a daily basis."

"Kenzie told me your relationship with the sheriff ended."

"That's what everyone thinks. I believe as much as I believe anything that my love for him is returned. I feel as if he's sailed away on a perilous voyage and asked me to wait, and every day I stand on the cliffs and watch for his ship, and all my friends think that he's either settled in a foreign port, or drowned. They pity delusional Maddie."

"But you're still on the cliff, watching the horizon."

"Yes, and I can stay here forever, so long as I trust."

"Is there a possibility you're wrong? Or that a temporary break became permanent?"

My cheek kept twitching upward, so I pressed my fingers against it. Down the street sirens wailed and grew louder as they swooshed past the building. When the sirens faded, I said, "Look at me, Ezra. I know what it is to be rejected, and I've needed to work hard to get anyone interested in me beyond a novelty fuck. I admit going too far chasing my ex, Claire, but I was acutely aware that she'd already moved on. This is different." I stood quickly, bumped my head against the angled ceiling. "This is different."

Pushing past Ezra, I went through the kitchen and back door, out to the courtyard.

Kenzie might stay another hour at dinner, so I wandered around downtown, avoiding the sheriff's substation and keeping to the shadows. I wanted another drink but didn't have any cash. The lights were on at Coyote Run Veterinary Clinic, and I was about to knock on the door when I recognized Emily Ayer's car in the side lot. I guessed she was having a goodbye party, too.

My next stop was the Country Squire, packed with diners and drinkers. Peering through the plate glass, I saw Abel at his regular barstool. I took a deep breath, opened the door, and crossed the room exactly like I'd instructed dog-phobic people to cross my center.

Abel's leather-covered journal was open on the bar, and he drank from a cut-glass tumbler while talking on the phone. "Is he dead? Okay, since you're already there, you take care of it, but I only need a two hundred words. Get it to me by eleven, and I'll run it tomorrow. Thanks." He scribbled a few notes and closed his journal.

"Hey, Abel. The usual start to the weekend?"

"Hot summer nights," he said, and used a cocktail napkin to

dab his brow. "Court records show a restraining order filed against you. You can thank me for not reporting it."

"I can thank you for lending me ten bucks." I held out my hand. "A loan. I'll pay you back."

"Why do you need ten bucks?"

"I'm inordinately thirsty and would like to buy organic, freshly squeezed orange juice at the market."

"They serve orange juice here."

I made the mistake of turning around. Everyone was staring at me, and one woman was pointing. "I'm blacklisted in every public venue. If you don't mind..."

Abel took out his wallet and handed me a crisp twenty. "Don't get falling down drunk and causing mayhem."

"Geez, Abel, it kills me thinking of all the sensitive fatherly advice I've missed out on over the years. See you." I left before he could respond, but not fast enough to avoid a thirty-something man in a red polo shirt, who sneered, "Cop hater!" as I walked by.

I headed toward the market, calculating my purchases. I could buy beef shanks for Bertie, and beer for myself. It took a minute for me to become notice the *clack, clack, clack* of footsteps behind me. I glanced back and saw the man who'd sneered, his leather dress shoes slapping down on the sidewalk.

Locals crowded in front of Rudy's Brewhouse, and I began trotting there, hearing the footsteps quicken and grow louder.

"If it isn't Mad Dog Whitney," a geezer said, and the others *har-harred.*

I stopped, pointed to the man following me, and said, "This cabernet-drinking, let-me-smell-the-cork *tourist* asshole is harassing me!"

"That's not—" the man began and stepped back.

Grizzled, ropy Rudy himself came forward, and frowned. "What's the problem, Maddie?"

"That tourist hit on me by the Country Squire. I turned him

down and said I always preferred an honest beer here, and he said only inbred rural yahoos like beer."

"That is a goddamn lie!" the man said. "She's the cop-hater. She hates America."

"He hates beer!" I screamed, and Rudy growled, "We got a rule here. No fucking politics," and pointed to the *Politics Free Zone* placard stapled by the front door.

I sidled away as Rudy and the old coots glommed around Polo Shirt. I sped down a side street and made a left, looking behind me every few seconds. As I approached an intersection, I heard loud voices and the crackle of radios. Down a cross-street, patrol cars, a fire engine, and an ambulance flashed red lights in front of a laundromat. People were gathering to watch, and some spoke loudly about a stabbing.

Bystanders moved to let a gurney roll into the laundromat, revealing the interior scene of crimson splattered across white washing machines. Richard Kearney and another deputy crouched over a body on the floor, and Oliver stood beside a sobbing older man. Oliver placed his hand on the man's shoulder and hung his head close as he spoke to him, the way I'd seen him do so often with distraught people in terrible situations.

And although I couldn't guess at what he was saying, I knew it would be exactly the right words for this man at this time, or maybe the words were irrelevant. Maybe Oliver's rough and warm voice and steady body were enough to provide comfort.

Then the crowd closed, blocking out my view of the laundromat's interior.

I crept closer, staying in the darkness, desperate for another glimpse of Ollie. Minutes later, EMTs pushed the gurney, now carrying a black plastic body bag, to the ambulance, and I had a flashing strobe stop-motion movie of Oliver catching the older man as he collapsed. Another flash revealed Oliver enveloping the grieving man in his arms.

When the crowd closed like a curtain on the scene, I knew I'd glimpsed a ship on the horizon. My heart soared with admiration for Oliver Desjardins, who always was and always would be *my* sheriff.

I returned to Penelope's Catering. Ezra and his crew had left, and others were drinking tea and coffee. Kenzie was deep in conversation with Beryl on a loveseat. I squeezed in beside my sister, whose small body generated warmth, and rested my head on her shoulder.

"Why are you shivering when it's so hot? Where have you been, and what have you been doing, Maddie?"

"No reason, nowhere and nothing. I love you."

She slid her arm around my waist, pulling me close, and turned back to Beryl.

Chapter Twenty-Seven

KENZIE AND I had returned home after midnight, and I'd spent another two hours reconstructing my whiteboards, so I wasn't ready to get up at 5:00 a.m. when the dogs began barking. I listened, but Bertie's sonorous woof wasn't among them, indicating that he recognized an individual or a vehicle. Perhaps an assistant was coming in early.

Vixen, who'd insinuated her head on my pillow, stepped all over my face as she climbed out the window over my bed. I didn't think she'd bite anyone, so I closed my eyes and waited. Soon I heard a car's tires crunching on the gravel outside.

The dogs calmed down, and I was drifting off to sleep when someone pounded on my front door.

I threw off my sheet and fumbled forward. "What the fuck!" I said, flinging open the door.

Claire, wide-eyed, her hair unbrushed, eye makeup smeared over one cheek, stood there, so pale, her skin almost translucent.

"Maddie. It's Oliver."

I tried to unscramble my hazy thoughts. "I didn't violate the restraining order. I only saw him by accident, I swear. I kept my distance."

She grabbed my hand in her cold ones. "I still don't know what's going on. He's been suspended from duty and charged with stealing evidence."

"That can't be—he was on duty downtown!"

"He called me at three and asked me to bring Zeus to you. I put him in a kennel."

I felt numb all over and stood motionless, because something was very, very wrong for Oliver to send Zeus away. "Tell me everything. I'll make coffee."

Claire barely registered the whiteboards as we went to the small dining table.

"I only have instant here. There's real stuff in the trailer."

"It doesn't matter."

I put the kettle on. "Where's Ollie now?"

She paced the length of the small room. "At Jim's office, trying to find a criminal lawyer with the right experience. Jim expects that Ollie will be arrested soon, and we'll have to make bail. We're waiting for a decent hour before we break the news to my parents. They'll be devastated."

"Abel Myklebust told me about evidence tampering in a drug bust. Does this have anything to do with it?"

"Maybe. He hasn't been charged yet, so we don't have details. Last night someone made an anonymous call when Ollie was on his way home after a drink."

"From the Bermuda Triangle?"

"Yes. The caller said he had guns and drugs. The dispatcher thought it was bullshit call and sent a cadet to intercept him. Oliver didn't take it seriously either and allowed a car search. The cadet found two handguns with serial numbers filed off and a few grams of meth in the spare tire well. He cleans the cruiser regularly, so they were planted recently."

"It could have been at the substation or at the Bermuda Triangle, or even when he was otherwise occupied...by a girl, for example." I scooped instant coffee into mugs and filled them with boiling water. "What does Andie Kleinfeld have to say?"

"Only that she can't discuss it." Claire sat, crossed her arms tight over her chest, and began rocking back and forth. Then she raised her green-gold eyes to mine, tears welling. "Maddie, I know how you dig for information—like those obsessive charts on easels. Have you found out anything that we could use?"

"Claire, he asked me to wait, so that's what I was doing. I assumed he was trying to convince someone that he was a dirty cop."

"He was working with Andie, not that either said so directly. I've never seen him as upset with anything as he was with the fentanyl overdoses. Usually the hard stuff comes from outside, but Oliver said fentanyl was being distributed locally. He didn't know who was distributing it because no street dealers would flip on the level up."

"Because the street dealers were more afraid of their sources than doing time. Nature abhors a vacuum, and when the cartels left after the fire on Mt. Hale, locals had room to expand operations. What about the girl? The one with Ollie in the photos?"

"He hoped she'd be his ticket in, but she was wary, and her place was probably a front, clean of any personal information."

"Where's the room? What's her name?" I said.

"He wouldn't say. I was sure you'd have a dossier on her by now."

"Believe it or not, Claire, I've been making a conscious effort not to obsess."

She laughed, spitting out her coffee, and began coughing. I reached over and patted her back, saying, "Was that funny?"

She was still coughing and laughing when she began crying.

After giving her water, I fetched a roll of toilet paper so she could wipe her eyes and blow her nose.

"Caring for Zeus means the world to Oliver. You can do something for our family, though. Ask Abel to hold off running any stories about this."

"We don't connect, but I'll do my damnedest."

"Thanks, babe."

The endearment threw me back, and yet this was a different type of intimacy. "Can I talk to Ollie? Can I see him?"

Shaking her head, Claire said, "That's why he got the restraining order. He wants to be sure you stay safe until all this is over. I've got to go to my parents' now. Everyone will be there."

When we went through the living room, she paused at the whiteboards. "I'd call this pretty obsessive for someone making a 'conscious effort' not to obsess."

"I suppose it does, Claire, but I've been hoping things will eventually come into focus.

"Maybe it's like a pointillist painting, and you need to step far enough away to see the pattern."

After Claire left, I considered waking Kenzie and updating her, but I knew she'd insist that I wait, and waiting any longer was unendurable. I carried a whiteboard back to my office in the trailer, wiped away my notes about Dino and Emily Ayer, and wrote *Who's the Girl?* across the top.

By 7:30 a.m., when Purlynn arrived, I'd already fed the dogs, hosed down the kennels, and made coffee. I introduced her to Zeus, and she said, "Isn't this Sheriff Oliver's dog?"

"Yes, and he's an awesome guy. Study up on German commands, because he's had Schutzhund training. We're boarding him for a while. I'm working on a project, so don't let anyone disturb me unless it's *absolutely* dire. Thank heavens Jaison will be back this afternoon."

I canceled the few appointments on my calendar and then called Abel. "Abel, I have a favor to ask. Oliver's been suspended."

"Talk to me."

After I relayed only the essentials, he said, "I get the distinct feeling that you're not telling me everything. Why would anyone plant drugs and guns on the sheriff? Isn't it much more likely that he finally got caught?"

"Not at all. The Desjardins family is trying to figure out what's going on, so please hold off on reporting the story."

"I can't do that."

"It's your paper. You can do whatever the hell you like."

"Okay, I *won't* do that. It's an important story."

"How can I change your mind?" When he didn't answer, I said. "How can I change your mind, Dad?"

"Don't call me that, Maddie. It sounds bizarre."

"It's even freakier saying it. How about this? I will trade you a juicier story if you delay reporting Ollie's incident."

"What's the story?"

"You have to agree first."

He made sharp clicking sounds before saying, "You're asking me to put a lot of trust in you, but you've never given me a reason to trust you."

"Okay, I'll sweeten the pot. In the meanwhile, feel free to write an article on the restraining order against me and how I've been kicked off the Midnight Runners because of my hostility to law enforcement and my history of arrests. Mention that I have not returned department equipment as legally required. I have repeatedly stolen valuable dogs, one of which I sold for hundreds of dollars. Mike and Cody at Coyote Runaway Brewery will give you a quote. On my last search for Dino Ayer, I broke into a cabin and pilfered snacks. I tricked my biological father into paying thousands to treat an injured dog with serious preexisting conditions. Most of my clients have dropped me, and my canine training feature with Sasha Seabrook is cancelled. That should provide several columns of filler."

"For something to be news, it must be new, and everyone already knows about you. Gossip is not on par with Desjardins' suspension."

"Maybe not, but Oliver and his family have never faced social hatred. Write about me instead. Please, Abel, I'll never ask you for another thing."

"'Never' is a long time, Maddie, but for you, I'll hold off on the suspension story for as long as I can."

If things could be lost in the Bermuda Triangle, things could be found in the Bermuda Triangle. I started with the low-res photo on their website. Despite the darkness, the girl's blue eyes were as bright as a Siberian Husky's. Using an online makeover generator, I changed her hair color to black and replaced her short waves with a long, straight fall. If I had been better at identifying faces, I would have recognized her when we met at the Crafty Looper.

When I realized Purlynn must have known about Ollie and Beth even as she was smiling and thanking me for giving her a chance, I felt a sensation like nails dragging over a chalkboard. I didn't trust her enough to ask her about Beth, so I called my girl on the inside.

"Zoe, it's Maddie. Do you have a minute?"

"For you, always. What's up?"

"Remember how we were talking about the part-timer with the long hair, Beth? I need personal info about her. Full name, address, date of birth. Her Social Security number would be helpful."

"She'll be in this afternoon. I'll pass the message onto her."

"No, don't tell her. I'm doing a little research."

"Oh! Is it about a puppy?"

"Yes, it's a background check for an adoption," I began, ready to spin a story. But she was my friend, and I loved her. "No, Zoe, it's not really about a puppy. Something else is going on in my life, and Beth is connected to it, but I can't ask her, or anyone else, because it's confidential. I don't want you to get in trouble with Mrs. Looper, and I understand if you can't do it."

"You wouldn't ask unless you had a good reason," she said. "Give me a sec."

I heard a computer's faint buzz and beep.

"Okay, her full name is Beth Lee Hale. Lee with two e's. I'll set off a flag if I access her SSI, but she's on the list for September birthday parties if that helps. She lives on Elshire," Zoe said, and I already knew the address would match the crash pad where I'd found Purlynn.

After I copied down Beth's phone numbers, I said, "Do you have a photo or two?

"She avoids cameras. I know because I've tried to include her in promo videos. If you change your mind about talking to her, she'll be here from eleven till four today."

"Thanks, sweetie. You're my favorite teenager."

"I know! Bye, Boss Bitch!"

It was easy enough to find Beth with a basic search. Her social networks showed a blurry old pre-long-hair photo and random photos of crafting projects, knit hats in animal shapes. She said she was in a relationship, and her friends were primarily crafters. She was from Capitola, her favorite color was peach, she was dairy free, and her favorite movie was *Mama Mia.* All of which seemed flagrantly bogus, a Potemkin Village identity, so I searched Capitola school records and couldn't find a trace of any Beth Hale.

An out-of-state company owned the Elshire crash pad. I left a message with the management company that I was conducting a credit check, but I didn't expect a return call. Over the next several hours, I hunkered down and combed the web for variations of "Elizabeth Lee Hale" within the county and then extended the search. I eliminated women who were too young, too old, or had the wrong birthday months.

Then, bingo, I located an Eliza-Bess Lee Hayle, the right age and birthday month in Hollister, who listed Capitola as a place she'd lived. But this Eliza-Beth was a devoted homeschooling mother who lived in a cozy suburb, and Hayle was her married name. Photos showed a sandy blond woman who bore a faint resemblance to Beth Hale before her hair extensions, and I'd put money down that doppelganger Beth was using a stolen identity and Social Security number.

I was contemplating my next move when the dogs went nuts, barking and yowling in greeting. I went outside to see Jaison coming through the gate, beat and rumpled from the long drive.

"You're back, you're back!" I threw my arms around him.

He laughed and said, "It's not like I was off to war."

"Did you have fun?"

"I had a great time. But I missed my girl," he said, and bent over to hug Heidi.

"There are donuts, and Zeus is visiting, and all sorts of crap is happening, but you don't have to hear about it now. I'm having a crisis. Can you manage things for the rest of the day?"

"Absolutely."

At 3:30 p.m., I went to the center and said to Jaison, "I'm going to be gone for the evening. Bertie can bunk down with Zeus."

"You're decked out for search and rescue."

"Nothing so exciting. I'm doing a little surveillance." As I spoke, Vixen was on the picnic table, swatting Zeus on the head with her paw. "I may as well take Danger Girl. May I borrow your Corolla? I need something generic and anonymous."

He wriggled a single key off his key ring and handed it to me. "Surveilling or stalking?"

“As Zoe says, po-tay-to, po-tah-to.”

Surveillance requires subterfuge, and I might need to pass as being on the way to or from a search. I transferred my gear and snacks from my backpack to a saddle harness that I buckled on Vixen. As backup, I stopped at the house and collected Kenzie’s blond wig and oversized designer sunglasses.

Chapter Twenty-Eight

I WAS PARKED down the street from the Crafty Looper when Beth walked out at 4:00 p.m., carrying a small bag with colorful skeins of yarn visible. A specific anguish encompassed me—a solitary, three-in-the-morning, the-rest-of-the-world-sleeps pain, sharp and hard and desolate, *I am alone, I am alone.*

She walked to an older-model black Chevrolet Malibu, and I trailed her, pulling over and parking when she turned into a gas station.

She was in and out in five minutes before stopping at a hardware store. After thirty minutes, I was about to follow her inside when she returned to her car with a large plastic bag.

She drove out Coyote Run, passing Curtis's Liquors, and heading toward Elshire, when she detoured to a side street with rundown shops. She parked in front of a storefront with a sign that said *Tendrils Salon*. Now I'd be stuck waiting for hours.

I was already sinking into the seat when I noticed that she carried the Looper's bag with her into the salon. I needed to get closer to see what was happening, but I didn't want to be recognized. I removed my T-shirt, leaving a tank top on, tugged on the hot itchy blond wig, and slid on the sunglasses before getting out of the car. I pretended to read the posters on the window of the café next door, while peeking into Tendrils.

Beth was talking to a woman in her early 30s with a smooth fall of dark brown hair and a blue twill apron over a t-shirt and jeans. They went to the back of the shop. I tried to act nonchalant and pretended to make a phone call when they came from the back to stand by the reception desk. The stylist had taken off her apron and wore a leather messenger bag.

I was about to hurry to Jaison's car when the stylist pulled her hair up, securing it with an alligator clip and revealing an elaborate tattoo on her neck.

I didn't move except to twist my phone enough to snap a photo of the woman, and then I returned to the Corolla. I enlarged the photo enough to make out the ship's masts and a Jolly Roger flag on the tattoo. I called the CPA who'd given her dog away. The phone rang and kept ringing. I hung up and called again.

"Offices of Heather Porter. May I help you?"

"Hello, this is Dr. Madeleine Whitney," I said, reaching to pet Vixen for comfort. "I have one quick question. You described the woman who took your dog as having a Jules Verne tattoo. Did you mean a pirate ship?"

"That's what I said. Jules Verne, like in *Pirates of the Caribbean.*"

"*Pirates of the Caribbean* is a Disney ride and movie. I think you mean *Treasure Island.* Robert Louis Stevenson wrote *Treasure Island.*" My phone beeped a low-battery warning, and I said, "But thanks!" and ended the call.

So Beth, who wanted a puppy and spent evenings with the doppelganger, was friends with the dog-killers. My temperature rose, and my heart thudded. I wanted to rush into the salon and throw her against the wall and scream as I kicked and hit her. I wanted her to feel a measure of pain that she inflicted on vulnerable creatures. *Breathe, just breathe*, I told myself.

My hands jittered so much that keying the salon address into my phone took numerous attempts before I pulled up their website. The "Meet Our Staff" page listed her as Evangeline.

Ten minutes later, the women left the salon. Beth carried the Looper's bag. She stopped by a trash bin while Evangeline looked up and down the sidewalk. An older couple was walking toward them. When the older couple turned into the café, Beth reached into the Looper's bag, took a small cardboard box, handed it to Evangeline, and dropped the Looper's bag with yarn in the trash.

Pieces of the puzzle came together.

I started my engine and watched as both women got in a nondescript silver-gray Ford Escape, the SUV that Heather Porter had seen. I snapped a photo of the license plate and then followed the Ford and kept my distance as Evangeline made aimless turns. "They're being careful or they're paranoid," I told Vixen, who was trying to chew off her harness. "Stop that."

Once again, my phone beeped a low battery warning. I fumbled in the glove compartment but couldn't find a charger.

Evangeline took a road bordered by grazing pastures before veering onto a minor artery leading to the highway. After almost ten miles, she turned onto another artery road that ran east through dense woodland.

She exited the highway, and I slowed, following as far back as I could. I lost the SUV somewhere on a steep hillside thick with pines, buckeyes, and evergreen brush. I retraced the route several times before I saw a narrow asphalt-paved lane and a sliver of gray catching the evening light. I pulled over into the shrubs.

No houses or structures were visible. My phone didn't show aerial maps or addresses for this location. It was a place to hide. My phone thought so, too, because it gave one last forlorn beep and the battery died. I put the phone inside the saddle bag.

Vixen's floppy velvet ears lifted, and she turned her head. I rolled down the windows and listened. Then I heard it too: barking somewhere in the distance.

"Okay," I told her, "I hoped I'd never say this, but I may need your help." I waited for over five minutes, listening for any human sounds before exiting the Corolla.

We walked to Evangeline's SUV, which was locked. The interior was clean and empty. Vixen sniffed at the door handle without much interest and turned to a pile of deer scat. "You're my cover, so come on."

I kept to the side of the narrow lane, stopping every ten yards to listen. Vixen listened, too, and when she heard a critter rustling in dry leaves, she froze in a point and then stalked toward the sounds. "Vixen, come!" I hissed, cursing myself for not putting her on a leash.

I crept forward again, calling low, "Vixen, Vixen!" Around a bend in the lane, a two-story brown shingle lodge came into view. Gleaming pickups, a Hummer, ATVs, and motorcycles were out front. A tall chain-link fence surrounded the house.

Unseen dogs began barking an alarm, my signal to get the hell away from here now. I called one last time, louder and anxious, "Vixen! Dammit!" I'd wait for her at the car, because she always knew how to find me. I took two steps backward and bumped into something that pressed hard on the base of my neck.

A man said, "Whatcha doin' round here, girlie?"

In my experience, the best answer to a difficult question is anything that will throw off the questioner. "Honey!" I said and turned around, smiling. It took all my will to continue smiling, even though fear began trickling through my blood like an IV drip. "Oh, I thought you were my boyfriend."

The brown-haired, brown-eyed man looked the way young men do: jeans, a black t-shirt, boots, a scruff of beard. Average height, on the thin side, and his complexion was pale with an unhealthy sheen, like lard. He wasn't handsome, and he wasn't ugly, and I would have forgotten his face in five minutes if I hadn't already seen him dozens of times in front of the Bermuda Triangle.

He tilted his chin upward. "Your hair's crooked."

I shifted the wig. "This thing is itching the hell out of me. Do you mind?" I pulled it off and held it like a dead skunk, with two fingers.

"Ah, hell, no. Who butchered that mess? Put the wig back on." His voice was incongruously soft.

I pulled the wig on, wriggling the sides until it seemed even. "Do you mind lowering your gun? I'm not exactly a threat to you. Is Oliver here? If not, maybe he's at the Bermuda Triangle, or at a friend's. I don't think he has softball today."

The man dropped his gun to his side. "Why didya think you'd find him here? No one's here. Nothing's here."

"This girl, a real vixen," I said, thinking *breathe, just breathe*. "She calls herself Beth. It's temporary. It'll blow over. These misunderstandings happen in relationships."

"We better go on up to the house. Give me your phone and your keys."

I pulled Jai's car key from my pocket. "My phone broke, and I haven't had the money to buy a replacement yet. I don't want Oliver to see me this way. I can't have another violation on the restraining order."

"Get going." He waved the gun.

As we approached the house, the dogs' barking grew frenetic, and the man shouted, "Shuddup!" and the dogs went silent.

"Well-trained," I said.

"Damn well better be," he said, and I knew the dogs obeyed him out of fear, not love.

Dirty boots, chain dog leashes, and teak wooden chairs were on the porch. "Stay back," the man said. He opened the door to an open-space living room, and a massive black pitbull with a snowy white blaze, cropped ears, a studded leather collar and scarred fur came forward with a low growl, his legs stiff, and a curl to his lips.

"No," the man said, "back it up, asshole."

The dog did as ordered, but his eyes remained fixed on me.

We stepped into a room steeped in a deep funk of drugs, sweat, gun oil, and sex. Stag-horn chandeliers hung from the beamed ceilings. The only natural light peeked through squares strategically cut out of the closed Venetian blinds.

The dog retreated to a place by a leather armchair, matching oversized furniture in the open-concept layout, with a staircase at the right. The far side of the room had a pool table, pinball machines, and a dart board.

A man was sprawled on a sectional in front of a huge flatscreen, while another wore headphones and played a video game.

An enormous marble island dominated the kitchen, which had a glass-front refrigerator, and a six-burner range. Handguns and semi-automatics were visible everywhere: on a dining table long enough to seat twelve, the kitchen counter, the bar top, and, of course, the gun rack.

Digital scales, glass pipes, hookahs, mirrors, and razor blades were scattered on every surface, and my shoulders jerked hard when I glimpsed wooden break sticks, used to pry open a fighting dog's jaws, by doors. Amateurishly printed dog-fighting magazines were stacked on an ottoman.

"What's your dog's name?" I asked, keeping me voice even.

"What's *your* name?" the man said.

Evangeline stumbled into the room, her lids drooping over her eyes, and collapsed on the L-side of the sectional, rocking a little back and forth, a line of spittle running from her lips, and Beth followed, holding a cocktail.

"So, Odie was telling the truth," Beth said, with a laugh, and I thought *Odie, Oliver Desjardins*. Beth nodded at the man with the gun and said, "This is the crazy bitch stalking the sheriff. Maddie, meet Josh. Josh, meet Maddie Whitney."

"Wanting my man back doesn't make me crazy." I sat on the

sofa, studiously ignoring the pitbull, who continued to be wary. And I was grateful for his presence, his dogness, among these monsters. "May I have a drink?"

"This isn't a fucking resort," Josh said. "Whitney? I heard that name."

Beth said, "Seven-and-Seven okay?"

"Sure, or a brewski."

She went to the bar and pulled a beer from the mini-fridge and brought it to me. "What's with the wig?"

"Remember how you told me you like to change things up? When we first met, I didn't recognize you from that photo of you and Ollie at the Bermuda Triangle because your hair was so different." I spoke evenly, as if I hadn't agonized over her relationship with Oliver. The pitbull edged toward me. I dropped my hand and felt his damp nose against it. He must be the favorite to have earned house privileges. "I thought maybe Ollie would like me better as a blonde."

Beth's laugh was a mean metallic thing. "Take the clue. He's over you."

"Maybe. Maybe not." I scratched the dog under the chin and then moved my hand to the back of his neck, gripping and relaxing the scruff the way a bitch grips her pup, and listened to his contented growl, and I wanted to weep for the cruelty this dog must have endured as well as the brutality he must have inflicted on others.

"So, let me get this straight," Josh said. "You're Maddie Whitney, and you followed Beth here because you think she's messing with the sheriff?"

"That's about the sum of it." To muddy the waters further, I said, "To be fair, Beth isn't the only one. Every woman in Coyote Run is after Oliver, and some of those bitches are elusive. Keeping track of them is a full-time job. Not that I'm jealous. I understand that a man doesn't want the same meal every night."

"You got that right," Josh said, sitting in an armchair. "Why are you so nervous? Cuz you keep twitchin' and jerking and shit."

"This is how I am. My internal wiring is fucked up. I have issues." I regretted never sending my mother the promised letter because I knew now what I wanted to say to her. I splayed my fingers across the pitbull's back; my hand was steady.

"What do you think about Red Meat Monster?" Josh asked. "He comes from UKC championship bloodlines."

"We call him Meathead," Beth said. "Josh, Maddie's that dog lady, the one who tracks down lost grandmas, but she didn't think I was good enough to have a dog."

"Sorry if it came off that way, Beth, but you told me what your boyfriend said about responsibility, and I didn't want to cause an argument. I didn't even know you were referring to Oliver, or..." Had she stared into Oliver's eyes when they were tucked into dark corners? Had she laughed at his corny jokes and touched him gently? "Anyway, I'm actually in the dog boarding business, not selling or adopting them out. I kennel pets while the owners take vacations or travel."

"Huh," Beth said. "I looked you up, and you were calling yourself a pet psychic."

"I did that for a while. It was a neat little trick until it wasn't." I finished the beer and stood slowly, my posture straight, shoulders back, and head up, establishing my place as an alpha with the dog. "Anyway, I apologize for disturbing you. A pleasure meeting you, Josh. Beth, I guess I'll see you at Looper's."

"Oh, fuck! *Oink, oink!*" Josh said and slapped his thigh. "Now I remember. Maddie Whitney, the girl who blew chunks all over the deputy. That was hilarious. Any connection to Raymond Whitney?"

I hesitated, and Josh said, "Yeah, you are. What is he, your ex?"

"Hell, no. He's my brother."

Josh let out a skeptical *tss*. "No, he's not. You look like a Mexican."

For the first time in my life, I felt a frisson of racial fear. "Different fathers."

"Yeah, well, me and Raymond did business together before that drunk asshole took off with a bundle of the cartel's cash. How's he doing?"

"No idea. We don't keep in touch. He's always been a tumbleweed."

"He was bragging on your family's dog business. You party hard like your bro?"

"Not lately. My legal aid guy instructed me to stay close to home, especially nights because of the assault charge and now the restraining order, both of which are bullshit, but irregardless, I have to be on the down low. I better get going."

"You talk a lot," Josh said, gesturing with the gun. "And all I hear is blah, blah, excuse. Park your ass and have a real drink."

I wasn't sure if I'd established my bona fides, but I didn't have a choice. I sat, and Beth upended a bottle of Crystal Head vodka in a glass pitcher, splashed in vermouth and ice cubes, stirred and then strained the martinis into tumblers with twists of lemon peel.

If I concentrated on each moment, I could function. The drink was smooth and icy, and the tumbler had a satisfying balance of weight and clarity. "This is a beautiful glass."

"Better be for what it cost. Baccarat," Beth said.

"Evangeline's a snob," Josh scoffed, and told me, "She's the one with the taste. Picked out everything. Only the primo shit for this lady."

The snob's eyes were closed, and her chest rose and fell with raggedy breaths.

"Everything here looks quality," I said. "No wonder Oliver likes hanging with you."

Josh snorted. "He's never been here. Now, I'm definitely interested in a sheriff who wants to earn outside income, but this place is only for people I trust, and I haven't made my mind up about him. Does he want action, or pussy?"

"Both," Beth said. "Maddie, what Josh is saying is, can we trust you?"

"As a general rule, you shouldn't trust someone you just met who asks you to trust them. But I'm cynical. I like to stay one step ahead of any jackass who's going to shiv me."

"You were one step ahead of my .45." Josh waved the gun.

I forced myself to laugh and said, "Got me there!"

Josh called to the gamer, handed Jaison's key to him, and said, "She's got a car somewhere. Check it out and see if there's a phone inside."

The gamer took the key and left.

I hadn't been aware of finishing my drink, but Beth refilled my glass. I had to sip slowly and keep my wits about me. "So, Josh, my brother liked hanging out at the Ring-a-Bell when he was here. He'll be bummed it got shut down. What did you say your business with him was?"

"I didn't. But it was a little of this, a little of that. He traded a gun locker for product, but he didn't have the combo, and we had to bust it open."

"I was wondering where he sold it. Our granddad's guns were in there, and I have a sentimental attachment to them. Do you still have them? Because I'd be willing to pay a finder's fee."

"We can check my stock later. How's your dog business going?"

"I've had considerable blowback from the incident with the deputy. I'm waiting it out, because people forget."

"We're always looking for useful partners," Josh said. "Money comes in and needs washing, or else I end up throwing it away on gadgets and trucks. I don't want to work hard to blow it all on crap that depreciates, *comprendo*?" His eyebrows went together the way Bertie's did when he studied a bug.

"You'd like to build wealth. That's exactly what I'm trying to do, Josh. I'm tired of living month to month and worrying about the books." In order to chit-chat with a dog-murderer, I concentrated on Meathead, the short bristly fur, the muscles on his thick neck, his ability to remain calm in the presence of a man who undoubtedly abused him. "You and me, buddy."

"What?" Josh said.

"Oh, I meant, you and me are both interested in multiple streams of income."

"I finally get to talk to someone who actually gets it!" he said.

"What do you mean? *I* get it. *I* was the one who came up with the idea for the Looper's hookup," Beth said, in the timeless aggrieved tone of a woman to a man taking credit for her ideas, and Josh glared at her as if she'd said too much.

"So, Donna-June Looper's in on your, um, import business?" I said. "I'm only asking because I want to sell branded items. Maybe you could tell me how to increase profits on imports."

"Donna-June knows shit about shit," Josh said. "It's 'save the diabetics' this and 'save the diabetics' that."

Beth topped off my glass, which had mysteriously emptied. "If you're gonna stay, I may as well make dinner. You like Italian, Maddie? I'm making Italian."

"What about a stir-fry?" Josh said.

While they went back and forth recalling and discussing what they'd had for dinner the past week, I scanned the room for exits. Josh was between me and the front door. The other man was closer to the back hall. The kitchen door was part-way open to a mudroom. My options were: Run out the front and be shot in the back or run out the back and be ripped apart by fighting dogs.

The gamer returned and said, "She's driving a piece of shit with almost two hundred K on the odometer. Nothing inside, but postcards from Las Vegas. Registered to Jaison something. No phone." He set the key by Josh's side.

Meathead went to the kitchen door and whined, and the gamer let him out, closing the door after him, and returned to the sectional.

"Beth," I said, "The chicken parmigiana and the stir-fry both sound delicious."

Chapter Twenty-Nine

THE WEAPONS AND DRUG paraphernalia were pushed to one end of the dining table to make room for us. I savored every bite of what I thought was my last meal—eggplant parmigiana with a creamy roux, succulent summer tomato salad, tangy three-layer lemon cake, and sweet cold java chip ice cream—and I said, yes, please, to refills of cabernet and espresso. I was drunk and buzzed and terrified and considering my fate.

The gamer served himself a plate, devoured it while standing, and returned to the sectional. Beth flipped through a cookbook while we ate, and Josh took calls throughout the meal, often leaving the table to speak out of my hearing.

The dogs outside began barking furiously, and Josh said to the gamer, "Find out what that is."

The gamer went to the window, putting his hand over his eyes to block the glare. "Something small in the bushes. Maybe a coyote fucking with the dogs."

Vixen, I thought, Vixen moves like a coyote.

"I can use the night goggles," the gamer said.

"Those are for security, not chasing wascally wabbits," Josh said. "You fucked up the last pair with paintball."

I finished my espresso and said, "Beth, this was a wonderful meal. You're a remarkable cook."

"I'm always trying to improve my technique and widen my flavor profiles. I watch all the cooking shows."

She smiled prettily, a lively sexy girl making dinner for her friends. I understood how she could charm Ollie, before I remembered the horrible things she'd done. "I can barely make a peanut butter sandwich. I bet Oliver loves your cooking."

"No fucking clue, because I've never been allowed to invite him, although somehow it's okay for his stalker to be here." She shot a look at Josh, who ignored her.

"I'm here by accident," I said. "Will you be seeing Oliver later?"

"Not tonight," she said, her lips set in a line, and I thought *she wants to be with him.*

Evangeline shuffled over and fell onto Josh's lap. She played with his hair, and he shared a cigarette with her. Her eyes wandered all over, finally landing on me. "Hey, you're Maddie, the broken-heart bitch who chases Odie, aren't you? You could be, like, a hundred times hotter with the right hair, makeup, and clothes. I want to give you a makeover."

"That's a sweet offer," I said.

She dragged a finger down Josh's cheek so gently my skin crawled. "Josh, what do you think—"

His phone buzzed again, and he held his forefinger to her mouth. He answered the call saying, "Yeah, yeah, they're primed. You make sure the location is locked down or it will be your ass."

He listened for a bit, and Evangeline leaned back to be close to me and said, "Big fight tomorrow. The one-year-olds have their first match, so we'll see who's got game."

Josh continued his conversation, saying, "Four vans should do it for transportation, and I don't give a fuck what the problem is with the lighting. You're supposed to be the video expert. It's your job to figure it out." He set down the phone. "I am not a goddamn party planner."

I could practically feel the adrenaline vibrating through my teeth. At some point in the evening, Josh had made a decision. He didn't care what I heard or saw because he had no intention of ever letting me leave.

I patted my napkin to my lips. "Thanks for a delicious dinner, and I hope we can meet soon to discuss business opportunities, but I really have to go." I pushed my chair back and stood. "May I have my car key?"

Josh drew on the cigarette until the tip glowed red. "I think you should stay until I feel comfortable with you."

Before I could respond, the man sprawled on the sectional stood, yawned, rambled to the table, and began eating the leftovers, like a beta dog who knew his place.

Evangeline smiled dreamily and said, "Hey, Josh, I can make her real pretty for you, for us. That will be fun, right?"

The thought of a three-way with dog-killers, one of whom was a light-toucher, made me want to grab a weapon from the nearby pile and go out in a blaze of glory, but I said, "I'd like that, Evangeline. Ask Beth, and she'll tell you I think you're a brilliant stylist."

Beth, who'd been sulking, said, "Yeah, she told me that your work is fantastic."

The man who'd been sprawling said to Beth, "You ready to go home?"

"Put the food in the fridge, and I'll load the dishwasher." When Beth pushed her hair over her shoulder, the wedding rings on her hand glittered, and, sure enough, the sprawler wore a wedding band.

"Evangeline, do you have any free spots for an appointment next week?" I said. "How long will it take to give me long hair like Beth's?"

"Hot fusion extensions, they're the best, will take hours since your hair is so short. I got a whole set-up right here."

Josh narrowed his eyes and said, "No time like the present."

"I need to get back..."

"What are you—Cinderella and you're going to turn into a pumpkin at midnight?" Josh motioned to the sprawler and told him to go upstairs and lock up all the guns and phones.

The man returned and whispered in Josh's ear.

Josh rose and moved behind me. He wrapped his arm around my waist and yanked my hips to his, and I felt his hot breath in my ear as he said, "You and Evangeline go have your girly time. I don't recommend you go out for a smoke or anything. In the yard, I've got dogs, and I keep them like I keep the sheriff: hungry."

And when he shoved me toward Evangeline, my knees buckled, and I grabbed the table's edge to stay upright.

Ah, fuck, I thought as I carried two tumblers and followed Evangeline, who swung a bottle of brandy by the neck, upstairs.

She pointed to a door and said, "That's the video studio. It's state-of-the-art." She opened another door to a room set up as a salon. "This is my hair and makeup room."

"What's downstairs?"

"Guestrooms. The basement is nothing but dog stuff. It smells terrible." She was slightly more lucid, but not operating on all cylinders. "My bedroom is through there. Do you want to see it?"

"Sure."

Double doors opened to an elegant ivory and celadon bedroom with a creamy rug over dark hardwood flooring. My eyes went to the closed laptop on an antique desk in front of casement windows ajar to the cool night air. "This could belong in a French Chateau!"

"I designed it," she said. "I saw a room like it in a movie, and I always remembered it."

"You have an excellent eye, Evangeline. What's over there?"

"The en suite." She opened a door to a spacious dressing room. Men's clothes, including a rack of leather jackets, were on one side and a colorful array of women's clothes on the other.

The dressing room led to an ivory and marble bathroom the size of my living room, with clothes piled in the corner and magazines scattered by the toilet. A brushed bronze paper holder held a cardboard roll with only a remnant of a tissue. A half-open pocket door revealed a laundry room.

"Josh never puts his stinky clothes in the hamper, and it's *right* here." She took the clothes to the laundry room and dropped them in a basket. "The cleaner comes twice a week, but he makes a mess every day. Look at that! He uses the last of the toilet paper but can't be bothered enough to change the roll."

"Men are like that, oblivious to all the effort you put in to make a beautiful home for them."

"I don't mean to bitch about Josh."

"Of course, you didn't. I can see how he provides for you. It's the espresso. It made me tense. Are you tense? I want us to relax together."

"Me, too," she said, and I followed her to a dressing table in the bedroom.

"Do you have anything low-octane to take the edge off?"

"No tolerance?" She opened a cloisonne box and took out an amber bottle. "These should do. The cleaner left them. How many?"

"I'll start with two. What the hell, give me three."

Evangeline dropped three pills into my cupped palm. "Down the hatch."

I popped them in my mouth, took a drink, and swallowed. "Aren't you going to join me?"

She pulled a glassine envelope from the box and said, "My custom blend." She tapped a tiny pyramid of white powder onto a mirror. When she wasn't looking, I spat out the pills and slipped them in my jeans pocket. Then I filled her glass to the top.

As she crushed the powder and cut it into lines with a razor blade, I wandered to the windows. Security lights illuminated a yard with dog fight training equipment: treadmills, pools, crates, a cattle prod. A dead cat hung from a rope. Meathead, another massive male pit, and a female pittie, her body distended from breeding, roamed the yard. A half-dozen dogs, scarred and damaged, were chained to steel stakes. Still others barked from elsewhere on the property.

My stomach clenched like a fist at the horror, and I took slow breaths. I couldn't help them if I didn't get through this.

"Evangeline, who was that guy who left with Beth?"

"Her numero uno mistake. She got knocked up and married at fifteen."

"That can't be legal."

"It is in Florida. Her mom's raising the kid. Beth is Josh's cousin, so he does what he can for her," Evangeline said, her words slow and careful. "She's fallen hard for Sheriff Odie, and she's been talking about divorcing and getting her kid back, and Josh says it could help business a lot having a sheriff working with us, but he's careful."

"What does Beth's husband think?"

"No one cares what he thinks. We all make accommodations."

"Like you and Josh?"

"We keep things open. You were checking me out. You like girls." She pulled off my wig. "Whoever did this should have their cosmetology license revoked."

"You're so beautiful, but I have to ask you one thing. When you attach the extensions, don't touch me softly. Be firm."

"Girls like gentle."

She grazed her fingertips on the back of my hand, sending a

painful shock all the way up my arm, and I jerked away. "I'm not a gentle girl."

"You're so weird!" She laughed. "Let's change your hair color, too. How about aubergine?"

"I'd love that. Can I use the bathroom while you mix the color?"

"Extra toilet paper is in the cupboard. Come to my salon when you're done."

I replaced the toilet paper roll, peed as fast as I could, and then peeked out to make sure the bedroom was empty. I grabbed a thick leather jacket and motorcycle chaps from Josh's side of the wardrobe and opened the laundry hamper and collected dirty briefs, socks, and shirts. I shoved everything in the bathroom cabinet.

I filled my tumbler with water, adding only enough brandy to tint it. Evangeline must have taken the enamel box to the studio. Using a glass paperweight, I crushed the pills she'd given me and mixed it into her drink.

I carried the drinks to the salon and handed Evangeline the spiked one. She swayed to a dance mix while she set up a rolling cart with hair extensions, clips, plastic rings, and something that looked like a soldering iron. "What's that?"

"It's the fusion tool. It melts the glue on the tips of the extensions to your hair."

"Does it burn?"

"Not unless you're careless." She spoke slowly and listed to one side. "Once your hair is done, we'll do your makeup. I'm not a nails expert, but you can use press-ons while the dye processes."

"Evangeline, I'm still super tense. Let's get our drink on before we start."

"Okay."

"Let's lie down, and I'll show you exactly how to touch me, so I won't make sudden movements when you're working."

She nodded, and her eyelids drooped. I supported her to the bedroom and closed and locked the door behind us.

"Finish your drink, Evie." I sipped my brandy-flavored water while she downed her drink. "That's my girl." She stood still while I removed her shoes. "Lie on the bed and let me give you a back rub. I bet it's hard standing all day."

She teetered onto the bed, and I straddled her back, sliding my hands under her shirt and massaging her skin, feeling the bones beneath, and she groaned a little when my thumb found a knot of tension.

"Evangeline, what's up with Purlynn Looper? Does she help you import?"

"We hoped she'd be useful. 'She's a dark one,' Josh said, and all she did was cry, cry, cry. Oh, I like that. Right there, *mmm*."

"Does Purlynn know about the drugs?"

"Can't trust someone crying, crying, all alone, boo hoo. Josh says can't rely on... Ooh, you got it." Evangeline's voice drifted off.

"Don't you feel bad about the dogs?"

"They like it. They like fighting."

"Beth wanted a puppy for fighting."

"Not for fights. She wanted a surprise for her son, like Odie's dog."

I brushed her hair away from her neck, seeing the tattoo again, and wanting to wrap my hands around her throat and squeeze until she gasped for air and suffered like the dogs had suffered. I wanted to shout at her and slap her until she listened and understood. I wanted to weep for her because she could have, should have, been someone else, someone decent.

I worked my fingers from the base of her skull all the way down her spine and then moved outward.

"So relaxed," she murmured, "that's...." Her breathing deepened.

"Evangeline," I whispered, and she didn't respond. She was

deep under, and I rolled her to her side so she wouldn't choke if she vomited.

I went to the door and listened, but only heard the dance mix coming from the salon. After wedging a chair under the door handle, I grabbed the laptop from the desk as well as an external backup and flash drives from the desk drawer.

I slid the laptop inside my shirt and tucked it securely into my waistband. After locking myself in the bathroom, I dressed in Josh's shirts and leather jacket. I stepped into his skidmarked briefs, yanking them over my jeans, and buckled on the leather chaps, folding up the too-long cuffs.

Josh must have stored his helmets elsewhere, so I did the only thing I could think of to protect my head. I fashioned a balaclava by layering filthy boxers and tried not to gag. Finally, I put on thick leather gloves.

Now that his aura of stink radiated from me, I opened the bathroom window and climbed on the ledge. The unchained dogs were out of sight, but I knew they would come quickly. I swung my legs down and then began lowering my body, straining as I gripped the ledge. I hung for a moment before using my toes to push away from the wall.

Breathe, just breathe. I relaxed my body, bent my knees, and let go. I hit the ground with a painful jolt and curled myself tight, hiding my face and tucking my hands under my body.

Meathead and the loose dogs didn't take the time to bark before they tackled me, muscle and fury and bone-breaking jaws, and I breathed in the horrible stench of my deflector shield.

Chapter Thirty

ANY POINT IN TIME can be divided into infinite points. At one of these fractional points before Meathead's jaws closed on my skull, his nose slammed on the brakes, which was enough to bring the other dogs to a halt. They circled and snuffled at me, recognizing their alpha's scent, confused by my own smell. Meathead pushed his head toward my tucked hand, in the way that pits do, insisting on a caress.

I opened my hand and reached out to give him a rub. "Pitbulls are such bullies for love," I whispered, and slowly sat upright, rearranging the boxers to see, and wishing I hadn't because it was too horrible, too horrible to see the carcasses piled in a steel trough, the tethers, a table with straps, hypodermic needles...

The chained dogs reacted as traumatized animals do: some slinking low in fear because they knew only cruelty from humans and others lurching forward, wagging their tails, frantic for affection or food.

There was no time to explore escape routes. I went straight to the wire fencing and scrambled to the top, the thick gloves both protecting my hands and making them clumsy, and then dropped onto the soft soil below. The moment Josh discovered I'd escaped, he'd search the vehicles, the lane, and the road beyond, so I had to stay far from those places and put as much distance between us as quickly as possible.

Vixen was nowhere to be seen, and I didn't dare call for her. Crouching, I scurried away from the security lights, aware of a throbbing ache in my left ankle. The easiest path was downhill, but that gave them an advantage when searching with infrared goggles or night scopes. I pushed through the scrub brush, the laptop jabbing my ribs, and up the steep slope, making every attempt to move behind tree trunks and boulders that would block my heat signal.

Even though I sweltered under the leather jacket, it protected me from the rough landscape. Pine branches wove tightly overhead, blocking the moonlight and starlight, and when I reached a tall thick tangle of wild rose, I dropped to the ground and crawled, the thorns ripping my exposed skin, but providing both visual and physical protection.

Perhaps Josh had taught his dogs to track, but I doubted it. If Ezra was a lover, not a fighter, Josh was a killer, not a hunter. Somewhere deep in my gut, a place without rational thought, I believed Vixen was safe from Josh because she was faster, smarter, mythical in her abilities.

As disoriented as a cave explorer, I thought of everyone I loved and everyone who loved me beyond what I deserved, and I thought of my dogs and Josh's dogs, destined to fight and die the next day. I thought of amazing brave Oliver risking himself to protect the vulnerable, and I thought about Bertie and the promise I'd made to his handler to care for him always. Most painful of all, I thought about my sister, and how I would ruin her joy if I died, and I thought about my kind, sweet mother, and how she had sacrificed her own happiness to love and care for an unlovable child.

I swallowed hard and dragged myself through the bramble,

only to tumble down a short, rocky incline into a creek bed. As I lay there, cold water trickled through the leather chaps and into the leg of my jeans. A rivulet slid under my collar and down my back, but it might have been cold sweat. *Night in the country is so lovely, and I will treasure this moment*, I thought, inhaling the green scents of water, Ponderosa pines, and brackens. Insects' chirps and frogs' croaks clocked the seconds. A breeze ghosted through branches and leaves.

There were no ambient sounds of machines or cars or airplanes or electronic devices.

Until there were.

Shouts and slamming doors and powerful engines and howling dogs sounded so close that I jumped up and splashed along the creek, propelled by the memory of the animal corpses and cattle prods. My ankle ached, and my lungs burned. I tasted mud and blood in my mouth, and my boots slipped on the mossy rocks. The roar of engines increased and then dissipated as ATVs scoured the hillside, and lights sliced through the darkness.

But I picked myself up after every fall and kept moving, thinking, *ten steps, another ten steps* like a mantra until I reached a hollow carved by the creek under a sequoia's roots. Hoping the overhang would block infrared sensors, I took a moment to catch my breath and think. I couldn't judge how long I'd been gone or how far I'd traveled, but I no longer heard voices or engines.

This wasn't search and rescue, where victims wait to be found: It was search and escape. I removed the jacket, chaps, and gloves, and hid them under a cover of dirt and branches. I adjusted the laptop securely in my waistband and confirmed that the flash drives were still tucked deep in my pockets.

Rather than taking the predictable route downhill along the creek, I traveled uphill, grabbing roots and branches to pull myself to higher ground. When I became too thirsty to go on, I dug into the gritty soil beside the creek with a stick. While water slowly seeped inside, I gathered moss for a filter and shoved the moss in the hole. I scooped handfuls of the most delicious water I'd ever tasted.

My sense of time was distorted, and I kept waiting for the sky to lighten as I clambered over rocks and wedged up crevices. My journey ended at the base of a bluff too steep to climb. I sat on a boulder and took the laptop from my waistband. I flipped it open, but the account was locked, so I burrowed under a layer of leaves and branches, a thick stick by my side.

A coyote yip-yip-yipped nearby, which didn't worry me much, because coyotes are canines. I covered my head with fern fronds to block out mosquitos. I thought I would never fall asleep, but exhaustion took hold and, as I was sinking into oblivion, I hoped that I would wake to live another day.

Sleep with dogs, wake up with bliss.

My arm curved around a warm furry body. I opened my eyes to gray pre-dawn light, and Vixen's tongue flicked out and gave me a raspy lick across my chin. I rubbed her back and felt the saddle bags and harness.

"Good girl! Good Vixen!"

When I rolled upright, pain shot through my leg. If I took off my boot, I might not be able to put it back on over my swollen ankle.

I unzipped the saddlebag. There was a chance the sheriff-coroner had closed my walkie-talkie account, but when I clicked the unit on, the screen showed my GPS location. A wan low-battery warning chirped, which meant I'd been given a bum batch of "new" batteries. Of course I had.

The screen didn't show Oliver's corresponding location because, in the highly unlikely event that he'd turned on his walkie-talkie, I was out of range, the signal obscured further by hills and trees. The closest road was a mile as the crow flies, but I was more like a dead duck than a crow.

Vixen rested her head on my lap, and I unwrapped a stick of jerky from the saddlebag. "I am considering my options, Danger Girl," I said as I fed her bites of jerky. "If I send a general distress signal, there's no telling who will hear it and reach me fastest. If we walk to the road, we might find help, or Josh might find us. Last option, we hike until we find a spot with a strong signal. Then we turn off the walkie-talkie to conserve the battery and wait until it's likely that I've been reported as missing before turning it back on. Sound like a plan? Yeah, it's a plan. You and me on an adventure."

In another hour, Jaison would realize I was gone. He'd check in with Kenzie. She had always been my advocate, and I knew she'd raise hell until the Sheriff-Coroner took action.

I scratched the ivory blaze on Vixen's throat. "I've come to appreciate your joie d'vivre, especially in this trying time. If I should expire soon, feel free to gnaw on my flesh, circle of life and all that. Perhaps my half-eaten carcass will seem like poetic justice when Dino's finger is eventually discovered in my freezer. Why didn't I get rid of it? Perhaps it would be like the dolls in horror stories with terrifying smiles that keep reappearing. No, I'm not being serious."

I slid the laptop in the saddlebag and zipped it closed. Laying the walkie-talkie beside me, I braced myself against the ground and stood, keeping my weight on my right leg.

When the walkie-talkie chirped a battery warning, Vixen turned her head. "Leave it," I said, but she snapped up the unit and skittered away. Even as I lunged for her, I knew it was exactly the wrong move, but I was in too much pain and too desperate and too exhausted and already in motion.

And Vixen sped off, carrying my last best option between her jaws.

* * * *

Using the sturdy stick as a cane, I hobbled to a small spot with a patch of sky and oriented direction from shadows cast by the rising sun. I aimed myself toward the road and walked forward, wishing I'd kept one of Evangeline's pills.

My needs were urgent, but my progress was glacially slow. I listened to bluejays squawking, squirrels jumping on branches, and a far-off airplane. I crossed an animal trail with deer scat and mountain lion paw prints. The morning grew hot, and the air smelled the way it does on the first day of the end of summer, glorious and heartrending in its finality. The brutal heat will wane, and the fears of fire will subside, and too soon the days will be frigid and muddy, and I would shiver and yearn for summer's brilliance again.

By the time the sun glared overhead, I was drenched in sweat and had reached a steep ravine, carved by a stream. Thick shrubs bordered the far side, and then I heard a roar, and, through branches, a lumber truck passed on an unseen road. I didn't sit as much as collapse on a fallen log and cried big gloppy tears because I was tired and I was sad and I was lonely and I was so close and yet so far and my self-recriminations were innumerable.

Then branches crashed, and dogs woofed and bellowed, and I turned to see Bertie and Vixen and Zeus rushing to me. They surrounded me, licking and wagging and jostling to get close, and now I cried big gloppy tears of joy and embraced them.

"Maddie! Maddie!" Oliver ran to me with Ben and Andie right behind. He pulled me up in an embrace, and I pressed my face against his chest and said, "It's you, it's you, it's not the doppelganger, but the real Oliver."

"Yes, Mad Girl, it's me," he said in the tender and rough voice I loved so much and missed for so long, and he held me tight while I blubbered happily, and everyone talked too many words and asked too many questions.

* * * *

Giddy that I'd been rescued, I guzzled water and ate two protein bars while summarizing the previous twenty-four hours. My companions constantly interrupted, lamenting my rashness and ignoring my justification that I'd only "infiltrated Josh's hangout" at the wrong end of a muzzle. "I'm sure Josh isn't his real name. I don't think any of them are using real names."

"No, they're not. Excuse me, but I have to make a report." Then Andie went off to one side.

Oliver and I sat on the log, his arm around my shoulders, and Ben pulled off my boot and said, "Let's see what you've done to yourself this time."

"I'm fine. Bertie's overexerted." I wove my fingers through Bertie's thick golden and ebony fur. "You shouldn't have brought him, Ollie."

"We knew he'd find you no matter what. Like you always say, Bertie's a hero."

"Even heroes have to retire." Wiping my eyes, I cursed myself for not accepting the obvious earlier. "Zeus would have found me. You and Ben would have found me."

Andie finished her calls and returned to our group, holding Josh's laptop and the flash drives. "Maddie, do you think you can hang tight here for a little longer? We can arrest and charge on felony animal abuse before they move and destroy evidence, but I don't want a lot of activity to tip them off."

"So long as my sister and Jaison know I'm safe, I can wait," I said. "By the way, Andie, you're damn fine in that gun belt and uniform. Khaki suits you."

"I wasn't aiming for fashion when Oliver woke me at four a.m.," she said.

Oliver squeezed my shoulder. "Kenzie knew enough to guess that you'd gone hunting for Beth, and she and Jaison came pounding on my front door. From now on, I'm going to superglue cell phones, extra batteries and chargers all over your body before letting you go anywhere."

"That sounds cumbersome. You could implant a microchip in my neck."

"Glad to do it," Ben said. "Don't let Maddie fool you. Those chips are only to ID, not tracking, which would require a...wait for it...battery and receiver, thereby defeating the purpose." He swabbed disinfectant on my inflamed skin.

"Ben, we've really got to stop meeting like this," I said, wincing. "At least I'm not being attacked by hordes of imaginary bugs."

"You've been attacked by imaginary bugs?" Andie said.

"It occurs infrequently, but powerfully," I said. "Like biblical locust plagues."

"Don't listen to her, Andie," Oliver said. "Maddie's never read the Bible.

"But she's well-informed on plagues, both historical and current." Ben wound an Ace bandage around my foot and ankle. "Maddie, how have you been walking on this?"

I held my hands palm up, seesawing them as I said, "Death, walk, death, walk, death, walk. I went with 'walk.'"

"I could tell you to see a doctor, but you'll only say that I'm an animal doctor, and you're an animal."

"I'm glad we've reached an amicable understanding on this topic," I said.

Andie said, "Did you hear anything else about Josh's drug business?"

"I don't have the specifics, but they knew Donna-June was heavily involved in charity work for diabetes. They offered to help her import insulin from Canada to test her out and gain her trust. I don't think she knew that they were using supply orders as a cover for counterfeit and illegal drugs from overseas," I said. "They planned to recruit Purlynn but decided against it."

"The Crafty Looper is the connection I was looking for," Oliver said.

"So, you were undercover."

"Not officially," Andie said. "Is that pointer the hunting dog you were trying to dump on me?"

Vixen crept to Bertie and dropped a green tennis ball in front of him.

"Hey, that's Zeus's," Ollie said, and the Dutch shepherd lunged for the ball, and Vixen snatched it back and sped in circles, making him chase her.

"No, I'd never let Danger Girl go," I said.

"Terrific decision, because if she hadn't carried the walkie talkie into the receivers' range, we'd never have located you."

"I estimated Josh's hideout to be within a twenty-minute drive of the Bermuda Lounge," Ollie said, "but that's a lot of territory."

"We divided the map along possible routes and drove across the grid crisscross," Andie said. "About ninety minutes ago, your location pinged and then vanished, but at least we had a starting point."

Oliver smiled. "Andie got a lesson in K-9 search and rescue," and Ben said, "Well, we started the search, but Vixen found us before we found her, and Bertie and Zeus took over from that point."

"So, Oliver's not in trouble with Internal Affairs?" I asked Andie.

"That's a complicated situation and one we can't share right now," she said, and Ollie said, "I didn't want you worrying about me, or putting yourself in danger."

"That's why you issued the restraining order."

He grinned. "No, the restraining order was to stop you from sending me demented letters with hunks of your hair."

* * * *

Andie made calls while we waited, sitting in the shade, repeating our stories and filling in details.

"Oliver, I promised Sasha I'd give her a big crime syndicate story. Can you call her to cover the bust?"

He raised an eyebrow. "No can do. We're casting a wider net, and everything's under wraps, so you're not going to talk to anyone about this. That includes Georgie Maguire and the shelter crowd, your sister, and all your cohorts."

"I don't see how I can keep it from them, Ollie. Kenzie and Jai already know I was in a crisis. What am I supposed to tell them?"

"Tell them you're not at liberty to speak," Andie said. "In fact, I'll tell them."

"Sasha is never going to forgive me," I said. "Ben, I'm sorry for keeping you from your appointments."

"It's okay. The situation qualifies as 'dire.'"

He smiled at me his familiar way, closed lips that turned up at the corners, rounding his cheeks under the beard, and I wanted so much to be friends the way we had been. I watched a hawk wheeling above in the blue, blue sky, and remembered Beau Blue playing on a day as clear as this, and I wondered at his escape and at my own, and I felt an ineffable sorrow, and said, "Does anyone else feel the change in weather? The air is different, and so is the light. Fall is coming."

Chapter Thirty-One

SIRENS SCREAMED IN THE DISTANCE. “Andie, is that for us? Does that mean you’ve got Josh?”

She nodded and said, “They were destroying evidence and packing up, but they’re in custody now.”

“Good,” I said. “Good.” I thought of this monosyllabic word, and how it was too easy to categorize people and events as either good or bad, and how this reductionist desire excused us from making an honest effort to have anything but a superficial understanding of others. I’d listened to Kenzie’s stories about abused and neglected children, and I wondered what horrors lay in Josh and his companions’ pasts. And I remembered that my own brother had traded with these criminals, that he was a criminal, too. Or maybe he wasn’t anymore. If I truly believed any dog could be rehabilitated, shouldn’t I believe the same of humans?

“What are you thinking about, Maddie?” Andie said.

“No, don’t ask her!” Ollie said, and Ben said, “You *really* don’t want to know,” and we were laughing as patrol cars, an ambulance, and a fire engine rolled to a stop on the road across the ravine and began the process of extricating us.

* * * *

I wanted to go home, shower, and sleep, but I was separated from my friends, and an uncommunicative deputy drove me to the sheriff's headquarters in the county's justice complex.

The EMTs had provided a cane, and I leaned on it as I limped into the cool of the two-story concrete building. People in the lobby stopped talking and stared as I was taken through the metal detector. But when a security officer tried to pat me down, I said, "I am here merely as a courtesy, and I'm leaving right now if you touch me."

I was so annoyed my eye twitched, and I turned toward the gawkers and announced, "Yes, you do recognize me. I'm a search-and-rescue expert here at the sheriff-coroner's behest because he can't find his ass with his own two hands."

The deputy grunted to the security officer, who waved me through, and the deputy led me down a hall, but grew frustrated at my slow progress and said, "Stay here."

I leaned against the wall until he returned a few minutes later with a wheeled desk chair, and said, "Take a seat." I plopped down, and he rolled me along the polished floors to an oak door at the end of the hall, where a man in a navy suit waited.

He said, "Please come in."

I lifted myself off the chair and limped into an enormous corner office with walls of awards and certificates and an enticingly wide sofa.

A woman and a man, both dressed in business clothes, stood beside Sheriff-Coroner Eastman, who was seated at a massive desk. He waved me toward an empty chair directly in front of him. "Hello, Ms. Whitney."

"Dr. Whitney," I said, ignoring the chair. I flopped on the sofa and swung my legs up. "I would have returned the walkie-talkie and rescue gear without a personal escort dragging me here."

Before he could answer, there was a rap on the door, and

Andie entered and said, "Hello, Sheriff-Coroner, everyone. Dr. Whitney, you beat me."

"Hello again, Assistant Deputy Kleinfeld," I said. "The only reason I'm here is to make sure you catch the rest of the dog fighting ring."

"We all have the same goal, to save lives," Eastman said. "Let's put aside personal differences for now, because we're racing against the clock. Can you do that?"

"Yes. Tell me how I can help."

So, they recorded my story and asked questions and conferred with each other. No one told me their names or positions, but the man's questions were legalistic and hers were about criminality. They finally said, "Thank you, Dr. Whitney. We appreciate your cooperation and may call on you again for further information. In the meantime, we ask that you keep this matter confidential. We may need to expand the investigation on a federal level."

"Confidential? Does this mean you're not going to clear my name as a cop-hater when I've risked my life to help you?"

The sheriff-coroner smiled his bleached-teeth politician smile. "To help us, or to help the ex-boyfriend you're stalking?"

"I think you mean the respected sheriff's captain that I assisted, you conniving SOB," I said, and his face flushed, a line appearing between his brows.

The man said, "We can order you as a witness not to disclose anything about this incident."

"That would be complicated and messy. My issues, particularly regarding conversations, are well known."

Andie stepped forward and said, "Dr. Whitney, is there any way we can persuade you?"

"I'm so glad you asked. I will consider confidentiality if the county promises not to euthanize the fighting dogs and to put me in charge of finding an appropriate sanctuary for their care and rehabilitation."

They yammered about killer dogs and told me I should be reasonable, and I yammered about acting humanely to the canine victims, and then they conferred in an adjoining room while I shoved handfuls of wrapped guest peppermints in my pockets.

When they returned, they said, "We agree to your requests, Dr. Whitney. We'll be in touch," and I said, "Sure, but let's not do this again," and casually swung my cane to knock over a bronze trophy on my way out because I was just that irritated with them.

The deputy who'd escorted me was nowhere in sight, but the wheeled chair was still there. I turned it so I could prop my left knee on the seat and hold the back, using my right leg to propel me forward.

Andie caught up with me as the chair was veering into the wall, "I realize that was difficult for you."

"Compared to dinner with killers, it was a piece of cake—although the killers did have actual cake."

"You're tired. Let me take you home."

On the ride back, I said, "What's happening with Donna-June Looper?"

"She was right upstairs from you. She's horrified her business was being used to funnel drugs into town and wants to do whatever she can to help," Andie said. "Purlynn thinks it's only another Saturday for her mother. When you see her at your center, can you please *not* tell her?"

"I will need some inducement, Andie," I said. "Do you remember the day we met? Because I was cheated out of my strawberry milkshake and fries from the Burger Hut. It's on our way back. Do you need authorization to approve this deal?"

"You *already* agreed to a keep quiet, but I think we can make an accommodation."

The air conditioning was too cold, and I slid down the window. "So, how's everything going with Claire?"

"Claire is..." Andie began. "How long were you with her?"

"Two years, most of it problematic, because we were never a good fit. She's so popular, and I resented all the time she spent talking to extraneous people about their boring lives when she could have been listening to the boring details of my day. Of course, no one is boring to Claire, which is one of the reasons she's so special. I wouldn't have fallen in love with her merely because she's beautiful, even though she takes my breath away."

"You don't resent me being with her?"

"She's her own person with her own agency." I considered for a minute. "Ollie's ex-wife gave me advice about him. She said that Oliver and Claire will always be closer to each other than anyone else. That's the way it is with twins."

"Does that bother you?"

"Honestly, Andie, it's a relief not to carry the burden of someone relying exclusively on me for emotional stability. How about you?"

"I appreciate the insight."

When I saw my sister, Oliver, and our search dogs waiting on the front porch for me, I said, "Stop! Stop!" to Andie, and gingerly swung my legs out of the car, hobbling to Kenzie, hugging and kissing her, pressing my face into her clean shiny hair, until she pulled away and said, "I was losing my mind with worry. Tell me what happened!"

"Nothing happened. I met a girl who was chasing Oliver, and she invited me to dinner. She was a terrific cook. I drank too much, tried to walk home, and got lost in the hills."

"We've had some misunderstandings, Kenzie," Oliver said. "Maddie and I have agreed to work this out privately, if you don't mind."

I grabbed her graceful, manicured hand in my scratched, bruised, and filthy one. "Why are you making that face?"

"It's a skeptical expression, because I know something else is going on. But if you want to keep it to yourselves, I'll respect that," she said. "Can you at least tell me what's wrong with your leg?"

"I sprained my ankle jumping from a second-story window."

"I'd be worried—*more* worried—, but you're a master of jumping out bathroom windows to escape."

"Escape what?" Oliver said.

Kenzie shook her head. "Bad dates, Thanksgiving dinners, massages with soft-touchers."

Andie made a U-turn and drove away with a honk of her horn.

"Who was that?" Kenzie said.

"Claire's girlfriend."

"I've missed so much since I've been gone," Kenzie said. "Maddie, if you're okay staying with Oliver, I have got to run to Spirit Springs. I'll be home late."

"I'm fine. Go, go," I said. "I need to get clean and pass out."

Walking even the short distance to my center was a challenge, so Ollie drove me there.

The dogs were ecstatic to join the rest of the pack, and Jaison came out and said, "Hey, Sheriff," and then he hugged me, lifting me off the ground. "'Bout time you got back."

Holding tight to him, I said, "Thanks for sending in the posse."

He set me down carefully. "Kenzie and me knew you wouldn't stay away from the pack unless something was wrong. I'm sure there's a story, including the whereabouts of my Corolla. Did you crash it?"

"No story except Maddie shouldn't go hiking in the woods at night. You'll get your car tomorrow," Oliver said. "She has to rest tonight."

"No worries," Jai said. "Purlynn and I have things in hand. Maddie, you take it easy. We'll keep the dogs here. Maybe not Vixen. She does whatever she wants."

"That's not such a terrible thing," I said, watching Purlynn across the yard. She smiled and waved at me and went back to filling one of the kiddie pools with water. Purlynn, the dark one with secrets, laughed as Vixen snapped at the stream coming from the hose.

"Ready?" Oliver said, and we slowly made our way to my cottage. I leaned against him going up the three steps inside.

He stopped moving at the whiteboards and Post-its. "Claire said you'd taken the express train to crazy town."

"One person's crazy town is another person's granular analysis."

He scanned my notes. "How does Dino Ayer's accident fit into any of this?"

"It doesn't. I was jealous because Ben paid so much attention to Emily. I didn't want to lose the only person in town who'll discuss retroviruses with me." I limped to the bedroom, sat on the bed, and began unwrapping the dirty bandage from my ankle.

Oliver sat beside me. He was quiet for a few minutes, before saying, "Maddie, about Beth..."

"No." I lifted my eyes to his and held on as long as I could. "No, don't you dare apologize for anything you did to stop those people. I wish I'd never seen what I did at that house, because I'll have to live with those memories forever. I also understand that you might have enjoyed being with them, because they were sexy and exciting, and the women were beautiful and talented. What a waste. What an awful waste."

"You didn't give up on me. No matter what, you trusted me."

I placed my hand on the side of his wonderful face. "Close your eyes," I said, so I could watch the crease on his brow soften and his mouth relax. "You trusted me to trust you," I said, and kissed him. "You know there are things I don't tell you, too."

"If you're silent, you have good reason. Keep your secrets," he said. "Now as to your stated opinions, that's another story, like your belief that showers are too dangerous for sex."

"Because they are. Hundreds of people go to the ER every day for bathroom-related injuries. I keep telling you to install both internal and external grab bars in your shower. All that glass, marble, and water, and you're begging for trouble."

"I can hold you while you wash. Because of your ankle."

"You won't try any hanky-panky?"

"Absolutely no hanky. Possibly a little panky," he said, and his phone buzzed. "It's Andie. I'll be back in a sec." He went to the living room and turned on the music to cover his conversation.

I couldn't stand smelling myself another second, so I pulled off my dirty, sweaty shirt, and threw it on the floor. I lay back and wiggled out of my jeans, gasping as the coarse fabric pulled against my sore ankle. I stood carefully and hobbled to the bathroom doorway and was leaning against it when Ollie returned.

"I'm off the hook," he said, letting out a long breath. "Internal Affairs scoured security camera footage at locations I've been at or near for the past week. Richard Kearney planted guns and drugs in my cruiser while I was responding to a domestic dispute."

"He called you a dirty cop."

"He thinks I am. A little cognitive dissonance there. Yeah, I said it, and you think I never understand your pretentious bullshit." Oliver grinned and came to the doorway, wrapping his arm around my waist to support me. "Kearney's been suspended, and I'm reinstated. Go ahead and say it. You *want* to. You *need* to."

"Say what?" My lips tightened in my effort, and then I gave up. "I told you so!"

"Yeah, you told me so. Now, I'm telling you something. I love you Madeleine Margaret Whitney, and I want to do all kinds of things to you, both hanky and panky, but you reek."

Laughing, I said, "Okay, but this is an exception, not the rule."

* * * *

I teetered on the edge of joy and heartbreak when I was able to touch and hold and taste and hear Oliver again. I raked my hand through his rusty gold hair and said, "Please let's try never to fuck this up."

He flipped me on my back and straddled me, tilting my chin so that I made eye contact with him. "No matter how hard people try, everyone fucks up, babe. But when we do, I won't give up. I'll do whatever is humanly possible to fix the fuck-ups."

"Me, too."

Oliver and I lay on opposite edges of the bed, reaching out to touch fingers, because we were still too hot, and I kept shifting my legs, trying to find a cool spot on the sheet. When Andie called again, I left to get water for us. As I was returning the ice cube tray to the freezer, I made sure the severed finger was safely hidden behind the frozen peas.

"Maddie..."

I slammed the freezer door shut and turned around, almost losing my balance. "Done with the call already?"

"Andie gave me an update on Donna-June Looper," he said, and picked up the glasses of ice water. "Come back to bed, and I'll tell you."

"I'm tired of being tired. I was laid up for days with an awful flu."

He propped up the pillows for me, and we sat side by side on the bed, drinking our water so quickly we emptied the glasses in seconds. "You emailed me about that. Repeatedly."

"I did?"

"I think you were delirious. I asked Jaison to check on you."

"He didn't tell me."

"You don't know everything. You don't know how I reread your letters and kept playing your messages to hear your voice. You don't know how it killed me to stay in the Bermuda Lounge knowing you were right across the parking lot, or how I felt turning you away when you came to the search party."

I pressed my face against his chest and said, "Tell me about Donna-June. Why her?"

"She met Beth in an online support forum for diabetics. Beth cultivated her friendship and introduced Donna-June to the black market of people selling their dead relatives' leftover insulin to those who needed it."

"Beth was grooming Donna-June."

He nodded. "Donna-June's a do-gooder. Beth and Evangeline took classes at Looper's—they loved the classes—and talked to Donna-June about local sick people who needed cancer, or anti-psychotic, or fertility drugs. They told her they knew someone who worked for a Canadian pharmaceutical manufacturer but driving the drugs across the border was risky."

"Let me guess: Looper's imports wool from Canada."

"Canada and all over the world. But dealers claim counterfeit and unapproved drugs are from Canada to give legitimacy. Beth convinced Donna-June to let her handle the imports directly, not inspecting them herself, because that would keep Donna-June's hands clean if anything should go wrong."

"She meant well." I yawned. "We should tell Purlynn..."

"Go to sleep. I'll talk to her."

As I watched him dress, I thought about Beth wanting a divorce and to get her son back and give him a puppy. Because, even in his guise, Oliver had given her hope for a different life. What an awful waste.

After Oliver left, I expected to pass out. But I couldn't stop thinking about how Purlynn would react to the news about Donna-June.

I sat up, flapped and shook my limbs until they ached, and then called my mother.

One ring, two rings, and then, "About time!"

"Hi, Mom, how are you?"

"Worried sick about us, sweetie. Do you hate me?"

"I love you forever and a day, Mom, and nothing could ever change that. But I'd like to understand why you didn't tell me."

She paused so long that I said, "Mom?"

"It's taken a long time for me to figure out why I did what I did, and I'm still not sure. I was so young and depressed with my marriage, and I was so ashamed that I'd broken my vows."

I expected her to bring up Jesse Whitney's known history of cheating as justification, but she said, "It was wrong. The longer I didn't say anything, the harder it was to admit."

"You thought I was your punishment."

"Heavens, no! You were always a blessing, Maddie, and that was part of my guilt, because it made me so happy every time you reminded me of your...of Abel and what I loved about him. He's so smart and clever, like you, and has all these odd little ways. He wasn't like anyone else I'd ever met, and you're both so beautiful."

It was uncomfortable and fascinating, seeing him through her eyes. "He could have helped financially so your life wasn't miserable. He *should* have helped."

"Wherever did you get the idea that my life was miserable? I had my children, and we always had a roof over our heads," she said. "Abel offered to support you, but I insisted you weren't his. I wasn't going to share you, Madeleine Margaret. I knew that God had given you to me for a reason—and this is what my pastor has helped me see—to be the guardian of someone special. When Kenzie and Raymond were born, I knew I was on the right path."

Confused and close to tears, I said, "I was the problem. I realize life was difficult for you."

"Stop seeing the glass as half-empty and look at it as having room to fill to the top, sweetie. I didn't think I could raise a family on my own, but I did it. If your...if Jesse hadn't divorced me, I wouldn't have learned to be strong and resourceful. I hope you kids learned something, too. Well, think of everything your sister does as a therapist and how successful you are! My heart's filled with pride for you girls. As for your brother, he's finding his way, and it may take time, but he'll get there. I pray for him. I pray for all of you."

I swallowed hard and said, "That's so thoughtful, Mom, even though I don't believe praying has any effect."

"Yes, sweetie, you've been telling me you're an atheist since you were thirteen. Why are you crying?"

"I'm not." I held a pillow over my face so she wouldn't hear me sniffle.

"Yes, you are. You and Abel are the same that way, too. You always act so tough, but you're sentimental softies." She laughed her sweet laugh. "If things hadn't gone the way they did, I wouldn't have taken the path that led me to Larry."

"Mom, I'm never going to be best friends with Larry, but I'm overjoyed you have someone who adores you and makes you happy."

"Happiness is a part of life, Maddie, but it's not the *only* part, or the most important part. When are we going to see you and your sister?"

"Why don't you come for Thanksgiving? You can stay in my old room. Coyote Run is officially a politics-free zone, so warn Larry not to wear any of those awful right-wing clothes and tell him we won't be fighting about anything but whether the mashed potatoes should be lumpy or creamy."

"You're being silly. Everyone knows lumpy smashed potatoes are the best."

"I wish that was the case, Mom, but Kenzie has started to make hers creamy. I hope you'll talk sense into her," I said. "Also, I want you to know that I'm trying to connect with Abel even though he's absolutely impossible."

Her laughter started as a giggle and developed into a full guffaw, and I said, "What's so hilarious? Okay, call me tomorrow, because I have too much to process now."

Chapter Thirty-Two

DESPITE MY DESIRE and need for sleep, my thoughts whirled, and I couldn't stand being in my own head anymore. I flip-flopped to my center at twilight, and the dogs gathered by the fence to greet me.

"Hey, Mad Girl!" Jaison rushed from the office trailer, and I leaned on him to the deck, where I dropped down, my legs hanging over the edge. "You're a mess. You oughta be asleep."

"My brain won't let me." I watched Bertie slowly come to me, and I bent over until my forehead met his. Vixen appeared from nowhere, licked our faces, and darted off again.

"He's wore out," Jai said. "That must have been some run he went on today."

"I was stuck in the middle of nowhere with Vixen being Vixen."

"But everything's all right with Sheriff Oliver?"

"Why don't you ask him through your secret back channel?"

"You think we'd ever abandon you?"

"It feels like a year since I borrowed your car," I said. "I think justice will be done for Beau Blue."

"You found the dog fighters?"

"I'm not at liberty to say anything about anything, so feel free to make assumptions. Is there any beer in the kitchen?"

He took off and returned with two bottles, and we raised them in a toast, and he said, "To you being out of the shit with the law."

"It's nothing they'll ever admit, so I'll still be hated by the good people of Coyote Run."

"Only the regular number of people hate you. You'll see."

"Ah, are you going all Magical Negro on me just because I need it?"

"It's still my long-term goal. I can't be your sidekick forever."

Looking into his dark brown eyes, I said, "The sidekick is required to be wacky, and that would be me. You're definitely leading man material. Except for being a little young."

He laughed. "Not as young as I was when you hired me."

"It's inevitable that you'll get your big break soon," I said, because I knew he was outgrowing his manager position. "Do you think the leading man gig involves dogs?"

"Absolutely. Stop jumping out of your skin. I'm talking about sometime down the line. You've found you a talented protégé, and with Purlynn here, I can take my skills someplace less pokey."

"How does Whitney & Bouvier Canine Rehabilitation Centers sound to you?"

"It sounds like a plan. Do I get to pick out our second location?"

"So long as it's in driving distance. I won't fly."

"I think it's gonna be someplace in Nevada. Nevada's the future," he said. "Now that we got that settled, after the sheriff talked to Purlynn, she flew outta here on a personal emergency. She didn't know if she'll make it in tomorrow."

"No worries. You and me, we can handle things on our own."

"Like old times." Jai sat next to me, pulled a blunt from his pocket, lit it and took a hit.

"This will knock me right out, which is what I need." I reached for the blunt. "To old times and to Whitney & Bouvier something-something. Change your name to Gouvier, so we can be WAG."

"No. You change your name to Raddie, and we can be Bouvier And Raddie Canine Center, BARCC."

"Have you been planning this for a while?"

The heat slowly dissipated, and we enjoyed a gentle buzz and bounced ideas about our partnership, and I extolled Bertie's grandness and Vixen's swiftness, and Jai reminisced about meeting his Rottie, and we threw balls for the dogs to fetch, and we declared justice done at Deputy Richard Kearney's suspension and waved our arms and shouted "Halleluiah!" and then I began crooning romantic Hall & Oates songs, and Jai yelled, "Hell, no!" but he joined me in the chorus of "Las Vegas Turnaround" as the sky transmuted into the exquisite cobalt of *l'heure bleue*, and night descended.

Purlynn arrived on time in the morning and came straight into my office. "Sheriff Desjardins told me you found out what's going on with my mother. I had no idea, and I'm still in a state of shock. Mom says she knew it wasn't legal, but she believed it was right if she could help save lives. I'm sorry her actions put you in danger."

"Your mother wasn't responsible for the dog fighters, and drugs have always been here."

"If I had been paying attention, I would have seen what was going on," Purlynn said, biting her lip. "But this last year has been rough...with my father leaving and all."

"Wasn't it a red flag that Beth wasn't a typical crafter?"

"There's no 'typical' crafter. We have all kinds of students and staff. Seriously, we once had a nun and a sex worker in the same lace crochet class, and they became best friends. That's the best thing about crafting; anyone can become part of the creative community."

"What's going to happen to your mom?"

"Her lawyer's negotiating a deal for her to turn state's witness. She may not get any prison time—even though she was already offering to teach classes to inmates. No matter what happens, she'll have to sell the house to pay the legal fees. It's too big and too empty, anyway."

"And the huge lawn is a fucking irresponsible waste of water," I said, trying to make her feel better. "Will you live in the fishing cabin, or will she have to sell that, too?"

"My dad gave the cabin to me years ago," Purlynn said. "My mother wouldn't live there anyway, because she needs to have a spa tub to unwind. We'll find a place in town."

"Doesn't your dad have any say?"

"The house and business are Mom's. Dad only wanted time to go fishing," Purlynn said. "I better get to work. Being with the dogs makes everything better, doesn't it?"

"I've always felt that way."

"Can you help me later with a Sheltie that keeps nipping children to herd them?"

"Yes, even though herding children isn't such a bad idea." I smiled, thinking of how Zoe would draw up a business plan to rent canine children wranglers to daycares and summer camps.

Kenzie snapped gleaming scissors open and closed in front of my face and said, "Please stop wriggling, or I'll tie you down and cut your hair the way I want to."

"You don't want to cut my hair at all. You want me to grow it out."

"Long, short, I don't care anymore, but I'm embarrassed to let you out in public when it looks like rats gnawed away hunks while you slept."

"No need to worry. I never go out anymore since I am universally vilified as a cop-hater."

"You're going out with me this evening. You need to dress up."

"For what? It doesn't matter. No fucking way." When I began to stand, she slammed her hand on my shoulder and pushed me back.

"Yes, fucking way. The Chamber of Commerce is presenting me with an award before the meat raffle and bingo at Grange Hall. You're my date."

"Award for what, and how come I'm hearing this now? Oliver and I have plans for tonight."

"Gotcha! I knew that would be your go-to excuse. Oliver says you're available. This is a new award: The Good Mental Health is Good Business Service Award.

"It sounds like a perfect opportunity for Ezra Brothers to flash his dental caps and network with the town's business class. Invite him as your date."

"That guy." She whistled out a breath between pursed lips. "If I invite him, he'll make it all about Ezra. The award's supposed to be a secret, but the chamber president told me because she wanted to be sure I'd show up. We need to act surprised."

"Act surprised on your own and buy me five tickets for the raffle, but only if they have venison."

Kenzie gripped the top of my head with her hand and snipped above my ear. "Don't make me call Mom and tell her you're not being supportive."

"My clients are still AWOL, Kenz, and the social media insults and threats are so horrible Jai won't let me read them."

"You can't keep hiding forever. Outsiders don't count for anything, and people here value you, and that's what matters." Kenzie ruffled my hair and stepped back. "It will have to do. I want you to be there by my side. Say you'll go."

"Okay, fine. Whatever."

* * * *

If I had a tail, it would have been tucked between my legs.

Kenzie teetered in heels, as pretty and vibrant as I'd ever seen her, gripping my hand tightly, and I trailed half a step behind, wearing an uncomfortable public appearance outfit, my cantilevered tits higher than my glum mood as we entered Grange Hall. The locals in the lobby noticed us right away, and I said, "I need to go to the ladies."

"I'm not falling for any of your tricks." Kenzie tugged me into the crowded hall, which was set up with long tables and chairs for bingo. In front of the stage was a display of plastic-wrapped hunks of meat in ice trays, and another table held the bingo ball spinner. A banner proclaimed *Coyote Run Chamber of Commerce Fun Night!!!*

The movie-night screen had been placed behind the podium on the stage.

"Déjà vu all over again. This place is filled with exactly the same people every time we come. They're trapped in suspended animation until we arrive, and when we leave, frozen again."

"Blah, blah, blah. Let's get drinks."

She had to let my hand go to take out her wallet, but the server, one of Penelope's staff, waved her money away. "On the house for the guest of honor."

"At least you're comped," I said, and Kenzie said, "You had no intention of paying anyway. All your friends are here."

"Lured by the meat." I smiled as Sasha Seabrook approached. "Sasha! I can't believe you came here to cover a hokey bingo night."

"She came to honor an esteemed Coyote Run citizen," Kenzie said, performing complicated eye jujitsu with Sasha.

"Kisses!" Sasha puckered her lips. "I'm not here as a reporter. I'm the presenter. I've never heard of a meat raffle before."

"The money goes to a food kitchen," I said. "But you take your chances. Early winners get their choice, and by the end, there's always the mystery meat, including roadkill. Cats, rats, skunks, whatever."

"Don't listen to her!" Kenzie pinched my arm. "Sasha, you look lovely."

"Thanks. So do you ladies. Maddie, what happened to your foot?"

"I sprained my ankle jumping out a window."

"Why were you—" Sasha began, and Kenzie said, "We'll spare you the details, but it involved dogs."

"Sasha doesn't care about canine anecdotes anymore," I said. "She wants to break big crime syndicate stories. She made me promise to give her any leads I discover."

My friend laughed. "Please! That was a joke. Besides, I realized I'm not an organized crime kind of journalist. My strength is uplifting human-interest stories. Horrible stories are the easiest way to get the most attention, and attention sells advertisements. Media competes for those detergent and car ads, telling scarier and uglier stories, and giving us a distorted view of the world and each other. Maybe I'm sabotaging my own career, but to heck with that. I want to dedicate my days to sharing stories about the best in people—and animals."

Kenzie agreed with her, and I smiled and said, "I promise to give you any feel-good stories I find."

Sasha winked. "Maybe you already have."

"Back in a sec, Maddie. Don't you dare sneak away," Kenzie said, and pulled her a few feet away to chit-chat and hob-nob and chin-wag.

I grabbed a prize list for the raffle from a nearby table. I wondered if there was any danger of trichinosis in the wild boar sausage.

"Hey, babe." Oliver, wearing his uniform, stood in front of me.

"Ollie! I thought you had the night off. Don't tell me you have to cancel our slumber party."

"Not slumber. *Lumber* because I'll be bringing the wood," he said, grinning. "That's still on my calendar. I bought raffle tickets for you." He handed me a strip of tickets and then pulled me close and gave me a lingering kiss, and when he let go, I kept my eyes closed to hold on to the feeling.

"Hello, ladies," Ollie said to my companions, who'd returned. "Wouldn't want to miss such a special event." He waved at someone across the room, and I looked up to see Sheriff-Coroner Eastman.

"Oh, great," I said. "Why's that major asshole here?"

"I *told* you this was a special honor," Kenzie said, and we were suddenly swarmed by acquaintances and neighbors coming forward to say hello and ask those banal things that people do, and I said *fine, fine, fine, nice to see you,* etc. My friends appeared, too: Jaison and his girl Julia, Zoe and her parents, Georgie and her husband, Hardwire, Beryl, volunteers and assistants from my center, and even Rudy took a break from the Brewhouse.

Claire Desjardins and Andie appeared, and Claire placed her cheek against mine and said, "Thank you for everything, you crazy marvelous bitch," sending me into a confused fangirl swirl.

I tried inching my way back toward the exit, but a body blocked me, and I turned to see Abel Myklebust, looming as he always did, awkward like me.

"Charley did an incredible job raising you. I want to say I'm proud of you."

"I haven't done anything."

"Yes, you have," he said. "I'm glad you're safe."

"Thanks, Abel."

"Abel," he said, sounding the name like *ah-bel.* "The Spanish pronunciation. My mother named me. I want you to meet her."

I looked around in a panic. "Now? Where is she?"

He laughed. "She's not here. But she's coming for Christmas. You'll meet her then."

"Okay. We should talk sometime."

"Come to dinner next week. Bring your sister."

I nodded, and then my attention went to Ben Meadows and his wife, who came forward. Ben grinned like a kid and held hands with Ava, who was bronzy from a summer in the pool. "You're finally back!" I said, hugging her close.

"Back to reality and our gorgeous house. The kids can't wait to see you."

"I can't wait to see them either."

We were interrupted by extraneous people who generated too much heat and too much noise and inspected me for too long. I smelled perfumes that were too sweet and colognes that were too spicy. Single voices merged into a discordant chorus, and the air tasted like biting into aluminum, and someone touched me lightly, burning like a stinging nettle.

I tried to break away, but Oliver held me tight. I shoved my face against the rough fabric of his shirt, blocking out as much of the visual stimuli as I could, and mumbled, "I need to get away." When my body jerked, my head hit his chin. "Sorry."

"Stay a little while. Don't disappoint people."

"I stayed long enough."

"I'll take you home soon. I promise," he said, but I was already shrinking into myself in order to keep from flailing and shrieking, and I tried to slow my breathing.

Finally, the lights blinked, and people took seats. Kenzie and Oliver led me to a front table with a *Reserved* sign. The Chamber of Commerce president gave a welcome address and spoke about an unnamed remarkable citizen, "one of Coyote Run's native daughters," and then I could smile for Kenzie, because she was remarkable, and I would endure this for her.

The chamber president introduced Sasha, who took the stage like the pro she was. I assumed she'd hand out a plaque to Kenzie, and all would be over soon. I became distracted by the sausages again, trying to recall what I'd read about a recent trichinosis outbreak. Had the pork been served raw and was the animal caught in the wild or raised in captivity?

Kenzie poked my arm repeatedly, but I didn't snap back to the present until applause filled the room, and Sasha stood on stage, smiling straight at me and saying, "Which is why I'm premiering my short documentary feature *Mad about Dogs* here tonight.

I turned to Kenzie and then Ollie. "What the fuck?" I tried to stand, but they held me in place.

The house went dark, and a title flashed on the screen, *Mad about Dogs, written and directed by Sasha Seabrook*, and my muddy, scratched face appeared on the screen as I glanced at the camera before walking away with Bertie. Sasha's voiceover said, "When I met Dr. Madeleine Whitney, she was leading a K-9 Search and Rescue team trying to find a disoriented senior in the middle of a forest."

I bent over, covering my head with my arms, but I couldn't stop hearing familiar voices, including my own, talking about me and my weirdness. They said special, unique, quirky, idiosyncratic, singular; pleasant euphemisms, but we all knew what they meant. There were clips of an interview when I pretended to be an animal psychic. And video of training sessions, karaoke at Rudy's Brewhouse, and Bonanza Days festivities. Sasha even included our last talk at Towering Pines Casino, when I'd been kicked off the Midnight Runners.

Every time I looked up, I saw myself with my twitches and grimaces, and I heard my peculiar inflections and obvious lies, and I felt nauseated, and it kept going on and on and on. I slid down, so I could crawl under the table, but Kenzie and Ollie held firm.

My skin was cold and hot and cold, and I thought I must be going into shock, when everyone clapped and stood and kept clapping.

The lights went up, and the sheriff-coroner held a plaque, and boomed into the mic, "Thank you, Sasha, for your moving and inspiring film, and now I'd like to present the Citizen's Award for Exceptional Bravery to Dr. Madeleine Whitney for founding and leading the Midnight Runners Search and Rescue team, and for being a loyal and respected friend of the Sheriff's Department. Come on up, Dr. Whitney!"

Everyone stared at me, and Kenzie urged, "Go on, go on," so I stood.

I moved slowly to the aisle. Then I turned and hurried toward the back exit, not caring that pain shot up my leg with each thud of my foot. I tore through the lobby and outside. I hobbled into the alley beside Grange Hall. My ankle hurt too much to even stand. I crumbled to the ground in a daze, my hands over my face, and that was where Oliver found me.

He sat beside me, and I said, "You'll get your khakis dirty."

"They're stain-resistant. Why did you run?"

"Because I was publicly humiliated!"

Oliver narrowed his eyes, and his lips went up on one side. "Even if that was true, which it's not, you've never given one damn about the opinions of people who are too ignorant to realize that you're smarter and more gifted than anyone else in the room."

"I'm the object of scorn and derision."

"Such a drama queen," said a husky, honeyed voice, and I looked up to see Claire Desjardins. My sister and Sasha stood behind her. "Try being a twin," she and Oliver said in eerie harmony, and laughed.

"As your therapist, I'm recommending that you get over yourself," Kenzie said. "But what do I know? I'm working with a man who thinks he's God's gift and pilfers my cosmetics."

"Maddie, I didn't mean for my short to upset you," Sasha said. "I shared my outtakes with friends, and they all said that I had to put it together. I even showed it to Sheriff Eastman."

"That's why he came?"

Sasha smiled. "As an elected official, he understands the value of free publicity."

They rubbed off the patina of embarrassment, and now I could recognize my rage. I glared at Oliver and Kenzie. "You held me down against my will. I *hated* all those eyes watching me. That's abuse."

"Oh, fucking hell!" Kenzie said, stunning me with the obscenity. "You always want people to hold you to give comfort. Okay, it was a terrible judgment call, and I—we—apologize, but don't I ever get to make mistakes? Why do I always have to be the reasonable one? Because if you want me to stay, you damn well better ease up on your expectations."

I opened my mouth but couldn't think of anything to say.

Oliver stood. "If you're not going in, give me my raffle tickets back. I feel lucky tonight."

"How lucky?"

"Grass-fed bison ribeye lucky."

I took his hand and let him pull me up. "I'm only going because I'm becoming vegetarian next week. If I don't win, I'm becoming vegetarian tomorrow. Also, I'm leaving as soon as prizes are distributed."

Kenzie said to the others, "Do you hear anything? Because I don't hear anything but *blah, blah, blah,*" and she bumped against my hip as we walked back to see all our friends.

Chapter Thirty-Three

ALTHOUGH SASHA'S SHORT FILM made me cringe, I appreciated her intentions and shrewdness, which not only promoted her own career, but resuscitated my business. Old clients returned, and new clients soon filled our sessions. When I began venturing into town, locals approached me, quoting lines and describing scenes, and I told Kenzie, "This is worse than being hated, because then no one waited for me to do something quirky or weird."

We were in the kitchen making a word cloud on a whiteboard, and she said, "Don't worry. I'm sure you'll do something soon that's offensive enough to wipe away all the goodwill. Remind me again why we're making this chart?"

"It's my way of convincing myself to ask for Beryl's help with a business plan."

"Just do it, the way you gave up meat."

"Kenz, I knew it was ethically and morally wrong to eat another sentient creature when I was ten. I don't want to be as slow processing this decision." I added "efficiency" to the word cloud, and said, "I have to run an errand. Will you be home for dinner or on a date with Ezra?"

"We have work-related meetings.

"He has a crush on you."

"He has a crush on himself, and I haven't seen the appropriate enlightenment on his side that I'm the prettier one."

"Well, fuck him, then, or rather, don't fuck him. Ben and Ava invited us to dinner. They're grilling, and I'm contributing eggplants."

"Are you glad to be friends with Ben again?"

"I was never not friends with him," I said, although things weren't the same. "Friendships evolve, though. Ours did."

Vixen scrambled through the window, leapt over the sink, and scampered out the kitchen into the hall.

"What is it with that dog?" Kenzie said. "I better see what she's doing. I think she stole my blond wig, because I can't find it anywhere." She set down her marker and followed Vixen down the hall.

I called Bertie to me, watching him carefully as I did these days, and we went to my cottage together. "You're in fine fettle, Bertie. Retirement suits you. Do you want to go on a field trip with me?"

It was well past time to put things in order. Purlynn had told me she was spending all weekend at the fishing cabin, packing some of her father's things and replacing others. I'd accepted her offer of wool blankets for the kennels and household items for the office trailer.

I planned to drop by unannounced and quickly bury Dino's finger in its original resting place. I wiggled on latex gloves and prepped the counter with paper towels. I held the frosty packet under warm water until it thawed enough to remove the foil. The finger inside was a grisly mud-covered thing, and I half-closed my eyes as I rinsed away the crust of filth and, no doubt, Vixen's slime.

I set the finger on the paper towels and rolled it dry.

A finger cut from a living body would have spouted blood. But the dark brown staining on one side of the finger, livor mortis, indicated that someone was dead *before* the finger had been severed, causing the blood to settle, not spurt.

"Ha!" I said to Bertie. "I *knew* it was impossible for Vixen to track Dino Ayer's scent from our location when you and Zeus couldn't."

The grasses on the path toward the lake were brown and beaten down flat. Bertie explored fresh smells and sights, sniffing ferns, deer scat, and tree trunks studiously before lifting his leg to leave pee-mail.

Purlynn's higher voice was in conversation with someone else, a man. I recognized Ezra's pleasing tones before I saw him carrying a cardboard box from the cabin.

Purlynn stood in the doorway, holding a roll of masking tape. "You made it!" she said, and Ezra said, "Hi, Maddie."

"Hey, Purlynn, Ezra. Busy day?"

"We've barely put a dent in things. Come on in." She bent to give Bertie a rub. "You, too, Bertie."

"Ezra, you might want to join us," I said, admiring the way he'd tailored his outfit by rolling his sleeve cuffs and tucking one side of a plaid shirt in his jeans.

"Let me put this down." He set the box on a pile with others.

They'd rolled the carpet and moved the furniture to one side of the main room. Wall plaques were stacked on the table, and wooden model boats were lined up on the floor beside cleaning supplies and furniture polish.

"I separated the shabbier blankets from ones that you might want to use for yourself," Purlynn said.

"Thanks, but let's have a little talk first." I sat on the floor and signaled for Bertie to join me. Purlynn leaned against the wall, and

Ezra used a wooden crate as a seat. "I have been trying to figure out a few things for weeks."

Purlynn scrunched her face. "What things? About the dogs?"

"That's usually my topic of choice, but no. I've been trying to figure out why Dr. Ben Meadows spent so much time treating Emily's Weasel, and, yes, I mean it the way it sounds." I paused. "Purlynn, I've been trying to figure out why you were so devastated by your father's permanent fishing vacation when you were still in contact with him. But mostly I've been wondering why the hell Dino Ayer buried his finger in front of Gordon Looper's cabin."

Purlynn blanched and seemed about to bolt, but Ezra grabbed her wrist, and said, "I'm sorry, but we have no idea what you're talking about. Are you all right, Maddie? I can call your sister."

"Oh, Ezra, it's not very spiritually enlightened to gaslight me," I said. "To continue, when the boat exploded, I wondered why my best tracking dogs couldn't follow Dino's trail here from our starting point, but Vixen, who runs off wherever she damn well pleases, dug up a morbid little treat, the finger Dino accidentally sliced off."

"Maddie, you underestimate Vixen's abilities," Purlynn said.

"I'm aware of her special genius, but Bertie and Zeus are superior, methodical trackers. Call me cynical, but I was suspicious of the beautiful, financially desperate widow and the huge insurance policy. Now that the policy has been paid off and the widow has left the country..."

"My sister would not murder anyone," Ezra said. "She loves, loved, Dino."

"That's hard to believe, but I believe it anyway."

"If you've come here to spin conspiracy theories," he began and watched while I unzipped my backpack and removed a plastic bag.

"No, I'm trying to restore something Vixen took to its rightful place." Holding the bag aloft, I said, "The problem was that I thought this was *Dino's* finger. But it isn't. This finger was cut from a dead man's body. Purlynn, this is your father's, isn't it?"

Her mouth hung open, and then she began crying so hard, her whole body quaked. Ezra tried to calm her, and I left the bag on the table and fetched a roll of toilet paper so she could wipe her tears and blow her nose.

Her story came out between crying jags, a phrase here, two sentences there, with Ezra's interruptions and additions.

The family had been in France purchasing vine stock with the last of their savings when Emily became ill. Doctors discovered she had non-Hodgkin's lymphoma.

The Ayer children had health insurance, but Dino and Emily's had lapsed, and they couldn't afford her chemotherapy. After googling frenetically, Dino had the brilliant idea of paying a shady veterinarian in Marseilles to write a prescription for his dog's alleged cancer.

"The medication is the same, but the dosages were different," Ezra said.

"But that's dangerous! She could have sold the vineyard."

"They already had a second mortgage on it. My sister was ready to die rather than make her kids homeless. I would have given everything I have for her treatment, but Dino and Emily kept it from me until I found her prescriptions and made her tell me the truth."

Purlynn rubbed her red eyes. "Aunt Emily was having serious bad side effects from the chemo. She went to Dr. Ben, pretending Weasel needed help. He knew right away what was going on."

"So, he began treating Emily?" I asked, and the puzzle pieces began shifting into place.

"He refused to," Ezra said. "But he monitored her health and made her promise to go to an MD. He's such a good man."

Relief washed over me, and I had never been so grateful to

learn that I'd been wrong about someone. "He's honorable and giving," I said. "Go on."

"We were losing our minds, Maddie," Purlynn said. "My dad, Uncle Dino, Ezra, and I met here to brainstorm ways to pay for her treatment. Dad left to get sandwiches at the Bait Shop. We didn't expect him to be back right away, because he always stopped to talk to his buddies, but after ninety minutes, I finally called him, and..." She sat beside Bertie and stroked his fur.

"We heard Gordon's phone ringing right outside. I was going to yell at him for taking so long," Ezra said. "But he never even made it to the path. I gave him CPR, but we knew it was much too late."

"So, Dino decided to cut off your father's finger and use his body in the faked boat accident," I said.

"It was all my idea," Ezra said.

"Don't cover for me, Uncle Ezra," Purlynn said. "Maddie, it was all me. I mentioned that my father had always wanted a Viking funeral, to have his body burned on a boat, and then I realized he could have the sendoff he'd dreamed about *and* help his friends. Uncle Dino didn't want to do it."

"I did, for Emily's sake," Ezra said. "It took a while to get Dino to go along with it. We stored Gordon's body on ice in Dino's boat hold and made our plans. The only complicated thing was keeping it all secret from Emily and the kids. I wanted to tell her he was safe and waiting for her, but I couldn't because she never would have accepted the insurance money."

"I watched from shore," Purlynn said, forlorn as she stared out the window to the lake. "While they drove away, I watched my father's Viking funeral all by myself."

"What does Emily think now? Where are they?" I said.

"She's grateful Dino's alive. Seeing the kids fatherless even for a short time gave her a different perspective on right and wrong," Ezra said. "They're somewhere where they can live cheaply and stay together. She likes her oncologist, and her condition looks promising."

"Ezra, what do you mean when you say love is truth and truth is love?"

"It's open to interpretation, depending on the situation," he said. "Use it as a shortcut to self-discovery."

"You concoct your so-called therapy totally by the seat of your pants, don't you?"

He shook his head and grinned. "Don't be a hater."

"Are you going to report us to the sheriff, Maddie?" Purlynn said. "Tell me so I can break the news to my mother."

"Give me a few minutes to think about all of this." If I'd had a whiteboard, I would have drawn a spider web chart showing the interconnectivity and symbiosis of the legal and illegal drug connections in a broken health care system. "Do you have anything to drink?"

They brought out a six-pack of Corona, and we went outside and sat on the dock, drinking while the water lapped the shore. The sunlight fell at a subtle angle on the trees and lake, signaling the progress of our journey around the sun. The worst of the year's heat was over, but we would have to wait several weeks before the rains came.

"Excuse me." I went inside the cabin, selected a model boat with a sunburst on the sail, and then picked up liquid charcoal lighter and matches by the grill.

Purlynn and Ezra watched as I set the boat at the edge of the beach, placed the plastic bag and finger atop it, and doused them in lighter fluid. Ezra and Purlynn looked at me, and she said, "Thank you."

We removed our shoes and rolled up our pants' legs before wading into the lake. I handed the matches to Purlynn. She struck one and dropped it on the boat, and orange flames flashed up. Ezra used a long stick to shove the boat farther from shore.

Purlynn was no longer alone as we stood witness to the conclusion of Gordon Looper's Viking funeral. I began singing Buffett's "I Have Found Me a Home," which seemed to suit the occasion for a man who had always been happiest on the water.

We watched as the fire burned out. Finally, the blackened remnants sank, and then Bertie and I went back to the ranch.

Oliver and I walked across the field with our shepherds, while Vixen stalked something by a shrub.

"You're quiet," he said.

"These last few months have felt like years."

"Mine felt like minutes."

"Time is like that, relative. Oliver, when are you going to give back my AC/DC shirt?"

"I'm keeping it. Makes me feel edgy."

"So, you've gotten over whatever issues you had with the band? What was the deal anyway? Did they come through town and start a riot, or bust up a hotel having an orgy?"

"If you must know," he said.

"I must."

"Do you remember the bowling alley that got bulldozed when Vineyard Garden Estates was built?"

"Sure, my grandfather was on a team with old Doc Pete. We have trophies stored in the attic."

"The sheriff's department team was Strike Force, and the sanitation department's team was AC/DC, named after the band. There was a cheating dispute, and the next day, a load of garbage was dumped on the sheriff-coroner's car."

"And?"

"And that's it. If you support AC/DC, it means you side with the sanitation department."

"Is my mouth agape?" I said. "I feel like it's agape, because that's the dumbest reason I've ever heard for a vendetta."

"I didn't come up with it. I'm only carrying on the tradition."

"Oliver Desjardins, don't even get me started, because I already feel like throwing these eggplants at your head."

"Are you sure Ben and Ava wanted the dogs to come, too?"

"They didn't expressly prohibit them, so yes." I gazed at Bertie, ambling with his feathered tail waving behind him. "Bertie has been teaching me to practice what I preach. I keep feeling sorry for him because he's aging, and I keep feeling sorry for myself because he prefers to be with the pack and not alone with me. I'm going to enjoy him enjoying his life as it is today."

"He has a great life, Mad Girl. Now all you have to do is spend time training Vixen instead of tacitly encouraging her wild behavior."

"I'm impressed you know what tacit means."

"I learned it when I misspelled tactic. Or maybe it was tantric, which I learned about, too. I even looked up mawkish, and I'm glad to see you're out of that stage and back to your ornery self."

"I was understandably sentimental having you back." I leaned against him and kissed his cheek. "But please don't endanger yourself again merely for a sappy tear-drenched reunion."

"Oh, just own up to the fact that you're a sentimental crybaby."

"Fine whatever."

"Looks like everyone is here."

Ben flipped something on the grill, his wife Ava poured wine for my sister, and the Meadows children played with squirt guns. After we shouted our hellos, I went to the kitchen to slice and dress the eggplant. When I opened the refrigerator, a magnet slipped, causing a postcard to flutter to the floor. I picked it up and saw a sunny tropical scene of white sands, turquoise water, and palm trees, with a banner saying *Greetings from Puerto Azul!* The reverse side had foreign postage and a handwritten one-line message: "Thank you for everything. *E.*"

The screen door opened, and Ben came inside. "Do you need anything? The garlic press is in that top drawer."

"I have everything," I said, still holding the postcard. "Thank you, Ben, for all you do."

"It's only a potluck, Maddie."

"Thank you for being patient when I was asking too much. Thank you for doing the right thing even when others thought you were doing the wrong thing."

"I don't know what you're talking about," he said, his voice low.

"Probably nonsense per usual." I attached the postcard to the fridge with the magnet, and when I smiled his way, he smiled back.

After I left the eggplant to marinate, we went outside arm in arm to hear excited crosstalk about the family's trip, Kenzie's work with Spirit Springs Institute, and planned construction of a barn. Some subjects were carefully avoided: Dino's accident and Emily's move; Oliver's temporary suspension and Deputy Kearney's firing; and the restraining order against me.

Vixen snuck close and grabbed a loaf of bread in a white bakery bag, running off, and I said, "Excuse me," and followed her, needing to be away from the chatter.

The sleek spotted dog sat by the creek, now the thinnest of trickles. I took the bread from her and said, "Let's stay a moment."

I thought of how Vixen's discovery of the finger and the Viking funeral bracketed the summer. I should be elated—and I was—by the return of Oliver and my sister and the capture of the dog fighters.

But unease crept low and dark, like a ribbon of smoke slipping under a closed door. I fretted that, if I became distracted by happiness, I would be unprepared to face trouble when it arrived. Not that preparation would help if the slumbering volcano in the distance erupted, or a meteor tore through the atmosphere, or the Black Death staged a comeback, or torrential rains caused suffocating mudslides.

Despite my brief stint as a pet psychic, I didn't believe in premonitions, but nonetheless, I sensed something powerful and dangerous approaching. It was as if our lives were governed by a trickster god, an agent of chaos.

A sliver of moon appeared in the darkening sky, and soon the Andromeda Galaxy would be visible, shining light that had radiated over 2.5 million years ago. The reverse was true, and the light we sent out would appear millions of years after we were gone. What would anything mean then?

All I had here and now was the ability to be grateful for my family and friends, for Oliver, for Bertie and all the other dogs who'd taught me how to live in the moment, and for Vixen and her unwavering exuberance.

And although I could not halt disaster, I could prepare for it by doing more than hoarding jam. I could endeavor to be worthy of those who cared for me. I could strive to be a kinder person, to help others, and find common ground with those I disliked. I could seek to repair my broken family, including Abel and my brother.

While I was no architect or general, I could lay bricks in a fortress of love. And when whatever came, came, I would reach out to my family, friends, and community, and together we would pick ourselves up, breathe, just breathe, and move on.

If you enjoyed this book,
please consider leaving a review. *Thank you!*

Visit www.martaacosta.com for more information about Marta Acosta's books and activities.

Made in United States
Orlando, FL
05 November 2024